JEN ST. JUDE

# *where you'll find us*



PENGUIN BOOKS

PENGUIN BOOKS

UK | USA | Canada | Ireland | Australia
India | New Zealand | South Africa

Penguin Books is part of the Penguin Random House group of companies whose addresses can be found at global.penguinrandomhouse.com.

www.penguin.co.uk
www.puffin.co.uk
www.ladybird.co.uk

Penguin Random House UK

First published in the USA by Bloomsbury YA and in Great Britain by Penguin Books 2026

001



Book design by John Candell
Printed in Great Britain by Clays Ltd, Elcograf S.p.A.

The authorized representative in the EEA is Penguin Random House Ireland, Morrison Chambers, 32 Nassau Street, Dublin D02 YH68

A CIP catalogue record for this book is available from the British Library

ISBN: 978–0–241–62778–5

All correspondence to:
Penguin Books
Penguin Random House Children's
One Embassy Gardens, 8 Viaduct Gardens, London SW11 7BW

FSC www.fsc.org MIX Paper | Supporting responsible forestry FSC® C018179

Penguin Random House is committed to a sustainable future for our business, our readers and our planet. This book is made from Forest Stewardship Council® certified paper.

*To everyone who makes me feel unlonely.*

*And for Z, who I will love with all of me, for all of time.*
*In every place. By any name.*

# *author's note*

Dear Reader,

In an attempt to be historically accurate, the language in this novel reflects the contexts and nuances of the characters' eras. Similarly, the transgender and nonbinary characters each have unique relationships with their own names and pronouns, and this is reflected in the text as well. Please read with care.

**Full content notice:** Transphobia, accidental outing, homophobia, racism, xenophobia, sexual assault (not on the page), suicidal ideation, imprisonment, HIV/AIDS and related discrimination, violence, death of relatives, death of an animal (not the dog!), fatphobia, bullying, cancer, dementia, vomiting

# *before*

MY PARENTS DISOWNED ME via text at the beginning of spring break. It was the day after my eighteenth birthday, so I guess their gift to me was waiting twenty-four hours to do it.

We had a blowout fight on the phone a week prior, but I'd still kept my plans to go home. I was dreading it because I knew we'd have to talk about what they found on my iPad, but I had nowhere else to go since my boarding school's campus would be closed over break. Plus, my dog still lives with them, and I'd do anything to see her. So, I got a ride from school to Pittsfield, took a train from Pittsfield to Boston, and flew from Boston to Indianapolis in a middle seat—especially miserable since I'm six foot one.

When I didn't see my parents waiting at baggage claim, I called them over and over again, more than fifty times. I got sent to voicemail just as many. They left me to stand by the other travelers hugging their families, chucking their luggage into trunks, and getting whistled at by airport security for a full two hours, until my phone battery was next to dead. Until, worst of all, I was out of snacks.

I thought maybe, generously, that they'd died in some freak accident, and that's why they weren't answering my calls. But they hadn't. They were just hitting the silence button, both of them, again and again, until finally Dad sent a text:

> Your mother and I thought more about the disturbing things we found on your iPad and after much consideration feel that it's best for all of us if you don't come home. We have been sick ever since and are heartbroken to lose our daughter. We will not be attending your graduation and will no longer be assisting you with your college tuition. Do not contact us again unless—

Unless I do things I cannot, will not do. I tried to respond, hands shaking (Campus is closed, where am I supposed to go? and Can I at least come say goodbye to Nugget?), only to find that they'd blocked me. John and Natalia Quick: parents of the century.

I used my 3 percent battery to call my girlfriend, Ramona, and she stopped the world to get me home to her. The Silvas booked me a direct flight from Indy to Miami, and the whole family met me at baggage claim with big smiles and open arms. Ramona had her long, blonde hair in beautiful French braids—her mother's work—and immediately offered me Tupperware filled with homemade brownies with sea salt. Her brother Auggie carried my suitcase to the car, though I didn't want him to, and Mrs. Silva kept stroking my hair.

On the way to their house, Mr. Silva insisted we stop to watch the hot pink sunset over the palm trees and ocean. As we stood on the beach, I thought about how I was supposed to be in Indiana with my parents, hiding the parts of me they wouldn't accept and missing Ramona. Instead, my arms were wrapped around her, her head pressed against my chest, my sneakers filling with sand. And I realized I wasn't missing anything at all. The worst had happened, but because I was with her, everything would be okay.

"Tell me everything," she said then, and because we weren't making eye contact it was easier to lie.

"They found out about us," I said, and she spun around to study me.

"I knew it," she said, looking sorry, slipping her hands around my waist. "I knew that's what happened." I put my head on her head.

I did not tell her the truth.

# *alone*

I ONCE MADE A promise I'd live until my high school graduation, but I'm starting to regret it.

I want to love the prom dress Ramona found for me because she thinks it's beautiful. It's olive, satin, simple. It belongs to the only other tall, broad-shouldered girl in our dorm, an Estonian tennis player I have never talked to. I don't know how much the dress costs, only that I can't afford it. Not now, anyway. If it were up to me, I'd tear it off and feed it to the pack of angry wild turkeys that terrorize the campus of Miss Stone's School for Girls, but I will instead have to protect it with my life.

In fifteen minutes, I will show up at Ramona's dorm room with a corsage of campus flowers I tied together with art room string. In fifteen minutes, I will match Ramona's gold gown just enough but not too much. In fifteen minutes, she will capture the two of us on her phone from every angle: her kissing my cheek, me kissing hers. Our smiles proof of our pride. Her camera roll an archive of our joy. Whatever happens next year, at least I can give her this: proof we were together now, in love now, happy now.

All of that in fifteen minutes.

For now, I'm alone in my dorm room, staring at my floor-length mirror, looking right through my reflection. The girls on the other side of our paper-thin walls are laughing and screaming, and I can hear them complimenting each other as they get dressed. *You're so pretty, Maren,* I catch. *You look amazing, Lena. Penny, please let me do a red lip on you. It's your look, okay, see? Don't you love it?* Penny does.

I look in the mirror and dare myself to like something—anything—about what I see. I guess I like the way my biceps look on full display, free of the barn jacket I wear even in summer. I guess I like the way my hair dried; soft, dark curls I can flip back or push away. I guess. What I like most, though, is that you can't see the lines of my boxer briefs under the dress's unforgiving fabric. No one will know I'm wearing them, but at least I do. This night is supposed to be special, after all—I don't want to feel totally pathetic. But it's hard when I'm wearing this dress that feels wrong in ways I can't totally explain.

Staring at myself, my mind wanders the way it does every day. I imagine myself as someone different. I dream of myself with a flat chest, despite my curves. I picture myself with shorter hair, despite my full cheeks. I tighten and harden everything I can. I stand how men stand. I change my face, tilting my head and jutting out my chin to give the illusion of a stronger jawline. I envision a suit that fits me without expensive alterations. I see me or someone like me in the space where my reflection stands: angles, brick, handsome. There, there, *there*. An impossible person, worlds and lifetimes away.

But with a blink, that person is gone and I'm left with me. Just me. In an olive, satin, simple dress.

And I only have fifteen minutes.

# *in fifteen minutes*

I KNOCK ON RAMONA'S door and even after three years of dating, my heart still catches while I wait for her. Lately, every single minute feels like a knuckle papercut: a constant, pulsing reminder that our shared world will end come graduation. We don't like to talk about it, but we are always talking about it. Except there's a whole lot I don't say.

Ramona opens the door and just . . . wow. Damn. Her blonde hair is pinned up carefully, strands falling to frame her face in all the right places. Her golden dress is red carpet material, and her makeup makes her look flawless. I instantly miss the birthmark on her cheek and the little scar on her chin, but I like this version of her too, both the artist and artwork. She makes a night like tonight look so easy. I feel a sharp, unfair pang of resentment, but push it down.

"You look stunning," I say, taking her face in my hands and kissing her on the forehead like I always do. She steps back to spin around, giving the full 360 view, before falling back into me.

"Oh, Calla, this *dress.*" She runs her hands up and down the silk of it and maybe I'm not so mad I'm wearing it after all. "Look at you! If I wasn't in love with you already, this would seal the deal."

I kiss her again, and when I pull back, she takes the opportunity to tease me. "I was half expecting you to show up in that ratty old coat you love so much."

"Hey, it's my signature look!" I say. I've never told her why I wear it so much; I don't say how much I wish I *was* wearing it right now. So she just laughs and rolls her eyes.

"Come in so I can do your hair."

She grabs my hand and tugs, and obviously I go with her. I put the wildflower corsage on her desk, and sit down on her wooden chair so she can do her thing. She's been looking forward to prom for forever. She literally got an app to count down the days. This night is for her, so I'll be exactly who and how she wants me to be.

But I'd be lying if I said guilt didn't play a part in that, too. Like, can't-sleep, can't-eat, nerves-on-fire guilt. Graduation wasn't supposed to be the end of the road for us. We were supposed to go to Alcott College together in the fall. Ramona had gotten into Yale, but chose Alcott instead because she wanted to be with me. It was our compromise school; out of all the colleges that recruited me for field hockey, it was the only one Ramona could see herself at. It has a strong poli-sci department, which she wanted. It's all-girls again, like she hoped for. They didn't offer me as much financial aid as other schools, but they gave me a partial scholarship, and my parents had a college fund for me to cover the rest. At least, that was the plan until a few weeks ago. Until I ruined everything.

After winter break, I left my iPad in my family's living room, forgetting to pack it since I really only use it to watch movies on airplanes. I figured I'd grab it when I went home for spring break, no big deal, but I didn't think about the fact that it syncs to my phone. My mom decided to use it to plan a vacation on TripAdvisor, and my very hackable passcode (Nugget's birthday. Honestly.) and autofill fucked me over. All she had to do was start typing "tr" and a million searches and sites centered on the same words popped up: *transgender, transmasc, trans, trans, trans . . .*

And then, from cruelty disguised as concern, she dug further. Poetry and novels. Porn. And somehow worse than the porn: lengthy, revealing posts on a trans message board. I can't even think about that part without getting sick to my stomach with shame.

*Do not contact us again unless you provide proof of seeking professional help.*

Ramona doesn't know this part of the story. She thinks I lost my parents and my tuition and our future because my iPad background was a photo of us. She thinks I lost it all because of *her*. And I'm a shitty, cowardly, awful liar for letting her think so.

I know I need to tell her what actually happened—and I should be able to. If anyone would understand, it's her. She's the president of Miss Stone's Gender and Sexuality Alliance. She's spent the last three summers interning at the Florida LGBTQ+ Democratic Caucus. She owns at least three T-shirts that say something about protecting trans youth. But there was a moment last year during spring break, on a beach in Miami. She was wearing a sapphire-blue bikini and an Unrivaled cap—how could I forget a single detail?—when our friend asked her if she'd ever date a guy and she said, "I'm a lesbian, hello?" Then they asked, what about a trans guy? "Obviously still a man. Obviously still no."

So, obviously, I've been replaying that moment in my mind at least once a day lately, secretly praying she's changed her mind since then, or that she loves me enough to change it for me now—if I even am a trans guy. Because despite all my research and reading and journaling, I still don't know. I so wish I knew.

The question has been there in the back of my mind for as long as I can remember, but committing to Alcott brought it front and center. It was supposed to be thrilling, me and Ramona going to college together. It was supposed to be a huge relief, but once it really started to sink in that I'd spend four more years at another all-girls school, I started freaking the fuck out. Couldn't eat, couldn't sleep, couldn't stop thinking about how I'm—

I mean, God, I couldn't even escape it when I *was* sleeping. I kept dreaming I showed up on the luscious, manicured Alcott campus, all my belongings in bags behind me, and they took one look at me and turned me away because they could tell I'm—

It doesn't matter, anyway. With Alcott off the table now, our future together already uncertain, Ramona doesn't need to know, not yet. Not tonight.

In her dorm room, Ramona's hair straightener slides right over my waves and flips them to shape them just so. She paints my face with her makeup, despite my skin being at least a few shades lighter than hers. Her nails are glittery, and I wonder if she'll get any on my cheeks.

I say, "Not too much, okay?" and kinda hate myself for it. She says, "Just trust me, Calla." And I do. Of course I do.

She winks at me while she smooths my hair and softly scratches her nails down my neck and across my back. She knows how much I like that. So much I'm hardly listening when she says, "And for the final touch . . ." She crosses the room to pick earrings out of her jewelry chest, and my stomach sinks. "I know these aren't really your thing, but it's prom, okay?"

The word *no* punches through me but dies at the back of my mouth. *Who cares if I wear earrings*? She does, and this night is for her. This whole look is for her. It's fine.

She holds up one set at a time and tilts her head, finally deciding on a dangly gold and crystal pair.

"Luíza got these for me in Rio," she says, her voice quiet. Luíza, her tia—her favorite, favorite person—had a heart attack last August and passed away at the age of forty-two. Luíza was a lesbian and an incredible activist, and to honor her too-short legacy, Ramona dropped out of her band to become even more politically involved. To say the least. She wakes up at the crack of dawn and stays up late into the night to phonebank, organize, email politicians, and draft petitions. She joined every progressive club on campus and is on the board of half of them. It's inspiring, but I can easily see it's all driven by her overwhelming, unbearable grief.

So, these earrings are special. And of course I'm going to suck it up and wear them.

"It's like they were made for you in this dress." She puts the earrings on the desk in front of me and I stare at them blankly until she gives me a look in the mirror. "Let's see, babe."

I haven't worn earrings since I was thirteen, so when I try to push the pin through my ear, I hit a thick wall of skin where the hole has healed over. I feel a flash of relief, and I'm about to say, "Never mind," but Ramona's face lights up.

"Oh, they're perfect," she says, clutching her necklace. So I put my thumb on the back of my lobe and pinch as hard as I can. After three tries, the earring rips through my ear and pierces my thumb. I take a sharp breath but don't let it show on my face, licking the prick of blood off my fingertip before she can notice.

I do the same on the other side. I'm quicker this time, but the pain is the same. When I'm done, I finally really look at the girl in the mirror. She does look pretty, and Ramona must think so too, because she's misty-eyed when she smooths my hair one last time.

"You okay?" I ask.

"More than okay," she says. A single tear slips down her cheek. Her makeup doesn't smudge at all, but she double-checks it anyway. "I'm *happy*."

"Me too," I say, standing up, spinning away from my reflection, leaning down to kiss her. Both of us pretending this moment's all that matters. "Tonight'll be perfect." And God, *God*, I hope it will be. After a year of mourning, of crying herself to sleep, she deserves it. So who cares if I hate this dress? If my ears sting? If I want to chuck these high heels at a dartboard and watch them stick? A perfect night is the only thing I can give her after ruining our future together. And it's the only thing that will beat my guilt down as it rises in my chest again and again and again.

She kisses me harder than ever before—satin lip gloss, hands locked on my back—then pulls away to say, "I love you, Calla Quick."

I whisper, "I love you too," and it doesn't feel like enough. I want to give her the world, but I can't, so I'll make sure tonight is perfect. If only tonight.

# *stand still, look pretty*

WE MEET OUR FRIENDS in the school gardens for pictures as the sun moves across the mountains. We clearly weren't the only ones with this backdrop idea. Dozens of our classmates and their dates from other schools and other lives pose in front of the willow trees and cascading rows of flowers. The beauty on the ground spills everywhere, peacocking, and the scent of jasmine nearly takes me out. This spring came to flirt.

"It's always so weird to see boys on campus," Ramona says. It only happens twice a year, on Family Homecoming and prom, and I can admit it is jarring. Ramona crosses her arms. "They always have this look on their faces like they're getting away with something."

I watch the boys, and yes, some of them are so smug I could smack them; their eyes sparked by mischief, darting around the throngs of Miss Stone's girls like coyotes in a henhouse. But many of them seem so . . . effortless, too. Clean; no makeup, no glitter. Sharp; hair combed and slick, suits and tuxedos that look like they were made for them.

I run my fingertips along the edge of my boxers, the only part of my outfit that feels right. The new holes in my ears throb as I watch one annoyingly handsome guy adjust the gold cuff links on his sleeves. He then stands behind his date and rubs her arms. Without even meaning to, I do the same with Ramona. She steals one of my hands and clutches it against the bones of her chest, as if to anchor us in this moment, and I feel a rush of impossible, desperate wanting. I wish we could stay right here forever, our future irrelevant, our years together here on campus not far behind us. Miss Stone's isn't paradise, not at all, but I was happy here at times. With Ramona, I'm the happiest I've ever been.

When it's our group's turn to take photos, we hand our phones to the girls behind us per the law of friendly-photo-taking-reciprocation, and Ramona directs everyone on where to stand.

"I have a vision!" she shouts, and everyone giggles as they fall in line.

"Ramona with the vision," Cho-Hee and Minali say at the same time.

"Ramona for president!" Lyndsey yells.

Our group has been steady since the end of freshman year, when one night we all snuck into the unlocked hockey rink, played broomball until the custodian kicked us out, then had a Disney Channel Original Movie marathon in one of our dorm's common rooms. Soaked to the bone with ice water, wrapped up in whatever blankets we could find, greasy bags of popcorn between us, we ranked all the movies from least to most queer.

The group is a mix of my world and Ramona's. Lyndsey and MK are my field hockey teammates, while Minali and Cho-Hee were Ramona's bandmates before she dropped out of Lilith Heir last semester to focus on her activism.

We all have the same dorky sense of humor, read the same books, watch the same shows, and have a shared playlist where we all add our gay little songs. We can communicate via emojis alone. And as of last summer, Lyndsey and Minali are also dating, so there's that too. I've always found groups are easy to hide in, and I've never felt so loved by friends in all my life. Or by anyone, really. It's strange and sad and terrifying to think it'll all be over in a few weeks, especially knowing I have nothing and no one on the other side.

Except Ramona, who has us all lined up, hips like this, hands just so, only our best sides on display. I smile and try to mean it because cameras know when you're lying. People shout at us to look at one phone, the next, and the next and to make a silly face and to look serious and to look in love and to shout SENIORS! and SUFFRAGETTES! and SAPPHIC! and I watch boys peel away from their dates and form huddles. Jump on each other. Punch each other on the arms, mess up each other's sharp, perfect hair. As we pose, one of them yells, "Looking good, ladies!" and I can tell it's meant to be nice. Not creepy. His date is not offended. And neither am I. If you're going to be a jealous dyke at an all-girls school, you're in for a hell of a ride.

Ramona calls, "Beijos!"

MK yells, "Thank you!"

But my mind sticks on *ladies*.

My cheeks burn and I look at the grass so I don't give anything away to whoever's camera flash explodes next.

# *prom*

RAMONA SPENDS THE WHOLE bus ride to prom looking at the photos of us, hearting all the ones she likes best. "Aww, look at this one." She zooms in and turns her phone to me, bottom lip out. "We're so cute."

She's glowing. I try to look that way too. Put my hand on my heart. "Frame-worthy."

"I'm sending it to my parents, they're dying for photos." I grin but feel another pang of unfair jealousy. The Silvas have been so good to me. Not only were they there when my parents abandoned me, they've invited me to live with them after graduation—the most generous gift—and I will have to take them up on it, at least until I figure something else out.

They keep offering to call my parents to try to talk some sense into them, and I keep shutting it down, but I'm terrified they'll decide to do it anyway. I've imagined it so many times, the way they'd start the conversation passionate and full of righteous fire. The way their faces would fall, just a little, when they heard the truth. The things they'd tell Ramona. I don't let myself think of what would come next.

The school buses take us to the Berkshire Hills Country Club, and it feels like a different kind of dream. It's pretty. Green, green, green. Huge windows, golf courses as far as the eye can see, sprinklers whirring. Ramona swears under her breath. "An environmental disaster."

We follow our friends down the steps of the bus and all of us try not to trip and die because of our long dresses. Except for Lyndsey, of course. Because Lyndsey thought ahead and bought a bomb ass suit from an expensive queer website. I know because I helped her pick it out. Lyndsey didn't pretend prom wasn't happening, wasn't happening, wasn't happening like I did and took the time to find something she was comfortable in. Granted, Lyndsey also didn't lose her family and entire future a month ago. And not to mention I have seventeen dollars in my bank account. My one trip to Goodwill was a total bust—a two-mile walk each way and not a single thing that looked halfway decent, let alone prom-worthy. But still.

At least I can move enough in this dress to pull half of Lilith Heir's band equipment out from under the bus and carry it inside. Even though the band's been broken up since Luíza died, they agreed to one final performance, and I for one am freaking excited to see Ramona in her element again. I miss the spark in her eyes she only gets when she's playing with the band. I know she loves her activism work, but nothing compares to how she comes alive onstage.

Inside the country club, the grand, high-ceilinged ballroom is buzzing with laughter and the steady beat of a dance song, and we stash the instruments to the side of the stage. Then Lyndsey and MK rush to grab the best table, closest to the desserts—my girls are competitive by nature—and whoop loudly when they just barely beat some other kids to it.

"Unsportsmanlike conduct," I say, sliding into one of the empty seats decorated with tulle and fake flowers.

"Season's over, Cap," Lyndsey says. "All bets are off."

"Plus," MK says, leaning close to me so she can whisper, "I asked that girl to prom and she said she was busy. And now she's here with that guy." I raise my eyebrows. I didn't know she'd asked someone out.

"Well, I've got a big wingspan," I whisper back. "If she 'accidentally' catches a stray elbow during a slow song, know it was me." MK laughs into her fist as the rest of our friends fill the seats around us, and I rub her back once to further comfort her.

"This is incredible," Ramona says, eyes bright, grabbing my knee under the table. "The committee did such a good job, and I love y'all, and I'm here with the prettiest girl in the room." I force a smile in the instant before she sighs and puts her head on my shoulder. "This is already one of the best nights of my life."

"I'm so glad," I say, and put my head on hers, "but I think the title of prettiest girl in the room goes to you."

"Oh, get a room," Lyndsey yells, so I lob a bread roll at her. She whips it right back to me, hard, but I palm it, no problem.

"Deeeenied."

"Dammit. You have the reflexes of a hummingbird."

The theme of the prom is Enchanted Forest, so a fake buck holds a sign that says Sweet Treats in his antlers beside us. The walls, rafters, and tables are decorated with evergreens and twinkle lights. Even I can admit it feels a little magical as we eat too-small salads and primavera pasta and Ramona refills my water again and again because she knows I tend to chug it. Then we hit the dance floor.

Under the string lights, the whole room is bathed in a soft, rainbow glow, and Ramona looks radiant. Mostly we dance all of us together, but whenever a slow song comes on, me and Ramona get close, and I rest my chin on her head and think, after tomorrow—or whenever I get the guts to tell her—will I ever dance with her like this again?

I love the scent of her, the feel of her, the brush of her skin against mine. I love her dark brown eyes and dyed blonde hair; a dare, she says, for people to underestimate her. I love her cute laugh, and I'm so grateful it's back tonight, when she's seemed so stressed, so tired, so sad this whole, long year.

I love all the ways she knows me.

I hate the ways she doesn't. The ways I haven't let her.

When her favorite MUNA song comes on, we both gasp before screaming the words. She looks at me like she's madly in love with me. She looks at me like I'm perfect. I am lucky, lucky, lucky. And I pray to anything, to anyone, I'll get to stay this way.

# *glow*

AFTER ABOUT AN HOUR of dancing, Cho-Hee rounds us all up, and pulls the six of us out of the room, down the hallway, and into the big stall in the bathroom. She opens up her purse to reveal a glittering selection of mini alcohol bottles.

"To toast our friendship, and because I'm nervous as hell to perform tonight. It's been too long."

"Over a year," Ramona says, her voice tight, because we all know why she hasn't wanted to perform. She picks out two bottles of tequila, while all the others pick their poison.

"I'm good," Lyndsey says. "But knock yourselves out."

"I'm good too," I say, nervous about what might come out of my mouth if I get even a little bit tipsy.

They all take their shots, and then Cho-Hee says through her grimace, "God, I'm so glad to be away from boys. They ruin the whole vibe."

"A guy fake-tripped so he could grope me!" Minali yells. "Lyndsey caught him, though."

"With my fists," she says, holding a boxing stance.

"I can't believe so many girls brought dudes as dates," MK says miserably. "Like, in the month before Pride? Pride eve?! Homophobic."

"I would rather eat glass than be with a boy again," Minali says, draping herself on Lyndsey.

"Women are so much smarter," Cho-Hee says. "And hotter. And cooler. And we just smell better."

"I'm so glad I've always known I'm a lesbian," Ramona chimes in. "I love loving girls." She loops her arm through mine and I feel the floor drop out from underneath me.

*I love loving girls.* The words cut through my mind as I twirl them around like a knife. I bite down on my bottom lip, hard, and find it difficult to breathe. Because this confirms it, right? I can't come out to her if I don't want to lose her. Hell, I can't come out to her if I don't want to be homeless after graduation, which is pathetic and selfish and manipulative for me to even think and—

"What about you, Calla? Would you ever date a guy?" MK asks, interrupting my spiral.

"What kind of question is that?" I choke out. I grab a bottle of tequila from Cho-Hee's purse after all. And then another one.

Everyone cheers, and they all cheer again when I throw the alcohol back. I barely react because I'm out of my body.

Minali laughs. "Damn, Calla, you gonna wait for the chaser or what?" I see now she has a Diet Coke bottle snug in her purse.

I shrug, and take another shot when Ramona does. She grabs my hands, and we kiss, and my whole body is screaming, *You can't tell her!* And *You have to tell her!* But I force my brain to shut the fuck up. I shove it all down. Deep, deep, deep, deep down. Then I realize my hands are sweating, so I pull them away from hers to wipe them on my dress while Cho-Hee buries the evidence in the trash under a few layers of paper towels. MK rushes all of us out of the bathroom, away from the scene of the crime.

"Act natural," she whisper-yells as we pass one of our teachers. I'm still trying to steady myself, and the rest of my friends all giggle in a way that is decidedly not natural, but the teacher lets us go.

As we chase each other down the hall, back to the ballroom, Minali yells, "There will never be a night like this again!"

And I know she's right. A wave of grief crashes through me. Then guilt, and rage, and self-loathing. I try to shove it all down, down, down again, but Ramona must read it on my face.

"Hey, *hey,*" she says, slowing her jog to walk with me. A single tear does slip down my cheek, and I wipe it away as quickly as I can.

"Is this about next year?" All I can do is clench my teeth and nod. "You're going to be okay, Calla. *We're* going to be okay."

"You don't know that."

"I do," she says, nodding quickly. "I promise."

I nod too, but I don't believe her. And I don't know how she can believe it either, even without knowing my secrets. She's always said she didn't want to do long distance. It's why she turned down Yale for Alcott. For me. She's said being apart would make her lonely and far too anxious. But now we'll be long distance for years, unless I somehow find a way to afford moving closer to Alcott. In the meantime, she'll make new friends, and meet new girls, and get a poli-sci degree and probably get an internship on the Hill to continue her tia's work and . . . who will I be, then? In every sense?

Maybe she's shoving it all down, too. Maybe she's pretending to be okay just as much as I am when I hug her tight to me, as we plant ourselves like a flag in this single moment. Still together, still in love.

"I promise we'll be okay," she says again, as she lets me go. "Just wait and see."

# *with the band*

BACK IN THE BALLROOM, I try as hard as I can to forget myself so I don't cry or freak out and ruin the night. After dessert—cupcakes painted like mushrooms, cakes decorated with edible flowers, and s'mores I avoid lest I ruin Estonian Tennis Player's dress—three student groups perform.

Celia and Jane, our resident "we're just friends" soprano/alto duo with absolutely insane sexual tension get up onstage to sing "For Good" from *Wicked*. It's so not the vibe, but half the room knows the words and sings along while rocking back and forth with their friends. Next, The Alphas cover "Girls Just Wanna Have Fun," because what's an all-girls school prom without it? And finally, Lilith Heir is up, for the first time in so long. I kiss Ramona's forehead before she runs onstage with Cho-Hee (lead vocals and bass) and Minali (drums). Ramona plays lead guitar, and yeah, it's hot. Lilith Heir is the best band this school has ever seen, and that's not just me being biased.

"That's my girl!" I yell as Ramona plugs her guitar into the amp, the tequila really hitting me, and MK jumps on my back, just as hyped as I am. Lyndsey's all the way by the stage, taking pictures of Minali. And I wish my phone wasn't in Ramona's purse, because I want to capture this moment too. Her smile is lightning bright, her cheeks flushed from excitement. She looks so colorful and alive. I hate how long it's been since I've seen her like this. My heart feels like it could burst.

Lilith Heir plays their most popular songs, "Cannibal Girls in Vegan Leather" and "Short Nails, Tight Tops," and I mouth the words I've known by heart for years.

"We've got one more for you," Cho-Hee says, and the whole band looks to Ramona, who steps closer to her mic.

"This one's for the love of my life. Calla Quick." Over my classmates' cheers, I recognize the first few chords to The Temptations' "My Girl." Lilith Heir's harmonies are perfect. They've added their own rock flair to it. The acoustics of the ballroom are weirdly good, and Cho-Hee's voice is gritty honey. But Ramona is making too much eye contact with me, and I feel other people watching me. Feeling jealous maybe of my hot-as-hell, cool-as-shit girlfriend. Or just sorry for me. Gossip at Miss Stone's is a wildfire sprayed with gasoline, so nearly everyone knows about my parents and the tuition money. I hate the attention, but I make sure to smile. I puff my chest out, try to look like I'm proud and unshakable.

But there's a lump in my throat the size of a grapefruit, and I kind of want to cry again, and I totally blame the tequila. Why did it have to be this song?

"My girl . . ." It's fine.

"My girl . . ." It's *fine*.

"My girl . . ." It has to be fine. It's nice, even. It's nice they're singing this song for me. It's nice Ramona picked it. But it's taking all my strength to hold my smile.

"Talking 'bout my girl—my girl!" It's just a song. Jesus, it's just a song.

I'm relieved when it's over. The song's final notes fade into riotous applause, somehow, impossibly, even louder than before, and I cheer louder than anyone, hiding the scream that's been building inside me. I hold my hands up in the shape of a heart and Ramona mirrors me until the applause dulls. They don't get off stage, so I assume they have another song on deck, but instead Cho-Hee sing-songs into the mic. "Callllllllla, will you come up here?"

My brows furrow in confusion as I look around me, as if there's another Calla they'd be talking about.

"Go, go, go!" MK shoves me forward as the whole ballroom starts chanting my name.

"Calla! Calla! Calla!" My mouth goes bone-dry, and my face burns red even though I'm suddenly freezing. But I move toward the stage in a fugue state, unsure of what's to come. I climb the stairs, careful to hold the bottom of my dress up, to take each stair slowly, one at a time.

# *spotlight*

LYNDSEY MEETS ME AT the edge of the stage and climbs the stairs with me. She pushes me toward the center, and wow, holy shit, why are the lights this bright? This is the opposite of mood lighting. Every inch of me is on full display.

Our head of school, Ms. Sinclair, disappears backstage. Once my eyes adjust, I see my chanting classmates beaming up at me. I look past them to the back of the room where the doors are propped open, as if escape is an option. I don't look at the boys in their annoyingly perfect tuxedos. I pray there's nothing in my teeth, and that my earlobes aren't bleeding, and that the lines of my boxers aren't showing.

Ramona takes Cho-Hee's mic and moves to stand right next to me. She puts her hand on my back, kisses my cheek, and takes a deep breath before speaking.

"I'd like to introduce my girl, Calla Quick. I don't really think she needs an introduction, though, does she?" My classmates cheer once again. "But, boys, let me quickly fill you in. She's beautiful, kind, generous, and just . . . my person. And last fall she led the Suffragettes field hockey team to their fourth state championship in a row."

"YEAH SHE DID!" MK yells, and a few dozen others whoop. Ramona hands the mic to Lyndsey.

"Calla's been the backbone of our team," she says. "As keeper, she sees the whole field from her cage, and so she knows the game better than anyone. But she was elected captain as a sophomore—a first in Miss Stone's history—because she really takes the time to listen. Our first year, I thought she was just *my* tall, goofy, hotheaded bestie, but then I realized she was *everyone's* go-to person. We all trust her with everything: our game strategies and dreams, our hopes and fears. Our secrets." I hold my polite grin but bite the inside of my lip. If I'm good at keeping other people's secrets, it's probably because I'm so used to carrying my own. But Lyndsey's tearing up, and it makes me tear up too.

She wipes at her eyes and continues. "Just as Calla sees the whole field, she really sees the rest of us too, on and off the pitch. And she loves us just as we are." I smile even bigger and try to look grateful, but I find it hard to breathe. Why are they talking about me like this? Is there a prom award I didn't know about?

Lyndsey hands the mic back to Ramona.

"She was recruited by Alcott College, applied early decision, and was accepted. She even got an athletic scholarship that would have covered half the tuition. Her parents were going to cover the rest. Until they found out the two of us are dating." I think I might actually pass out, because I can *hear* how sorry people feel for me, and my heart rate gets really fucking weird.

I grip Ramona's shoulder just to stay standing. I half expect my parents to burst through the door and yell, "That's not what happened!"

"We don't need to tell the whole story," I try to whisper, but it catches on the mic and everyone laughs uncomfortably. Am I still smiling? When Ramona talks again, it sounds like she's underwater.

"She tried to apply for financial aid but her parents make too much money for her to be eligible."

*And it's fine,* I think. *I don't want to go to Alcott. I don't want to pretend for four more years. I don't want it on my resume forever. I don't—*

"What Calla doesn't know, though," she says as she turns to beam at me, "is that even if her parents aren't giving her the support that she deserves, she's not alone. I really wanted to believe—and deep down I knew—that Miss Stone's school is a family. Which is why"—she turns to me, glowing—"I made an appeal to our classmates, our alumni, our community." In my peripheral vision, I see Ms. Sinclair emerging through the curtains again. Holding something. "Girls help each other. Women help each other, and I couldn't be more thankful for how everyone came together to help Calla."

In what feels like slow motion I turn to see that Ms. Sinclair is holding a big ass check. Made out to me. For the amount of $36,000. The rest of my first-year tuition at Alcott College. Lyndsey reaches into her suit jacket to pull out the official Alcott College field hockey uniform. She hands it to me, and I can barely feel it in my fingers.

"Courtesy of Alcott's Coach West," Lyndsey says, still emotional. "She's so damn excited to have you."

She motions for me to hold it up, so I do. I unfold the silky tank jersey and the too-small skirt, and I don't think I'm breathing. If I thought the room was loud before, that was nothing. If Ramona was underwater, my classmates are in the trenches of the ocean. I honestly couldn't tell you what anyone says next. Not Ms. Sinclair, not Ramona. Not Minali or Cho-Hee or Lyndsey or MK.

Who waves a piece of paper in front of me and says, "Just sign right here and it's official!"?

Who says, "Calla, say something!"?

Who shoves the mic in my face? Why did the lights get so bright again? And holy mother of God, why is this dress so tight?

Am I going to throw up?

I'm going to throw up.

"I'm sick," I say, or at least I think I do. I run down the stairs, my heel catching on the last one, and I fall with a gigantic thud, my right wrist folding horribly underneath me. I hear a collective gasp echo through the thick, watery air.

I want to die on the spot but I can't. Instead, I get up and run.

# *escape*

WHEN I GET OUTSIDE the ballroom, thoughts race through my mind all at once: *What the fuck just happened?* and *What the fuck is wrong with me?* and *I ruined Ramona's perfect night* and *Jesus Christ, my wrist hurts,* and *Is it humanly possible to be this embarrassed and not die?* I might die. I honestly might. And maybe that's fine. I have never wanted to die more than I do right now, and that's really, really saying something.

But what the fuck? What the fuck. I should be ecstatic and grateful and relieved. Instead, I feel like I'm going to explode. My blood pressure is plummeting. The edge of my vision starts to fade to black and I know I might be only minutes away from throwing up or passing out or both. The first bathroom I see happens to be the men's room, so I throw myself through the door and into a stall. A couple of surprised dates yell something but I still can't hear well or see well or feel anything other than nausea and despair.

I should be *happy*. I should be fucking happy. Ramona loves me. She loves me so much she raised the money for me to go to California with her. I could go to Alcott after all. And if I'm not going to come out anyway (how can I, while living with the Silvas?), I *should* just go to Alcott. I should play field hockey, and dorm with Ramona, and build the rest of my life with her, and graduate and—

Just shove it all down. Forever.

I get sick and it tastes like tequila no chaser, and it totally ruins primavera pasta for me. I barely hear the disgust of the other guys in the bathroom before they quickly scurry out. I consider drowning myself in the toilet but there has to be better ways to go out.

It's quiet for a minute, but then the door opens again, and even in my sorry state, I feel her before I hear her.

"Calla?" Ramona calls, her voice high with panic.

"I'm in here," I choke out. I think I might get sick again, but just spit instead.

"Are you okay? Do you want me to come in?"

"No. I'm just . . . so . . . embarrassed."

"I'll be right here outside the stall, okay?" When I don't say anything, I hear her slide down the wall, heels scratching against the tile. "And you shouldn't feel embarrassed. Didn't you see? Everyone loves you. Everyone cares about you."

I spit again and I have to cut it with my teeth. Disgusting. She's right, people do care about me. But they shouldn't. As ungrateful as it sounds, sometimes I wish everyone was like my parents. I wish they'd disown me, unclaim me, hate me. Maybe then I could just run away. Disappear, no strings attached. Be someone new without hurting anyone.

"God, why are all men's rooms so gross?" she mutters, and I laugh a little, because it did reek in here even before I got sick. I flush, and pull myself up to sit on the toilet. I use a ball of toilet paper to wipe the sweat off my forehead but there's nothing I can do about the stains down my chest, on my back. The Estonian tennis player is going to feed me to the evil wild turkeys. Fine. Better than drowning in toilet water.

It's quiet for too long. I know I should say something, but I think if I do I'll start crying. I should be thanking her, telling her how excited I am, how grateful. I should say how much I loved her performance. The song for me. All of it, everything. I should and I can't.

"Was it the tequila?" Ramona asks finally. "Or the dinner?"

"I don't know," I whisper. The next silence lasts so long it grows teeth.

"Are you well enough to sign the commitment letter? I promised Coach West she'd have it tonight." *Oh.* So that was the paper someone was waving in my face.

"Tonight?" I say, and try to keep my voice neutral. But God, *no*. Not tonight. Not now. I need time to think.

"Yes, tonight," she says, annoyed. "I thought you'd be happy, I thought . . . What is going on, Calla?"

"Nothing."

"Something."

"I don't know."

"What do you mean you don't know?"

"I don't know," I say again, louder.

I can't sign that letter. But God. Fuck. What am I thinking? Throwing away my only chance at college for . . . *what*? What else can I do besides pull it together, accept the money, act grateful? Go to Alcott with Ramona, play field hockey, graduate. Forget the impossible thing. Forget the dream that should only be a dream. Remember I'm damn lucky.

And I'm going to tell her that. I swear to God, I open my mouth to tell her that. Maybe it's the stall door between us, opaque as a confessional. Maybe it's the boulder-weight of my secrets; the truth finally crashing through. Or maybe it really is just the tequila.

Because instead, I say, "My parents didn't cut me off because I'm dating you."

A beat of silence. "I don't understand, I thought—"

"They cut me off because they went through my iPad and found . . . I mean . . . I don't think I'm a girl, so . . ."

I'm glad I can't see her face, but that means I also imagine the worst in the stretching silence.

"What?" she finally says.

"I said I don't think—"

"No, I heard you," she says. "You said you're not a girl."

"I said I don't think—"

"So you're a . . . boy? Or nonbinary?"

"No. Yes. Or, I don't know, but—"

"You're telling me this now? Here? Like this?" Ramona's voice is something worse than angry. It's cold. Hurt. And I don't know what to say, because she's right. How did I mess this up so badly? I wanted to give Ramona one night. One perfect night after ruining our future together. Why did I not tell her sooner? Or later? Or never? How is it humanly possible for someone to be this self-centered and confused?

The door to the bathroom swings open, and a group of boys pour in, whooping.

"Oh, sorry," one of them says when he sees Ramona. "I thought this was the guy's room."

"It is," Ramona says. "I was just leaving." The door creaks again, and I know she's gone.

# *in limbo*

I DON'T FOLLOW RAMONA right away. I just pull my legs up to my chest so the boys don't clock my heels and listen to them talk about their dates. Their after-party plans. Me.

"Did you see that chick totally eat it?"

"Timber!"

"Think I felt the room shake."

They laugh at me—really laugh—and I'm reminded I'm not one of them. I never will be. It makes me feel sick all over. It makes me hate them.

I punch my knees until the boys are gone. Then I force myself to leave the stall, wash my hands in the sink, and rinse my mouth out with lukewarm faucet water. I swish and swish and swish and know it's not enough to erase the smell of vomit from my breath. I finally look in the mirror and hate what I see more than ever. Streaked mascara, foundation like mud down my cheeks, flattened hair, haunted eyes. Does everyone hate themselves this much? Am I a narcissist for thinking that I'm special in this way?

I wipe at my face with wet, scratchy brown paper towels until I look borderline presentable. Because I have to find Ramona. I have to make things right.

I'll apologize. I'll take it back. I'll beg her to let me take it back. I can't lose her, not like this. For what? For *what?*

I don't have to look hard for her. She's right outside the bathroom, arms crossed, talking to Ms. Sinclair, Lyndsey, and MK.

"You good?" Lyndsey says, at the same time Ms. Sinclair says, "Should we call an ambulance?"

"No," I say, ignoring the dull throbbing in my wrist, "no, don't do that. I'm okay. Just . . . overwhelmed."

"Maybe you need some fresh air," Ramona suggests, and her voice is softer now. She holds her hand out to me and I take it, and I'm so relieved I could cry. "I'll go with you."

"Yeah," I say, "I think that'll help," even though my blood floods with dread.

Outside, I'm surprised to find the sunlight still lingering, though a white sliver of moon punches through the twilight sky. Ramona doesn't let go of my hand. Some of our classmates are scattered around the front of the building, chatting or laughing or texting. We silently walk away from them along a manicured pathway, until it abruptly ends. We take our heels off to walk on the luscious green grass. We still don't make eye contact.

When it feels like we're far enough away from the country club, I take a deep breath and begin.

"First, I want to say thank you. For raising the money. That was—"

"Calla, please. Stop."

"I mean it, though. I can't believe you did all that."

Ramona waves me off. "But . . . okay. So . . . what you said in the bathroom. Are you trying to tell me you don't want to go to Alcott anymore?"

"I do," I lie. I know it sounds like a lie. I hate myself for it.

"It's an all-girls school, Calla. And you just told me you . . . might be a boy?"

"No," I protest. "I'm not." I'm not sure if I'm lying still. But I don't want to lose her. I can't. "I'm not a boy. Or not like. Just a boy."

"But you're not a girl?"

I should say that I am. I should lie one more time. I should take it back and we can laugh about this—tequila? Never again!—and move on and what does it matter?

I should, but I hesitate. I miss my chance. She sighs and says, "Look, I'm sorry. Let's start over." She takes my hands in hers, dips her head so my downcast eyes catch hers. "Thank you for trusting me. I love you and you're safe with me. But I need you to talk to me. I just want to figure this out."

I don't deserve her kindness in this moment. She should be screaming at me for wasting her time, wasting everyone's donations, ruining her night. But she's not, so the least I can do is tell her the truth.

"I don't . . . I don't think I'm a girl," I manage, but my voice cracks.

I sense her body stiffen, and the tension shows in her too-chipper voice. "Okay. That's okay. I mean, that's great! So, what do you mean by that?"

What I mean but don't say: My body feels like it's in this so-wrong dress all the time. What I mean but don't say: I could barely look at the boys in tuxes tonight without wanting to die. What I mean but don't say: When our teachers yell out, "Ladies!" I feel smaller than I ever have. What I mean but don't say: When I have to wear my field hockey skirt, I wear boxer briefs underneath my spandex. What I mean but don't say: When you touch my chest, I can't feel it. Because it's like it's not part of my body at all.

And: I've been dreaming of being someone else, somewhere else. With a different name and a different body and different clothes and a different life.

And: I'm sorry.

What I say: "It's hard to explain."

I hazard a glance at Ramona and see her nodding slowly. Her face scrunches up like it does when she's trying not to cry and my heart breaks even more. "Okay. That's fine. I just. I mean. I thought Alcott was your dream."

"It was. Or, I don't know, they recruited me, and you got in too, and I wanted to be with you . . ."

"I turned down Yale for Alcott. For you," she says, an edge returning to her voice.

"I know." Of course I know.

"You let me do that, Calla." She says my name like it's an accusation.

I stare down at my hands in hers, praying she doesn't let go. "I know. I'm sorry. I didn't know this would happen. When we got in, I just started spiraling. I wasn't planning on coming out, I—"

"I spent *so* much time raising money for you." She grips my hands harder. "I haven't even started studying for finals. The other Lilith Heir girls wanted to make an album as a last hurrah, and I said no, this was more important. God, I even spent all my phonebanking hours calling alumni for donations instead."

"Ramona, I didn't know any of this. If you had told me . . ." What? I would have told her to stop? I would have told her the truth? "I didn't ask you to do all that," I say finally, more frustration in my voice than I mean. I know I'm not allowed to be upset, that I'm the bad guy, but my voice shakes anyway.

"You shouldn't have to ask me. I *wanted* to help! Be a supportive girlfriend!" She pulls her hands away from me then. She hugs herself, putting space between us.

I cross my arms too. "And I'm grateful, Ramona. I am. You're the best, but I just . . . I don't know if I can . . . If I want to . . . Because I think I'm . . ." I can't get the words out, because it feels like if I do, my whole world will come crashing down.

She takes a deep breath and exhales slowly. She doesn't look at me when she says, "Because you think you may not be a girl. But you also don't think you're just a boy. So you're nonbinary?"

I nod, because it feels true enough. "I think so. I'm still . . . figuring it out."

"Are you going to transition? Is that why you don't want to go to Alcott?" I can tell she's trying to keep her voice measured, like she wants to pretend there's not a right or wrong answer. I know better.

"I didn't say I don't want to go." At least not out loud.

"That doesn't answer my question, Calla."

A group of girls from Miss Stone's breaks the silence that follows, giggling as they head toward us, carrying their shoes in their hands too. There's a walking path lit up by small lanterns in the trees, and without speaking, the two of us head that way.

Ramona puts her heels back on when we get to the gravel. I would rather walk barefoot on stones and sticks and dirt than put mine back on.

When we're hidden by the trees, Ramona presses again. "Just answer the question."

"Which question?" Though I know exactly which question.

"I asked if you're planning to transition."

"I don't know," I say, and that's true too. I have no idea how that would work. My parents took me off their insurance. I have seventeen dollars. How would I afford it? Who would take care of me? And then, the most important piece: "Would you still want to be with me if I did?"

I don't dare look at her. She slows her pace, and I slow to match.

Her voice is softer when she says, "Calla, you know I'm a lesbian, and for me it's never been fluid. I've known my whole life that I don't want to date a man. Including a trans man."

"I know that," I say, and feel like I'm drowning. "But, Ramona, it's *me*. Can't you just try to love me still, while I figure it out? Just wait and see?" I know I sound desperate. I am desperate. I can't lose her too. I can't.

"I don't have to try to love you, Calla." She puts her arms around my waist and presses her head into my chest. "That part is easy. I'll *always* love you. No matter what." Her tears wet my skin, and I silently beg: *Choose me. Want me. Stay.*

"Then can't we just try? It's me," I say again. "It's us." She looks up at me and I wipe her tears. She nods quickly, a pained smile painted on her face.

"Okay," she breathes. "You're right. Let's try. Let's see. You're going to change, and maybe I will too. I could surprise myself. I could surprise us both."

Only then do I exhale. Tears of surprise and relief cloud my vision, and I blink them away as fast as I can. I kiss her hair and hold her hand as we start walking again, afraid if I let go, she'll change her mind.

"And you can still go to Alcott. There are probably so many genderqueer people there. We can still be together," Ramona says, snuggling closer into my side.

"I mean, we can be together even if I—"

"I'm not doing long distance, Calla. I would have gone to Yale if I wanted to do long distance."

"But we were going to when—"

"When we didn't have a choice. Now we do, thanks to all those donations."

"I know," I say, and let a *but* die in my throat. *But* I can't go on testosterone and play field hockey. *But* I can't go to Alcott without field hockey. *But* I don't want to live like that. *But* I'm so tired of hiding so much of myself. *But* if I decide I'm just a man, Alcott will be at the top of my resume, outing me for the rest of my life.

"So you'll sign the commitment letter tonight?" I know I have to. But.

"Does it have to be tonight?"

"Calla. Yes. What else is there to think about? Coach West said she really can't wait any longer. She has other recruits in waitlist limbo. I almost told you earlier, but she said she would wait until tonight."

My vision blurs and I trip on a root or maybe nothing at all. I feel sick to my stomach again, and even in the evening wind, sweat rolls down my temples. I don't want to go to Alcott—I can at least admit that to myself—but I also don't want to lose Ramona. She's asking me to choose. The answer should be easy. It's not really a choice at all. But all I can think is: *I need more time, I need more time, I need more time*.

Without warning, rain comes fast and roaring, the whole forest crackling around us. I try to cover her, to protect her from the deluge, but we're both soaked to the skin within seconds. For an instant, I'm grateful for the distraction, for the seconds of silence it buys me.

"We need to head back!" Ramona shouts over the wind, grabbing my hand and pulling me back toward where we came from. We start at a walk, the trail turning to mud underneath our feet, but a massive crack of thunder sends us running.

With every step, my stomach tightens. Despite the storm, I wish we could stay in the woods, in this moment where Ramona still loves me and I haven't signed the next four years of my life away. But the rain falls harder, and we run faster, back, back, back. Back to prom. Back to our friends. Back to the piece of paper waiting for my signature.

*I'm so lucky*, my head says. *This is a good thing*. My heart is louder, its beat thundering through me: *I need more time, I need more time, I need—*

# *lost*

THE STORM OBSCURES WHAT little was left of the setting sun's light. We do our best to navigate the dark and the downpour, but we hit a patch of slick mud and literally skid to a stop, gripping on to each other to keep from falling over. When we find our balance, I realize we're standing at a fork in the road.

"I don't remember there being a split," Ramona says.

"Me neither." I try to think back to a moment when we might have veered left or right, but I was more focused on trying to save my relationship than where we were walking. I pat my sides looking for pockets, for my phone, but of course nothing is there.

"Shit, I left my phone in your purse," I say.

"Shit, I left my purse in the ballroom."

Shit, shit, shit.

"It's okay," I say. "We can't be too far either way." We stare into the thickly knitted trees and try to make out something familiar, something different.

"I think it's the right one," Ramona says, and of course I trust her, the girl with the answers. Thunder cracks overhead, making both of us jump. "And even if it's not, it's better to figure it out sooner than later."

But we barely take five steps before lightning strikes, and all around us turns a hot, white, angry blue. It cracks like gunshots, like fireworks, so close we stumble forward and hit the forest floor. Then there's crashing, ripping, rushing, and we spin around to see a huge tree fall behind us. We both flinch when it strikes the ground, instinctually shielding our eyes with our arms. When we look again, smoke rises from a small fire where the tree was struck, but it's quickly extinguished by the rain. Still, the scent of char is everywhere, sharp and suffocating.

We're both too stunned to scream. That lightning almost hit us. The tree came even closer. And now its wreckage is blocking the path entirely.

"Ramona," is all I can manage to say.

"I'm right here," she says as we reach for each other. "We need to find shelter. This storm . . ."

As if on cue, a new, crueler wind picks up around us. It's raw and loud and relentless. We get up and run forward because we have no other choice. We hold on to each other as if our lives depend on it. Our teeth are chattering, my skin burning, feet cramping. With each step we take, it's harder to stand, and it feels more and more possible that we might not make it out alive, and God, that would be my fault. All this is my fault.

"I think I see a light!" Ramona says, voice almost carried away by the wind. My heart unclenches at the thought of finally seeing the lanterns around the country club, but instead, we come to a clearing.

The sky above it is impossibly cloudless, though the rain keeps falling. There are more stars than I've ever seen. They feel so close. They light the world before us: a field dripping with feathery, bloodred flowers. A white, weatherworn house with a door that same bold, unforgettable crimson color. Rocking chairs on the front porch. Every window aglow. The chimney smoking. Ripples blooming across a small pond with every strike of a raindrop, and on its edge, a weeping willow tree. Chickens run around next to a coop, unbothered by the storm.

"Someone's home," I say desperately, gratefully.

"Someone's home," Ramona echoes.

I'm so relieved I could fall to my knees. Instead, I squeeze Ramona's hand, and we run.

# *home or something like it*

WHEN WE KNOCK ON the door, nobody answers. I pull away to knock again, this time louder, this time harder. Silence, still. In my desperation, I turn and try the silver handle, and the door opens gently into the house.

"Wait," Ramona says. She takes a step back and looks around us, like someone might emerge from the woods to help us. "We can't just go in."

"But—"

"Shouldn't we wait until someone opens the door? It's not polite to just—"

"Ramona," I say, my voice pleading. My words are cut into pieces by my chattering teeth. "We can't stay out in this storm. We're wet and freezing and—" Lightning strikes another tree nearby. Ramona jumps and the sound stays on my skin.

"Fine," she says, folding her arms tighter across her chest. "But if there's an ax murderer in here, I expect you to protect me."

"Obviously. Done."

We quickly step inside.

Warmth wraps itself around us, and the scent of maple sugar hangs in the air. I'd think I was dead or dreaming if my wrist didn't hurt so badly.

"Hello?" I call. "Anybody home?"

Directly in front of us, a wooden staircase leads to a second floor. To our right, a huge kitchen is clean white, wood, and teal. To our left, in the living room, a record spins on its player while a fire blazes in the hearth. Thank God. Thank God. Thank God.

"Is this 'Prove It on Me Blues'?" Ramona asks.

I shrug and my teeth chatter harder as if in relief, and we immediately sit right in front of the fire. I expect my freezing skin to burn, but the heat is perfect and strange and soft. Along one wall sits an old piano. Along another, a bookshelf filled with colorful, leather-bound books, gold etchings down their spines. Beyond a huge, green velvet couch, a big window overlooks the pond and the willow tree, and despite the storm, the view feels peaceful. They must have hosted a party recently, because streamers twist across the doorways, and a confusing balloon bouquet sways in the corner.

"Trick or Treat, Happy St. Patrick's Day, Grand Opening?" Ramona reads.

My eyebrows furrow as I take it in; then I realize we've tracked mud across the floor. I start to say something about it when thunder booms outside, shaking the whole house. Ramona grabs my hand, and we clutch each other as if that will save us.

We startle at the sound of scraping on the hardwood, and soon a bear-size German shepherd bounds down the stairs. He falls down the last few steps, but scrambles to pick himself up before running right toward us. I brace for him to rip my throat out as any good guard dog would upon finding strangers in his home, but he just snuggles his huge body up against us, nuzzling his head into Ramona's lap, the fur around his snout a distinguished gray.

"Hey, baby," she says, scratching his ears. His tail thumps against the little table with the record player, and the scratchy, defiant blues track skips on the beat.

"Signs of life," I say. "Hey, big buddy. My dog at home is smaller than your head." He pulls away from us, leaving behind a coating of fur on our dresses. Then he wiggles his butt, psyching himself up to jump on the couch. It takes him two tries, but he gets it, and the cushions sag under his weight.

"There you go, old boy," Ramona says.

"Are you home alone?" I ask, as if the dog will answer. He only gives a self-satisfied sigh as he settles onto the couch.

Whoever lives here wouldn't be that mad we came in to seek shelter, right? The art and the record, the dog and the maple scent, all signs of someone kind. Cultured. Gentle. Still, when I hear footsteps coming down the stairs, I imagine it all—a serial killer, a gunslinging homophobe, a bigger German shepherd—but to my even deeper relief, it's a girl around our age. She pauses halfway down the stairs and leans on the railing to study us. She's white, has long, curly red hair, and is wearing a bedazzled jean jacket over a vintage Sarah McLachlan tour T-shirt. I let myself breathe again. Her smile is immediate and amused.

"Fresh blood!" she calls. Ramona and I must look horrified because she quickly adds, "Not literally. Chillax."

"Yay! Welcome! Hi!" says a warmer voice from the other

end of the room. We turn to see a Black boy in a blue, white, and maroon geometric sweater that looks like it was ripped from *Saved by the Bell*. His hair is shaved on the sides and big up top, and his fingers are covered in something pink. He waves at us with jazz hands. "Please accept my most elaborate apologies. I didn't hear you come in. I was in the pantry."

"No, no. We're sorry for barging in," I say. "We got caught in the storm and dragged in all this mud—" But when I look back at the carpet, it seems perfectly clean.

"No one cares," the girl cuts me off with her thick New York accent. "Tell us, what year is it?"

Ramona and I look at each other, confused by the question. "You mean, on Earth?" I say blankly.

"Yeahyeahyeah," she urges me on.

"It's 2026," Ramona says warily.

"2026! Everyone's gonna freak. When was our last house-guest from, 2011?" she asks the boy.

"Yes, it's been so long since we've had anyone new. Nobody since Tyler, and it felt like he only stayed for a minute. God, I wish he'd stayed. Love of my many lives."

Ramona and I exchange another look. Fifteen years since their last visitor? These people hardly look old enough to drive, let alone run some kind of hotel in the middle of the woods.

"Sorry," Ramona says, "but do you have a phone we could borrow? We left ours at the country club and need to call an Uber." The two—friends? Lovers? Siblings?—exchange wide-eyed, amused stares.

"What's an Uber?" Geometric Sweater asks. "Is it a robot? Oh my God, wait, no. Is it a flying car? Finally."

"Um, no. It's a car share service? Like a taxi?" Ramona says.

"You download an app and order a ride and . . . You've really never heard of it?"

"We're a bit behind the times," the girl says, and the boy snorts out a laugh. When I look closer, she's not wrong. These kids seem like they're crazy about vintage, both of their outfits thrift finds of a lifetime. Together, they look like they're living in the 1990s. The girl even has blue eyeshadow, for fuck's sake.

"Okay," Ramona says slowly, "but you must have a—"

"I have to know," Bedazzled interrupts her, still leaning on the banister, batting her eyelashes at us. "How's Whitney? Mariah? Sophie B.? Celine? Alanis? My girl Sarah?" She pulls at her T-shirt.

"Ambrosia, diva, darling," the boy says, "let them settle in a little."

"Ugh, fine. Okay, but one question: Who was president after Obama? Seems like y'all were finally making progress, huh?" Something hardens in me, and even sweet, polite Ramona glares at her. They're messing with us. They are completely messing with us. And maybe I'd find it funny any other day but not today. God, not right now. Rage lights up my chest.

"What's your problem?" I bark, and Ramona puts her arm in front of me as if I'm going to charge up the stairs and tackle the girl. I wasn't going to, but Ramona's right that I want to. Bedazzled just smirks and cracks her gum, then blows a bubble the size of her face.

"I'm just curious, is all."

"Are you . . . like . . . MAGA?" I ask.

"My name's Ambrosia," she says.

Ramona interrupts before I can scream. "I'm Ramona. This is Calla," she says. "We're students at Miss Stone's, and we're lost, and soon our teachers are going to realize we're missing and panic. We might get in huge trouble. Can you lend us a phone or not?"

"Sorry, love," Geometric Sweater says. "I wish I could, but there are no phones here."

"No phones?" I ask dryly.

"No phones."

"IPad, laptop, anything?"

"Nope," Ambrosia says as she finally comes all the way down the stairs. Ramona and I look at each other in disbelief, as she sits in the tiny slice of couch not taken up by the massive dog. "You can send off some smoke signals in the backyard if you want to. It won't get you very far, but knock yourselves out."

I want to bite her head off but Ramona presses her arm into my chest as a warning, so I shut up. "Okay, so, how do you get in touch with people?" she asks gently, trying to keep her voice measured.

"We don't," they say together.

"So, what? Are you Luddites? Or living off the grid or hiding from—"

"Blondie, take a chill pill," Ambrosia says, the dog's head now firmly planted in her lap.

"Her name is Ramona," I remind her.

"I'm Lionel," Sweater says. "See, the thing is, things work different in this house." When neither Ramona nor I respond, he continues. "Time doesn't exist here. Like, imagine this house is an island. Imagine time is a stream going by, and each year is a boat. Or maybe each lifetime is a boat? Or is it every instant? Anyway, it's like each of us docked here at this house and time has been passing us by since. But if we ever return to the stream of time, we'll be pulled back to the very moment we left. Right back to that same boat. Make sense?"

Ambrosia claps her hands together and guffaws. "Lion, wow. Jesus, wow. That cleared things up, huh?"

He rolls his eyes and waves her away. "At least I'm trying to explain. You just want them to flounder."

"No. Well, yes. But mostly I've just learned to let Sunny do her thing."

Ramona and I share a look that says, *Are these people high?* While they don't seem violent, something clearly isn't right, and part of me wants to get the hell out of here.

Ambrosia leans forward and gives a smile that's almost sympathetic. Almost.

"Look, ladies, it'll all make sense soon enough. You're not in any danger, and for now, Lionel is making dessert"—Lionel waves his frosting hands again—"and I'm going to take you upstairs to get some dry clothes, okay?"

I bristle at *ladies*, even though I look like one, I know. I must admit—however foolish, however unfair—I'm disappointed Ramona doesn't correct her. But why would she? We need their hospitality, their shelter, their clothes. Another violent crack of thunder reminds me of that. Lightning strikes, too, bright as daylight. We can't leave yet.

"Like I said, I'm Ambrosia," she calls back over her shoulder as Ramona and I reluctantly follow her up the stairs. "Just Ambrosia. No last name, you hear me? Have you ever heard of Madonna or Cher?"

"Uh, sure," Ramona says, turning around to shoot me a bemused grin. "Who hasn't?"

"Right, so, like that."

All along the walls, up the stairs and on the second floor, are striking framed portraits. There are five of them, all of people around our age, seemingly from different time periods. There's one of Lionel, and it so captures his charming smile, the gap in his front teeth, his big brown eyes. There's one of Ambrosia too, and she looks larger than life—high glam makeup, hair pinned up with butterfly clips, a choker necklace with a star charm at the center. Her tongue between her lips, playful.

One portrait in particular stops me: an androgynous person with light brown hair slicked back; one strand out of place. Heavyset and handsome. A button up shirt that looks like it belongs to a cowboy. Freckles sprayed across a long face. And a stare that holds me there in the hallway for at least a minute. For too long. I feel so much gender envy I could melt into the floor.

"Coming?" Ambrosia calls from the top, and I take three stairs at a time to catch up.

# *perfect place for a cult*

UPSTAIRS, AMBROSIA DIPS INTO a bathroom to grab us towels to wipe the muck off our legs. They're impossibly soft. Delightfully warm.

"Are these . . . eucalyptus scented?" I ask.

"Sure, babe," she says, shrugging. "Whatever you say." Then she leads us into the only room with an open door. It's a massive closet lined with shelves and racks of carefully organized clothes. No, *costumes*. Vintage costumes from as many decades as the people in the photos. I walk over to study the fabric, and my jaw drops at how well preserved they all are. There are suits, dresses, pants, and sweaters that look like they're decades, maybe even centuries, old. It feels like a museum, and I don't feel clean enough to even be standing near them.

"Good selection, yeah?" Ambrosia says. She sweeps her arms wide. "Take your pick." Ramona reaches for the sleeve of a white cashmere sweater, but stops short of pulling it off the hanger.

"Are these your clothes?" she asks.

"Yes. And no. We all share everything."

"You and Lionel and . . . Sunny, was it?"

"And Kiyo, and Abe. You'll meet them soon."

"And you're all . . . what? Friends?" I ask, pulling a men's sherpa jacket out. It's rugged. It stirs me. I put it back quickly.

"Lionel and I, well. He's my best friend. We came in as a duo, same as you two. And Sunny and Kiyo are, like, so in love. Abe mostly hangs with Kiyo or the animals. Man of few words, usually. Barely even talks. But we're all family here. Kinda have to be after all this time." She's being cryptic again, but I don't care to press her on it. I just want to get warm and then get the hell out of here once the storm stops. And I want this wet dress off my body. Forever.

"Anyway," Ambrosia says. "I'll leave you to it. Feel free to use any of the other rooms if you don't want to change together." She shuts the door gently, and after a beat, Ramona and I start stripping. I look for something simple, neutral, and warm. I choose a nondescript outfit—black sweatpants and a tan hoodie—and change into them quickly.

But I can't help but sneak glances at the suits, the jackets, the blazers, the vests. The pressed shirts. The shoes. Oh God, the shoes. I want them so badly my mouth tastes like metal, and I realize I've chewed through the side of my tongue. I dream about stepping into the leather and laces, but I just as soon look away and shove my hands in my pockets. What would Ramona think of me in those clothes? Would she raise her eyebrows? Would she think I'm handsome? Would she smile and lie?

"Okay, what the hell is going on here?" she whispers probably too loudly, grounding me. She's still tugging on jeans but they're sticking to her wet skin. "No phone? No computers? And that whole time river thing? What the fuck?"

"I'm just as confused," I whisper back. "But we should wait it out, right? Until the storm is over at least? Unless they have an umbrella and a flashlight and . . ." And maybe in the meantime Coach West will fill my spot and Ramona and I won't have to continue that fight because I'll no longer have a choice.

"No, you're right," she says. "Your lips are still blue. And I feel like I'll never be warm again. We should at least stay until hypothermia is off the table."

"Yeah, okay," I exhale.

"You don't think they're serial killers, right?" I see her doing calculations in her head. "I mean, they're, like, our age."

"There are definitely eighteen-year-old serial killers."

"Probably not very good ones."

"I don't think I even want to meet a bad one," I say, dozens of documentaries flashing through my mind. "What if it's a cult?"

"In a farmhouse?"

"A farmhouse is a perfect place for a cult!"

"Wait, did you even see a driveway?" Her eyes get even bigger. "Or a street? Is this house just in the middle of the woods?" I was so rattled when we got here, I hardly noticed, but I think she's right.

"This shit just keeps getting stranger."

"Maybe we're dreaming?" Ramona suggests. "Here, hit me."

"What? No!"

There's a booming knock on the door, and we jump. Ramona has only one leg in her jeans still, and she almost falls over, but catches herself on my arm.

"You two good?" Ambrosia calls. "If you don't like anything, I can call Sunny and she'll—"

"We're good," Ramona answers. "Almost ready."

"Sweet. See you downstairs in a sec." Ramona pulls her arm away from mine and finishes getting dressed, glancing at the door every few seconds.

"I'm feeling more and more freaked out by the minute."

"We'll leave as soon as we can," I say, though the thought of going back to prom makes me want to die. "As soon as the lightning stops."

"Yeah, okay."

"And I'll fight them if it comes to it, remember?"

Ramona throws her arms around me, and we stay like that for a minute, just holding each other. When she pulls away, I kiss her forehead. The thunder cracks again, so loud, so close.

"For a second back there, I didn't think we were going to make it."

I don't know if she means as a couple or in the storm, but I don't dare ask.

"Me too," I say, breathless. "But we're okay."

We're okay.

# *kids these days*

I FEEL UNSETTLED AS we trudge back downstairs, but the German shepherd manages to ease my anxiety. He's thrashing with joy. I don't know if anyone has ever been so excited to see me in my entire life. It almost makes me like myself.

"What's your name, doggy?" I ask as he throws his body at my legs and covers my new pants in fur.

"Dash!" Ambrosia and Lionel call from the kitchen.

"Dash!" Ramona repeats as she combs his clean, sleek fur with her fingers. "You're so handsome, Dash."

Lionel pokes his head through the doorframe.

"He's really become Abe's dog, but Dash hates the rain. It's rough on those old joints, so he decided to hang inside with us. You hungry for dessert? Come eat."

Ramona and I look at each other quickly. Are we going to risk eating their food? Miss Stone's School for Girls has trained us to be polite, but the classes were severely lacking in lessons on how to identify poison.

"Definitely," Ramona says, taking the polite route even though she had at least ten macaroons at prom simply because they were decorated like woodland animals.

She marches into the kitchen, confident as always, and I'm right at her heels. On the counter: a huge wooden bowl full of bright fruit, the pink cake Lionel was frosting, and a royal blue glass vase filled with the most colorful collection of wildflowers I've ever seen.

Ambrosia sets the round oak table in the corner of the room, her red curls falling into her face as she lays plates down at seven seats.

"Your house is beautiful," Ramona says, and touches the bottom of the birch tree chandelier dangling in the center of the room. "It's very farmhouse chic. Rustic but elegant."

"Thanks," Ambrosia says. "Kiyo's the artist. She made that chandelier, isn't it divine?"

"And it's really Sunny's place," Lionel says with a shrug. "House of Sunny. Though she never makes us feel that way." I try to keep up: Dash is Abe's dog. This is Kiyo's art. This is Sunny's house. Lionel's the baker, of course. And Ambrosia, well. She's the worst.

"How long have you lived here?" I ask.

"Feels like forever, doesn't it, Lion?" Ambrosia says as she jumps up to pull a water pitcher down from a shelf. "Sparkling water, anyone?"

"Sure," I say. I'm not thirsty at all, strangely, but I must be dehydrated by now.

"It really does feel like forever. Time's a blur," Lionel says, sounding amused. He gestures toward the table. "Take a seat, make yourself at home." We do, but they don't yet. It feels like a trap.

"And how . . . I mean. How did you come to live here?" Smooth, Cal.

"Same as you," Ambrosia says. "We found this place right when we needed it most. During a storm, naturally."

"Ambrosia and I grew up in New York," Lionel says, putting a truly ridiculous amount of rainbow sprinkles on the cake as a final touch. "But we didn't find each other until, well. Later."

"Now we're inseparable, aren't we, darling?"

"Absolutely, buttercup."

"We're both a little too much."

"Better than not nearly enough. And you know the gays have to stick together." Lionel winks at us. He licks frosting off his finger and makes a sound like it's *good* good.

Ramona and I lock eyes immediately, and I know we're both thinking the same thing: They're gay, and that shouldn't make us trust them more. But it does.

"I'm bisexual, technically," Ambrosia says, pouring water into each of the glasses. "I mean, have you freaking seen *Titanic*?" It looks like there's glitter in the water she's pouring, but I don't dare ask. "And you two? Are you friends or—?"

"We're dating," I say, even though dating doesn't seem to cover the depths of us. The years of closeness. The way we are tonight and always.

"We've been together for three years," Ramona adds, sending me a soft smile, taking my hand.

"You two must be schoolgirls," Ambrosia observes, then smirks. "You looked like you came from homecoming."

Even though everything's okay now between Ramona and me, I still wilt at the memory of just a few hours ago. The dress, the song, that gigantic check. My wrist, still stinging, the bathroom. The tears Ramona tried to hide.

"We did," I say. "Well, prom. We're seniors at Miss Stone's."

"Right, you said earlier," Ambrosia says. "Prim and proper, just like perfect Polly."

"Polly?" Ramona looks at me with a question, but I can't think of any Polly.

"Polly McCarthy. I think she rowed crew there in the eighties, right, Lion?"

"That rings a bell. I mostly just remember that her teeth were snow white and her hair was mad permed."

"She was a Miss Stone's student in the eighties?" Ramona asks.

"Right."

"But she lived here. With you. When she was . . . older?"

"Uh, nope, she was a senior too."

I may have gotten a B- in stats this year, but even I know that makes no sense. Tonight has been confusing enough without them playing this game, and I'm getting sick and tired of it.

"Why are you doing this?" I ask.

"What do you mean, pumpkin?" Lionel says sweetly.

"Why are you messing with us?"

"We're not, Jesus," Ambrosia says. "Just making friendly conversation."

"Bullshit," I say.

"Calla . . ." Ramona warns.

I ignore her and direct my question at Ambrosia, challenging her. “Then explain to me how Polly McCarthy was a senior in the eighties while you’re eighteen in 2026.”

“We’re eighteen in 1997,” Lionel says. “Or 1998. It was New Year’s Eve, so hard to say.”

“And now we’re eighteen here, forever,” Ambrosia says as she sweeps her arms around the room.

“Fuck off,” I say, and push my chair away from the table. Ramona shoots me yet another withering look as I stand and cross my arms against my chest.

“I think what Calla means to say is that we’re confused,” Ramona says, her politician mask still perfectly in place. “We’ve had a long night, and we appreciate the hospitality—really, we do—but what you’re saying feels impossible.”

“Kids these days,” Ambrosia says, smirking, after a small, tight silence. “So entitled. So aggressive. No rainbow cake for you.”

“Ambrosia, sweetheart,” Lionel says, carrying the cake to the table. “You must remember what it’s like to be new.”

“As if. That was, like, thirty years ago.”

“What do you *mean*?” I ask. “What is going *on*?”

From behind us, a new voice says, “Oh dear.”

# *sunny and kiyo*

A BLACK GIRL WITH a wavy bob and a long, flowy, emerald velvet dress stands in the doorway. She's as tall as I am. She's full of gravity; all eyes go to her. And she's painfully beautiful, made more so because she's shaking her head at Lionel and Ambrosia. She turns to me with her eyes full of apologies.

"Are they giving you trouble?" She uses one arm to clutch her pearls—literally—while she drapes her other arm around a smaller Asian girl with short hair, a silk blouse, and what can only be described as trousers. She's holding a folded umbrella beaded with rain.

The shorter girl says, "Ambrosia and Lionel must be the worst welcome committee of all time."

"Excuse me," Lionel balks. "I baked them a cake. With sprinkles. And look!" He rushes into the living room and returns with the balloon bouquet.

"Happy St. Patrick's Day?" Trousers says, narrowing her eyes to read the gold print.

"It's all we had in storage, okay? And I thought, you know, they're *lucky* to be here!"

"Grand opening?"

"Of our home!"

"Trick or—"

"Treat!" Lionel points at the cake.

"Yeah, you two are horrible at this. But I'd be worse. On purpose," Trousers says.

"She's kidding," the girl in the gown assures us, nudging her partner with her hip.

"We're just having a little fun, Sunny," Ambrosia says, tongue out. "It's been so long since we've had new toys."

"New *friends*," Sunny corrects her as she floats farther into the kitchen.

"I'm Ramona," Ramona says, standing up to offer her hand to Sunny, who shakes it daintily. Ramona continues to handle this weirdness better than me—as she does most things.

"Ramona, it's a pleasure. I'm Sunny Ruffin," she says. "Welcome to our home. And you are?"

"Calla," I say, arms still crossed. "Calla Quick."

"And you must be Kiyo." Ramona offers her hand to the other girl. Kiyo looks her up and down, scowling, and without taking her hand, crosses the room to hang the umbrella on a hook.

"Yes, that's Kiyo," Sunny answers.

"Don't mind her," Lionel says. "She'll warm up."

"If you're lucky," Kiyo mumbles, still not looking at us as she pulls a kettle and tin canisters down from a shelf. When she opens their lids, bittersweet botanical scents drift across the room. It's intoxicating. I'd maybe ask for some tea too if I didn't think she'd bite my head off.

"Anyway, sorry to have missed your arrival," Sunny says. "We were reading in the barn and I just had to finish the chapter I was on, come hell or high water."

"Well, you're just in time for the pink rainbow maple cake," Lionel says. "A bake for the gays."

"Isn't everything you make for the gays?" Ambrosia says.

"Technically yes, but sometimes I like to hit people over the head with it."

"Your maple cake *is* one of my favorites," Sunny says. "Even if I don't have much of a sweet tooth."

"Criminal," Lionel whispers, and Sunny playfully hits his shoulder.

"Wait, wait, tell us," she says, turning back to us, clutching her pearls again. "What year is it?"

"2026," I say, my voice tight with frustration.

"2026!" Lionel and Ambrosia echo me.

"2026!" Sunny cheers. "The world spins on."

"They're Miss Stone's students," Ambrosia says. "Like 1980s Polly."

"Jesus Christ," I mumble, and roll my eyes. Sunny looks at me like I kicked a puppy, and Ramona steps in front of me.

"Please excuse Calla," Ramona says. "We're just confused by . . . all this. By the things that you're saying about this house and time and . . . I'm sure you understand."

"Are we dead?" I ask abruptly. "Dreaming? Are you actors? Are we all on drugs? Oh, God, Ramona, we got hit by that tree, didn't we?" This is my coma dream. That has to be it.

"Oh dear," Sunny says again. "It is confusing, it is. Let's sit down for cake and I'll tell you a story."

"Should we wait for Abe?" Lionel asks, but Sunny waves him off.

"He's tending to the animals. I'm sure there will be plenty left for him, yes?"

I sit at the table with everyone else and stare at the cake, pink and sprinkled and beautiful. I still don't think I should eat it.

"I have an egg allergy," I lie.

"Me too," Ramona says quickly. "I mean, um. Dairy." Another lie.

"Well, don't worry, we account for all allergies," Lionel says, and I swear he smirks like he knows we're full of shit. "The cake is perfectly safe for you both to eat."

My knowledge of baking is minimal—is it even possible to make a cake without eggs or dairy?—but I have no other good excuses. I take a bite because everyone else does, everyone except Ramona, who pushes her plate away gently. The cake is the perfect level of sweet. It melts in my mouth and lingers there, a swirl of fruit and sugar and cream, and I never want to eat anything else ever again.

"This is the best thing I've ever tasted," I say begrudgingly. "You should do this for a living. Wow."

Lionel beams. "Well, sweetness, I already do."

I send Ramona a look that says *you sure you don't want to try this?* But she just shakes her head quickly and shoots me a look of concern.

Sunny puts her fork down and reaches both hands across the table. "I'm going to ask three things of you before I tell my story, all right? First, take my hands." We do, but reluctantly, and she squeezes gently. Her skin is soft, her nails a loud shade of pink. "Second, I need you to feel how real I am. All of us are as real as you, flesh and blood." She does feel real—realer than a coma vision, fever dream, or ghost. Realer than me, probably. "You see, right? You feel it?" We nod again. "Finally, I need you to suspend disbelief. It's hard. Believe me, it is. But it'll be worth it."

"Play the game, newbies," Ambrosia says, mouth full of cake. "Sunny Says."

Sunny rolls her eyes. "Sunny says ignore Ambrosia. Now, I know just where to begin."

## SUNSHINE (SUNNY) RUFFIN

## 1911–

In 1911, George and Ruth Ruffin had their fifth and final child in Philadelphia—another son! Or, at least, so they thought. Time would prove them wrong.

Their youngest child was beloved, bright, and bubbly, and so they called her Sunshine. She was doted on, as youngest children are, even if she only got hand-me-down clothes and toys and had to sleep on the floor of George Jr. and Little Leroy's room in the apartment on Columbia Avenue. Even if the adults in her life often ran through all her brothers' names before they could remember her given name—George, Will, Eugene, Leroy . . . ? But it was okay, she thought, that they always forgot that name. She preferred her nickname. It made her feel like light.

She was, in particular, Ruth's favorite child. Oh, Ruth never said that, of course, but everyone knew. Sunshine was always at her side, helping with her sewing, curlers, and cooking. They learned to dance the Lindy Hop and the Charleston together, and when

George, bone-tired from his job at the factory, yelled for them to hush, they'd collapse into each other, giggling.

Ruth let Sunshine try on her high heels and wedding pearls, and she never said anything rotten about it. When Sunshine was five, Ruth even gave her a doll from her own childhood. It was naked, and missing an eye, and the hair looked like it had been styled by a tornado, but Sunshine hugged it to her chest like it was the most precious thing in the world.

"I confess: I felt sad when you were born. I wanted a daughter. All these boys and little old me." She pulled Sunshine into her arms then, and kissed her head. "But I didn't know I was holding *you*. My beautiful child. I wouldn't trade you for anyone."

"I love my dolly, Mama," Sunshine said, smoothing the toy's hair, "but won't they tease me?" She looked at the door, where just outside her brothers were roughhousing on the couch.

"If they do, they can make their own supper," Ruth said, "and *you* can have all of their dessert." Sunshine smiled, and Ruth smiled bigger. She used one finger to lift her daughter's chin, and looked her right in the eyes. "Your brothers can be mean, I know. And it's a mean world, especially for folks who look like us. I want you to promise me, right now, that you'll never let anyone take your joy. Your sparkle. Your *light*. You'll need it in this life. It's the only way you'll survive it."

Sunshine promised. And she had to be the light of the family—ask anyone—when darkness came in 1919. When the Spanish flu swept through Philadelphia like a match to dry branches, taking Ruth and not-so-little, but my God, far-too-little Leroy from the world. Sunshine was only eight, and she couldn't understand how this could happen to her. She needed her mother, desperately. But she also understood everything; the impossible weight of the loss. The way it devastated her father so much he stopped going to work at the factory.

Sunshine knew her role: the smiling one, the creative one, the one who reminded the rest of them that they had to keep going, even if her nightmares kept her up well into the night. She could hide so much at night in a too-quiet Philadelphia.

When the flu died down and the world came back—slowly, carefully, devastated—the New Year's Day parade did too. The Mummers parade stretched from Broad Street to Columbia, spilling out right near the Ruffins' apartment. Sunshine's brothers were so excited for it they woke up early, dressed in their most colorful clothes, and packed candy bars and bubble gum in their pockets. They got a prime spot, right on the corner, and made sure Sunshine could see it all from her view on their shoulders—the bands and the clowns, the costumes and balloons. And the men in women's clothes strutting down the street, twirling parasols, leaning into each other and laughing.

The parade was all men, and most of the men were white. Sunshine was used to that, even if it always took a bite out of her heart. But that's why time froze when she saw a Black person in a red ballgown, a slit showing off her leg, a big hat full of feathers balanced perfectly on her head. Black curls danced down her back. A longing beat like a drum in Sunshine's chest, and all she could think was: *her, her, her, her, her!* She was the most beautiful person Sunshine had ever seen. Her wanting was so loud, and because she was only eight years old, and because she didn't know it was considered wrong, she said, "Isn't she something?"

"That's a man, Sunshine!" Eugene said, and George Jr. and Will howled with laughter. "Don't be a fairy." Sunshine felt her cheeks get hot. But even though she was the youngest, she knew they were wrong. So what if she was a man? She was gorgeous. She was radiant. She was . . . light.

She locked eyes with Sunshine as she passed, and they shared a smile. Sunshine pretended she could keep that smile, pretended she could put it in her pocket.

Every January 1st, Sunshine looked for her in the parade. She found her every time, each year more elegant than the last, and when Sunny was thirteen, she made sure to lose her brothers in the crowd. When she spotted the woman, Sunshine caught her breath and ran into the street, jogging beside her.

"Please excuse me," she said, looking around to make sure no one was going to drag her back to the curb. "I just wanted you to know I think you're very beautiful."

"Thank you, sweetheart," she said. "I think you're very beautiful too." Sunshine's heart stopped. A word she never thought she could claim, *beautiful*, just like that, planted on her like a kiss.

"You're a woman, aren't you?" Sunshine asked. "Or more than a man, at least." The words were an accident, a spill. But the person just put a hand on her back with a softness Sunshine hadn't felt since her mother was alive.

"Come see me at Cecil's Barbershop, would you? Then we can really talk."

Sunshine went the very next day. A chubby little dog met her at the door, tail wagging. The woman was there, out of her parade glamour—her wig gone, gown traded for black pants and a tidy white shirt, no makeup, looking like any man in the neighborhood—but her shine was still there. It lived in her eyes, danced in her movements. Sunshine sat patiently on a small wooden bench, her heart beating loudly in her ears, until the last customer left. Then the barber motioned for her to come sit in the chair.

She said to call her Florence. She said she was an invert (Sunny filed that word away), a feminine mind in a man's body. She said she was born this way, that it's written all over her body, that nothing could change her. And did Sunshine understand? She did. And did Sunshine want Florence to make her over? Of *course* she did. Florence locked the door and spun the open sign to closed. She did Sunshine's makeup, lightly, but it changed her whole face. Sunny's hands were shaking as Florence went in the back and returned with a wig.

"Isn't she gorgeous?" Florence said, tucking fake hair behind Sunshine's ears. Another word Sunshine didn't think possible: *she.* But she knew suddenly it wasn't only possible but inevitable. She touched a finger to her pink lips, she shook her hair back and forth, she fluttered her eyelashes. The dog jumped up against her shins and put its head on her lap, as if to signal approval. Florence finally remembered to ask for her name, and she said: "Sunshine. Sunny for short."

But only minutes later, Sunshine thought she heard a knock on the door, and phantom or not, her floating heart turned to stone. She jumped out of the chair and scrubbed her makeup off in the bathroom, convinced when she stepped out into the world everyone would know what she did. What she was. That word! Invert. Something beautiful. And, like a treasure, something to hide. She barely said thank you or goodbye to Florence. She ran all the way home.

And when—months later—her longing for her reflection won out over her fear, she returned to Cecil's, a so-sorry ready on her lips. But Florence was gone. Moved to Harlem, the new barber said. "Like the rest of the fairies and sinners."

For five years, Sunny filed that away too. *Harlem. A place for people like me.* A place that could be a home if she needed one.

When she was eighteen, she suddenly, desperately did.

# *dream made real*

WHILE SUNNY IS TALKING, my head spins. Is she saying she was born in 1911? Is this a game? Performance? Mental illness? Or my own hallucination? The relentless pain in my wrist feels like proof positive it's something real, but what do I know? I keep rotating it to keep feeling. Under the table, Ramona holds my other hand, tapping her foot against mine like a series of question marks. I tap back with the same question: What. Is. Going. On.

Sunny accepts a cup of tea from Kiyo, and wraps her fingers around it while she breathes in the steam.

"Anyhow, since Florence wasn't around to do my makeup, I had to do it myself. I stole some things—I'm not proud of it, but I did. Saved up for others when I could. Got up in the middle of the night when my father and my brothers were asleep to learn how to dress, to do my face, to style my hair." She lovingly pats her carefully styled waves. "But we only had one bathroom, and one night Eugene woke up and stumbled in." Kiyo puts her hands on Sunny's shoulders. Her softness must be reserved only for Sunny, who makes eye contact with me. "He woke up the whole house. Probably the whole town. You can guess what happened from there, can't you?"

I look down at the half-eaten cake in front of me and steel myself against tears. Yes. I can guess.

How many of her family's words were echoed by my parents nearly a century later? Did they call her sick? Perverted? Did they threaten to call the police or a priest? Did they wish she'd never been born, and claim she ruined their life, and tell her she's an embarrassment? A disappointment? A tragedy? Their own daughter. Their own sister. The people who'd known her all her life?

Yes, I can guess. Yes, I can imagine.

"That's awful, Sunny," Ramona says kindly, but with too much pity. She grips my hand tighter.

"I had to leave. I headed toward Harlem and . . ." Her eyes glaze over for an instant, and Kiyo rubs her shoulders, as if to comfort her. "And then, well. Let's just say, there was a storm, and I got all turned around. Just like the rest of you. I was lost and cold and alone and I thought I was going to die. I started dreaming of a house and a friendly dog to greet me. I dreamed of a willow tree and a fire to warm me. I dreamed of a place where I could be Sunny all the time. Where people loved me for all of me." She looks up at Kiyo who squeezes her shoulders.

"You don't have to talk about it, Sunny," Kiyo says. "They've heard enough."

"I'm almost done, darling, don't fret," Sunny says before turning back to us. "I got lost and then this house appeared in front of me, Dash waiting on the porch, my dream made real, and I'm awake as ever. I've been here ever since."

I do the mental math. "So you're saying you've been here since . . . 1929?"

"That's right."

"But you're . . . still eighteen?" Ramona says slowly.

"Yes. In body and mind."

I state the obvious. "That's impossible."

Amusement sparkles in Sunny's eyes. "Yes, Calla, it is. Do you want to see other impossible things?"

# *impossible things*

"DID YOU LIKE THE cake we just ate?" Lionel asks us as if in response to Sunny's question.

"It was incredible," I say, but I don't get the relevance. He stands up from the table and heads to the counter where he cut it. Impossibly, the cake is sitting on the white tile just as it was when he made it. Whole. Frosted. Sprinkled within an inch of its life.

"Okay, so you made two," Ramona says.

"Do either of you want an apple?" Ambrosia asks.

"Sure," I say, humoring them. She pulls one from the bowl, bright red and shiny, and instantly another identical one appears in its place. I mutter *whatthefuck* and Ramona gasps.

"Or how about a flower?" Sunny says, pulling two stems out of the vase of rainbow wildflowers, one for each of us. Two fresh ones bloom instantly.

"Magic tricks," Ramona says but sounds unsure. "Sleight of hand."

"Sleight of bowl?" Ambrosia offers, taking a huge bite from the apple. "Why don't you pick a record? This party could use some tunes."

The others stand and head to the living room. Ramona and I reluctantly follow. We walk toward the stack of vinyls piled haphazardly next to the record player.

"Choose something good," Ambrosia says. "Something fun. Something we can dance to."

Ramona picks one up. "But none of these are labeled."

Sunny gestures for Ramona to put it on. So, she takes the purple record from its sleeve, puts it on the player, and drops the needle. Within seconds, the opening notes of Lilith Heir's "Cannibal Girls in Vegan Leather" fills the room. I clap a hand over my mouth. Ramona and I look at each other in awe, in horror.

"We never recorded this," Ramona says breathlessly. "We've never recorded anything . . ." She falls onto the green velvet couch and grips the arm so hard her knuckles turn white.

"How did you . . . ? Where did you . . . ?" I look from Sunny's face to Lionel's, from Ambrosia's to Kiyo's. None of them seem surprised by our reaction. Kiyo looks straight up bored, studying a small sketchbook she's pulled out of her trouser pocket.

"Now this is what I'm talking about," Ambrosia says, moving her shoulders to the music. "This track is fresh."

"This is my song," Ramona says. "It's my band, Lilith Heir. I wrote this two years ago."

"No shit!" Ambrosia says, sliding onto the couch beside her. "It's good, girl. It's like if the Spice Girls were gritty and gay. Wait, do you know them?"

"Ambrosia," Ramona says, seemingly snapping out of whatever stupor the song put her in. "Do I know them? I'm so honored to tell you this: Scary Spice is bi."

"No shit!"

"Allegedly she hooked up with Ginger once."

"Don't play with me, Blondie."

"I'm so serious. Hand to heart. And do you know about Whitney?"

The song plays on and I sit down on a chair, dizzy. Ramona is distracted now by sapphic celebrity gossip, one of her all-time favorite topics, but I'm still spiraling out over this impossible Lilith Heir song. There's no explaining this away as a prank, a trick of light, or sleight of hand. How do they have this? How is it playing? How is any of this real? I'm so freaked out half of me wants to run out the door, but I don't.

I don't run when they have us pull unmarked books from the bookshelf, and open them up to find works we've each been meaning to get to—Cory McCarthy's *Man O'War* for me, Tegan and Sara's *High School* for Ramona. I don't run when they have us throw water in the fireplace and nothing, and I mean *nothing*, happens to the flames—no smoke or sizzle or wavering. And I don't run when the storm stops suddenly outside, and a rainbow that looks close enough to touch cuts the dark night sky. It seems to flow through the willow tree and stream into the pond. It's so beautiful it's almost cartoonish.

"Now that's just showing off," Sunny says, shaking her head as she takes in the colorful display.

Ramona and I are stunned into confused—and maybe convinced—silence. I sit on the edge of the fireplace and feel the heat of the gentle, eternal fire lick at my back. Maybe they're telling the truth. Maybe all this is real. And if so . . . then what? Everything I've ever known about time and reality and life itself is wrong? Stars cloud my vision and I grip the stone hearth to steady myself.

"Okay," Ramona finally says, and I can see the blur of her sitting down on the couch, Dash jumping up beside her for pets. "So . . . impossible things happen here?"

"Impossible things," Sunny says.

"And time stands still?" Ramona asks.

"Yeah, dude," Ambrosia says, eyes wide. "We can live forever here."

"And you all found this place the same way we did?" I ask. "Lost in a storm?" They all nod and share knowing looks with one another.

"We call the land Amaranth," Kiyo says, "after those flowers you saw in the field. In ancient Greek, the word means immortal."

"Amaranth appears to inverts who need it most *when* they need it most," Sunny says.

"Introverts?" I ask.

"No, darling. Inverts. Girlish boys and boyish girls and everything in between." My heart leaps because I swear Sunny looks directly at me when she says it.

My mind rewinds back to right before the storm, to my silent plea. *I need more time*—to figure out who I am and what I should do. And then I stumbled into a weird, queer forever. The absolute absurdity of it all makes my whole body buzz. I almost laugh out loud.

"There are some small conditions, though," Sunny continues. "If you leave you can never return. However, you are under no obligation to stay. If you walk back past the field of flowers, you'll go right back to the exact moment in your life before you stepped into the clearing."

"How do you know that if you've never left?" Ramona asks.

"We had brothers visit, once, early on, when it was just me and Kiyo. Didn't we, love?"

"Herman and Hubert," Kiyo says, barely glancing up from her drawings. "Knucklehead and Chucklehead."

"Herman stayed for, oh, two years? Then he left, told Hubert about us, and lo and behold he found it next. That's how we know what happens when you leave here. You lose no time at all—Hubert said it was like Herman was never gone. Unfortunately, he also said Herman couldn't remember anything he learned from future guests that would make him rich quick. Rats."

"So the younger brother went back too?"

"Oh, yes. So long ago. Many others have come and gone since then."

"And now there's only you four, and—" The front door swings open and there he is. The person whose stairway portrait stopped me in my tracks. He's soaked to the bone, dressed in denim and a boxy white shirt, a soft smile on his lips. He shakes rain out of his hair, and my heart stands still.

Dash howls joyfully as everyone yells, "Abe!"

# *abe*

"NEW KIDS," ABE SAYS, voice soft with wonder. He looks back and forth between me and Ramona, and every time he lands on me, I want to look away. Suddenly I feel self-conscious about my matted hair, god-awful posture, and sweatpants. I wish I'd picked something more presentable, but I can't change now.

"Dry off and come meet Calla and Ramona," Ambrosia says. "Girls from Miss Stone's." Again, I don't correct her, and this time I'm only disappointed in myself.

Abe kicks his muddy boots off, then takes the stairs three at a time. He comes back quickly, wearing sweatpants now, too, so I feel a little better. He sits wide-legged on the only remaining chair, and Dash makes sure to greet him.

Abe is handsome. Sturdy. And, God, I hate assuming but . . . possibly trans. Like Sunny, he seems comfortable in his skin, and I feel a deep, hot stab of jealousy.

"Sorry to miss your arrival," he says. "The goats have been so needy lately. Especially Sylvie, poor girl."

"Abe's gifts were the animals," Lionel says. "Well, all of them but Dash."

"Gifts?" Ramona asks.

"That's part of why we like new guests so much," Lionel says. "You bring presents!"

"Ah, yes," Sunny says. "Amaranth gives a gift to everyone. Something wonderful, different, and new. Sometimes it's a tangible, physical thing—a room, an object, or supplies. Other times it's an abstract feature. Sometimes both."

"So your gift was . . . ?" I ask Sunny.

"As the first one here, it's hard to say. At the very least, the magic books. But possibly this whole world was my gift, where people like me can live safely, free to be ourselves. Forever." That word again. It sticks in my mind. An unimaginable fantasy. What would I do with forever? Who could I become?

"My gift was endless art supplies," Kiyo says dryly. "Lionel's was the pantry, thank heavens. Ambrosia's was the playroom. Abe's was the animals."

"And don't forget his man cave," Ambrosia says, leaning forward to slap Abe on the knee. He blushes and rolls his eyes.

"It's a toolshed," he says.

"It's like if a Home Depot and a hurricane had a baby. Enter at your own risk."

"Will we get gifts too?" I ask, hopeful.

"Calla," Ramona says, "we're leaving in the morning. I don't think there will be time for gifts." My heart sinks. Right.

But Sunny only smiles. "Of course, but if you *did* stay, you would get a gift, yes." Her eyes fall on me. "Amaranth chose you.

It brought you here for a reason. It sees into the deepest parts of all of us and gives us exactly what we need."

I didn't think my heart could beat faster or harder, but it does. A small part of me genuinely believes Sunny, believes all of them. She says I'm here for a reason. Could that be—despite all logic and rationality—true? What if my gift gives me answers? What if it helps me figure out what I should do next year? With the rest of my life?

"And how long does it take, usually? For a gift to appear?" I ask.

"It's hard to say," Sunny says. "Never terribly long."

I turn to Ramona to see if she's curious about our potential gifts, too, but her face is as stony as her voice when she says, "Unless it happens tonight, we'll be gone."

"Well, what if—"

"Calla. People are probably looking for us. You have a commitment letter to sign. We could get in trouble."

"Time isn't passing outside Amaranth," Kiyo says. "Thought we covered that."

"Even so," Ramona says firmly. "We're leaving in the morning."

My shoulders sag. Would it really be the end of the world if we were gone for a little bit? I don't want to worry anyone, but with everything we've seen tonight, is it really that crazy to believe time is standing still outside Amaranth? That here, we have all the time in the world?

"A lot can change in a night," Abe says. I swivel my head and find him staring at me. When I meet his gray eyes, he holds my gaze. "In a moment, even."

Does he sense my desperation? Can he tell how badly I want to stay?

"Let us show you around at least," Ambrosia says. "You still have time to experience all that Amaranth has to offer."

"Please," I say. "That would be great." I stand up before Ramona can protest.

# *the house at amaranth*

FIRST, LIONEL LEADS US back into the kitchen. The plates and mugs from earlier have disappeared.

"When Ambrosia and I got here, the kitchen just had staples. You know, bread, rice, and milk. Those poor souls were eating the same things over and over again, for years. Can you imagine? I'd be gone, bye-bye! Adios! Au revoir!" He opens every drawer and cabinet one by one to reveal the mismatched plates, pots, silverware, and spices. "But I show love by feeding people, so I guess that's my magic," he continues. "On my second day here, the cupboard started spitting out new ingredients. I'm working on a cookbook, even."

"Ooh, can we see?" I ask.

"Okay, I *want* to be working on a cookbook."

He pulls the teal pantry door open, and I'm confused to see the inside completely empty.

"Wait, where's the food?" I ask.

“Step in, loves. One at a time.” I motion for Ramona to go first, so she takes one stride in and gasps. She reaches forward and starts stacking coconuts in her arms.

“I love baking with coconut,” she says, grinning at me. “It reminds me of my tia and her quindim. Whoa.” The coconuts just keep coming, and fast. Lionel and I lurch forward to help catch them, and even still, some hit the floor with a *thwack, thwack, thwack*.

“Are you Brazilian?” Lionel asks.

“Mm-hmm. My dad’s family still lives there. But I’m from Miami.”

“I’m Puerto Rican and Haitian,” Lionel says, “but I grew up in Brooklyn. I do speak Creole and Spanish, though.”

“My Portuguese is mid at best, but when I’m there it just flies out of me. It’s wild.”

“Maybe you can teach me some,” Lionel says with a smile before turning to me. “Your turn, Calla.”

“I’m just, like, British and Italian or something.”

“No, pumpkin. Your turn in the cupboard.”

“Oh, ha.” I don’t know why I’m nervous, aside from the fact that I can’t cook for shit. I step inside, and find . . . hot dogs. Which I don’t even like. There are also buns, s’mores ingredients, bags of Fritos, and cans of chili.

“I don’t get it,” I say, handing the items out two at a time to Ramona and Lionel, who is excited for some reason.

“Oh, *fun*!” he exclaims, beaming. “This means we’ll have a campfire later.”

“Why doesn’t the house just make the food for us?” I ask, shaking a Fritos bag. Lionel slaps his hand to his chest, offended.

“Where’s the art in that?”

# *treasure*

"NOW ON TO THE best part of the house, if I do say so myself," Ambrosia says with a flourish. She leads us down a flight of plywood stairs to the basement, dancing down each step. It's drafty and smells like, well, a basement (what *is* that smell? I love it), but it's filled with stacks of board games, a pool table, pinball machines, beanbags, and some '90s style inflatable chairs.

"Is this—?" Ramona starts, but Ambrosia finishes.

"—a Tamagotchi? Yes. Yes, it is."

"Holy history," Ramona says, fingers trailing along a shelf of vintage treasures.

"Excuse you." Ambrosia winks as she opens a drawer to reveal Game Boys, a CD player, and a Bop It. "This shit is cutting edge. And there's a karaoke machine, too; you'll love that, Blondie."

"Um, absolutely yes."

"So your gift was . . ." I pick up a tie-dyed Beanie Baby and pop it like a baseball.

Ambrosia spreads her arms wide. "This whole rec room. Because I'm fun. Duh," she says. "I used to dream of a room like this when I was growing up. I didn't have any toys or friends or nothing. Had to entertain myself."

"This feels like something out of a movie," I say.

"I know, right? Like I said, it's fun. I'm fun. Unforgettable. These nerds were just, like, reading and painting for a hundred years before I came along." Ambrosia is bouncing around the room, eager to show off her Nintendo 64, Koosh balls, and air hockey table.

"You can probably tell me and Lion are the most stoked to have you," she says. "We haven't had too many new guests since we got here. Maybe five? And, clearly, none of them stayed."

I want to ask her why they left, why she's stayed, but it feels too personal to ask someone I just met. I expect Ramona to remind her, yet again, that we're leaving in the morning, but instead she squeals. She's pulling the karaoke machine Ambrosia mentioned out from where it's hiding under Legos and plastic figurines. It's bright pink and Barbie-themed.

"Okay, this is iconic," she says, trying to untangle the plastic cords.

"You think so?" Ambrosia says, and I'm surprised to see she's bashful. "I kinda thought it was tacky."

"One decade's tacky is another one's treasure," Ramona says, and plugs the bright pink block into the wall. "Should we sing tonight?" she says into the microphone. The tinny sound fills the whole basement.

"Are you kidding?" Ambrosia says. "I've been waiting forever for a duet partner!"

She nearly knocks Ramona over with a hug. Ramona catches her, laughing, and I see that spark in her eyes for the first time since we got here. Since she was onstage, earlier tonight, singing her heart out to me. Since I ruined our night and the rest of our lives.

Even still, Ramona smiles at me over Ambrosia's shoulder. I smile back, but it falls as soon as she looks away. Because I now know I'm the reason why that spark faded, long before prom. She'd spent so much time collecting donations for me, planning her life around me, giving up parts of herself to help me—yet doing the same for her by signing that commitment letter feels like an impossible ask.

But impossible things happen here at Amaranth. Maybe my night here will fix me. Maybe it'll make Alcott feel . . . well, possible. Because all I know for sure, watching Ramona now as she flips through the karaoke machine's song catalog, is that I don't want her to lose the light in her eyes ever again. Especially not because of me.

"Darlings, don't let Ambrosia's playthings distract you for too long. There's more to see!" Sunny calls down the stairs.

"Coming, Sunny!" Ambrosia says into the microphone. She grabs Ramona's hand and drags her toward the stairs, and I'm relieved when Ramona does the same to me as they pass.

Sunny waits for us on the second floor landing. "I know you've already seen the boudoir," she says as she twirls into the middle of the oversize closet, "but I must tell you it's my favorite room in the house. If you ever need fashion advice, I'm your girl. I can make a paper bag look like a ball gown. I can turn a frog into a prince."

I wonder, pathetically, if she could help me like what I see in the mirror for once in my life, but I don't dare ask. Not here. Not now. Not in front of Ramona.

Sunny leads us quickly through the other three rooms on the second level, which feels a bit cramped for five people living there. The first room is pink, pink, pink. It's filled with soft light, a pile of folded blankets, and a magenta chaise lounge.

"This is my writing studio, though you're welcome to use it for whatever you'd like. There's a desk, blank notebooks, books on craft . . ."

"You're a writer?" I ask. Sunny sighs wistfully and drapes herself across the chaise.

"I am. Unfortunately. I've been working on a novel for . . . well. Forever. I like to think I'm almost done, but who's to say?"

"A novel! What's it about?" Ramona asks. Sunny sighs again, but I can tell she's fighting a smile.

"It's based on a doll like me, finding a place like this but in the big city. Though, unlike me, she has to go through absolutely *horrible* things to get there. I really put her through the ringer, Maud."

"Poor Maud," I say. "I'd love to read it."

"Mmm," she hums instead of answering, before continuing down the hallway.

"Here's the bathroom, appropriately named, because all that's in here is a bathtub." Sure enough, the wallpapered pastel heaven has only a giant clawfoot tub sitting in the center surrounded by towels and candles.

"I have questions," I say. Sunny laughs, and I have to smile because the sound is so warm.

"Because time stands still here, you won't ever have to

relieve yourself. You're not even digesting food, not really. It's an illusion."

"I miss pooping!" Lionel yells up the stairs, and the whole house fills with laughter. I immediately want to ask if people get their period here, because I would do unspeakable things to stop mine forever. But I'm way too embarrassed, and Sunny is on the move again.

"And, similarly, the bedroom." Sunny steps into the last open door, where we find a single bed, a lamp, and a nightstand with a stack of books.

"*The* bedroom?" I ask. "One bedroom for seven—I mean, five people?"

"That's right. Sleep isn't a necessity here," Sunny says. "Night and day are illusions, too. I suspect Amaranth upholds the ruse to keep us sane. But I like to sleep every now and then. I need my dreams. And we've found newcomers like you are quite attached to the routine of it." I have so many questions, about how they share the space and what they do with their days and if they ever get sick of each other, but Sunny is already heading back toward the stairway.

Behind her, I focus on taking one stair at a time, but when Sunny says, "Abe'll show you around outside," I nearly trip.

# *the grounds*

ABE AND DASH ARE waiting for us by the back door, and so are boots in just our sizes.

"Think those should fit," he says. "It's a little hard comparing boots and high heels." I realize he grabbed the boots for us, that he's been waiting patiently by the door, and my heart swells at the gesture. But then I picture him examining my stilettos and that makes me want to walk into the pond outside, never to emerge.

Regardless, the boots are a perfect fit. Tan and steady.

Ramona and I follow Abe across the porch, down the stairs, and past the firepit. Dash pants and trots beside us through the field of amaranth flowers, kicking up mud. The bright, white stars still take my breath away, and besides the grass squishing under our feet, the only sign of the storm is the smoky rainbow still streaking the chalkboard sky.

My eyes land on Abe, striding a couple steps ahead. He walks with his hands in his jacket pockets, head bowed. Something about it feels so masculine and natural in a way that makes me ache with jealousy. I try to imagine what he thinks of me. Can he see the unsureness in my gait? The way I hunch my shoulders to hide my chest?

Can he see I'm like him?

If I told him everything I dream of being, would he roll his eyes? Ask me why I haven't done anything about it yet? Would he call me a fraud? A coward? Or would he hug me and tell me he sees it? That he can imagine me different. Boyish. An impossible person possible.

He must sense me staring, because he turns and immediately meets my eyes. Heat rushes to my face and I quickly turn away. And Jesus, why am I being so weird? It's not like I've never talked to a trans guy before. I've talked to many, many trans guys—on the internet. I just haven't gotten to hear their voices or stand close to them or smell their cologne, which for Abe is like campfire and evergreen and . . . yeah, I think that's goats. Surprisingly, it works. So does his big, bulky, sherpa-lined corduroy coat. So do his sweatpants that bunch at the top of his boots, already muddied, already weathered. I feel myself pulled to him like a magnet, but Ramona breaks the spell.

"Sure is quiet out here," she says. She's never been good with long silences, always playing music or NPR in the background, regardless of what we're doing.

"I like the quiet," Abe says as we cross the lawn, "and my space. So I'm grateful for all this incredible land." He's soft spoken with a slight accent, though I can't place it. It's not Southern, not quite. I wait for him to say more, but he's a man of his word. He likes his quiet. He likes his space.

"Do you grow anything here? Plants, food . . . ?" Ramona asks.

Abe shakes his head. "Nothing grows here."

Ramona furrows her brow. "But the flowers, the grass . . ."

"Exactly the same as when I got here. Without time moving forward, things just stay as they are. Kiyo and I have tried to seed thc wildflowers. She hates that they only survive in vases here, but they never take. It's all strange, isn't it?"

"Do you ever get used to it?" I ask.

He shrugs. "I reckon all of us have gotten pretty good at accepting things as they are. Even if we don't understand it."

We reach a red barn, with one side half covered in what must be a Kiyo mural in progress—there's an outline of a brown two-story house under a swirling, colorful sky. Outside the barn is a grid of fences. Four goats of different colors wobble up to us, big-eyed and bleating, and Dash puts his tongue through the fence to give them kisses.

"All the farm animals were part of my gift. Meet the goats: Sylvie, Agnes, Dorothy, and Nellie."

"They're so sweet," Ramona sings, and they really are. They push their heads into my hands, and Abe gives us pellets to feed them. They eat out of our palms with their goofy, gross tongues and I can't help but giggle. I feel light for the first time all night.

"They remind me of my dog, Nugget," I say, and Abe smiles at them like a proud father.

Next, we meet dozens of chickens, who scatter when we come close, and two black cows named Bert and Ernie. They're tucked away in a barn stall, fast asleep. I only know they're alive because their stomachs rise and fall. They're cuddled up together, heads side by side. They seem so peaceful, so comfortable, like they want for nothing.

"They're in love," Abe whispers, leaning into me.

"Aww," I say, and immediately hate how high my voice is. "Gay cows."

"They're actually both girls," Abe says. "Ambrosia named them. I'm not very good at naming things."

"Obsessed," Ramona whispers. "Do you milk them?"

"Nope," Abe says. "Don't have to."

"Because nothing grows here," I say.

"Nothing grows here," he says with a grin. "Thank God."

Beyond the cows' stalls is a main hall lined with bales of hay, and the rest of the structure is clearly for the houseguests' use. There's a reading nook surrounded by piles of books that I assume are Sunny's. There's an art studio that must belong to Kiyo with buckets of paint, half-finished canvases scattered around, and portraits of old houseguests that no longer fit along the stairwell. There is drawing after drawing of Sunny—in different lights, at different angles, with different expressions. It's romantic. Abe smiles as we pass it, knocks on the doorframe as if in reverence, but I guess it's not an official part of the tour.

"That's pretty much it," he says.

"What about the 'man cave' Ambrosia mentioned?" I ask, and raise my eyebrows at him. He looks away from me quickly.

"It's . . . uh. It's just a toolshed. It's not worth seeing, really."

"I like tools," I say, "and sheds." I instantly regret it, because Ramona squints at me.

"Since when?" she asks.

"Since . . . since always."

Abe studies me, and either decides I'm ridiculous or genuine before smiling.

"Maybe later, then," he says. And I desperately wish Ramona wanted to stay at Amaranth so there could be a later. So we could have all the time in the world.

## *campfire*

BACK IN THE FIELD, the amaranth shiver. The stars, silver before, seem golden as we head back toward the house. The stillness of this place calms me as we walk, and the absolute, total quiet is unlike anything I've ever known before.

It's interrupted only when Lionel yells, "Campfire!" as soon as we're within earshot of the firepit. He's stacking the food in an orderly line, along with what looks like a few bottles of champagne. Ambrosia is carrying a pile of blankets so high I can't even see her face, and Sunny and Kiyo are folded into each other, deep in conversation. When we get there, Abe kneels by the fire, angling the logs of wood to form a pyramid.

"Do you want to help me light this?" he asks, and it takes me a minute to realize that he's talking to me.

"Uh, sure," I stammer, and kneel beside him. Our fingers touch when he hands me the matches to strike, and I feel too warm already.

"This fire's different from the hearth," he says, adding kindling around the logs. "Only lives as long as you need it to." He holds the logs upright, and I place one match and light another and another, and then as the flames rip into being, we step back and watch them riot.

"Now we're cooking with gas," Kiyo says.

"Well, fire," Abe says, but she just pats his shoulder.

We all settle into a circle of black chairs that are far more comfortable than they look. There are seven, exactly. Were there five before we got here? Kiyo hands out long, thin sticks for roasting, and Dash puts his paw on Lionel's knee to beg patiently for a hot dog.

"So you're from the 1920s," Ramona says to Sunny. I can hear the doubt in her voice, but if Sunny notices, she doesn't let on.

"1929," she says. "Which I've been told is the dawn of the Great Depression. Yet another reason for me to stay."

"1948 for me," Kiyo says. "Yes, a few years after the Second World War, and yes, I was in a Japanese American internment camp. But I'm not some living history textbook. None of us are. We're people, so mind your own beeswax."

"Right," Ramona says. "Of course." I only nod awkwardly. Kiyo clearly isn't too fond of dredging up the past.

"1959," Abe practically whispers.

"1997 slash eight," Ambrosia and Lionel say together.

Ambrosia lets out a big sigh. "The best of times for us queers—"

"I still hate that word," Lionel interjects. "Reminds me of grade school bullies."

"—and the worst of times. Lion and I have *the virus*," she

says in the voice of a monster. She's trying to joke it off, but I can tell by their faces that it's not funny. It's not funny at all.

Ambrosia throws her arm around Lionel. He puts his head on her shoulder and looks at his hands. "We can't leave or we'll die," Lionel says, not able to manage the same lightheartedness as Ambrosia. "So we're stuck here."

"Not that we want to leave," Ambrosia says. "Right, Lion?"

He shoves a hot dog in his mouth in response.

"It's still hard, I'm sure, to feel like you don't have a real choice," I say. The fire cracks loudly in the hush that follows. I suddenly feel so incredibly shallow and selfish for thinking my problems are so impossible to overcome. But I know my shame doesn't help them, and this isn't about me at all. "Are you . . . wasn't HAART . . ."

"Sweetness, HAART costs eighteen thousand dollars. At least. Per year. We don't have that kind of money, and neither do our parents."

"Not that they even know we're positive," Ambrosia scoffs, and Lionel looks down sheepishly. "We're both on all sorts of waitlists, but that's no guarantee."

"Right," I say, feeling foolish.

"I can't imagine what you all have been through," Ramona says, sounding genuine. "I mean, I can *imagine*, but I can't—"

"Yeah, yeah," Ambrosia says, grabbing a champagne bottle by the neck. "Look, we're only telling you all this because it's your first night. But in general, we don't like to talk about it. Any of it. Ever. We left our old lives behind for a reason, and we want to leave them there. Okay?" I don't try to argue. Ambrosia switches subjects. "You're in the hot seat now, babes. You're Miss Stone students? And you're seniors? In 2026?"

"Right. Tonight was—is?—prom," I say, to a chorus of oohs and whistles.

"Let me guess," Sunny says, "you had to go with fellas but you secretly wanted to go with each other?"

Ramona actually laughs out loud. "No," she says, and puts her hand on my arm. "We went together. A lot of girls do."

A heavy silence falls over the group, and Kiyo's head snaps toward us. "You were allowed to go together?" she asks earnestly.

"Yeah, of course," Ramona explains. I can see realization dawns on her then, just how recent our history is. "Or I guess, not *of course*. You said your last guest was from 2011? Well, we've made *some* progress since then. Most of the time it doesn't feel like enough, but in the U.S.—and in a lot of other places—gay people can actually get married. For now, at least. My tia was a lawyer in D.C. before she passed. She played a huge part in getting it legalized." I send her as much love as I can in a glance.

"Marriage! For crying out loud," Sunny says breathlessly, and even Kiyo lets joy flicker across her face as she reaches for Sunny's hand.

"How mainstream," Lionel says, brightening.

"To gay marriage," Ambrosia says, holding another bottle up as an offering. "So the queens can be miserable too." She pops the cork and it bubbles over her hand. She licks it off her palm before taking a swig from the bottle. She hands it to Ramona next, who tries to hide her disgust but fails miserably.

"Oh, no, thank you," she manages, and Ambrosia rolls her eyes.

"You can't get AIDS from spit, Blondie," she says. "Besides, germs don't exist here. No one gets any kind of sick, ever."

"Oh my God, no," Ramona stammers, mortified. "I didn't think tha—"

"So, you went to prom together," Ambrosia plows on, leaning forward to offer the bottle to me. Unlike Ramona, I take it. "And you're dating. And you're seniors. At Miss Stone's." She says this last part with a horrendous British accent.

"So what's next for you?" Lionel asks. "You know, once you leave in the morning." That is the last question I want to think about right now. I take a sip of the champagne and stare at the fire.

"Well," Ramona starts when I don't answer, "the plan is Alcott College, an all-girls school. We both got in. Calla's going to play field hockey and I'm going to study political science. I want to be like my tia and fight for human rights."

"Ramona's an incredible organizer and activist," I say, finally finding my voice. It's easier to talk about Ramona's future than mine. "She's been fighting for queer rights all across the country. Especially in Florida." Lionel winces at my word choice, and I mouth, "Sorry."

"I can tell you're so proud, Calla," Sunny says.

"I really am," I say, and smile, and Ramona returns it even bigger.

"An activist, huh," Ambrosia says, looking only at Ramona. "You going to be a lawyer, too?"

"That's the plan."

Ambrosia's eyes flick to me. "And you, Calla?"

I want to tell her to mind her own beeswax, but I don't think it'll land well. Acid burns in my throat but I fight to keep my expression neutral. I take another sip of the champagne to stall.

"Is field hockey a job?" Sunny asks.

"Oh, no," I say. "Well, it would be, sort of, because I got a scholarship and I'd need to work to keep it. But I would have to study something, too, if I went there."

"Why are you saying 'if'?" Ramona says sharply.

"When. I meant *when*, sorry. I'm still getting used to it." I bring the bottle to my lips again and hope it helps hide my lie.

"How wonderful," Sunny says, flushing. "I always wanted to go to college, but there aren't many options for a girl like me. Did you just get the news?"

My face goes hot, and I massage the back of my neck to calm the heat growing there. Maybe it's that they're magical strangers from history. Maybe it's that I'll never see them again. Maybe this champagne hits harder than the bottle I swiped at my cousin's gender reveal party last summer. Whatever the reason, I say too much.

"No, I mean, we got accepted back in March. I just couldn't go for a while, because my parents aren't going to pay the tuition anymore. Because they found out I'm, uh, trans. Or I might be trans. But anyway, now I can go, thanks to Ramona, who's amazing and raised all this money for me. So I am going. I am going to Alcott."

"And you'll sign the commitment letter the minute we get back," Ramona says, and I can't tell if she's encouraging or chastising me. I only nod, and stare into the flames of the fire.

"You seem . . . thrilled," Kiyo says.

"I am," I say too quickly.

Everyone is still looking at me, and I shift around uncomfortably in my chair that's feeling less and less comfortable and more and more like quicksand.

"Trans," Sunny says softly. Firmly. "I'm afraid I don't know that term, exactly. What does it mean?"

"Tranvestite?" Kiyo guesses.

"Transsexual," Ambrosia offers.

"We don't use those words anymore," Ramona says, and reaches over to put her hand on my arm.

"Well, some people do," I say.

"It's kind of like RuPaul, right?" Lionel suggests.

"They had *Drag Race* in the nineties?" I ask, surprised.

"RuPaul is a race car driver now?"

"What? No, *Drag Race* . . . Never mind."

Ramona motions impatiently for me to continue. She looks like she's also waiting for answers, ones I don't really have yet. "It's not like RuPaul, no. He has a drag persona, but identifies as a man. Trans, or transgender for us is like . . . well, you, Sunny? Like, you were born in what the world thinks of as a boy's body, but you're really a girl?"

Sunny considers that for a moment. "Hmm. Well, I'm not just a girl, see? Like I said, I'm an invert. A third sex. There are signs of it on my body. I have feminine hands, hips that sway, gorgeous gams, a higher voice than most. Girlhood in my body." She holds out her hands and stands up to twirl about. "Perhaps that's true for you too," she says to me. "You're quite tall and muscular."

"With the posture of a man," Kiyo says.

I swear I don't mean to look at Abe but I do. He locks eyes with me and grins. "Strong hands," he adds, and my heart thumps.

For the first time in a long time—maybe forever—I feel seen. None of them challenge me, question me, or roll their eyes. They're curious. They see my favorite parts of myself and consider them proof of what I've felt my whole life. It's weird how a group of strangers—from a different century, if they're to be believed—are making me feel so right. So real.

"Excuse me," Ramona says indignantly, "but masculinity isn't a gender. It doesn't just belong to men, just as femininity doesn't just belong to women. Your body doesn't define your identity."

I wilt at her words. "Ramona, that's not what they—"

"Unless you'rc an invert," Kiyo interrupts me with a wink. "Like Calla."

"She's not an invert," Ramona says, raising her voice, but quiets it as she remembers herself. "She's nonbinary."

"Meaning, not a boy or a girl, exactly," I clarify.

"Right, see? A third sex," Sunny says, beaming. Ramona looks like her head is going to explode.

"Never mind," she says. "Okay, so you're an invert. Kiyo and Ambrosia . . . ?"

"Girl power," Ambrosia declares. She holds up a peace sign and Kiyo mimics her.

"And Lionel and Abe are guys," Ramona says, looking a little too eager.

Abe looks around like, *who, me*? I feel such intense second-hand embarrassment I could walk right past the flowers and back to reality.

I wish this conversation would end. I don't know why I started it. Did I start it? I drink more champagne just to have an excuse not to look anyone in the eyes.

"Oh, you think I'm—I don't know what you think." Abe blushes in the firelight and laughs a little. "I'm actually a girl, to be honest. Just butch."

"Invert," Sunny says, and he shrugs a little.

"But you use he/him pronouns. Your name is Abe," Ramona says, flustered and maybe even a little annoyed.

Abe starts to answer, but Sunny puts a hand on his shoulder to stop him.

"At Amaranth, we're whoever we want to be," she says protectively. "This is a home of abundance. This is a place of acceptance."

"Right, so, if you want to be a man—" Ramona starts, but Kiyo cuts her off.

"Ramona, do you like your name? Do you like being called a 'she'?"

"Yes, but what I'm saying is—"

"Calla? Do *you* like your name and being called 'she'?" Kiyo prompts.

The champagne starts to churn in my stomach. Ramona's gaze is hot on my skin, but I don't see a point in lying anymore. I shrug and shake my head at the same time.

"All right, so what would you prefer?" Kiyo asks.

"I don't know," I say quickly, as if I haven't thought about it a million times.

"Sunny was a family nickname, but I chose it to be my only name. Although, you may call me Sunshine if you're feeling formal."

"I picked Abe," he says, "for a few reasons."

"Obviously, I chose Ambrosia," she says, spinning to drape her legs over the arm of her chair. "It wasn't a gender thing, it's just, who's going to remember an Amy?"

Everyone looks to me. I pull my knees up to my chest as if to create armor.

"Maybe just . . . Cal," I say. I pretend like I'm coming up

with it on the spot. Like I haven't hesitated writing the last two letters of my name on assignments, forms, signatures. Like I haven't tried it out in coffee shops, just to hear the sound.

"Cal," Sunny says. "And should we use 'she' for you? Or 'he'?" I don't think anyone has ever asked me directly. At Miss Stone's it's either a performative parade of cis girls announcing "she/her" where I have little choice but to echo them, or more typically, it's just assumed that we're all girls. But the truth is, when I try on he/him pronouns in the most secret parts of my mind, they don't feel totally right either, at least not yet. It's partly why I haven't talked to anyone about this before—I didn't know what I'd tell them. I didn't want to lie. I wanted to wait until I was sure.

I take a swig from the bottle to stall again, to try to figure out how to tell them that without sounding silly, but champagne goes down the wrong pipe and I cough violently into my sleeve. Kiyo leans over to whack me on the back, and I try to catch my breath.

"Sorry," I say, when I can finally speak again. "Um. I mean. I guess 'she' is fine." I hate myself for it.

"You can be anyone here, honey bear. We can do better than 'fine,'" Lionel says, as if he can read me.

Soft stares are sent my way from all around the circle. Ramona even begins rubbing my arm as if to encourage me. If I can't say it now, surrounded by queer strangers I'll never see again after tonight, with my girlfriend who says she loves me no matter what, will I ever? Isn't this what I've been waiting for?

"I don't know if this is something you've heard before, but in our time, people use they/them pronouns? Like, for one person.

So instead of 'she did this' or 'that's hers,' you'd say 'they did this' or 'that's theirs.' It can mean a lot of things, but for me it would mean I don't really feel fully like a girl or a boy. But 'she' is fine too, if that's tricky. They or she. She's fine too."

"You said 'she is fine' three times," Kiyo says, crossing her arms. "Which means it isn't." She holds eye contact with me for far too long, and it's louder than anything else she could say.

"They," Lionel repeats. "Like when you don't know the gender of the person you're talking about, you say they." It feels a little on the nose, like it communicates all my confusion and questions about who I am.

"Only now it's the opposite," Abe says, petting Dash's head. "Now, we know Cal more." He smiles, and it truly feels like the fire is warming every hidden part of me.

Ramona pulls her hand away from me abruptly, and I turn to see her reaction. To check in on how she's feeling, what she's thinking, how she's looking at me. But she's not looking at me at all, and I'm confused because she was just comforting me. She was just encouraging me.

"Ambrosia," she says. "How about that karaoke?" Ambrosia's out of her chair and shoving the rest of her s'more into her mouth before Ramona's even finished speaking.

"Um, hello, yes," she says, wiping marshmallow off the edges of her mouth. "I thought you'd never ask."

"I beg your pardon," Lionel says, "where's my invite?"

"And mine?" Sunny says. "I was born to shine."

"Where was this energy for the past thirty years?" Ambrosia says, throwing her arms into the air.

"I want to hear more Lilith Heir songs," Sunny says to Ramona. "They're quite good. And just in my register."

To my surprise, Kiyo gets up too, her gaze locked on Sunny.

"Oh, I gotta see this," she mutters, smirking.

Suddenly it's only me and Abe in the firelight, smoke rising up between us as everyone else chases each other into the house, laughing. And though it's the most embarrassing thing I could possibly do—and I've done *a lot* of embarrassing things tonight—I nearly start to cry.

Because Ramona's hand was on my arm and then it wasn't.

I just came out. Again. Maybe more honestly this time. Maybe more completely. And she ran. Did she run? Or did she really just want to do karaoke? Did she just not think it was a big deal? Is that a good thing?

What if she didn't mean it when she said she'd always love me? What if she thought she would in theory, but she can't in practice? And Jesus, how many times has she told me that she can only love women? That she only *wants* to love women? What was I thinking, telling her? What was I—

"Cal," Abe says loudly, which tells me it wasn't the first time he called my name.

I blink myself out of my spiral and turn to him. "Sorry, zoned out for a minute there."

"You . . . all right?" he asks, eyebrows furrowed.

"Yeah, yeah," I say quickly. "Just processing everything." I sweep my arms wide like I'm talking about Amaranth.

He considers me for a moment but soon looks to the fire. "I'm going to stay out here for a while," he says, stoking the flames even though they've been burning just fine on their own. "I'm not much of a singer."

"Is that an invitation for me to stay or a hint I should let you have your quiet?"

"An invitation," he says quickly. "It's a beautiful night, and it's early yet."

"Aren't all nights the same here?" I ask. He shrugs a little.

"More or less." His eyes flick up to meet mine. "But you're here. You and Ramona, I mean. And the stars are brightest after a storm."

# *stars*

ABE'S RIGHT. IF I thought the sky was something before, it's everything now. Stars as clear as crystals, as big as planets. I feel as small as an atom, no room for fear or stress or questions. The tightness in my chest melts away, and when I try to say something, I find I can't speak.

For a long time, I don't try again. I just sit, alone and not alone, and I pretend I'll never leave here. I let myself feel their forever. I let myself forget for the first time in so long.

"For a few years here, I was really interested in constellations." I practically jump at the sound of Abe's voice. I remember myself then, and him too. His voice is soft, deep, quiet. I envy the casual way he's sitting now, relaxed into the chair, Dash between his knees, the dog's head lovingly perched on his leg.

I scan my body to fix how I'm sitting. To slouch my posture. I cross my arms and drop my shoulders and try to cave my chest in while still sitting tall. To mirror him without him realizing

I'm doing it. But it doesn't really matter. He's still looking at the sky.

"I think the only ones I know are Orion's Belt and the dippers," I say.

"The bears! Ursa Major and Minor. Two of my favorites." He lights up, and that lights me up too.

"Any other favorites?"

"All the animals, of course. Especially the dogs—Canis Major and Minor."

"I know the zodiac ones, I think. Leo the lion, Pisces the fish, Aries the ram, Cancer the crab. Uhhh. Taurus, the bull. I'm a Taurus."

"I'm a Capricorn. The goat," he says, nodding toward the pen where the goats are sleeping.

"You had astrology in the fifties?"

Abe smirks and raises his eyebrows at me. "Sure. Star signs have been around since ancient Greece at least."

"Right." I blush. "Duh."

"There's more than just the zodiac animals, though. Like, look there. Super bright. That's Aquila."

"Aquila," I say, but can't quite follow where he's looking.

"Here," he says, and nods for me to come closer to him. I push myself out of the chair with my uninjured hand. I crouch down beside him, and he takes my arm and guides it across a triangle shape.

"See there? It's an eagle," he says. "The bird that carried Zeus's thunderbolts."

"That's cool," I say, more focused on his fingers on my skin than where he's pointing me. With his sleeve slipping, I notice he's wearing a wooden watch—odd, since time stands still here.

I want to ask about it, but he pulls his arm away and covers it up quickly. Thinking better of it, I hurry back to my chair.

Weirdly breathless and sweaty in the cool night air, I reach for the champagne and take a long, deep sip. I offer it to him, but he declines. I choke out: "Do they all have stories? The constellations, I mean."

"They do. I think a lot of cultures have stories about them, but Sunny's only read the Greek ones to me. I'm, uh, not the best reader myself," he says, sounding embarrassed. His eyes stay trained to the sky. "To be honest, though, the myths are mostly violent and depressing. I always thought the stars deserved better."

"Maybe we should make up our own stories for them," I say.

"Oh, I'm not very creative."

He leans his elbows on his knees and for what feels like the millionth time I wonder how he's able to look so naturally masculine. I wish I could ask him every question I have tonight about what it means to be a girl who's not a girl at all, or a butch who's not a boy, but something like it, and how does he do it? And how can I do it?

But it's way too soon, even if I only have tonight. I don't know him like that. I don't know him at all.

"Okay," I say, trying to forget myself again. "I'll start. Gemini. That's your cows, Bert and Ernie."

"A-moo-zing."

I laugh. "Ooh, or those stars there? A slice of strawberry maple cake."

"That cake does deserve to be memorialized."

"It really does. Okay, your turn."

"Hmm," Abe says, blushing in the firelight. After a beat, he grumbles, "I don't know. Sorry. I told you I'm not very creative."

I point to somewhere he clearly can't follow. "That one—whatever it's called—looks like a pineapple under the sea."

Now he's the one to laugh. He shakes his head, hair falling into his eyes. "What?!"

"Yep, yep. Center of Bikini Bottom."

"Again, *what?*"

"See? It doesn't have to make sense. Just try."

"All right," he says, licking his lips, looking skyward. "That square right there is a hoedown."

"That cluster is a bunch of people waiting for their order at Taco Bell after midnight."

"Taco what? That triangle is a sock hop skirt."

"That bright, flashy one is a flamingo on vacation in Vegas."

"On vacation from what?"

"His problems."

"Flamingos don't have problems."

"They have to stand on one leg all day. They can only eat shrimp. They live in catty, gay communes. How dare you minimize their plight."

We go on and on, our stories getting more and more ridiculous. At one point, I have Abe laughing so hard he gets good tears in his eyes.

"Whew," he says. "Wow." He wipes them away, then stares at the house, where silhouettes now dance in the kitchen light. I can't help but stare at Abe's freckles, sprayed like stars across his cheeks, and think about the stories I'd find in them.

He starts to hum something under his breath I almost recognize, but not quite.

"Thought you weren't much of a singer," I say, and he returns my teasing smile with a sheepish one.

“Didn’t even realize I was doing that,” he says. “Guess I forgot myself for a second.”

“Me too,” I say, under my breath. Because for the last little while, I forgot to hate how high my voice is. I forgot to hunch my shoulders to hide my chest. I forgot to worry about what Abe thinks of me. Or what Ramona thinks of me. I forgot to worry about next year or tomorrow morning or anything at all.

But then the back porch door opens with a crack, and my whole body remembers. Ramona tumbles out into the night, and my throat tightens again.

# *small talk*

"HI, LOVE," RAMONA SAYS, sitting on the arm of my chair.

"Hey," I say, putting my hand on her knee. My stomach tightens, wondering again why she left the campfire, but she has the spark back in her eyes and a lightness about her. Maybe I was worried for nothing. "How was karaoke?"

"The *best*," she cries. "Oh, you two should have been there. Sunny did 'Material Girl,' and the nineties kids did 'Barbie Girl,' and I was living." She says *nineties kids* like she believes them now. And I believe them too, which is such a wild, impossible thing.

"Nice," I say, and half of me feels relieved when she gently scratches her nails down the back of my neck. But the other half of me wishes she'd been gone longer. It's just, I was having such a nice night with Abe. It was so easy to be myself. I felt so free. We were really clicking. We were really *laughing*.

Not that it isn't that way with Ramona, too. Usually.

“We should get some rest,” Ramona says to me.

I’m not even a little sleepy, though, nor am I ready to leave this campfire, this moment, this place. “If we only have tonight at Amaranth, shouldn’t we just stay up and take it in?” I suggest.

“We have an early morning ahead of us,” she says in a way that makes me think it’s not about the early morning at all, and more about Ramona getting me alone to talk.

So I say, “Okay.” I stand up and fold my blanket, place it on the chair nicely. “’Night, Abe. ’Night, Dash.” Dash scrambles up for me to pet him, but Abe stays seated.

He waves a little, pulling his blanket tighter around himself. “’Night. I’ll stay up to watch the fire die.”

We pass through the kitchen and say good night to the others, and as we walk up the stairs, my mind races. Is Ramona mad at me? Scared of me? Hurt? I said too much. And, somehow, not enough.

But as soon as we get to the bedroom and shut the door, she pushes me onto the bed and throws her arms around me. She kisses both of my cheeks, my forehead, my lips, and I’m so relieved I could die.

I kiss her back, hard, and pull her on top of me. She buries her head between my shoulder and my neck, and I’m overwhelmed by her special, intoxicating prom perfume. Her familiar Dove shampoo. The smoke of the campfire, sharp and new. Will it linger when we leave here tomorrow? Will any of this follow us home?

“I love you,” I say, mostly just to hear her say it back.

“I love you, too, Cal,” she whispers. I like the sound of it. I hold her tighter. My heart races. I can still have it with Ramona too: freedom. Ease.

"I'm sorry, too," she says. And I expect her to say for leaving me behind at the fire. "I shouldn't have pushed that gender conversation. I didn't know they'd say such outdated, offensive things, which is why I was, like, 'okay, bye, conversation over!' "

My brows furrow. "What do you mean?"

"Like, Sunny saying she's not trans, that she just has woman traits on her body. And Abe saying he's only butch. I just wanted to scream: Trans men *are* men! Trans women *are* women!" Ramona continues. "They don't understand because they don't have the knowledge we have. I didn't want to cis-plain it to them, though."

But isn't that what she's doing? Trying to tell Sunny and Abe who they are? The words and terms may not be the same, but the feelings are. I feel my gender in my body, like Sunny. I feel it as a contradiction, like Abe. And part of the reason I've never told anyone about those feelings is because I didn't have the right words for them yet. I felt like I couldn't come out until I picked one label, or was able to prove that I want to change, plan to change, will change. But the people here didn't make me plant a flag in the moon of myself, like: *These are the words for me and this is who I am, now and forever*. They made it seem kind of . . . simple. Who do you want to be right now? Well, here you are.

"Anyway, I'm sorry if you felt offended," Ramona says, and I realize how long I've been quiet. "Just, the outdated words they used? Even *I* was offended."

"I wasn't offended, actually," I say finally, carefully. "I liked hearing how they think about themselves and their genders. They're not ignorant or wrong. They're just using different words. They have different contexts. It all made sense to me."

"You know what I mean, though," Ramona says.

"Well, sure, in 2026, Sunny's probably, maybe a trans girl, and Abe is probably, maybe a trans guy, but we're not in 2026, are we? And even if we were, who knows? Those labels still may not feel a hundred percent right to them."

I feel her tense beside me.

"Why are you arguing with me on this? I feel like you're being difficult on purpose."

"I'm not trying to be difficult," I say, but it comes out through clenched teeth. "But it's like you're pushing them back into the binary. And they're telling you they don't live in it."

"Oh my *God,*" Ramona says with an incredulous laugh. "Don't treat me like I'm some ignorant, cis idiot. It's *me*. You know me." She means she fights for trans rights every day of her life. She means she has more trans friends than I do. She means she knows better.

"I'm not trying to be difficult." I try again to be level. "It's just, when people tell you who they are, you should believe them."

"I believe them, Cal," she says, pushing herself off my chest to sit up. "And I believe you, too, when you actually tell me things. You're trans? You want to use she/they pronouns? Okay! Awesome. Now I know. But I had to find out these intimate, important details about the love of my life alongside a bunch of strangers."

Guilt rushes through me. I hate myself for hurting her. But at least I'm still the love of her life, even if she's staring down at me with tears in her eyes. I sit up too.

"I'm sorry, okay? I should have told you earlier. I wanted to tell you." I'm at least half lying. Again. "I'm still figuring it out, and they just straight up asked me. You and I didn't have that much time to talk before the storm . . ."

She searches my eyes and nods slowly, like she's convincing herself that's true.

"Then let's talk. What exactly did your parents find on your computer, Cal?"

*Fuck.*

"I—" I don't know what I'm about to say because God knows I can't lie and still look Ramona in the eyes. I want to tell her everything and have her hug me and choose me and know that she'll still love me. I want to tell her nothing, because all I can think about are the cruel things my parents said, and how close I came to losing Ramona just hours ago. Either way, I have to say *something*. My voice cracks as I start over. "They went through all of my internet history. Which included poetry. And journal entries. And porn, I mean—"

Ramona shakes her head, hard, and kisses me, and presses her forehead to mine. "You know what? I'm sorry. You don't have to relive this right now. Tonight's already been a lot."

"Understatement," I whisper, and though I'm happy to hear her laugh, and to not have to talk about the porn or my Google searches or journal entries, I can't help but wonder if she just couldn't stomach it.

"Let's get some sleep," she whispers. "We can talk about all this when we get home tomorrow, okay?"

"Yeah. Thanks."

"And then you can figure yourself out at Alcott. It's all going to be fine."

What else can I say besides, "Right."

As we crawl under the covers, I don't dare ask her if she

really believes the houseguests now, or if she thinks we're still losing time at home, or if she's actually physically tired, because I'm really not at all. When she does fall asleep on my chest—or at least pretends to—I lie awake and stare at the ceiling of this impossible, magical house and think about Sunny and Kiyo and Ambrosia and Lionel and . . . Abe.

My blood warms and my heart quickens as I think about our time by the fire together. How he wanted me to stay with him. How I made him laugh so hard he almost fell off his Adirondack chair. How Ambrosia said he barely talks, but he wasn't quiet with me at all.

Another question I don't ask Ramona as I rub her back in the dark: Don't you think Abe is wonderful? If I could look like him, talk like him, walk like him, be like him . . . if I could be laid-back and soft, strong and handsome . . . would you think I'm wonderful, too?

I don't want to leave when the Amaranth sun pretends to rise. *I need more time*, I pray again. *I just need time*. I don't sleep. I can't. And I don't need to. I hear the others laughing in the kitchen still, deep into this world's illusion of night, and I want to join them. Want to know them. But Ramona's arm is across my chest, and I don't want to let her go.

# *day 1*

RAMONA WAKES TO THE smell of pancakes. I never slept, so I don't need to wake up at all.

Before we go downstairs, we stop in the closet room again to pick out clothes for our trip home. Ramona and I both choose simple clothes good for hiking: thick pants, thermal wicking layers, water-resistant jackets in case we end up in the same storm in that same moment on the other side, like the others said we would. I have no sense of how far we went last night, and we have no way of checking a map, so we have to be prepared.

"Looks like we're ready to go," Ramona says.

"Mm-hmm," I mumble as we start downstairs.

But with each step we take, my heart sinks deeper and deeper at the thought of going back, at the thought of leaving this place. It's actually magic here. I became more and more sure of that the longer I lay awake. Amaranth appeared to us for a reason, and now, we're about to walk away from it all. We will never get forever, and we will never be able to come back. I so want to stay here, to disappear from the world. To never have to think of my parents or that Alcott commitment letter or coming out ever again.

Ramona is holding my hand so tightly, it's like she knows I might pull some shit. And in the light of a new day, or something like it, I try to think with my head instead of my stupid, desperate heart, and consider that maybe she's right. We'd be foolish to stay here. Irresponsible. Or worse, cruel; making people search for us somewhere they'll never find us.

By the time we get to the kitchen, the houseguests are all sitting at the table. Lionel is wearing rubber duckie–patterned cooking mitts, balancing plates of chocolate chip and blueberry pancakes. Ambrosia looks like she's going to a concert, dressed in a glittery halter top, her hair twisted into little buns on top of her head. Sunny is wearing a bathrobe, but she makes it look terribly expensive, and she has to tear herself away from the page she's reading to greet us. Kiyo is using a knife to cut her pancake into a snowflake design. Only Abe isn't there. A sharp prick of disappointment pokes at me. He doesn't care enough to say goodbye, and I feel . . . hurt. Like, really hurt. Like, irrationally hurt. But who am I to him after only one night? To any of them?

"Good morning, sunshines," Sunny calls, putting her book down. "You sure look ready to leave us."

"We wish we could stay longer," Ramona says, "but I don't want people to worry."

"They're not," Kiyo says. "We've explained that more than once."

"Sure, I know," Ramona says, "but what if?"

"What if what? You're wrong," Kiyo says. "Zero time has passed. But it's nothing to me, go if you want to."

"God," I say. "You don't have to be so—"

"You know nothing about how I've had to be," she says, eyes hard.

A tense moment of silence follows before Lionel breaks it. "Annnnyway," he says loudly, clapping his duck mittens together. "I did pack you baskets for your journey home, should you choose to leave still. Plenty of trail mix, fruit, and water. A little chocolate, you know, something sweet to remember me by." He gives us a wink.

"Things like food can come back with us to our world?" I ask.

Lionel barks out a laugh. "We don't think so, ducky, but you never know. And I just thought the baskets look cute."

"Before you go, Blondie," Ambrosia says, standing up from the table to put her hands on Ramona's shoulders. "There's something you might want to see first."

"Oh?" Ramona says, humoring Ambrosia.

"Yes, *oh*. Follow me."

She leads us down to the basement, through her 1990s wonderland, and pauses at a door. She puts her arms out to gesture at it. "Ta-da!"

"Is that . . . new?" Ramona asks, and Ambrosia nods quickly.

"Very glad I came down here this morning," she said. "That's some fast magic, Ramona Silva. Amaranth didn't have to work too hard to figure *you* out."

"What do you mean?"

"I'll let you do the honors," Ambrosia says, stepping aside. Ramona looks between the two of us before reaching forward to turn the knob. She steps into the new room and covers her mouth with both hands.

"Oh my God," she whispers. I finally take my eyes away from her face, so full of wonder, and look at the room. It's a recording studio. There's a whole wall of colorful, beautifully crafted guitars, a sound booth, keyboards, drums, a harp, and a very intimidating cello. The walls are sparkling with pearly vinyl records. It's impressive, even to me, and I don't know the first thing about music. I know only that I've loved every song Ramona's ever written. I know only that she is bouncing with excitement, and I love seeing her so awestruck, so hungry.

"This is the studio of my dreams," she says finally, squeezing my arm before running over to the wall of guitars and touching each one of them gently. She pulls down a bright orange electric guitar and whispers, "You're telling me none of this was here before?"

"That's what I'm telling you, Blondie," Ambrosia says, running her hand across the harp strings. "You think I'd have made you sing on a plastic Barbie machine last night if it was? All this is because of you. All this is *for* you."

"Wow," Ramona says. "*Wow.*" Her voice breaks, and tears spring to her eyes.

"It would be a shame, wouldn't it, if you left right now without even taking all these axes for a spin . . ." Ambrosia says, slinking around the soundboard.

Ramona turns to me. "What's a few more hours, right?"

"Right," I say, hope coursing through me. "Take as much time as you want."

# *suit yourself*

AMBROSIA IS JUST AS excited about the recording equipment as Ramona is. She sings "Damn I Wish I Was Your Lover" into the microphone, and I slow clap.

"Okay, pipes," I say.

"Isn't she great?" Ramona says excitedly. "Her range is incredible."

They orbit each other around the room, joy rolling off them in waves. They tune the guitars and fiddle with the knobs and start jamming. When I start to feel like a third wheel, I leave the two of them alone to geek out. Upstairs, I eat pancakes with Lionel, Sunny, and Kiyo.

"That may be the fastest anyone's gift has manifested," Sunny says, putting her hand on my arm. "She must be special, your girl."

"She is." I'm proud but unsurprised. Ramona's gift could have been so many things—*she's* so many things—but Amaranth saw right to her true passion. The recording studio is the most perfect gift she could have gotten. I can't help but wonder about mine, what Amaranth may see in me, though I know we'll probably leave before it comes.

"Since Cal's staying this morning," Sunny says to Kiyo, "why don't you paint them, darling? I so hate when people leave without a portrait."

Kiyo grimaces. "Now?"

"No time like the present." Sunny turns to me. "You saw the ones in the stairwell, right? All Kiyo's masterful handiwork. Some of us dressed up when we posed for ours, but it's really whatever you feel most comfortable in. Do you want to wear what you have on or change into more distinguished duds?"

"Oh, uh." I think of the closet, about the suits and tuxes, the vests and sweaters. I remember the button up shirts and the shiny leather shoes. The work boots and the sherpa jackets, the chinos and the blazers. I want so desperately to try them on, but what if I can't pull them off? What if I look like a poser, like I'm trying too hard? What if Ramona comes upstairs and doesn't like what she sees? Or feels like I'm not including her again? I cross my arms against my fleece and shrug. "I think this is fine."

"Suit yourself," Kiyo says as she takes one more bite before heading out the back door, and I realize I'm meant to follow her.

In the barn, she motions for me to sit on a stool in the corner of her workspace. She fixes my posture and angles me a bit to the side, then studies me for what feels like way too long.

"Hmm," she says more than once as she's mixing paint together, and it doesn't sound like a good thing.

"Thanks for painting my picture," I say, mostly so I don't have to hear another disappointed "hmm."

Kiyo shrugs. "Sunny asked me to. And everyone gets one."

"I know, but—"

"Sunny is sentimental. And with the other world always trying to silence us, or erase us, or kill us, this is the one place—the *one* place—we can be remembered. So, I do my part." She nods toward the wall of past guests. "Although, it sounds like things are different in 2026. Two girls allowed to go to prom together. Gay marriage and all that."

"In some ways, yeah, things are different," I start, shifting in my seat. "But all that's still true, too. Our government's still trying to erase us. They still want us silent or dead."

"It's funny, then," Kiyo says, her eyes on the canvas.

"What is?"

"Usually when we get houseguests, they're blown away by this place. They think Amaranth is a miracle. They come to us broken, completely without hope, searching for a home where they can live freely as themselves because the other world won't let them. Meanwhile, you and Ramona are ready to leave. Eager, even."

"I'd stay if I could," I say. "Trust me, I would. But I can't let Ramona leave alone." As soon as the words leave my mouth, I feel guilty. Like it's some kind of betrayal to tell Kiyo something I haven't told Ramona: That I don't want to leave. That she's making me go.

"She'd be fine," Kiyo says.

"I'm sure. She's always fine."

"And you?"

"Never." I laugh, but Kiyo doesn't.

"Never?"

"I'm just . . . I've been having a hard time." I rub the back of my neck.

"So you're broken? Completely without hope? Searching for a home?"

"Something like that." I shift uncomfortably on the stool, feeling guilty again. Ramona is my home. At Miss Stone's or Alcott and after. Anywhere. But . . . what if only *I* was the one meant to find this house? So I could have more time to figure out who I should be. So I can show up for Ramona fully and confidently. So I can know for sure what I want. Sunny said people come to Amaranth for a reason—

I notice, suddenly, Kiyo's paused her painting and is looking at me.

"And here I thought Abe was the quiet one," she says. "It's like pulling teeth with you."

"Sorry," I say. "I'm just in my own head right now about gender stuff and what it means for me and Ramona. And what happened with my parents. But . . . I know you probably think it's all trivial."

"I don't." She sounds so sincere, it makes me want to change the subject.

"Well, anyway. Enough about me. I'd love to know more about you. I mean, so, you're into art?" I say, smooth as ever.

"Clearly," Kiyo deadpans as she continues her brushstrokes.

"That mural outside is gorgeous."

"Still working on it."

"Where did the idea for it come from? Is it just your imagination? Or based on a real place?"

"It's where I grew up, in California. My childhood home."

When she doesn't elaborate, I figure that's all I'm going to hear about that. So I try the one other subject I've noticed Kiyo seems happy to chat about. "You've been with Sunny for a long time, huh?"

"You're like the host of that radio show with your Twenty Questions," she says. But there it is: She glows, unable to stop the smiles that spread across her face. "Sunny's perfect, isn't she? She loves me as I am. We started dating soon after I found this place."

"You got here in 1948, right? How did you find Amaranth?"

Kiyo looks over the canvas and quirks an eyebrow at me. "Wouldn't you like to know?"

"Sorry," I hurry to say. "I shouldn't have asked. You said last night you don't like to talk about this stuff. I'll shut up."

"I'm kidding," she says, but only after making me sweat for a second. "I'll tell you. I don't know why, but you've got the kind of face that makes people want to talk. Maybe it's your big buck eyes." She meets my gaze then. "But don't think this makes us friends."

I put my hands up. "Never."

## KIYO TAMURA

## 1930–

Before the war, Kiyo Tamura's life in Northern California was full of blossoms. She lived in an apartment directly above her parents' flourishing flower shop, Bay Area Blooms, where they let her paint bouquets on the windows, and the bright, fresh scents of lilies and chrysanthemums drifted out the door.

Kiyo's mother, Harue, always wanted to be "just like the other Americans." Maybe it was the pressure of being a second-generation immigrant, having watched her own parents struggle and sacrifice. Or maybe she thought fitting in was good for the family business, that it helped them attract a wider clientele. Or maybe it was simply human: Harue wanted to belong. So she curled her hair and wore pretty floral dresses down to her knees, and she used the same fabric to sew Kiyo miniature matching numbers.

"You look so nice, Kiyo-chan," she said every morning as she wrapped Kiyo's hair. "Don't you think so?" Kiyo always smiled sweetly and nodded, because even though she hated the dresses, even though she and her mother both knew she'd come home with dirt stains and scraped knees, the patrons always said she was "cute as a button," and slipped her pennies and candies when her parents weren't looking.

When she was old enough, Kiyo clung to her father, Jiro, as he pedaled the delivery bicycle around Berkeley, freshly cut stems and ribbons spilling out of the handlebar basket. The roads were treacherous—cars whipped around corners, radios blaring, engines roaring—but on those familiar streets, Kiyo felt so safe and free that she often closed her eyes, face tilted up like a sunflower to catch the warmth of the sun.

Then the bombs fell on Pearl Harbor in 1941, and President Roosevelt signed a bill in 1942 ordering all Japanese Americans be detained. In a few months, white men in navy suits came knocking on the door of Bay Area Blooms, saying things Kiyo didn't understand, but there were no words needed. Her parents' faces said enough—something horrible was happening.

They locked their doors. They closed the shop. They whispered late into the night, their words muddled under the staticky sound of the radio. The flowers of Bay Area Blooms started to wither and rot. Kiyo tried to preserve her favorites—the celosia and snapdragons, the marigolds and zinnias—by pressing bruised petals into book pages.

Her parents hardened themselves. They didn't cry as they packed their belongings into suitcases, so Kiyo didn't cry either—even when the military came for them, as promised, and told her the books and all their petals would have to stay behind.

The men in uniforms forced the Tamuras at gunpoint out of their home, onto a cramped bus, and then onto a train so overcrowded Kiyo could hardly breathe. She held on to her parents' coats with steeled fists, and though the windows were covered with paper, she watched the world blur by through the tiny sliver of glass they'd somehow missed.

Colorado was like nowhere Kiyo had ever seen. Not that she got to see much beyond the barbed wire fences. Camp Amache was like a small, dilapidated city, with long, army-style barracks housing far too many people. They'd barely finished building it before they shoved over seven thousand people into one square mile. The guards acted like the camp was a gift, because there were mess halls—where Kiyo's mother would work, preparing meals—laundry, toilets, and showers. There were hospital houses and schools. But Kiyo's dad had to wake up early every day to help with construction. She hugged him goodbye each morning as he left to build their prison.

There were fifty kids in Kiyo's class. The books they studied with were ripped and stained with a strange brown liquid, and they always had to share. To make matters more annoying, the boy who sat behind Kiyo always kicked her seat. Every day she'd turn around and ask him nicely, through clenched teeth, to stop. How did he not understand she was already on the verge of tears every day? Wasn't he? Wasn't everyone? They were so far from home. They'd lost everything. And worst of all—they didn't know how long the war would go on, or if they'd even make it out alive.

Still, he didn't stop, until the girl in the back of the room got tired of it. One day, when the teacher was outside, she walked up the aisle, took her textbook, and whacked him in the head. "Knock it off," she said, and then winked at Kiyo. It was the first time Kiyo had smiled in months. The other kids howled with laughter, and when the teacher came rushing back in, the girl was already back in her seat, an angelic look plastered on her face.

After class, Kiyo chased the girl into the crisp fall air.

"Hey!" she called, and the girl slowed to a stop. "Thank you." Kiyo loved the girl's maroon jacket, and the way her hair was pulled back with a single barrette. She was so pretty, so very pretty, and made prettier by her irreverent smirk. Kiyo nearly forgot what to do when she stuck her hand out toward her.

"Kiyo," she said, taking the soft hand in her own.

"Marion."

Just like that, Kiyo had something to look forward to every day, for the first time in so long.

It was so easy between them. They made each other laugh, braided each other's hair, and talked about everything they missed in California; for both of them, the flowers most of all. Colorado—or at least this patch of it—was nearly barren, and the inmates could only grow practical crops like vegetables, beans, and hay. Marion was the only beautiful thing in Kiyo's gray, cold world, so she wanted to give Marion beautiful things too. She used whatever she could find around the camp to create little gifts that made them both blush—paper flowers ripped from textbooks, a bracelet made of threads pulled from discarded clothes, a kite fashioned out of twigs and newspaper.

When they were thirteen, the girls discovered they could rig the faulty door to the schoolhouse so that they could sneak in during the evenings, before curfew. They'd play tic-tac-toe and hangman. They'd try to draw each other; Marion drawing goofy stick figures, Kiyo sketching works of art that had to be erased before morning. When they were fourteen, they'd write their names on the chalkboards with hearts.

"Marion loves," she said as she scrolled in loopy handwriting, then collapsed into giggles.

"Marion loves who?" Kiyo said, and wondered why it made her throat tight.

"I'll tell you if you tell me," Marion sang.

"Tell you what?"

"Who you love! Who you like."

Kiyo pouted. She didn't want to play this losing game. But Marion made her play. All the time.

But one day Marion changed it up. "Who do you want to kiss?" she asked, wiggling her eyebrows, sticking her lips out as if to taunt her.

Kiyo was tired of the game. So tired, she just said, "You. I want to kiss you."

She regretted it immediately, because Marion got very serious and very still. What a silly thing to say. Girls didn't kiss girls, everyone knew that.

But Marion said, "Do it." So Kiyo did.

They didn't talk about it. Not that night, or when they kissed again the next time, or when they took it further. What was there to say? There were no words for any of it.

Only, there was one, they would learn.

In the end, it wasn't the secret kisses, or the not-so-secret clasped hands, or the way they tangled up in their small, horrible beds that gave them away. It wasn't even the gifts that Marion had hidden in her bed like a private shrine. It was what happened in the mess hall at dinner after Marion had a terrible day. She was telling Kiyo all about it, as she always did, when her eyes filled with tears. Kiyo reached across the table to push the hair out of Marion's eyes. To tuck it behind her ear, because Marion had stopped wearing her barrettes in an attempt to look older.

Without warning, a soldier approached their table and slammed the end of his gun into the wood. It shocked the room to silence, and all eyes were on the girls. All eyes were on Kiyo—except for her mother's. Kiyo only glanced at her quickly but saw that she was staring at the floor.

"Are you a homosexual?" the soldier shouted. A word they'd never heard before.

"No," Kiyo protested. But the word was out there and people were staring, and then they were all whispering it, *homosexual,* a new ghost in an already too-haunted place. After Kiyo's heart rate slowed, her cheeks cooled, and the mess hall returned to its normal volume, she tried to laugh it off, but Marion looked stricken. After dinner, when Kiyo tried to go to her unit—block 6, barrack 8, unit C—Marion's father opened the door instead.

"Don't come here again, Kiyo," he said. His words were harsh, but his voice was soft and his eyes were sad. "It's too dangerous now."

Kiyo's parents agreed—she was never to be seen with Marion again.

"How could you draw so much attention to yourself?" her mother said, voice shaking. "To all of us?"

"They could kill you," her father yelled. "If they think you're—" He either didn't remember or couldn't say the word. "Look at me. Do you understand?"

"But I'm not what he said," Kiyo pleaded. "That word—"

"Their word, their camp, their world," he said. "Our truths do not matter to them. Neither do we."

"But—"

"But what?"

*But I love her,* she didn't say.

Kiyo waited in the classroom alone almost every evening, and Marion never came, so she picked up the chalk and drew.

She couldn't sketch the depth of that longing, the cutting, physical pain of it. She couldn't draw the loneliness, the sharp but shapeless haunting. All Kiyo could do was watch Marion from afar and trace her over and over again with white chalk on the blackboard. She had to wipe it all away every night, but it didn't matter. She never really captured Marion, not in a way that felt real. Maybe that was the biggest heartbreak of all.

In 1945, the camp closed abruptly. Thank God.

And yet.

The Tamuras returned to California to find their landlord had disposed of all their belongings and placed new tenants in both the apartment and the shop. Bay Area Blooms was now a tobacco store, and the stench made Kiyo so nauseous she thought she might vomit. To calm herself, she tried to remember what her bouquets looked like painted on the windows. Then she tried to remember the details of Marion's face, or her voice, or the scent of her. Kiyo found that she couldn't, and so she did vomit, right there on the sidewalk.

"What now?" Kiyo asked when she could, wiping her mouth with her sleeve.

"We stay patient. We endure," her father said. "We put our heads down and work."

"We start over," her mother added. "Just like our parents did."

Kiyo didn't want to endure, not anymore, and if she had to start over, then she wanted to do it somewhere, anywhere, with Marion.

She was patient over the next three years, while the Tamuras lived in a government-issued trailer and worked odd jobs to get back on their feet. After school, Kiyo went to bag groceries, and though she did give most of her earnings to her parents, she tucked a dollar away each week just for herself. For Marion, really.

In 1948, Kiyo learned from a neighbor that Marion's family had resettled in Boston. While her parents were away working, Kiyo scribbled an apology—could she really leave them like this?—and pinned it where her parents would see, then she used every last hard-earned, hard-saved dollar she had to travel across the country to see her friend.

She protected a bouquet of California flowers on bus after bus, all the way to Massachusetts. A dangerous thing for a young woman to do alone. An unthinkable thing for a Japanese American girl in the wake of the war, even years later. But she had to. She *had* to.

She'd been patient. She'd put her head down and worked hard and endured. It was time to start over, just once more. It was time, again, for beautiful things in beautiful places with a beautiful girl. She deserved that, Kiyo thought, after everything.

When Kiyo arrived, Marion's husband opened the door.

# *unfinished*

"I DROPPED THE FLOWERS and ran away," Kiyo says. "I never looked back, even when I realized I didn't have enough dough to get home. Even when the storm hit. Had to run until I couldn't run anymore. And now I'm here."

She goes quiet, and I barely know what to say. My stomach hurts from outrage burning a hole right through it. It's one thing to read a history book, but another to hear the pain of it all, hot in her voice. I wish I could tell her things have gotten so much better, that everyone learned from it, that it's never happened again. But I can't say that. I can't lie. It's happening now.

All I can say is, "I'm sorry. That's horrible, Kiyo."

"Save it," she says. "At least it all led me here, to my home. To Sunny. A beautiful place with a different beautiful girl. A 'home of abundance,' as she likes to say."

"I know. But that doesn't mean it wasn't wrong. It doesn't mean it doesn't hurt."

"It was a long time ago," she says, but looks away from me. She lets out a rueful laugh. "You can see why none of us like to revisit the past much."

"Thanks for sharing your story with me," I say. "I'm honored you trusted me."

"Honored." The word drips with sarcasm. "I'm sure. Don't make me regret it, though. And don't ask me for more." But I think I see a small hint of a smile.

"Does it count as *more* if I ask how you fell in love with Sunny?"

"No," she says, and then her smile is so much more than a hint. "I'll talk about Sunny all day for free."

While Kiyo paints, she tells me stories of their early years here, just the two of them. How the Chucklehead, Knucklehead Brothers—her words, not mine—ruined their peace, but ultimately gave them peace of mind that they weren't missing anything back home. I have no sense of how long we're there, but eventually she quiets. I sense her mood shifting. She swears under her breath and furrows her brow.

"Everything okay?" I ask.

"Yes," she says in a way that definitely means no. "Can you loosen up, maybe?"

I try to relax my shoulders, and smile bigger, but she frowns, so I straighten up and smile less. She only frowns deeper. She moves from neutral to miserable, and without any warning, she picks up the canvas and throws it onto the floor. I jump in my seat, and see for the first time what she's put on the page: It's still muddy and sketchy, but it's me. It's such an accurate portrait, it stops my heart for a second.

"Forget it," she says. "Today's not the day."

"What? But it's my only day."

"It's just not working. You're uncomfortable, I can tell. *That*"—she points accusingly at the canvas—"is not you."

I rescue the canvas from the floor and stare at it, and it feels almost like a mirror.

"What do you mean? It looks just like me."

"It may look like you, but it's not *you*," she says. "It has to be perfect. I have to get you right, otherwise, it won't help you be remembered." She turns to walk out of the room, leaving me there clutching the canvas.

"Was it the fleece?" I call, only half kidding.

She appears again in the doorway and studies me. "You don't have to look so sad about it," she says. Only then do I realize I'm frowning, knuckles white around the painting.

"I'm not, I'm just . . ." Just what? Disappointed Kiyo couldn't take the lines and shapes of me and fit them together in a way that made sense? Hoping I'd like myself better in paint than in real life? "I guess I just thought it would be cool to have a piece of me here when I leave. That sounds so entitled, wow, it's just . . . your portraits are incredible, and—"

"Can I show you something?" Before I can answer, Kiyo blows past me, straight to a big wooden hutch that lines one wall. She opens the door to reveal vibrant blue plates, bowls, and tea sets veined with gold. She carefully removes one of the larger bowls and holds it up to me. "Have you heard of kintsugi?"

I shake my head, and she rotates the bowl so I can see all of the shimmering cracks.

"It's the Japanese art of healing broken pottery with gold. And the metaphor is probably obvious. We shine through our scars. All these lines are from mistakes houseguests have made over the years. A cup knocked off the table at a birthday party. A bowl dinged during a passionate argument at family dinner. A plate thrown across the room because someone's heart and hurt were too big." She hands me the bowl. Lets me study the cracks.

"They're stunning," I say. "Are you showing them to me because you think I'm broken?" I'm joking, but she gives me a knowing look.

"You just arrived here—of course you are. We all were." She starts backing away, out of her studio. "I hope you find your gold here, sport. But you'll have to fill in the cracks yourself."

With that, she's gone.

Standing alone with the bowl still in my hands, I say to no one, "What just happened?"

I want to be annoyed with Kiyo, but there's no use pretending she's wrong about me—I know she's right. And apparently, it's obvious even to a stranger that I've been broken for a long, long time.

I map the bowl's golden veins with my fingers and wonder what, if anything, could mend me. Could make me whole.

If I'd picked the right clothes—whatever that means—would that have made a difference? If I'd thought of a happy memory while Kiyo painted, would that have been enough? Like the time Ramona and I tipped a canoe in Windsor Lake, or Ramona running onto the field to kiss me after I stopped a wild shot in the final second to win state, or Ramona perched on my shoulders at Boston Calling—

Ramona is my gold, I think. For three years, she's been holding me together. Giving me somewhere and someone to belong to. Making me make at least a little bit of sense. She's more than my girlfriend, she's my best friend, and without her, I'll completely fall apart. There's a lot I have to figure out, but I realize none of it matters if I'm not doing it with her.

After putting the bowl back as carefully as I can, I head back to the house to find Ramona. Tell her we can leave whenever she's ready—I'll be right by her side. But when I get inside, no one is around. A chorus of laughter bubbles up from the basement, and I hear Ramona, Ambrosia, Sunny, and Lionel all talking over each other.

I move to head downstairs, but my eyes catch on the stairs to the second floor instead.

And then before I even choose to do it, really, I walk up. I lock myself in the closet room, stand in front of the floor-length mirror, and wonder what Kiyo saw—or worse, didn't see—in me. The fleece isn't anything special but it's *fine*. It's not good or bad, just completely neutral. But I hate it now, because she hated it, so I peel it off and throw it in a hamper before turning to the rest of the clothes.

What was Kiyo looking for? What am I looking for, even? I should know. I'm dying to know.

I take a deep breath, pull a simple black suit from the rack, and begin.

# CAL QUICK

## 2008–

In Bakersville, Indiana, a town just on the edge of Indianapolis, John and Natalia Quick ignored their kid. It wasn't on purpose, exactly, they were just *so* busy. John worked long hours in sales for a soulless big pharma company, Natalia worked odd hours as a fitness instructor, and they rushed through their short time at home. Their daughter, Calla, was obedient, and rarely complained. She was quiet, sure, but doing all right in school. She was good at field hockey, apparently, though they could never make it to any of her games. When they asked her how her day was, she always gave them one-word answers. They didn't have the time or energy to press. It made her easy to ignore. They bought her a puppy to keep her company; a tiny, trembling Italian greyhound she named Nugget.

When Calla wasn't at school or field hockey, she spent most of her time with Nugget or a pack of boys in the neighborhood. They sat in the same rows of bus seats to and from school and spent the afternoons climbing trees, riding bikes to 7-Eleven, and pretending to be superheroes. These boys were Calla's ticket to herself because she could hide among them. When they were together, people saw *kids* instead of *girl*. When they were together, Calla felt less *girl* and more *friend*. They called her Cal. They let her borrow their big T-shirts and ballcaps. They forgot the parts of her she wanted them to forget. It helped her forget those parts of her, too, which felt like freedom.

Jackson Laurier, a funny golden-haired boy who drew bubbly graffiti comics in permanent marker all over town, was her best friend. He told her once she felt like a brother. He told her once he didn't think of her as a girl.

"Because I'm not," she said, and he high-fived her.

John and Natalia hated that Calla spent so much time with Jackson and the boys, but they hated her moping around their house even more. They seemed to think their boyishness was contagious, making Calla into too much of a tomboy, even though most of the boys weren't even particularly boyish. If anything, Calla was the one who destroyed them in soccer, begged them to search for frogs in a neighborhood creek, and dared them to use fresh mud as a slip-and-slide. It wasn't ideal, but at least John and Natalia didn't have to entertain her. They didn't have to pay for summer camp, or after-school care, and that was reason enough to let it go.

But during the spring of Calla's sixth-grade year, COVID-19 shut the world down—and the Quick family had no choice but to tightly orbit each other. Calla's classes moved online, John's job became fully remote, and though Natalia streamed Pilates classes through her laptop, it was not enough to quiet the violent anxiety of a global pandemic. Natalia needed something louder, and right there, only rooms away, was her lonely, moody daughter. Calla was trapped at home too, and more impenetrable than ever. She even tried to hide her first-ever period from Natalia, who only found out when she discovered bloody pads shoved to the bottom of the bin while taking out the trash.

"You're becoming a woman!" she called through Calla's slammed door as she slipped tampons underneath it.

"Go away!" Calla yelled, hysterical. Nugget barked, as if to defend her. Natalia laughed at Calla's angst. Typical preteen. Typical PMS. Typical kid living through a pandemic.

But there were other problems with Calla, besides. She was chubby, too tall for her age, and had inherited her father's football-playing shoulders. What kind of mother would Natalia be if she didn't protect Calla from a world that would eat her alive if she didn't put in more effort? Calla could be pretty, Natalia thought, if she'd only let her make her over.

"It's for your own good," she said, as she straightened Calla's hair with a chemical that smelled like death and left sores on her scalp.

"You have to take care of yourself," she said, as she counted out pretzels to the perfect portion size. "No one else will."

The final touch took bargaining, though not much. The wager: If Calla got her ears pierced, she could go outside and play with the boys, who'd started playing pickup soccer again. Natalia wasn't worried about the virus, truth be told; it was just like the flu, wasn't it? The whole thing was liberal propaganda and she was sick of it. It was August, after all—half a year since the lockdown had begun—but Natalia knew Calla was so desperately lonely she could use her freedom like currency. Sure, Nugget was excellent company, but she wasn't much of a conversationalist, and Calla had barely talked to Jackson or anyone all summer. With fall sports already canceled, she'd miss a whole year of field hockey too. So when Natalia bartered with the earrings, Calla said, "Fine. Whatever."

John held her down on the floor of the bathroom. He had to put his knee on her chest while Natalia pinched the needle in one hand and a cube of ice in the other.

"You won't even feel it," she said. "This is how Nonna did it for me and all my sisters."

Calla felt it. The needle, twice, ripping through each ear. Worse, the pressure on her wrists, her father's knee on her sternum. Worse still, the look they both gave her when it was over; one that said, "Well, that didn't really help much, did it?"

But Calla didn't cry—would have rather died than let them see that—until she was alone again in her room, Nugget curled into a cinnamon swirl on her lap. She didn't understand who she was staring at in the mirror; this thin girl, this starving girl, whose boobs kept growing anyway, no matter how little she ate, no matter how many sports bras she layered. Even though she knew it was her, it didn't feel like her at all.

"I hate you," she whispered to the girl in front of her, through clenched teeth. "I hate you," she whispered to her parents, rooms away. "I hate you," she whispered to the whole world, for shutting down, for leaving her home alone for so long.

"Not you," Calla said, when Nugget tilted her head with concern. "Never you." For some reason that made her cry harder.

Then Natalia appeared in her doorway, and didn't bother to ask why Calla was furiously wiping tears from her cheeks.

"I can play outside tomorrow, right?" Calla asked, catching her breath between every word.

"Yes," Natalia said. "You've earned it."

# *in the closet*

THE FIRST SUIT FITS all wrong. I look like a parody of a used car salesman from the 1980s. I take it off quicker than I put it on. I rip blazers, jeans, sweaters, and chinos from the wall and pile them on the floor. I'm surprised to find binders, and my whole body buzzes with hope. I've never been brave enough to buy one, not that I could afford it anyway. But when I put one on, I feel claustrophobic. It squeezes me like a vise, and I start to hyperventilate. It would be worth it if I looked flat. Instead, I just look like I have a huge uniboob, like I'm smuggling a giant water balloon in my shirt. I try two more, just in case. I growl every swear word I know while I wrestle myself out of them as fast as I can.

I try the rest of the clothes on, and some of them aren't *so* bad—a pair of blue trousers, a nondescript gray sweater. But I still feel desperately disappointed by what I see. I still wish it were someone different in the mirror every time. I still dream of a man—or maybe not quite a man—standing there instead, and then feel sick because I want it so badly and I can't have it.

But who cares? Who *cares*? What does it matter? Why *should* I get to have it? We don't always get what we want. Jesus, Kiyo's story—and Sunny's—reminded me of that, to say the absolute least. I'm lucky to have a gorgeous, smart, powerful girlfriend I can love in public and get to go to a good college and play a sport I'm great at and be completely healthy, unlike Ambrosia and Lionel.

I'm fine. I'm *fine*.

I keep pulling clothes on despite myself: pressed linen, soft cashmere, thick jackets. As nice as the clothes are—expensive, quality, dreamlike—everything looks at least a little ridiculous on me, too baggy or too tight in all the wrong places. Proof they weren't meant for me.

And yet.

My heart skips when I pull out a navy tux with black satin details; structured and classic, but still interesting. When I hold it up in front of me, it just feels right. I put on a button-down shirt, try to close it over my boobs, but it gaps between the buttons. I get a bigger size and it looks frumpy, but I figure I'll tuck it in.

It doesn't look better tucked. And the suit is worse. I still look like *woman, woman, woman*. My chest is so pronounced, I'll never be able to hide it. My ass is so big, it gives me away. Even though no one's watching, I'm embarrassed by how wrong I look. How hopeful I was. I rip it off quickly, and pop a button in the process.

"*Dammit*." I crawl around on the floor looking for it and accidentally catch a glimpse of myself topless in the mirror, something I always try to avoid. Something that makes me feel sick and small—and too big—and devastated. I stop mid-crawl to stare at the girl, a stranger, in front of me. I cross my arms in front of my chest and look away but it's too late. I'm undone. When I see her, that girl, I want to hate her—have hated her—but I don't. Maybe I even love her. But I feel planets away from her.

I watch tears roll down her cheeks onto a discarded sweater. I watch her pick it up and use it to cover herself, to wipe her tears away. I watch an unexpected sob escape her—shamefully—as she gets up to hastily put all the clothes back on their hangers as nicely as she can. She pulls the sports bra and T-shirt and fleece back on, defeated. Then her bad wrist gets caught in the sleeve at a strange angle and it hurts so badly she just gives into the sobbing. She avoids the mirror.

I avoid the mirror. Because as much as it doesn't feel like it, that's me. And soon we'll be leaving here, and I'll be back in a dress at prom—if the houseguests are to be believed—and I will be walking through the woods toward Miss Stone's. Toward Alcott.

There's a knock on the door, and I quickly quiet my ridiculous crying. Steady myself. Yell as normally as I can, "Just a minute." I take deep breaths and try to massage the pink splotches out of my face. I still feel hollowed out and strange when I open the door, and I'm mortified to find Ramona there in the hallway. With Abe. They both look at me with eyebrows furrowed. Dash is sitting between them, at attention. He tilts his head at me and whines.

"Hi," I say, because I've got nothing else.

"Hi," Ramona says slowly. "Abe, um, heard you crying, so he came to get me."

"Ah. I'm guessing that room is not soundproofed," I say, and force a smile.

"Not so much."

"I didn't mean to pry," Abe says. "Was just hoping to get clothes that weren't muddy."

"No, no, it's fine. I, uh. I just lost a button," I say. "It ruined the shirt. And it was a really beautiful button. So I felt . . . bad."

"You're crying because you lost a button?" Ramona questions, clearly unconvinced.

"And because my wrist really hurts."

"Why?"

"I busted it when I fell off the stage."

Ramona reaches toward me with concern. "I didn't think it was that bad. You haven't even mentioned it . . ."

"We were, uh, kind of preoccupied after it happened."

She stiffens. "Right."

An awkward moment passes. "Did you . . . want to get going?" I ask. Because what does it matter if we stay? I should just go, rip the Band-Aid off and give in to what's inevitably going to happen. But Ramona surprises me by folding her arms across her chest and looking at the floor.

"I was actually, um, really hoping maybe you'd be okay with us just staying the afternoon?" She lifts her eyes to me, and they're bright with hope. "This music studio . . . I mean, Cal. It's amazing. Ambrosia and I are halfway through recording 'Florida, I Love You,' and I'd love to finish. We sound *good.* Our voices are perfect together."

"Yeah, cool," I say. "If you want to stay, I'll stay." Even though I feel so defeated now, I really do just want to go home, gift or no gift, Alcott or no Alcott. But I haven't seen Ramona this excited about anything since Luíza died—not even prom—and I want to give her this.

"Thank you," she says. She throws her arms around me and kisses my cheek, and I catch her with my uninjured arm.

"I guess I'll just, um . . ." I try to think of somewhere to be that would be out of everyone's way, that won't send me back into another emotional breakdown. "Go for a walk."

"If you want," Abe says, "I could make you a splint for your wrist."

"Oh. That's really kind, but . . ." But he's the last person I want to be around right now. Watching him be everything I want to be and can't be will almost certainly send me back into a gender panic meltdown.

"I know you won't be here that long, but it'll help with the pain in the meantime since nothing can heal here. I have some experience. You may have noticed I made one for Sylvie, the goat. She thinks she can fly."

"No, really," I say. "I'm fine."

"You'd get to see the famous toolshed."

"And we know how much you love tools and sheds," Ramona says, smirking, and I know she's kidding but it feels like a dare.

"I did say that." I take a deep breath. "All right, Abe. Splint me up."

# *simple guys*

WE'RE QUIET THE WHOLE way down the stairs, out the door, and across the field toward Abe's shed. I can't help but think about how cute Abe's smile is as he watches Dash jog alongside him, and how annoying that is to me in this moment. Even with his rosy cheeks and long eyelashes, his masculinity is effortless. An afterthought. And his clothes fit. If I were really a guy, wouldn't I be more like that? Wouldn't I walk more like him? Talk more like him? Move more like him?

God, I wish I were more like him. But I'm not, so I need to stop thinking about it. Get over it. Shove the impossible down.

The small, tan shed appears in our sightline on the edge of the trees, unassuming. Its door is predictably amaranth red. It looks like an everyday tree house, though it's firmly planted on the ground.

"I'm getting nervous," he says, and I force myself to look at him again.

"Did you forget how to make a splint?"

"I've made the shed seem so mysterious. It's really nothing special."

"I'm a simple guy," I say, and hold my breath. He doesn't laugh or treat it like a joke. He just exhales, so I do too. Our eyes meet and immediately fall away. I study my boots.

"Neat," he says. "Me too."

When we get closer, he opens the door and waves me in. Dash darts in before me and cuddles into a pile of carefully arranged blankets in the back corner.

"Sorry for the mess, it's just . . . how my brain works," Abe says. "No one else really comes in here."

"It's so fine. You should see my dorm room. And my handwriting. And my gym locker."

The shed is decidedly unglamorous compared to the rest of the property. It's full of sawdust and plywood and half-finished furniture covered in blue tarps. It's chaotic with clutter. Shovels, animal feed, hammers, and axes are scattered about, and for a split second I think, *Ramona was right about the serial killer thing after all.* But Abe starts to tidy the place, tucking things away as quickly as he can.

Then he clears a pile of jackets off a bench for me to sit on, and I notice, behind him, shelves filled with whittled wooden animals. They're either creepy—another point for serial killer—or insufferably adorable. As is the scene I imagine next: Abe sitting here in a starlit room, carefully carving an elephant holding a picnic basket with their trunk.

"You made those?" I ask, and he gets even more flustered.

"I did," he says. "It's just . . . a way to pass the time."

He gathers supplies—gauze and some wooden rods and

tape—and sits down next to me. He rolls up his sleeves and I notice his wooden watch again. It's the purple red of amaranth, and I wonder if maybe Kiyo helped him use the flowers to dye it, but before I can ask, he motions for me to give him my wrist.

"So you fell?" he finally says.

"Yeah," I say with a grimace. "I'm not great with heels." I try to make my voice lower. To copy his posture. And I feel like a fool, and I remember my reflection, and I want to disappear. *Stop thinking about it, Cal,* I scream at myself. *Get over it. Shove it down.*

Abe raises his eyebrows. "I'd have liked to see that," he says. "You in heels. I'm sure it was charming. Sort of like a giraffe on stilts. An octopus on a unicycle. A bird on ice skates." I smile to myself, my breath steadying.

"That'd be quite the circus."

"You ever been to the circus?" Abe asks, sounding strangely excited.

"Me? No. But I've seen them in movies and stuff, obviously. Wait, do you know what movies are?"

Abe holds back a smile. "I'm not *that* old. I've seen movies. They were even in color, with sound and everything."

"Right," I say, feeling silly again. "I'm just bad at history. Clearly."

"You know who you remind me of a little?" he says, measuring gauze and cloth against my skin.

"Who?" I'm terrified of his answer, of what it will reveal about how he sees me.

"You probably don't know him. But there's this actor who died a few years back—at least for me—James Dean?"

"Of course, I know James Dean," I say breathlessly. Like I

haven't studied his photos. His slender build and easy, queer, West Coast masculinity.

"He dated this actress, Pier Angeli. You look like her."

My heart falls. Speaking of circuses, I feel like the world's biggest clown.

"My mom is Italian," is all I can think to say. I must sound or look defeated because Abe's eyes widen.

"Oh," he says. "You're not as pretty as her, if that makes you feel better."

"It really doesn't." I laugh.

"No, no," he says, eyes even wider. "I just mean you're not as feminine. It's just your big eyes and your hair and—ugh."

"Is this why you're usually quiet?"

He turns beet red and takes a deep breath, but he's grinning too. "Cal. I'm begging you. Let me start over."

"It's really okay," I say, waving it off. "I get it. I look like a girl."

"Well, you don't, actually. Because you're not one." He says it like it's easy. "I'm just going to stop talking and keep fixing your wrist."

He motions for me to give it back to him. I do, and it's starting to hurt like hell holding it out and straight and suspended. But he's careful as he works to set it and wrap it. He's gentle, unlike our trainer at Miss Stone's, Ms. Bannon, who doesn't give a shit if she's pushing me too far or not, if she's hurting me or not. She once told me to take an Advil and a nap after I broke a finger and lost two fingernails during a game.

"I think it's just sprained," I say.

"Not just," Abe says, and lifts his eyes to meet mine. "It's pretty bad." Abe makes a slight wrong move and I wince. He makes more eye contact to check in on me, and I nod for him to keep going. I can feel the heat of his body, the rhythm of his breath, and I try not to look at him.

"See? You're shaking," he says. "That's a pain response." It is. But it's not why I'm shaking.

"Are you a doctor or something?"

Abe laughs. "No. I can barely read, to be honest. Just helped out a lot of animals." He clips his homemade wrap in place and pulls his hands away. "Hopefully this stops you from moving it in ways that'll hurt." Sure enough, now that he's done, the pain has eased considerably, even if it feels a little funny. Even if I'm still shaking a little.

"Thanks, Abe," I say. "This helps a lot."

I move to get up to leave, but he says, "Can I ask you something?"

"Um, sure, yeah," I say, settling back into my seat.

His brow furrows, like he's thinking really hard about what he says next. "Last night you said you like *they* or *she*."

"Yeah. Sorry, I know it's confusing."

"It's not. I was just wondering . . . is one better than the other? What I mean is: Having us use both 'they' and 'she,' is it an invitation to know all of you? Or is 'she' just a compromise? Or an apology, even?"

Direct hit. For a second, I think he might be making fun of me, but one look at his face—his eager gray eyes, his concerned eyebrows—tells me he's asking sincerely. For a second, I can't speak. "Oh," is all I say when I finally do.

"Sorry, maybe I just didn't understand. I'm not very smart, like I said—"

"No," I stop him. "You get it. A lot of people do use it as an invitation, to let people know all the different pieces of themselves. But for me, I guess . . . I guess it is an apology."

Abe waits for me to go on.

"Last night was the first night I've shared any of that. I guess I figure if I tell people they can still use 'she,' then I don't have to feel upset when they forget to use 'they,' or choose not to. And I don't have to feel disappointed in myself when I'm not brave enough to correct them."

He nods once, definitively. "'They' only, then."

"Thanks," I say, looking at my hands, already playing with the edge of the tape on my splint. "I just think they/them fits me best, you know? But people will sometimes forget, even if they're trying. Because it's different and new, I know that. And I have long hair or whatever, and I still look like, well, this, and—" God, I'm rambling.

Abe puts his hand on my shoulder.

"We're all human, and I can't speak for the others, but I won't forget. It's important to you, so it's important to me." He stands up to leave, as if that settles it.

"Thanks. Again. And 'he' only for you?" I ask, and he nods once more.

"It suits me best. Hey, you wanna chop some wood with me? Lots of downed trees from the storm."

"I don't know how helpful I'll be," I say, waving my splint around, giving him an out.

"I'm not worried," Abe says, turning his back to me as he gathers axes and a saw. But he twists to smile at me over his shoulder. "You seem strong."

# *in the wood*

ABE SHOWS ME HOW to hold the axe, and I raise it up into the air with one hand and bring it down with a satisfying crack. It lodges in the log, and he has to help me pull it out, but I slam it down again and again even though it's clear I'm never going to actually split the wood that way.

Abe grins at me. "Feels good, right?"

And it really, really does.

We make quick work of the wood together. He pushes, I pull, I push, he pulls, and each time the saw blade goes straight through, clean to the forest floor, I can't wait to start again.

"Do you cut the trees down in between storms too? For firewood?" I ask. He nods.

"Always feels a little dangerous, doing it alone. Wish you were staying. I could use the help."

"Wish I was too." I give a weak smile, but longing pangs in my chest. I push it down, swing the axe over and over again, and try to forget. A bead of sweat rolls down my chest, and ugh, the last thing I want right now is boob sweat. But I look up to see Abe's sweating too. He pushes it back into his hair, and I mean, Jesus Christ. Come *on*. How did he even make that look cool?

When the sawing is done, we carry the pieces back through the trees to the edge of the pond, where the firepit is marked by cinders. He helps me balance the wood under my arm with the bad wrist, and we go back and forth, wordlessly.

In the quiet, I can hear my own breath. When I move, my mind stops spinning. I forget to want to be someone else with every beat of my heart, because I like the person I am in the woods. I'm strong and sweaty and unfeminine. I feel alone, in the best way. Abe is nearby, but he's not watching me. He just helps me when I need it.

Next, we tend to the animals and plants, and I like who I am in the yard too: grass-stained and earthy, tender, and thoughtful. We're still quiet, except for when we're laughing—when one of the chickens won't stop following me around, and when Nellie, the black goat, runs in circles, and when Dash dances on his hind legs every time Abe says, "Good boy!"

All the while I'm waiting for Ramona to come find me, to say she's finished recording her song, that it's time to leave. But instead, light starts to fade from the sky.

"How long have we been out here?" I ask Abe, who's watering the amaranth.

"Hard to say. Time moves different here."

"But last night felt so long, and today was like . . . it's like I blinked and the sun is setting. We didn't even have lunch yet."

"And I'm sure Lionel was gravely offended, but without

hunger it's hard to remember to eat sometimes." He looks at his watch, then smiles sheepishly and shakes his head.

"What does it say?"

He holds it up. "Nothing. It doesn't work, but I always forget and check it anyway. I just wear it because I think it makes me look more like a man."

I let out a small laugh. "Well, it is very handsome," I say, and both of our cheeks flame. I quickly turn toward the house. "Um, I should probably go find Ramona."

I start out alone across the field and watch with both horror and hope as the pastel and neon sunset roars across the sky at a breakneck pace. We were supposed to get home before nightfall. Has Ramona been looking for me? I've been easy to find, right? Is she pissed at me right now?

Inside the house, the windows are lit with an amber glow, and when I burst through the back door, I find Ramona in the kitchen with Lionel and Ambrosia. She's wearing an apron. Her hair is tied up in a messy bun on the top of her head, and she's covered in flour from head to toe. They all are.

"Cal!" she says.

"What in the world?" I ask, taking in the floury scene.

"We're having a food fight!" Ambrosia yells.

"I can see that," I say.

"Those two started it," Lionel says. "I am but a victim caught in their crossflour. Watch out!"

I duck into the living room to dodge a flour ball Ambrosia winds up to throw at me, and I hear it hit the wall with a thud.

The three of them descend into a fit of giggles, and I call through the din, "I hate to interrupt, but Ramona, the sun is setting."

"Okay, temporary truce!" she says to the others, and comes

to pull me back into the kitchen. "I saw. I guess time just got away from me." She giggles again. I study her face. It's so serene. She's smiling. She's glowing. Shouldn't she be freaking out?

"I thought you wanted to leave before it got dark . . ."

"I did," she said. "But that was before the recording studio."

"And before I spent all damn day further convincing her the magic of the place is real," Ambrosia says.

"And before I promised we'd throw a party tonight if you stay," Lionel adds.

"A prom do-over," Ambrosia says, "since your first one sucked."

My stomach drops. How much did Ramona tell them? Lionel and Ambrosia must think I'm a complete asshole now.

None of them seem mad, though. Ramona even takes my hands into her powdery ones. "I had such a good time making my music today. It's been way too long. I've been so burnt out, between school and organizing and everything else . . ."

"That's awesome," I say, even though me and my problems are probably the "everything else" she's talking about.

"I just feel so lucky I got this day. Maybe if we stay one more night, you'll get your gift too, Cal. I want that for you," she says, tucking a stray hair behind my ear.

"Yeah?" I smile. Despite my failed makeover montage in the closet earlier, my heart soars. Spending time with Abe outside has shown me what else Amaranth has to offer, and now I get one more night. *I get one more night.* I knew I wanted to stay, but I can finally admit to myself how badly I want it.

"Yeah!" She reaches up to kiss me, and I soften.

"Now, for the love of God," Lionel says, "would you all go clean up so you can help me make the truffle ravioli? We have a black-tie event to cater!"

# *secret ingredient*

IT ONLY TAKES ABOUT four seconds for me to realize that black tie means, well, formal attire. And I am instantly angsty all over again. I try to distract myself by helping in the kitchen, but I can't cook for shit.

"You don't know how to properly chop an onion?!" Lionel gasps, looking over my shoulder, hands to his cheeks like *The Scream*. "You didn't even take the skin off! *Cal!*"

"In my defense, I've been eating cafeteria food for years, and I only have one hand."

He starts muttering to himself in Creole, and while I can't understand him, I can't imagine he's saying anything flattering.

"Would you like to share with the class, Lion?" Ambrosia says.

"I said, there is still only one competent cook in this kitchen. I can't wait to leave this place."

"He's joking," Ambrosia says to Ramona. "He says it all the time and he's always joking."

Lionel uses a cookbook to shield his face from them as he mouths to me, "I'm not joking." And is that part of the joke too? He shoots me another look I can't quite read, and out loud says, "Even if I wasn't joking, I can't leave. We all know that."

"Why would we want to, anyway?" Ambrosia says. "This is like gay paradise, and home is . . . hell."

"I knooow," Lionel says like they've had this conversation a million times before. "Doesn't stop me from missing my sister. I have a twin, Roseline. Have I mentioned her?"

"No," Ramona says. "You haven't."

Lionel's face lights up. "She's the best. I think you'd really like her. Her and all our friends, actually!"

"I'll remind you that most of our friends are dead or dying," Ambrosia says, bitterness lacing her usually chipper tone. "In the ugliest, worst ways possible."

"You really don't have to remind me," Lionel snaps.

"All right, all right. *Sorry*," Ambrosia says begrudgingly. "Why are we even talking about our old life? There's no point in dwelling on the past. And anyway, I'm basically your Amaranth twin." Ambrosia kisses his cheek, and Lionel's face sours.

"Sure are, boo boo," he says, but there's that darkness in his eyes again, and a hint of frustration in his voice. It doesn't seem like anyone else hears it, though, because Ambrosia is back to mincing garlic and belting "It's All Coming Back to Me Now," like nothing happened.

Ambrosia—I have to admit—is doing the impossible: She's doing Celine Dion justice. Which almost distracts me from the fact that she runs her hand down Ramona's arm whenever she sings, "When I touch you like this!" Now all I can focus on is how blatantly Ambrosia is checking out Ramona. Every time

Ramona turns away, Ambrosia looks her up and down. Right in front of me.

I try to shake it off because I'm not jealous. We're never jealous. We trust each other. And I mean, I get it. Ramona is the most beautiful girl I've ever seen in my life, and these kids hardly ever get new houseguests. Of course Ambrosia's thirsty. Of course she's trying to drink Ramona in before we leave. That's fine. It's fine.

At least, it's fine until Ambrosia pulls Ramona by the apron strings to be close to her. Until she says, "Blondie, you've still got a little flour right there," and uses her thumb to wipe it off her cheekbone. They're so close they could kiss.

"You trying to steal my girl, Ambrosia?" I joke but don't joke.

"Wouldn't dream of it," she says, and Ramona hits me teasingly with a kitchen towel.

"Good, because I may only have one arm available but I can still fight."

"Oh my God, Cal," Ramona says, and rolls her eyes. "Don't be toxic." But is she blushing at Ambrosia's attention?

I chop the onions with a quiet fury.

"Easy, killer," Lionel says to me, voice low.

"Sorry." I slow my chopping to a steady beat, but his gaze lingers.

"You're carrying fire."

"I'm fine. Honest."

He gives me a knowing look. "It's okay, sweet pea. I am too. That's why I'm reassigning you to something that involves fewer sharp objects."

Lionel has me peel and prep the carrots, a pretty straightforward task. But next to me, his eyes well up, and I wonder if taking over the onions was just a cover.

When Ambrosia and Ramona are distracted, I arrange the chopped pieces of carrot so they read, U OK? on the counter, and nudge him to read it. He chuckles sadly, grabs more carrots, and stands beside me, arranging them. He starts shaping H-O-M-E-S, and I try to save him the trouble.

"Homesick?" I whisper, and he nods. "I don't blame you. I bet New York was such a fun place to grow up."

"*Fun* doesn't even begin to cover it. My childhood was heaven," he says so only I can hear. "My family, they're wonderful people. I miss their food and their music and their gossip. I miss my chic mother and soft father. And the way my sister and I would hide flashlights under our pillows, and pass notes back and forth while we were supposed to be sleeping." He fans his face. "Ugh. I don't want to cry, although it is nice to remember. We don't do that much around here . . ."

"I'd love to hear more stories about your family, if you ever want to talk," I say.

"Thanks, Cal," Lionel says on a smile, tears threatening to spill over. He fans at his face again. "Okay, we have a lot of cooking to do, and you're no help. No offense."

"None taken. And, hey, tears are usually the secret ingredient, right?"

"Right," he says, returning to the onions. "But there's plenty of tears at Amaranth already. Don't let the others fool you. It's a sanctuary, sure, but the *cost* of it . . ." He trails off.

"It sounds like you have a lot to miss back home."

"I really do." Lionel shoots a fleeting glance at Ambrosia to see if she heard him, but she's belting into a spoon. "I really, really do."

# LIONEL TOUSSAINT

## 1979–

Before Lionel Toussaint found Amaranth, he was already a homebody. He liked to be in his family's Flatbush apartment more than anywhere else in the world, and he liked the company he kept there: his twin sister, Roseline, his mother, Carmen, his father, Pierre, and his two grandmothers, Abuelita and Maamaa. They were close-knit and loving, Abuelita and Maamaa doting constantly on Lionel and Roseline. Their pride and joy. Their reason for living. Their babies.

Their house on Beverley Road faced east and was always sunlit. It was weatherworn on the outside but meticulously kept inside. "No one needs to know how nice we have it in here," Pierre said as they watched the paint chip more and more over time. "They might try to take it."

"Safest to blend in," Carmen echoed. Lionel took that to heart. The condo's three bedrooms were tiny, even by New York standards, but the kitchen had enough space for everyone to stand around as meals were prepared, gossiping and yelling at each other in a hybrid of broken Spanish, English, and Creole, singing along to the new English pop songs Lionel and Roseline came home from school singing. They had their own language no one else could quite speak. Not completely.

Lionel was deeply proud of his mother and Abuelita, who had moved with the rest of their family from Puerto Rico to New York in the 1950s and built a life. He was deeply proud of his father and Maamaa, for escaping Baby Doc, a cruel and vindictive dictator, for making it to the United States, for finding such beautiful love there. They were people with bravery and dreams. They were people with stories.

And they still were, here in New York. Pierre, an activist back in Haiti, stayed home to take care of the twins and the grandmothers, who were aging swiftly. Maamaa in particular needed help coming up and down the stairs, and who could help her if Lionel and Roseline were at school? Carmen got her nursing license and was beloved at Brooklyn City Hospital. She slowly but surely climbed the ladder, promotion after promotion landing her the job of Head Nurse.

Lionel was proud to be part of his family, which meant, too, that he was proud to be Haitian and Puerto Rican and American all at once. And more than proud, he felt lucky. To love his family so deeply. To spend so much time together in the kitchen, cooking dinner, singing, laughing, throwing uncooked rice at each other and hearing it rattle on the floor. He was proud even when he wrote COOKING in scribbly letters under his favorite things in second grade and the other boys at his table snickered.

"Cooking's for girls," someone said, and Lionel felt defiant.

"Why?" he asked. "We all have to eat."

"Because it's girly," someone else said.

"What's more manly than taking care of people?" Lionel asked.

"Feeding people? That's big love." He wished Roseline were in his class to defend him. If his classmates could only see Pierre, they'd know what he meant. He knew these kids were wrong. He felt bad for them for thinking the way they did.

He never thought for a second cooking made his father less of a man, or made Lionel less of a boy. Those fears came later, when he was eleven and had a crush on Theodore Huxtable on *The Cosby Show* and pretty much the entire cast of *The Outsiders*. He watched that movie with his family and made sure to keep his face stony. Neutral. Chill.

After, when Roseline asked from her squeaky, glow-in-the-dark inflatable chair, "What did you think?" Lionel responded, way too loudly and way too quickly, "It was fine."

"Oh. I really liked it," she said, and shrugged, and Lionel felt his stomach sink. It felt so gross to half lie to her, even about something like a movie. He felt a little sick over it, but maybe that's because he knew it was the start of space growing between them.

There were already other things he didn't tell her about: that he tried on her clothing sometimes, just for fun. That he wanted to tag along when all the Toussaint women went shopping together. And that he only felt God at church when this one particular boy was in attendance. His round glasses and sweaters. His new shoes and big smile. He was sent from above to keep Lionel committed to the Catholic Church. *Patron saint of sexy,* Lionel thought to himself every time he saw him, then immediately did the sign of the cross, and said every prayer he knew. Twice.

Then HIV/AIDS swept through New York over the next few years, devastating hospitals and communities and families. Lionel watched the news. He read the papers. He heard his neighbors whispering. He listened to his mother crying, late at night in the kitchen, recounting the horrors she'd seen at the hospital.

"It's unthinkable," she said as Pierre comforted her, tried to feed her fried plantains she just pushed to the side. "Where is God?"

Lionel listened against his will, from his bedroom, from under a pillow.

"Don't you want to know what's going on?" Roseline asked from the doorway, voice trembling. She was wearing a yellow nightgown, her hair set in rollers. She was looking for someone to comfort her, to listen, to care.

But Lionel rolled over and said, "No." He listened to her crying alone as a restless, unsleeping fear crept over him. Because he knew people who felt like he did were some of the most susceptible.

And that fear only deepened when the FDA labeled Haitians a high-risk group for AIDS.

"Four H group?" Carmen spat after a late-night shift. "With the homosexuals and hemophiliacs? With the drug addicts? Dios mio."

Lionel felt sick to his stomach.

The whole thing sparked the dormant activist in Pierre, and he dragged his family across the Brooklyn Bridge and into Manhattan with thousands of other Haitians.

"We don't give AIDS!" people yelled.

"Discrimination!"

"The United States is racist!"

"Why don't we ban the FDA?"

Yes, Lionel thought, and shouted alongside his father, his family. Two big signs bobbed above the crowd in front of them: AIDS Is Behavioral Not Racial. And: We Are Not The Sinners.

"That's right!" Pierre called.

"We are not like them!" Carmen yelled.

Lionel locked eyes with Roseline, but quickly looked away before she could read him. His heart pounded. His traitorous heart, always betraying him. He started to sweat, and though the April day was warmer than it should be, he knew that wasn't why.

*I am like them*, a small voice rang in his heart. And then, the shadow of a thought, *Do I have to choose?* And, quieter, further still: *Am I going to die?* He kept marching. The crowd almost crushed him.

If he had to choose, his choice was easy. His family was everything to him. What did he need love for, anyway? But that was when it was just an idea. That was before the first day of junior year, when the patron saint of sexy sat next to him in history class, with his bright white smile and cashmere maroon sweater, smelling of cinnamon.

After years of yearning, Lionel knew every inch of him: His fancy sneakers, high cheekbones, wavy brown hair, and those Goddamn glasses. But there were new surprises, too, now that he got to be so close to him. His name was Rex Jones. He had asthma, and sometimes had to whip out an inhaler. He got nervous when the teacher called on him, and had a bundle of keychains on his backpack so big it sounded like someone was dumping out a junk drawer every time he walked into the room.

When Rex and Lionel got paired up for a report on the Constitution, Rex invited Lionel over to his place, and Lionel thanked Jesus, Mary, and Joseph every step of the way there. Rex lived in a fashionable brownstone building with a chandelier in the front lobby, rugs as soft as pillows, and a baby grand piano smack in the middle of the living room.

"Do you play?" Lionel asked Rex, just to have something to say. Rex smiled shyly, and took a seat on the bench.

"I dabble."

"Let's hear it, then."

Rex didn't just play "A Whole New World." Maybe things would have been all right if he had. But on top of that, he sounded like

Aladdin. And not only did he sound like Aladdin, he made eye contact with Lionel the whole time. And not only did he make eye contact with Lionel the whole time, he changed the "princess" lyric to "prince."

And, well. The rest was history. Because now, Lionel knew what he needed love for. He needed it because it made him feel electric and wanted and whole and special and *alive.* It made his body burn with longing, with hunger, with want. It made his heart sing, his worries fade, his purpose in life settle. He was meant to be with Rex. It was the most natural thing in the world. It was serendipitous, the two of them years in the making. It was full of passion and tenderness and feelings Lionel never knew he could have, but that ripped him all the way open. He needed love like he needed air.

And though he still had all his fears chirping in the back of his mind, he felt safe. He was a virgin, after all, and Rex was too, and they kept it very PG-13 (except for the couple times they didn't). And Lionel met him at church—or, if not met him, watched him there. Always sweetly bowing his head, prayerful. Rex sang him a Disney song, for heaven's sake! The boy had asthma and wore sweaters and glasses and played piano! He was rich, even! His cupboard was stocked with brand names. And Lionel was a kind person. A good person.

He was so loved. So how could it happen to him?

# *formal attire*

**AFTER EVERYTHING IS PREPPED**, cooked, and plated, Sunny, Kiyo, and Abe join us in the kitchen.

"We decorated the barn," Sunny says brightly, stealing a bruschetta bite. "It looks enchanting, if I do say so myself."

"I still don't understand why we're throwing them a party," Kiyo says, grabbing a piece of arancini. "They stayed an extra night? How special."

"Darling, don't be a party pooper before it's even started. And anyway, it's not *just* for them. It's for all of us. Maybe especially me. You know how I love to put on my glad rags and look spiffy."

"You do look stunning," I say to Sunny, and she does, in a white flapper dress, fur shawl, and long strands of pearls. She throws her head back and laughs.

"Oh, what a doll you are," she says. "But this isn't my dress for this evening. In fact, I should go get ready. We all should."

My stomach sinks again, and panic pops like fireworks in my chest. "Is it okay if I just wear this?" I ask, gesturing to the world's most cursed fleece jacket.

"They're a doll *and* a hoot," Sunny says, before spinning out of the room. I take that as a no.

"Seriously," I say to the rest of them. "I'm not really in the mood to dress up."

"Cal, come on," Ramona says. "It'll be fun. Just wear the dress from last night."

"I'd rather not," I say, but don't elaborate. I don't want to hurt her feelings. She found that dress for me. She loved it. She loved me in it. It's not her fault I hated it.

"Okay, well. There's that whole closet. I'll find you another dress," Ramona offers. But I must make a face because she adds, "Clothing isn't gendered, you know."

"I know that," I say, but the thought of wearing a dress here, now, again, makes me want to die on the spot. "I just don't see myself ever wearing a dress again, if I'm honest."

She stops folding napkins and raises her eyebrows. "What? Ever? Why? There's no one way to look nonbinary."

"I know that," I say again flatly.

"There's always menswear!" Ambrosia says. "You'd look so cute. I can see it now, a little bow tie, something that still makes your tits look good. It's all about the tits."

Ambrosia does a little shimmy, making Ramona giggle again (have I ever heard her *giggle* this much before?), and now I really do want to fucking fight her, but I try to keep my composure.

"I'm not . . . no," is all I can manage.

"We'll help you, Cal," Lionel says. "Me and Kiyo make quite

the styling team, and Sunny's a master tailor. We even get Abe looking fresh on party nights." Kiyo makes a face like she very much does not want to be on my styling team.

"I'm not too jazzed about the dress code, either," Abe offers, giving me a sympathetic smile. "But it'll be worth it for the food."

"Yes!" Lionel practically sings. "See? Food brings us all together." And then, wistfully: "My dear, sweet father taught me that."

I reach out to put a comforting hand on his arm, and he smiles over at me. Then Sunny clears her throat from the top of the stairs, and we all turn to look.

Sunny was not joking about her party gown. When she descends to the living room, she looks like a young Josephine Baker and like a billion dollars in an intricate, gold-beaded dress, a matching headpiece, big gold cuffs on her biceps, and of course, her signature pearls—a 1920s dream. Kiyo actually tears up when she sees her, and I have to look away. It feels like I'm in on a private moment between the two of them, even with all of us in the room. I imagine Kiyo will paint this girl, this dress, this moment, and it will be exactly right.

"Us next!" Ambrosia declares, grabbing Ramona's hand and dragging her up the stairs.

Ramona and Ambrosia take forever picking out dresses together, and I bite the edge of my thumb the whole time. I make small talk with Sunny, Lionel, Abe, and Kiyo and try not to be jealous. Not of the incredible, still-wet portrait Kiyo did of Ramona that's now hanging in the stairwell (how long were we out chopping wood, truly?). Not of Ambrosia, who is really not a threat, I remind myself. Ramona loves me, and Ambrosia looks like a red-headed version of the Cool Crimp Courtney doll in the basement—a walking parody of the most over-the-top 1990s styles.

But I'm still relieved when Ramona appears at the top of the stairs. We all whistle and clap, as she walks down like a debutante. She's in a royal blue dress that fits her like a glove, that makes her brown eyes pop. She's dripping with diamonds, and her high heels give me PTSD but she looks damn good in them.

"Well, hello, gorgeous!" Sunny says.

"Lucky Cal," Lionel says, nudging me. "She's a stunner, folks!"

"Thanks, y'all," Ramona says. Her eyes turn to me then, and I can't help the smile that spreads across my face. I feel so proud when she sits down next to me, puts her hand on my knee, and kisses me on the cheek.

"Hold on to your hats, ladies and gents!" Ambrosia announces her arrival, and we all turn to the stairs once again.

Lionel gasps and calls, "Jessica Rabbit?! Is that you?"

Clearly, Ramona styled her tonight. Her long, red hair is shaped into swooping waves. Her strapless, red silk dress has a slit all the way up her leg, and she's a natural walking in her crazy high stilettos. Her usual powdered blue eyeshadow has been replaced with a subtle gold. She looks like a model. And her tits, I must admit, look great.

Ramona can't take her eyes off Ambrosia as she twirls around the room. It shouldn't make me so desperately sad. It shouldn't make me hot with jealousy. But. Well. It does.

"All right, fellas," Kiyo says, looking around at Abe, Lionel, and me. "Let's get snazzy."

"Cal's not a fella," Ramona reminds her, rubbing my knee protectively. "She's nonbinary, remember?"

Where was that energy when everyone was calling me a girl yesterday?

"Oh. Right," Kiyo says, and, surprisingly, "Sorry."

"No, it's okay," I say. "I . . . I like it." It's the first time anyone's called me a boy, or something like it, since . . . well. Since it became obvious I wasn't one. I have to stop myself from smiling too big over something so small.

"Okay," Ramona says coolly, pulling her hand away. "Noted."

My smile melts away as I follow Kiyo, Lionel, and Abe up the stairs.

With the closet to ourselves and a divider set up for privacy, Kiyo lands immediately on a green plaid suit with a white bow tie. She changes behind the wooden room divider, then brushes her short hair with her hands in the mirror.

"Looking good," I say, and I worry I'm being too familiar, but she grins. Lionel pretends to faint and Abe slaps her on the back.

"You make this look easy," he says.

Lionel chooses a classic black tuxedo with hot pink shoes and a hot pink tie, and his eyes sparkle as we cheer as he and his reflection moonwalk together.

Abe is a little flustered, but he tries on three suits—plain black, white linen, brown wool—and lands on the third one with a definitive nod. For the first time, I realize how much he hides his body in his corduroy jackets, oversize button-downs, and big sweaters. I feel a spark of shame looking at his chest because I know he wouldn't want me to. But, quickly, the shame is swallowed by recognition. His shape doesn't undo his masculinity. If anything, for me, it strengthens it. He should read as a girl like I do, but all I can see, so obviously, is a boy. A man, almost. Handsome. Could someone look at me and see what I see in him? As I look at Abe, it feels possible.

"You look very academic," Lionel says, massaging Abe's shoulders. He blushes and looks at the floor.

"You know I'm anything but. The only textbook we had was the *Book of Mormon*." He tries to smooth his vest down as Kiyo slicks his hair back.

"I agree with Lionel," I say. "You look like a gentleman and a scholar." Abe meets my eyes. I smile softly, and he smiles too.

"You're next, Cal," Kiyo says, and my heartbeat ramps up.

I walk around the room, pretending to look, knowing I've already tried on at least a dozen outfits and all of them were wrong. The thought of putting them on in front of the others makes me nauseous. I eventually just pull out a pair of simple chinos and a polo shirt.

"Do you think I could get away with this?"

"Absolutely not," Lionel says, and shakes his head.

"Sunny will eat you alive," Kiyo agrees.

"You wouldn't live it down for decades," Abe adds.

I put them both back and stare at the racks and racks of useless fabric in front of me. I don't know what to do in this moment. All I know is I really want it to be over.

"I could just . . . I'll just wear a dress," I say, pulling out a simple black one. "It's fine."

"Didn't I tell you we can do better than *fine* here?" Lionel says. He stands and starts sifting through the suits. "I think you'd look dreamy in this." Lionel pulls a purple suit with big shoulder pads.

"Or this," Kiyo says, grabbing a red jumpsuit that looks like it belongs to Rosie the Riveter.

"Or this," Abe says. He's holding out the tux I was so hopeful about earlier—the navy one with the satin details. I can't help but let out a laugh. Abe flushes. "Sorry. Too mid-century? Is that what you call it?"

"No," I say quickly. "I actually love that one. It's just that I tried it on earlier and I really wanted it to work, but . . ."

"Well, let's see it, then," Lionel says, and when I hesitate, he takes it from Abe and puts it in my hands. "You don't have to wear it tonight. Just try it."

"Okay," I say with a sigh. I change behind the divider. When I step back out, I don't dare look at the others' reactions. I stand in front of the mirror and let my eyes fall on my reflection. It's still so painful. Seeing the way my body curves in all the wrong places, the way the shirt gaps over my chest where the button popped off earlier. I have to hold the fabric closed with my uninjured hand and pray to the Good Lord Elliot Page I don't flash anyone. My eyes find every part of me that feels wrong. My hips are undeniable. My eyelashes are too long, cheeks too round, face too feminine. Still. Again. Obviously a girl.

"See what I mean?" I say quickly. I try to rush back behind the divider but Lionel steps in front of me.

"Hold on, buttercup," he says. "Let me look."

He takes my hands and pulls my arms out from my sides, scanning me from top to bottom. He even drops one hand to spin me around a little. After a mortifying moment, he says, "You look good. The suit just needs some help. Kiyo, would you get Sunny?"

She nods, and an excruciating amount of time (seconds) later, Sunny bursts through the door.

"Say no more," she says, though no one has said anything at all.

Kiyo closes the door behind them as Sunny looks me up and down, tilts her head, then reaches for new pieces. Or rather, the same pieces but in different sizes. She scans the wall of accessories quickly and reaches for a box of pins. She hands me the stack of clothes with an encouraging smile and then shoves me behind the partition. This time when I emerge, my reflection looks like a little kid trying on their father's clothes.

"I know, I know, you're swimming in it," Sunny says, hands up. "Just turn away from the mirror and let me work my magic."

"You really don't have to—"

"Shhh," Lionel says. "Let it happen." Sunny takes the blazer off me and hands it to Kiyo to hold.

"I'm good with a pen *and* with a pin." Sunny smiles as she starts to pin the pants around me, tightening them in the places they bag. She then has me take them off so she can sew the fabric in place. It's tedious, and she takes her time, and I already feel guilty because I know it won't make a difference and I'll end up in a little black dress and everyone will roll their eyes and groan and talk about how I make things more difficult than they need to be. But Sunny is determined, so I don't stop her.

Once the pants are done, she motions for me to tuck in the too-big white, starchy dress shirt, and she pins that too. And then she does the jacket, which takes the longest, and I feel more and more exposed while all of them watch. And more and more anxious when I realize Ambrosia and Ramona are downstairs, together, alone. Beautiful Ramona and hot-as-hell Ambrosia and me, probably looking goofy, trying way too hard to be someone I'm not.

"All right," Sunny says finally, grabbing a pair of shiny black shoes. "Now, don't look in the mirror yet, Cal. And no one say anything. Let them have their own reaction. And, Cal, if you hate it, I won't be offended. It's not my best work. I was rushing."

"Promising," I say, as I struggle to tie the laces with my hand in a splint. Wordlessly, Abe bends down to help me, and when we straighten up, he puts his hands on my shoulders.

"Don't say anything," Sunny warns.

"I won't," he promises. "Just . . . here. You don't need it but. A finishing touch." He takes his watch off. The one he wears to make him feel more manly. He puts it on my wrist and fastens it.

"Thank you," I whisper. I don't think I've ever meant it more.

"On the count of three," Sunny says. "Three, two—"

I turn around early because I can't bear it any longer.

"*Oh*," is all I can say. I reach forward and touch the glass. Because in front of me, for the first time—Cal. Me. Exactly how I've always wanted to look. It's not perfect—so far from it—but it's close enough. Despite, despite, despite—there I am.

There. There. *There.* Here. It's the exact feeling I've waited for my whole life, that I'd started to give up on. For once, I don't dream of being someone else, somewhere else. For once, my eyes don't go right to all the parts of me I wish I could change. I just see Cal. I just see me. And I like me.

"Is this Amaranth magic? Like, is the mirror playing a trick?" I ask.

"That's just you, angel," Lionel says, smiling wide.

"Swoony," Kiyo adds. "Sunny, you're something else."

I turn back to my reflection. "I really look like this?"

"Does that mean you like it?" Sunny claps her hands together.

I don't want to speak, because I don't want to cry, so I just go hug her.

"I love it, Sunny," I say, when I'm confident I can.

"The right fit can go a long way," she says, and hugs me tighter.

"They like it!" Lionel cheers. "But, I mean, how can you not? You look like a Hanson brother."

"Like a who?" Kiyo says. And then, disturbed, "Wait, Abe are you . . . crying?"

"No," he says, but we all turn to see him wipe a tear from his cheek. "Fine, yes. I, uh, lost a button."

"A button?" Kiyo asks.

"Well," Abe says, and locks eyes with me. Grins. "It was a really good-looking button."

My whole body flushes and I duck my head, hoping he won't see.

"I'm confused. Is this a Mormon thing?" Kiyo asks again.

"Oh, who cares," Lionel says, already heading toward the door. "There's a feast waiting in the barn. Let's go party!"

Sunny grabs Kiyo's hand and they follow Lionel out of the room. Abe isn't far behind, glancing back my way for a split second before disappearing through the doorway. But I linger for just a moment. I look at myself one more time, in case I never get to feel this way again. I stand up straight. I tuck my hair behind my ears. I tug on the jacket so it settles. I feel proud. I feel euphoric. I feel . . . found.

# *but*

WHEN I HURRY TO follow the others down the stairs, the girls are already whooping and applauding. As I make my grand entrance, I look right at Ramona.

"What do you think?" I call, striking a pose as if I'm on the cover of *GQ*. I pretend to fiddle with my cuff links. Casually stick my hand in my pocket. The others playfully catcall and whistle, but I watch Ramona's eyes find me. Clear as anything, I see her face fall.

It lasts only an instant—something between disappointment and frustration, and I try not to let myself think the word *disgust*. Then she picks her cheeks right back up, plasters on her politician smile, and claps robotically.

"Look at you!" she says, voice high. So high.

"That only took forever," Ambrosia says. Lionel elbows her and she adds, "But worth the wait!"

Ramona stands and hugs me, and I try to pretend I didn't see her reaction. Maybe I misread it. Maybe she was just surprised. But she taps my back like I'm a stranger or a weird uncle. When she pulls away, she simply says, "C'mon," and runs toward the door. Everyone spills out of the kitchen and heads in the direction of the barn, Dash included.

I stand alone again for a minute, watching them all cross the field under the moonlit sky. I catch my reflection in the window pane, just the hint of me, and I'm giddy all over again. *There,* I think again. *Me. Cal.* I can't stop looking at myself. I can't stop smiling. I even laugh out loud, though there's no one to hear it. Sunny is a genius, and I'm grateful. I'm not hopeless. I'm not impossible. I'm there, right there. Right here.

But as I step out into the night, tears sting the back of my eyes because Ramona didn't love it. That much was obvious. And as much as I don't want to risk our relationship, I don't want to lose this version of myself either. The one that feels lighter than air. Happy, free, and easy, all on my own. My body feels—for the first time—like home. I didn't know it could feel like this, but now that I know, how could I ever let it go? How could Ramona ever want me to?

I cross the amaranth field to the barn and see that it's strung up with lights and dripping with beautiful, swirling, hand-painted streamers. At the center of the hall, there's a big, round table set with decorative dishes, vases of wildflowers, and crystal glasses. The record player, relocated from the living room, blasts "Rhythm Is a Dancer," and Lionel buzzes around the buffet table, hyping up his miso-glazed salmon, stuffed bell peppers, and ravioli.

I make a plate of food I know I won't eat and sit between Sunny and Ramona. She barely even looks my way. I push ravioli around with a fork as everyone discusses the top song the year they came to Amaranth: "Singin' in the Rain," "Now Is the Hour," "Lonely Boy," and "Candle in the Wind."

Then, over dessert, they go over all the houseguests who came and left: a lesbian actress from the 1950s, a football player and a beatnik poet from the 1960s, a comedian from the '70s, and Polly McCarthy from Miss Stone's in the '80s.

"Oh, and there was that two-spirit person, briefly, in what, 2000? Kohana," Lionel says. "The way she described it, it sounded like how you describe being nonbinary, Cal."

"Cool, yeah. Two-spirit identities are exclusive to Indigenous people, but they can fall under the nonbinary umbrella," I explain. The first thing I've said since we sat down.

"See?" Ambrosia says. "Everyone in our other lives thinks we're sickos. Thinks we don't even deserve to live. But we're as natural as the mountains and the sea. And just as beautiful, too. Or, I don't know, I'm assuming. I've never seen a mountain in real life."

"You've never seen a mountain?" Abe asks, sounding almost outraged. But Ramona only wears heart eyes.

"I love that," Ramona says to Ambrosia. "Lyrics, maybe?"

"I'm telling you, Blondie," Ambrosia says. "If you stay just *one* more day, we could write and record a new song too."

"You know I have to get back," Ramona groans, then looks at me. "We have to get back." Ambrosia pouts like she's joking, but it turns into something genuinely sad. Her bottom lip even trembles. Ramona reaches across the table and puts her hand on Ambrosia's arm. "Hey, you know I loved today."

Their eyes meet, and the two of them share a look that says so much and lasts so long, it makes me uncomfortable. I clear my throat.

"So, uh," I say, turning away from Ramona and Ambrosia. "What do you all miss the most from your other life?"

"Seasons," Sunny says almost automatically. "I love summer fashion. And do you know how long it's been since I've seen snow? Here, it's either springlike or storming."

"I miss California," Kiyo says. "Other Japanese people. And my mother." She refills her champagne flute, downs it, and fills it again.

"Nothing," Ambrosia says fiercely.

"Everything," Lionel sighs. "My whole family. Brooklyn. Cute boys on every corner. Movie theaters and malls and roller coasters."

"Maybe Cal's gift will be a roller coaster!" Ambrosia says, hopeful. "Imagine it right in the middle of the clearing?" With the way my emotions have been over the past forty-eight hours, it probably isn't out of the question.

"Whatever it is, I so hope it comes tonight," Sunny says. "For all our sakes. Since they simply *must* leave in the morning." Her words are playful, bubbly like the champagne we've been drinking all night.

"I want Cal to get their gift too," Ramona says. "Trust me, I do. And, honestly, I love it here. I wish we could stay, but . . ." Ramona trails off, looking to me.

"But maybe one more day is okay?" I say.

Ramona considers it for a moment, making my heart hopeful, but ultimately shakes her head.

"I think we should go. Just in case."

"Yes, we know," Kiyo says, smirking. Downing half of her new glass. "So you can fight for rights that the rest of us will never get to have. So Cal can recommit to your relationship. Oh, *so* sorry. I mean, to that fancy school. Or just to being a g—"

"Kiyo," Ramona snaps.

It's like all the air gets sucked out of the room. Or at least out of me. My head whips toward Ramona, but her eyes are locked on Kiyo, cheeks flaming.

"How much champagne have you had, darling?" Sunny asks Kiyo, shooting her a warning look.

Ramona puts her fork down. She takes a deep breath. "Kiyo. I told you those things in confidence," she says flatly. I feel a prick of betrayal, but still take Ramona's hand under the table.

"You can't just say hurtful shit like that," I say.

Kiyo grabs her champagne flute and leans back in her chair as she takes a big swig. "It wouldn't be hurtful if it wasn't at least a little bit true."

"So, Abe, what do you miss from home?" Lionel asks loudly, trying to change the subject.

"Well, it's not true," Ramona says, ignoring Lionel. "I mean, I want to go to college with Cal, but I don't want her to be a girl."

"Right. You just want *them* to go to a school for girls."

The look Ramona gives Kiyo is murderous.

"First of all, she uses 'she' too."

"That's not what Abe said."

Ramona turns her murderous look on me for a moment, but plows on. "I just want *them* to go to the school we chose together, which means securing the field hockey scholarship. And they want that too. It's their dream school. It doesn't matter that they're not a girl."

I'm quiet for too long. It does matter, but I can't say that.

Ramona stares at me. Everyone stares at me.

"Right?" Ramona prompts.

"Yes," I say defensively. But she just keeps staring at me, and I'm suddenly so sick of lying. Not only that—I'm sick of being lied *to*. My mind flashes to that look Ramona gave me when she saw me in my tux. And in my gut, in my heart, I know Kiyo is right. It wouldn't hurt if it weren't at least a little bit true, and it's true that Ramona doesn't want me like this, while this is all I've ever wanted.

I move my napkin from my lap to the table.

"Let's talk outside."

# *more truth*

WE WALK TO THE firepit, far enough from the barn that no one will hear us. We sit side by side in Adirondack chairs in the chill and darkness of a night with no fire. I put my hand out. Ramona doesn't take it.

"What's going on?" she asks.

I force myself to keep eye contact. Fold my arms to steady my shaking hands against the cotton and silk of my jacket. Take in a deep breath. "Ramona, I love you. I can't imagine my life without you. But I . . . I don't understand why I have to go to Alcott if it doesn't feel right anymore." Ramona opens her mouth to speak, but I hurry to continue. "Why can't we do long distance? At least until I can afford to be near you."

The anger in her voice is immediate. "Because, Cal! I turned down Yale, Luíza's alma mater, just to go to Alcott with you. I didn't even *want* to go to Alcott, not really, and now you want me to go alone? I worked so hard to get the funding for you, and I know you didn't ask me to do that, but you were sobbing for weeks! It was so hard to watch. I thought if you could go to Alcott it would help, but apparently not."

"I can't begin to tell you how grateful I am that you did all that. It's the nicest thing anyone has ever done for me," I say. I choose my next words carefully. "But I can't go just because I feel guilty."

Ramona's face hardens, and I can tell she's trying not to cry. "So you don't want to go? Officially?"

I try to picture it one last time: Being Cal in California. Questioning how much I can change before Ramona leaves me. Putting my head down, pushing myself down, just to survive four more years of pretending.

I try to picture it for the first time: leaving that version of myself behind at Amaranth. The version that is willing to hide to make everyone else more comfortable. The version that can't stand what they see in the mirror. The version that hates themself. Gone, forever.

It feels terrifying. It feels irresistible. It feels . . . possible.

"No," I barely breathe out. "I don't want to go. I'm sorry."

Ramona turns away from me. She's trying to hide that she's crying, but I can see her back rising and falling. I can hear her trying to get her breath under control. And I'm sorry, I'm sorry, I'm sorry. It breaks my heart to break her heart. My chest physically aches, and all I want to do is turn to Ramona for comfort—how messed up is that? When I reach out to put my hand on her back, she shrugs me off.

"I need a minute," she says.

"Take your time," I say. We have so much of it here.

I look at the stars, still and bright—not as bright as last night but still otherworldly. I count them just to have something to do besides break down. If I stayed here forever, could I count them all?

When Ramona finally turns back to me, she says, "I just don't know how we got here." She sounds so hurt. "It feels like you changed your mind overnight."

"I know," I say, holding my own hand now, rubbing my palms together. "But I've been feeling like this for a while. I did want to go to Alcott with you. I really, really did. The whole time we were looking at schools, the only thing I could focus on was being with you. But once we committed, I just got this sinking feeling. I kept looking at the website and the brochures, at all the girls smiling on the quad. I looked at the field hockey uniforms with their short little skirts and skin-tight tops, and all my emails from Coach that started with, 'Hey, lady!' And I . . . I don't know. I just started spiraling. I found myself staying up late every night researching trans and nonbinary stuff, and reading queer poets, and I got into this forum and . . . I don't know. Things started to click."

"Okay, but even at Alcott you can still figure out what you want, and who you are, and I'll be there with you the whole way."

I can't look at her when I say, "Yeah, but if I go to Alcott, I won't be able to take hormones because of field hockey. And I don't even know, you know, how I want to transition, or if I want to, but I want the option."

"It's only four more years."

"But it's *four more years*. And then it's on my resume forever. Having an all-women's college on there will out me for the rest of my life."

Ramona studies my face. Shakes her head. "You keep saying

you don't know if you're nonbinary, or a guy, or if you want to transition, or what you want, or who you are—"

"Because I don't know."

I watch my knuckles turn white as I clasp my hands together as tightly as I can. I concentrate on the pain while I wait for Ramona to say something.

Her voice is quieter when she finally asks, "Do you think maybe you *do* know, you just won't let yourself accept it because you're scared of what it means for us?"

I could protest. I could double down, saying I know for sure that I'm not a guy. But it would be a lie.

I hate the sob that escapes my throat. I hate that I can't save us. I hate that I'm losing my best friend. But most of all, I'm relieved to finally tell her the truth.

"Maybe I'm close to knowing," I say.

Ramona moves to sit on my lap. She takes my face in her hands. "That makes me really happy, Cal. Even though it also makes me really sad."

*Why sad?* I almost ask, but I already know. I study her face, every inch of it: the scar on her chin, the birthmark on her cheek, her big, soft lips, and unforgettable eyes. Even now, her beauty leaves me breathless. Even now, I love her more than ever. It's not enough.

"I think this is the part where I'm supposed to beg you again. To choose me still. Love me still. Just wait and see. But I won't. I know it's not fair to either of us."

Ramona smiles sadly and pushes a lock of hair out of my eyes. "When you came down the stairs wearing this suit tonight, it was one of the worst moments of my life."

"Um, ouch."

"No, listen. It was one of the worst for me because I could tell that, for you, it was one of the best. You were glowing. You look *incredible*, Cal." Tears fill her eyes again and spill onto her cheeks. "But all I could see is you walking away from me. Choosing another life, another path. Because even this"—she trails her fingers along my lapel—"is just not for me. I want it to be. More than anything, I do. I wish I could change myself for you, just like you've been trying to do for me."

"It's just a suit," I say.

"We both know it's not just a suit. It's a beginning, right? Otherwise, going to Alcott wouldn't feel so impossible for you." She runs her fingers along the back of my neck and I feel the whole world slip away, because I know this will be the last time. "I don't want to get in your way, Cal. We're only eighteen. Our three years together has been its own lifetime, but we have so many more to live."

"But I wanted them all with you," I say, my voice quiet and desperate.

"I wanted them all with you too," she replies, choking on the last word.

"Why does it have to be so all or nothing?"

"Because we should both get it all, everything we want, just how we want it. I love you too much to give you some half love. You deserve to be wanted fully, for exactly who you are."

That's a nice thought, but every time I tell someone who I am, I lose them. My parents. Her. No one's ever loved me—all of me—and all signs point to no one ever will.

"I understand," I say flatly, feeling numb. "I just don't want to lose you."

She grabs my chin and forces me to look at her. "You're

not losing me. You're still my best friend. I'll be here with you through all of it, even if it's different than we expected. I love you, and this isn't your fault, and there's nothing wrong with you. You're perfect."

"I love you too," I say, voice barely above a whisper. I think I might pass out. I think I might throw up. I think I might die, actually. Then I look down at Abe's watch, a perfect fit on my own wrist, and remember how I felt when I saw myself in this tux for the first time. Free. Safe in myself. Happy, all on my own. That feeling floods me again, pushing me back into my body. I try to hold on to it because it's the only thing that's going to get me through this.

"And you're perfect, Ramona. I've always known that. We're just . . . not perfect for each other."

She hugs me then, tighter than she ever has before, and we both cry until we can't cry anymore. When she pulls away and I kiss her, long and hard, I know it's for the last time. And I think she does too.

"If this is right"—she wipes my tears away as hers fall on my cheeks—"why does it feel so wrong?"

"Because we really thought it would be us, in the end. Or at least I did."

"I did too," she says. "Man. We were really something, weren't we?"

I pull her back to me. Hold her tight. "We still are."

She leans into me as we look at the sky. I smell her hair, her perfume, her skin one more time and I try to feel in my muscles and bones how much I loved her. How much I still love her. I hope I'll remember it all forever.

Because it's over. It's really over. I can't believe it's over. It's wild how quickly a world can shatter. But once my lungs finally, finally steady, I feel like I'm breathing fully for the first time in days. The full truth is out. The worst has happened. My heart is broken, but hope is already burning in the cracks.

"I think Ambrosia wants to climb you like a tree, by the way," I say, just to lighten the moment.

"Too soon," Ramona says through a laugh as she slaps my knee. "And anyway, it's just a creative connection."

"Uh-huh. I think I know what it looks like to have the hots for Ramona Silva."

"What, are you my wingman now?"

"Maybe."

Ramona laughs. "Life comes at you quick."

I blow on a pretend finger gun. "Cal Quick."

"Oh my God," she says, throwing her head back in mock despair. Then, full of wonder, "Oh my *God*."

I look up and see it too. Shooting stars chalking up the night sky. Bright, bright, bright. It's a show. It's a miracle. Maybe it's a sign everything will be okay. Or it's just Amaranth magic, odd and extraordinary as usual.

"This place," I whisper, and she squeezes my knee.

"This place," she echoes. Seconds later, we hear the others, whooping and shouting. We turn to see everyone jogging across the field toward us.

"The stars!" Lionel yells, arms open wide as he runs.

"They're shooting!" Ambrosia calls, jumping on Lionel's back in celebration.

"That's new!" Sunny says breathlessly as they finally get to us. "Cal, that's your gift!"

My jaw drops and I look to the sky again. "Really?"

"It has to be!" Lionel says.

"What a beautiful gift," Ramona says, kissing my cheek, "for a beautiful person."

It is beautiful. It's breathtaking.

But what does it have to do with me?

Ramona stands and goes to Sunny and Lionel and Ambrosia, the four of them bouncing and twirling in the starlight. Abe and Kiyo trail a little behind, both walking slowly, hands in their pockets, looking to the sky. Abe must sense me staring, because he turns his face to me and breaks out into the biggest smile I've seen from him yet. Another gift.

And then, even through all the cheering, I hear it. My brows furrow as I look down at Abe's watch.

"Abe," I call out. He comes closer, that smile still playing on his lips, but it quickly fades when I extend my arm for him to look at the watch. A flash of confusion crosses his face, and he deftly removes the watch from my wrist. He studies it, puts it to his ear, shakes it.

"It's . . . ticking," he says.

Then there's another sound that we all hear: quiet but sharp, like a funeral toll. Everyone freezes, listens.

"What was that?" Kiyo asks.

"It sounded like a bell. Or a chime," Lionel says. "I think it came from the house!"

"Cal brought us *two* gifts!" Ambrosia yells, already walking backward toward the house. "Oh, you spoil us!"

She and Lionel both take off, and Sunny follows, practically dancing. She shoots me an excited glance. "See? I told you you're here for a reason."

# *tick*

IT DOESN'T TAKE LONG to find a grandfather clock, taller than I am, right in the middle of the living room. It's a gorgeous mahogany, its glass stained into a beautiful mosaic. We all crowd around it, and my heart starts to jackhammer in my chest.

"A clock. Huh," Ambrosia says. "Not sure what we need this for."

"It shows the same time as my watch," Abe says, looking down to his wrist and up again.

"Your watch?" Kiyo asks. Abe shows her and everyone leans over for a look.

"Huh," Ambrosia says again, sounding less excited as she sees the second hands move.

We all stand in silence, watching the grandfather clock. Then the minute hand ticks forward, and it sounds like the cocking of a gun. The mood in the room switches from excitement to confusion.

"Everyone saw that, right?" Abe says. His hands are shaking.

"Yes," Sunny says, voice barely above a whisper.

"Does that mean . . . it couldn't mean—" Kiyo starts, but Sunny cuts her off.

"No. Don't even say it."

"Are you suggesting time is passing?" Lionel says.

"Time can't be passing," Sunny says firmly.

"Maybe it's nothing," Ambrosia says, panic creeping into her voice. "Maybe it's just, like, a really pretty clock. Or maybe it does something rad. Like in *Back to the Future* or whatever." Ambrosia runs her hands along the clock, looking for a handle or doorknob to unlock further magic. But then it ticks again, and she jumps and startles away.

Silently, we watch it tick again, and again, and again, dread building heavy in the room. Until Abe says, horrified, "I think I have to pee."

"I think I'm hungry," Lionel says.

"I think I'm, I'm tired," Kiyo stammers.

"*No!*" Ambrosia yells, and it's like the breaking of a dam. Everyone erupts into questions and shouting. Sunny puts her hand to her heart, a haunted look frozen on her face.

"Is that why the stars were falling?" Lionel asks no one in particular. "Because time is passing?"

"If that's the case, some fucking gift Cal brought us," Ambrosia says. The venom of her words has everyone turning to me.

"I don't . . ." I start but don't quite know how I plan to finish that sentence. "I don't know what's happening. I just wanted more time to—"

"You asked for *time*?!" Kiyo's voice is loud and hard. "The whole point of this place is that time doesn't exist!"

"No, that's not what I meant! I meant I wanted to stay here, to have the space to figure myself out. I never imagined . . ."

"Well, clearly something got lost in translation."

My blood goes cold but my suit suddenly feels too hot, too tight. My gift is a curse. This is my fault. It has to be, doesn't it? I mean, how many times had I begged for *more time, more time, more time*? Is Amaranth that literal? Did it read my mind? Did I just ruin everything, all this, for everyone?

"If time is passing, what does it mean for our other lives?"

"Are we going to age?"

"What about illness? What about HIV?"

There are more questions, more shouting, until Sunny throws her hands in the air and yells, "Would you all be quiet?!" with the gravitas of an elementary school teacher. We shut up.

"It must be a test," she says, turning away from us. She paces back and forth. "Yes, yes, that's it. A trick. Time isn't really passing. It just looks and feels that way." She sounds like she's trying to convince herself, but I want to believe her. *God*, I want to believe her. I can't be the person who ruined Amaranth for everyone. I can't be the one who destroyed forever.

"Why would it test us like that?" Ambrosia says.

"That's the question, isn't it?" Sunny says. "Maybe it's asking us what we would do if time began. It's creating urgency. How would we live? Who would we be?"

"Why does it care?" Ambrosia says, exasperated.

"Because Amaranth protects us," Sunny says, desperation slipping into her voice. "That's why it's paradise."

"But, Sunny, if time *is* passing . . ." Lionel says, and lets his words linger.

"I have to sit down," Ambrosia says, and she looks faint. She throws her heels into a corner and curls into a ball on the floor. Ramona sits down beside her, rubbing her shoulder. There's a tight, heavy silence that feels like it could crush us all.

"I really do have to pee," Abe says, running upstairs, where hopefully the bathroom is now more than just a bath room. Dash rushes after him, and he stumbles on the steps. The fur on his face seems, suddenly, whiter.

"This is your screwup," Kiyo says, rounding on me. "You brought time here."

"Darling, let's not rush to conclusions," Sunny says. "We don't know what's happening yet."

"The stars are moving. The clock is ticking. And what the fuck, Abe had to pee," Ambrosia says, pushing herself to sit up. She leans against Ramona.

"Sunny," Kiyo says. "Cal needs to leave. Now." She turns to me, getting up in my face.

"Beat it," she growls, a shove punctuating each word. I stumble backward but don't try to fight back. "Leave. Right now."

"Love, stop, it's not their fault—"

"They've ruined *everything*," Kiyo spits in my face. "We're either going to die here or return to the worlds we came from. Where we'll *also* die, miserable and hated and alone."

"Slow down," Sunny says. "We just need time to think. We need to be patient."

"Sunny," Ambrosia says. "I agree with Kiyo. Cal should go. Every second counts for me. For Lion. You don't understand how fast it can get so bad."

"Listen, I'm worried too," Lionel says, "but that doesn't even make sense. When has anyone's gift disappeared when they left, huh? Never."

"And what if we need Cal to fix it?" Sunny adds. "What if they leave and we never get answers?"

"Either way, we don't have time to waste," Ambrosia counters.

"*Sunny,*" Kiyo pleads, facing her now. Sunny tilts her head for a few seconds, considering, before placing her hands gently on Kiyo's shoulders and moving her away from me. Then Sunny takes both of my hands in hers, holds them tight, and locks her eyes with mine.

"It seems we are a house divided. The only fair thing to do is vote."

My cheeks burn as I stare at the floor and wish I could melt right into it. I can feel everyone's eyes on me, and it makes me feel so small. I am so ashamed. I am so alone. I almost—but don't, can't, won't—rip my hands from Sunny's and run.

# CAL QUICK

## 2008–

The first thing Calla did when she left her house for the first time in months was take those Goddamn earrings out. She showed up at the soccer field at the end of the road with bloody lobes, the studs tucked away in her jacket pocket.

"Hey!" she called to Jackson and the rest of the boys, excited for them to be excited to see her after all that time, but they didn't even look her way. "Hey!" she called again at the edge of the field, louder this time. When they still didn't acknowledge her, she ran onto the pitch, stole the ball, and blasted it as far as she could.

"What the hell, Calla?" Evan called.

"Get out of here," Mason said, "we're in the middle of a game."

"So what? I'll wait until you need a sub," she said.

"So what?" Tatum mocked her high voice.

"Guys only," another boy said. A kid Calla didn't even recognize. "Unless you want to suck my dick after."

"Bro," Mason said. Giggling. "Look at her."

Calla's mind went blank, free of the comebacks she was usually so good at when the guys picked on each other. But this was different. It wasn't the usual teasing. It was mean and gross and laced with a danger she didn't yet know how to describe.

"Jackson?" Calla called to her friend. They'd just been texting the other day, joking and talking about a show they both watched. But now, he was too busy staring at the ground to even look at her.

"We decided it's weird you follow us around," Evan said. "Go play with the other girls."

"I'm not even a girl, though," she blurted out, and knew immediately by the feral looks on their faces it was the wrong thing to say.

"Prove it," the new kid said.

"Dude, no!" Mason said, laughing more.

"*Jackson,*" Calla pleaded. He wasn't going to say anything? Wasn't going to defend her? Tell the other guys to get lost?

"You should go home, Cal," was all he said.

But she couldn't go home. Her parents would know something went wrong, and she could never, ever tell them what happened. And, God, what had happened? Evan taught her how to tie her shoes. Mason saved his Sour Patch Kids for her every Halloween. Tatum always hugged her hello and goodbye. The only hugs she could ever remember.

And Jackson. Jackson had given her a valentine—wasn't it just last February?—that was a cartoon of the two of them sitting on bubble letters that said, BFF. Underneath, it said, LUV U CAL PAL. That was only weeks before the world shut down. What had happened? What had she done wrong?

Calla couldn't go home, so she sat at a bus stop and tried to hate the boys, her friends, but only hated herself instead. She used rocks from the side of the road to make white scratches on her skin. She watched the green-and-white IndyGo buses pass by. She thought about getting on one, but she didn't know where they went, and she didn't have any money, and she knew she'd get in trouble.

A few weeks later, when schools opened for the first time since March, she wished she didn't have to get on the bus at all. She sat as far away from Jackson and the boys as she could. She hid behind her mask and her hoodie, pressed her forehead into the dirty window glass, and pretended she didn't exist.

But that got harder and harder to do, because after a few months, something strange started happening. Every time she walked down the hallway, crowds of boys followed her, mooing like cows. Every time she talked in class, her classmates knocked on their desks, snickering. For two whole weeks, she didn't understand what they were doing, and she didn't understand what she'd done to deserve it, and no one would answer her when she shouted, "Why are you doing this?" They'd only laugh and run off like they'd gotten away with something.

Finally, after weeks of torment, a girl in her English class slid Calla a piece of paper. It said:

*Since u want to know: @jacksond00dlez* 🙁 *Sorry*

She didn't have a cell phone, so couldn't look it up until her parents let her use the family laptop for homework that night. She typed in the username, hit enter, and held her breath as the page loaded. And then there they were, for anyone to see: drawings by her best friend, little pictures of someone who could only be her, with cartoonishly large breasts. *I HAVE HUGE KNOCKERS,* one of them said. *ME AND MY MILK JUGS,* read another caption. And finally, the one that made her sickest, *THIS GIRL THINKS SHE'S A BOY,* with a speech bubble that read, *"ARE THESE CHESTICLES?"*

She slammed the laptop shut. She put her head on the desk and hit it there, over and over. She lay on her bed and cried into Nugget's fur. She didn't sleep at all. The next morning, she spotted Jackson at the end of the hall, and without a word she marched over to him and punched him right in the jaw, sending him flying into a locker. She hadn't planned to do it—though no one would believe her. She broke his jaw. She hadn't meant to do that, either.

For a full hour, Calla was humiliated beyond her wildest imaginings. The shock of it numbed her as she sat in the principal's office with Jackson, his parents, her mom, and the school counselor, while they discussed everything that had happened. While they looked at the pictures together. While she crossed her arms over her chest and tried to squeeze herself out of existence.

She felt numb as she was forced—by everyone, but especially her mother—to apologize to Jackson.

She felt numb when Jackson was forced to apologize too, even though he could hardly speak, and to delete the account in front of them.

She felt numb when they let Jackson go, and as the counselor—a woman older than her grandmother, with tattooed eyebrows and a sweater covered in kittens—asked Natalia and Calla to stay behind. Calla assumed she wanted to talk about the ways boys looked at her now, what the principal had called "sexual harassment," but it was another one of Jackson's cartoons that was up for discussion.

On the way home, Natalia was silent, but when she pulled into the garage, she turned the car off and sat there. She did not unlock the doors.

"You think you're a boy, Calla?" she asked, voice trembling.

"No."

"That's not what those boys said . . . what that woman said . . . *God.*

I'm sick. So which is it?" When Calla didn't answer, Natalia yelled, her voice panicked. "Do you think you're a boy? Or are you a liar?"

"No!" Calla yelled back, but collapsed into herself, finally, finally crying. "I'm not a boy and I'm not a liar. I'm not anything," she said. And it was true. She felt like nothing. She felt like no one.

"Do you think you're a boy?" Natalia asked again. Calla didn't speak. But even bad moms have a mother's intuition.

"Get out," Natalia said, and when Calla didn't move, she screamed it. It was a strangled, murderous sound, so loud Calla's hands flew to her ears. Natalia screamed it over and over again, "Get out! Get out! Get out!" So, when she recovered from the shock of it all, Calla did. She slammed her door on the way out, and she ran.

# *losing time*

BEFORE THE VOTE, SUNNY makes everyone gather proof that time is, in fact, passing. A banana with a single bruise. A strawberry soft in a spot the size of a pinhead. Even more damning, eggs from the chickens. A toilet in the bathroom. All of us hungry, tired, and at least half convinced.

The fire in the living room hearth dies for the first time. Abe relights the flame and we gather around it as time keeps moving. As night's hours—real hours—tick on. The grandfather clock keeps the score.

"Cal should stay," Ramona says, before everyone is even settled. She sits on the couch with Ambrosia and Lionel. Abe finds a chair, with Dash at his feet. Sunny sits on the fireplace and warms her hands by the flames, Kiyo standing by her side. I stand in the doorway, my shoulder leaning on the wood frame. I want to be close to an escape.

"Ramona shouldn't even get to vote," Kiyo says, her leg up on the fireplace. "She's biased. They're dating."

"Not anymore," Ramona says softly.

"Wait, what?" Ambrosia says, leaning deeper into Lionel so she can turn to stare at Ramona, who looks at me with panic in her eyes.

"It's okay," I say, playing with my splint, trying to smile. "We broke up."

Lionel gasps. "Here? Tonight? What happened?"

Abe shifts in his chair uncomfortably and bends down to pet Dash.

"Dating or not," Kiyo says, "they've only been here a few days."

"They were still called here," Sunny says. "They were still chosen. Amaranth gave them gifts, and we have to believe it's something good."

"This isn't a gift."

"We don't get to decide that."

"How can you say that, when . . ." Kiyo trails off, her voice cracking. She wipes tears from her eyes, and the sight of it chills me. Sunny's tears come too, and she shakes her head and reaches out across the fireplace to hold Kiyo's hand.

"I vote for Cal to stay," Ramona says again, unwavering.

"I vote for them to leave," Kiyo says, her words angry, her expression broken.

"I vote stay," Lionel says. "We need answers."

"I vote leave," Ambrosia says, and I don't know why it stings as much as it does. She turns to me, an apology written on her face. "Nothing personal, Cal. It's just Lion and I . . . we need time to stop. Badly."

"Stay," Abe says. To me, he says, "Please."

"That's three votes to stay," Ramona says. "Two votes to leave." A hush falls over the room, and as if to taunt us, the grandfather clock chimes twice.

Only Sunny remains. Of course Sunny will want me to stay, won't she? She said we were all called here. She said I was chosen. She said this is a gift. But she's still holding Kiyo's hand. They have a whole conversation in just a glance, and my stomach falls. Sunny presses her lips together, then turns to me.

"I'm sorry, Cal," she says. I nod quickly back at her and force myself to turn to stone.

What a fool I was to hope.

"I understand," I say. "I, um. Thank you for letting me stay here and . . . well. I'm sorry. I'm just really sorry." I swear the clock ticks louder, like a hammer on wood that can't be ignored.

"You didn't do anything wrong," Abe says. I shrug.

"I did. Even if I didn't mean to."

"I'll go too," Ramona says, coming to stand by my side.

"Well, you can't leave yet, either of you," Sunny says. "It's three to three. It's a tie."

"But there's no one to break it," Ambrosia says. "Shouldn't your vote count for double, Sunny? Amaranth was yours before it was anyone else's."

"I never wanted to be alone here. I never wanted this world to be only mine," Sunny says. "This place is ours."

"Then who's the tiebreaker?" Kiyo asks frustratedly. "Dash?"

"There's no one left," Ambrosia protests. "And we're running out of time."

"Cal didn't vote," Abe says, his voice solid.

"Why would they get a vote?" Kiyo asks.

"They found Amaranth, same as any of us."

Everyone starts arguing, and I try to tune them out—those who want me to stay, if only to fix this, and those who want me to leave, in case that's the key.

"Abe's right," Sunny says finally, loudly. "Cal's the tiebreaker. It's only fair."

"I can't," I say, shaking my head quickly. "I can't make that choice for you. I've already done enough."

"It's a choice for *us,*" Sunny says. "This is your home now too." Kiyo scoffs, but I don't look at her.

"In Amaranth we trust?" Lionel says, and I can't tell if he's being sarcastic or not.

"Yes," Sunny says emphatically. "Exactly. It has our best interests in mind. It keeps us safe."

"What do you say, Cal?" Abe says, eyes locked on mine. "Will you stay? Please?"

I look around the room, at Abe and his dog, their shared eager expression. I look at Sunny and Kiyo, both teary and fearful, and Lionel and Ambrosia, who are holding each other's hands too tight, despite their different votes, their hope reaching in different directions. And, finally, I look at Ramona, who is looking at me with so much love. Despite it all, she's still my person. She's still right here with me. She still wants to follow me home.

"How am I supposed to do this?" I ask, my throat tightening. "How am I supposed to decide for everyone?"

"You're not deciding," Sunny says. "You're voting. Same as everyone."

If I thought for sure leaving would fix things, I'd do it, but they've told me gifts stay even after houseguests leave. And what if Sunny's right? What if it's staying that's the answer? Leaving is so final. Leaving can't be undone.

"Cal," Abe says my name softly. He must be able to tell I'm torn, because he locks eyes with me again and asks sincerely, "What do *you* want?"

I want more time with Abe, in the woods, under the stars. I want Lionel and Ambrosia to be okay. I want Sunny and Kiyo to get their forever. I want Ramona and I to figure out who we are now, and I want her to keep making music, because she's been happier here than I've seen her all year. And I want time at Amaranth to figure myself out. I want to fill my scars with gold.

"I'll stay. See if we can't fix things." I don't know if it's right, but it's what I want.

Ramona hugs me, but my eyes stay on Abe. He gives me a small half smile. Kiyo storms out the back door, slamming it behind her. Sunny stands to follow her, but gives my shoulder a squeeze before she goes.

"I know we're losing time," Ambrosia says with a yawn. "But I'm so tired."

"We must need to sleep now," Lionel says.

"There's only one bed, though," Ramona says.

"I call dibs," Ambrosia says. "But you can join me if you want, Blondie."

"We *just* broke up, dude," I say, and Ambrosia shrugs.

"Can't blame a girl for trying!"

In the end, Lionel and Ambrosia share the bed. Abe and Dash go to sleep in the shed, and Kiyo and Sunny share the chaise in Sunny's writing studio. Ramona and I take the cushions from the couch and make a makeshift mattress on the floor. I am tired down to my bones, but I lie awake, staring at the ceiling, listening to the grandfather clock tick.

When the house goes still, I come undone. I let new tears fall silently as Ramona sleeps beside me. Because in a matter of hours, I managed to destroy two forevers: the one I imagined with Ramona, and Amaranth. Even if it was right to end things, even if I don't know how things will work out here, all of it is my fault. It's all my fault, it's all my fault. And I have no idea how to fix it.

# *morning*

EVEN IF I DON'T know how to fix time, thankfully it seems like Sunny does. Or at least, she has a theory. We all gather in the kitchen the next morning, and while Lionel huffs and puffs around the cabinets (which do replenish still, thank God) the rest of us sip tea and eat toast with jam and butter.

Except for Abe, who comes late and looks miserable. He puts his head in his hands on the table, and I want to check on him, but Sunny begins her speech, which she's promised is very important.

"I've called you all here this morning because I have a theory about Cal's gift. About our new time."

"Let's hear it," Ambrosia says. I may be imagining it, but she looks a little pale.

"Like I said last night, I think Amaranth wants to create a sense of urgency. I thought about it deep into the night. Urgency for what? But don't we all have projects we've been working on for decades? Wouldn't this push us to take action? Mortality creates art."

"Mortality creates death," Lionel says.

"Shh," Ambrosia shushes him. "So, what are you saying, Sunny?"

"I'm saying, I think we're being pushed to finish our projects. My novel, for example. I talk about it all the time. I think about it all the time. And yet, it's only half written."

"My mural," Kiyo says. "On the barn. My old home, my family's flower shop. I haven't touched it in years."

"I did want to do a cookbook," Lionel says, frowning at his bruised peach.

"I mean, hey, it can't be a coincidence that up until two days ago I had nothing," Ambrosia says. "I spent all my time cleaning up after you people. Playing video games. Chillin'. But thanks to Blondie, I mean, what if we make an album?"

"Yes!" Ramona says, reaching across the table to hold her hand. I can't help it, my throat feels tight. But Ambrosia's eyes light up. "Oh my God, yes. It'll be so good."

"You'd stay? Until we finish it?"

Ramona chews her bottom lip and breathes deeply, but she doesn't take long to answer. "Listen, I'm scared. I have so many things at home that are important to me, but you all matter, too. And I think this place has been good for me." Ramona looks at me and offers a shy smile. "I've spent too much time on other people recently. I want to keep phonebanking and canvassing and writing petitions, but I also need to take care of myself. Music makes me feel ready to fight."

I smile big at her, even though my heart hurts. "I think Tia Luíza would be happy to hear that," I say.

"So you'll stay," Ambrosia says.

"I'll stay. At least until we finish the album." Ambrosia nearly tackles her out of her chair.

"Abe doesn't really have a project, though," Kiyo says, the anger from last night still lingering in her tone. "Neither does Cal."

"I do, actually," Abe says quietly.

"Really? What is it?" Lionel asks.

Abe shifts in his seat. "It's private."

"Well, that's not strange at all," Kiyo says sarcastically.

Abe puts his head in his hands on the table again, and he really looks like he's about to die.

"In my defense, I just got here," I say, trying to get attention off Abe. "But I don't really have any skills. I'm good at field hockey. I'm not sure how that serves me here."

"Perhaps you and Ramona are just helpers," Sunny says. "You haven't been here long enough to dither and dillydally like the rest of us."

"So Ramona will help me," Ambrosia says. "And Cal will help everybody else?"

"Cal help *me* in the *kitchen*? Gag me with a spoon," Lionel says.

"Hey," I say, pretending to be wounded.

"I'm just playing, muffin," he says. He most certainly is not.

"Well, that works for me," I say, ignoring Lionel. "I'll be a floater."

"We have a plan, then," Sunny says. "Be diligent. Be purposeful—"

"Be gay," Ambrosia says, and steals the bruised peach Lionel has been glaring at all morning.

"Oh, no," Abe says pathetically. He covers his mouth, stands up, and sprints outside.

There's a beat of silence before Kiyo says, "I should probably . . . or someone should probably—"

But I'm already on my feet, following Dash out the door and down the stairs.

Abe doesn't make it very far before he doubles over on the grass and vomits. Again and again. It's violent, like he can barely take a breath. I want to comfort him. I don't know how. Dash waits patiently, worriedly, feet away, and I sit on the porch steps with my legs stretched out and shaking. I look at my hands, the ground, my sneakers. Anything but him. I hate the sound of his retching, and hate even more the fruitless dry heaving he does after. The helplessness of it. It makes me feel helpless too.

When it's over, he starts laughing, and that only freaks me out more.

"You okay?" I ask.

"It's been a long time," he says weakly, when he's finally able to speak.

"Yeah, it's not fun." I think of prom, which, strangely, does feel like years ago. "Let me get you some water."

I assure everyone inside Abe's okay, though I'm not so sure. When I return with a glass, he sits next to me on the porch, his face a terrible shade of gray. He brings the water to his lips and takes a tiny sip.

"I'm sorry you had to see that." His voice is hoarse.

"Don't worry, I wasn't watching." Abe nods gratefully. "Are you sick, do you think?"

Another wry laugh. "Something like that."

I reach out to awkwardly rub his back, but Abe jumps the moment I touch him.

"Sorry, I—"

"No," he says, wiping his mouth. "That felt nice. It's just, no one's really touched me in a long time, I guess."

I try again, and I can feel the muscles in his back relaxing under my palm. His face softens. I don't say anything, because I know he likes his quiet. But soon he takes a deep breath and says, "I got you something."

I raise my eyebrows. "You got *me* something?"

He digs around in his pockets. "Something little. Very little. I figured last night was hard for you. With the breakup and your, uh, gift. And Kiyo, I mean, geez Louise. She's my best friend here, but that girl came out swinging."

"She's just scared."

"Yeah, I know. But aren't we all?"

He opens his hand, and inside there is a single button, the pearly black one that popped off my shirt.

"When did you—?"

"Early this morning. It was under a stack of sweaters." I move my hand from his back and he places the button in my palm.

"Thank you," I say, so embarrassingly sincere I immediately have to make a joke. "Definitely a button worth crying over, don't you think?"

Abe smirks. "Oh, definitely. I know what it's like to lose buttons. When you finally find the right one, well. Nothing like it."

"I feel complete now."

"As you should. Such a perfect button."

"Irreplaceable."

"So . . . circular."

"I'll sew it on my wrist, which feels like it's healing, by the way." I smile at him, and hold the button at the end of my shirt. "See? Heart on my sleeve."

He looks away, toward the sky, and I worry I took it too far. But he says, "Anyway. I know it's silly. I just wanted you to remember something nice from last night. You in that tux was . . . you looked great."

"Thanks, Abe," I say, trying to hide my blush. "You did too."

"And I'm real glad you stayed," he says, so quiet I could almost convince myself I misheard him. Then Dash runs from Abe's side to put his head on my lap. "He is too, see?"

"At least someone is," I say, petting Dash. "Not sure why any of you would want me here at this point."

Abe looks back at the kitchen, where we can hear the low murmur of everyone else chattering away.

"Don't get me wrong, I love the others. But you remind me a lot of myself, which makes me feel . . . unlonely," he says.

My heart leaps into my throat. For him to think that, for him to see some of himself in me, even when I keep forgetting to deepen my voice and change my posture, it means a lot. "That's the ultimate compliment. I kinda think you're the coolest."

"Even after you saw me puke my guts out?"

I laugh. "Especially now. Nothing cooler."

"Just two simple guys," he says, hitting my knee with his.

"Two simple guys," I say, and we smile at each other. Because we both know we're anything but.

# *personal delivery service*

FOR THE REST OF the day, everyone puts their head down and hustles to work on their projects, trying to stop time. I just make myself present, available. It's the very least I can do.

Abe disappears into his shed, and since being around Ramona and Ambrosia doesn't sound very appealing to me right now, and Kiyo definitely doesn't want me anywhere near her and Sunny, I hang in the kitchen. Lionel doesn't trust me to help, but he uses me as a taste tester (best job ever) and an ingredients fetcher. Mostly, I like listening to his stories.

"Roseline was always my sous-chef," he tells me. "She had no interest in cooking, but I bribed her with Pogs."

"Pogs?" I ask.

"They're these little cardboard circles with cartoons and pictures on them. We didn't even play the game you're supposed to play with them. Just made a museum gallery for our Barbies."

I smirk. "My mom gave me *so* many Barbies."

"Did you make them kiss like we did?"

"That might have been the only thing I did with them."

He laughs as he motions for me to hand him cavatappi. As he stirs, his expression turns sad. "You know, I still haven't told Roseline I'm a gay man, let alone that I'm living with HIV. My own twin. Isn't that horrible?"

"Of course not," I say. "It's often the hardest to come out to the people you love the most. It's the scariest thing in the world." I would know.

"It really is," Lionel says more to himself than me.

I hop up to sit on the counter next to where he's working. "You know, I put off coming out to Ramona for a long time. And I mean, it absolutely suuuucked," I groan, and laugh so I don't cry. "And, yeah, in some ways, my worst fears came true. But Ramona knows me so much better now, which means she can actually love *me,* even if it's just as friends. Maybe you should give Roseline that same chance."

He sighs. "Maybe. That's why I'm so close to Ambrosia, even though she drives me crazy sometimes. She *knows* me knows me. She's seen me at my very worst and very best, and she thinks I'm fun and funny and talented! She doesn't treat me like I'm just a tragedy waiting to happen. But still, it's not the same as what I have with Roseline."

"Are you scared Roseline will treat you that way? Like a tragedy?"

Lionel's eyes well, and he wipes away unfallen tears with the back of his hand. "I don't want to just be her gay brother with HIV. Someone to worry about, or pity. Or worse. I've lost so many people because of this disease, Cal, you can't imagine. I couldn't take it . . ."

I put my hand on his arm, stilling his anxious stirring. "I don't think you'll lose her. It sounds like she really loves you, even if it might take her some time to get past her own fear. That's why you have Ambrosia, too. One person can't be everything for you. We can only be so much to each other."

"But you can't promise me," he whispers. "You can't promise Roseline won't leave. No one can."

"No. But if you do lose her, you'll grieve and you'll survive it. You will. You've already survived so much."

"You too, dumpling." He smiles up at me, putting his hand on mine. "First your parents, and, well, I'm sorry about you and Ramona."

"It's okay," I say, though it's more complicated than okay. Though my chest is still physically aching. Though my whole world has been undone. "Like I said, we can only be so much to each other."

"Mmm," he hums. "We have to patch ourselves together with scraps of love."

"Crumb by crumb," I say. "Sorry, that was cheesy."

"Cheesy, breezy, beautiful. Cover girl! Speaking of cheesy, gorgeous, can you fetch me the gouda?"

In addition to taste tester and ingredient fetcher, Lionel also turns me into his personal delivery service. While he whips up every dish imaginable and scribbles his recipes down chaotically and aggressively in a big leather book, he plates meals on trays and sends me off to feed the others.

Which is helpful, because it's also an excuse to bother everyone. I bring colorful, meticulously plated amaranth grain bowls to Ramona and Ambrosia, who have lyrics and sheet music spread out all over a blanket in the field. Their legs are overlapping, but they pull them apart when they see me. Ambrosia looks gorgeous—curls loose, braless in a sundress that makes her blue eyes pop—and I know I'm not allowed to be jealous. I am anyway. I'm so jealous it hurts.

I bring a bowl to Sunny, who is flitting about her writing studio, pinning notes around the room, pressing a pencil to her lips, thinking. She is glamorous as ever, but I can't help but notice the bags under her eyes. The worry lines around her mouth.

"Thanks, doll," she says, barely glancing at me or the food. She shoves it in a corner haphazardly. It's for the best I delivered it, because I can only imagine the horrified face Lionel would have made at her ambivalence toward his culinary masterpiece.

And at Kiyo's ambivalence too. Or straight up disgust, though that may just be for me personally. She glares at me and the bowl from where she's perched on her ladder outside the barn, hair slicked back with sweat, sleeves rolled up, painting. Her mural is breathtaking. Something only a genius could conjure.

But I don't say that. "Anything I can help with?" I ask instead.

"No," she says. "You've done enough."

My final stop is at Abe's shed, and I realize I went here last because I'm anxious to see him. I wonder what his project might be, what about it is so shameful or personal or precious that he wants to keep it private. But I don't get to see him. He yells for me to leave the tray by the door, with a horribly weak, "Thank you."

He does the same thing when I try to deliver dinner, a gnocchi Lionel promises will melt in your mouth. When I go back out a few hours later to check on Abe and collect his tray, it's still outside, untouched.

"I'm worried about Abe," I tell Ramona when we settle into bed. "He seems really sick."

“Have you asked him if he’s okay?”

“Well, no, but—”

“Or what you can do to help?”

“Well, no, but—”

“Oh my God,” she sighs, and rolls her eyes as she pushes my shoulder. “Boys.”

So the next morning, when I find Abe retching in the woods, I wait by the shed door for him, holding a tray of fruit and pumpkin waffles, and a stew for Dash. When he’s done puking his brains out, Abe spots me and leans up against the wall next to me.

“I know,” he says, wiping his mouth. “I’m a total dreamboat, right?”

“It’s actually really hard for me to handle,” I say.

“Anyway, thanks for—”

“Hey, listen. I don’t mean to pry, but I’m worried about you. Are you okay? Is there anything I can do to help you?”

For a minute he just stares at me. Then he takes a deep breath and looks at the ground. “Kiyo usually helps me but she’s obviously busy. So, sure, I guess I could use some help.”

“Anything.”

“You remember everything I showed you the other day about how to feed the animals?”

“Hay and grain for the goats and cows, feed for the chickens?”

“Yeah. Not rocket science, but . . .”

“No problem. I got you.”

He nods, gratitude written all over his face. “I owe you one.”

So when I’m not helping Lionel, I spend the rest of the day—and the next and the next—alone with the animals. They’re happy to see me. The goats eat right out of my hand, the cows moo their hellos, and the chickens make me feel like I'm living my farmhouse dream. The only downside is they all poop now, but I hold my breath and deal with it.

"Life would be so much easier if I could google how to make fertilizer," I mutter to myself, voice pitched lower than ever, just for me.

Because there's no one around to hear me, and with everyone else obsessively wrapped up in their projects, there's no one to impress, no one to perform for. I start to dress like a whole man—construction boots, baggier pants, and plain shirts. I spend hours in front of the mirror, cutting my hair shorter and shorter. With a foolish, freeing conviction, I snip layers to my shoulder, then my chin, then the top of my ears. It takes me a few tries to get it just right, and though I'm sure it's a hack job disaster that would make a barber faint on the spot, I can't stop staring at myself. I can't stop touching it.

And when I deliver food to Abe next, he actually opens the door.

"Look at you," he says, taking in my new look.

"It's a mess, I know." I run my hand self-consciously through my hair. "Especially the back. I couldn't do much with that, because, I mean. I can't see it. But one good thing about time is it'll grow."

"You should cut it again, just like this. It suits you."

I look at the ground, because I must be glowing, and I don't want him to see it. I shouldn't need his validation. I shouldn't even want it. But fuck, it feels so good to have it.

Dash rushes out of the shed and jumps on me gleefully.

"Hi, boy," I say. "I've missed you. Have you been taking good care of your dad?" I scratch his ears and smile up at Abe, but he looks like he's seen a ghost. He bites his lip and studies me for the longest time.

He says finally, "Will you keep a secret?"

It's such an unexpected question, all I can do is nod.

Abe motions for me to come inside the shed. I sit on the bench where he made me the splint and take it all in again: the bed he set up for himself on the floor. The little wooden animals, and one in progress, too, a bird of some kind. The room smells like sawdust and Dash, who has already curled up again in his little bed.

Abe putters around nervously, tidying things that don't need to be tidied. Whatever he has on his mind must be big.

"Is your secret about your project, or . . . ?"

He nods. Hesitates. "Just . . . don't tell anyone else, okay?"

"I promise."

# ABE TURNER

## 1941–

Abe Turner was born Abigail Jensen in Park City, Utah, to a bishop and a homemaker who belonged to the Church of Jesus Christ of Latter-day Saints. Abe and his seven siblings spent most of their time at temple, and though Abe was the oldest, they all prayed over him the most.

He was boyish, even in the conservative clothes they had to wear. He'd cut slits up the middle of his skirts so they felt more like pants, and his mother would cry because they couldn't afford new ones. He chased the girls at Sunday School and tried to kiss them, and his father decided that was beyond prayer and necessitated a beating. The younger siblings would stand outside the door, listening, while Mr. Jensen tried to make Abe regret himself—force him to change. When he was done, Mr. Jensen straightened his tie, opened the door, and left his child curled up on the bed.

"I'm trying to save your sister's soul," he'd say to the other children, and they believed him. They feared their father, but they feared

Abe more. What was wrong with him? Was it catching? Could God's love stop it? Betrayals of betrayals, they each accepted fifty cents from their father to follow Abe around at school, and report back on his every unrighteous move.

Eventually Mr. Jensen pulled Abe from school, just for good measure. He ordered Abe's mother to only teach him lessons from the Bible and the *Book of Mormon*, so that one day he'd be similarly dependent on a man. Obedient and subservient. Entirely submissive.

Only, Mrs. Jensen wasn't all those things all the time. On almost every occasion, she tried to stop the beatings. She'd put herself in between her husband and her child, yelling that God wouldn't want this. Jesus couldn't want this. This is not the way to salvation. She'd stroke Abe's hair after and say, "You're loved, you're loved, you're loved." She'd beg him to just behave, please. She couldn't disobey her husband, but she also couldn't bear to watch this anymore.

Things did change when the family doctor noticed Abe's bruises, and it was only a matter of weeks before Mr. Jensen was asked to step down from bishop. Not because of the violence, necessarily, but because he "couldn't control his daughter." How are you to lead a ward, they asked, if you can't even save your own child's soul?

Mr. Jensen had to start working on the railroads, which didn't pay nearly enough. He was gone more and more, and they ate less and less, until he joined the U.S. Army and was sent to war in Korea. He did not come home.

If the prayers and beating hadn't changed Abe, this did: his mother sobbing alone in the bathroom—uncontrollable, inhuman wails that poured up from somewhere deep and lonely—then wiping her face and returning to the kids like nothing had happened at all.

Until one day she simply stopped in the doorway, and said, "No one ever thinks about me."

Abe burned with shame, because it was true. He rarely thought about his mother: what she needed, what she wanted, what she felt. There was no room for that, not with seven children. And didn't Abe owe her most of all? The eldest? The wildest? The one who ruined their lives, who sent their father to an early, unmarked grave?

Abe decided to become what her mother needed: a daughter. Abigail. She stepped up. She cared more for her siblings. She tried to be pretty; she was almost of marrying age, after all. She grew her sand-brown hair long and let the sun pull out its highlights. She was pious and religious and chaste. And when a new boy in town, picture-perfect Wilford Sorensen, asked if he could court her, she said, without hesitation, yes. A true, honest-to-God blessing. He hadn't known her before. He didn't know her history. He saw her as she wanted him to see her: the perfect woman, the perfect wife.

They married at seventeen—early for their community, early for their time—because he had money and her mother needed the help. Because Wilford claimed it was the Lord's will. Because they couldn't have sex before marriage. And Wilford really, really, really wanted to have sex.

Their wedding was a joyful occasion—Abigail so happy to see her mother happy, her siblings proud of her for once in their lives, the first dance with Wilford something like romantic. She loved the way he looked at her, the way he wanted her.

But her wedding night, their first time, left Abigail stunned. She couldn't talk for two days after. It had been painful, for starters, which she hadn't expected, and Wilford hadn't seemed to care, which confused her deeply. He was a good man. He had only been kind to her. So then why had he kept going when she was shocked and silent? Why hadn't he asked her a single question about how it felt, about what she wanted? Why did he only throw a towel over her blood, and tell her it better be cleaned up by morning? And how had he not noticed when she lay in bed all night, awake, crying? Silently, but still.

He slept soundly. He tried it again the next day. She felt broken, hollowed out. Damned.

And she told herself: This is for my mother. This is for my siblings. This is for me—because what do I have? No real education. No money. No chance at survival.

No chance at salvation.

And, yes, there were times when she remembered who she used to be: boyish and irreverent and free. Childish, she'd think. Impossible. Her biggest dream, buried, buried, buried, all the way down.

Until she missed her period. And she threw up on the front steps of the temple and the women around her shared conspiratorial looks and she knew, she knew, she knew, she could not survive it. What kind of mother would she be? Parenthood was brutality or sacrifice. Marriage was an early grave.

But where could she go? What could she do?

Then one day, not long after her morning sickness began, she and Wilford drove past a sign for the circus.

"What's a circus?" she asked him. He shook his head, and took his eyes off the road to stare at her with contempt.

"A bunch of freaks," he said. "Not a place for righteous people like us." Abigail felt her heart beat faster. She was not like him—he, Abe, was not like him.

So, as if to prove it, Abe stole his husband's clothes. He walked five miles in Wilford's clown-size shoes. He traded Wilford's watch for a ticket—a painful decision, Abe loved that watch—and settled in as the lights dimmed and the audience hushed at the start of the show.

The ringleader was a flamboyant man with a mustache that twirled upward. His clothes were colorful, glittery, and so tight they left little to the imagination. Abe had never seen such a man. He couldn't take his eyes off him. And then there were the others: the bearded lady, a whole cast of clowns, the male trapeze artists who looked like ballerinas, a butch lion tamer who put her head between the teeth of the beast.

These people filled Abe's body with butterflies. He thought, at first, it was fear flapping inside him—how different they were from anyone he'd ever known. How dangerous and confusing and strange. But as the show went on, and his heart beat harder, he realized what he was feeling was something more like recognition; a piece of himself outside himself. Something familiar in so many of the stars of the show, bowing and curtsying, puffing their chests out, all of them proud.

But what was that piece of himself? What was the word for it? Was it simply, like Wilford had said, "freak"?

After the show, Abe wandered into a tent where the performers were all flitting about, calming animals (God, those poor animals), taking off makeup and leotards and glitter. He didn't know what he expected—to be turned in to the police or Wilford? To get kicked out?—but it wasn't kindness.

He found the lion tamer first, and she smiled at the sight of him. She looked him up and down, and said, "I noticed you in the audience. I like your look."

"I like your look too. And that lion act. That was . . . wow."

"They call me Flora the Fearless, but my real name's Barb. What's your name?"

"Abe Turner." His mother's maiden name.

"Nice to meet you, Abe Turner. Now if you'll excuse me, I have an elephant to feed."

"Wait. Please take me with you." Abe hadn't even planned to say it, but he had. It was out there.

The tamer put her hand on her hip and considered him. Abe continued, "I just . . . I ran away from my husband and I . . ."

"Then you're wise, at least. I know that much. But we're not a free ride," she said. "Do you have skills? Would you be able to help around here?"

Abe looked beyond her, to her corral of horses, lions, and monkeys.

"I'm great with animals," he said, his mouth dry with desperation. "I could help you with the animals." He'd helped raise seven siblings. He'd taken care of their sheep, chickens, and goats. How different could a lion be?

Barb smiled. "Yeah? All right, then. Let's see if that's true."

# *the project*

“SO, YEAH,” ABE SAYS, still looking at the floor. “I ran away with the circus. And then not too long after, I set some of the animals free and had to run away *from* the circus, so here I am.”

My mind is racing, my heart pounding, but I don’t let it show on my face. I take care with what I say next. “Abe, you’re . . . pregnant.” I say it like a fact, not a scandal.

He doesn’t respond. Just pulls the tarps off pieces of furniture scattered around the shed.

I can’t help it: My jaw drops. There’s a dresser and a rocking chair. A crib. It’s white, and on the headboard, he’s carved sheep jumping over the moon. He leans on the crib and nods, face crestfallen.

“I’m pretty sure,” he says. “But they haven’t been able to grow here. Until now.”

“That’s why you’ve stayed?” I ask.

Abe nods.

I imagine him back in the 1950s, choosing between birth and a possibly fatal abortion. I imagine his stomach and breasts getting bigger and bigger, reading more and more as *woman* and *mother* as he got smaller and smaller and smaller.

"And no one knows?"

"Just you, now. And maybe Dash. I think that's why he's glued to me."

"I'm really honored you trust me with this. But . . . why?"

He puts his hand on his stomach. "I have this gut feeling this won't change how you think about me."

"It won't," I say quickly. "It doesn't. But for what it's worth, I don't think it would change how the others see you either. They've been so quick to accept me—"

Abe shakes his head. "It wasn't always like this, Cal. Even though I'm a girl, they see me as a boy now. A man. I can feel it."

"And that's what you want."

"Yes. *Yes*. It took years, though. Decades. When I got here, Sunny was already so much herself. She was so confident in who she was, and I was so far from how I wanted to be. It took sixty years for me to figure it out, for me to choose it, and for them to really see me."

Sixty years. His boyishness seemed so natural to me. Easy. Thoughtless. Effortless. I've been jealous. But apparently, I've also been wrong.

"Why do you think I'm usually so quiet? I have to think about every word. Deepen my voice. I worry I'll forget myself."

"I get it," I say. God, do I get it.

"I know," he says, "which is why I can forget myself around you. But I don't want them to forget I'm a man." He plays with his watch. He doesn't look at me. He hunches his shoulders to hide his chest, just like I always do.

"Being pregnant doesn't make you less of a man. Whether you want to keep the baby or not."

"I do want to. I *really* want to. That's the rub. But I know having this baby will change how the world sees me. Forever."

"Maybe," I say, because I can't lie to Abe. "But mostly, I just see someone gentle and strong. Thoughtful and easy to be around. Funny and . . . and handsome. You'd be a great father, if you want that."

He looks up at me, finally. I almost think he's about to cry, but he raises his eyebrows playfully instead. "You think I'm handsome?" He makes it easy to joke it off, but I don't.

"Of course I do."

We're both silent for what feels like forever. He puts the tarps back on the furniture and I know I've said too much. I'm kicking myself and trying to think of an exit line when he picks up a pair of scissors and says, "You said your wrist was healing. Do you want me to take your splint off?"

"Um, yeah, thanks," I say, and he kneels in front of me. I have the urge to run my hand through his hair but obviously don't. I mentally slap myself instead. He makes quick work of taking the splint off, slicing through the fabric, taking the wooden pieces apart.

"Feel okay?"

"Yep. Great."

"You sure? It's still shaking a bit, which is a—"

"Pain response," I finish. "I know. But I'm not in pain."

He looks up at me with his gray eyes, and I think he's going to ask me why it's shaking, then, and I'm not going to be able to answer him. "While we're at it, do you want me to cut the back of your hair for you?" he asks instead.

I exhale. "Sure."

He straddles the bench, and I turn to do the same so he can get a good angle. He runs his fingers through to untangle the knots. It hurts a little. It feels so good. I hear the first *snip* of the scissors.

"So . . . what happened with you and Ramona?"

My heart sinks. Of course he, and probably everyone, wants to know. I want to make something up, something easier than the truth. But I've been learning that doesn't serve anyone, and if he's trusting me with his big secret, maybe I can trust him too.

I tell him again about Alcott, and my parents, and Ramona raising the money. About how I want to become someone new. About how I hid that from her for so long, even if I didn't mean to. It sounds awful when I say it all out loud.

"Oh," he says, when I'm done rambling.

"I know, I know," I say, putting my hands over my face, careful not to move too much as he keeps slowly cutting. "It was selfish and cowardly. But she'd just lost her favorite aunt last summer and she's been grieving and I just . . . I don't know. I'm the worst. I should have told her sooner."

I'm glad I can't see his expression, can't see him judging me. Because what I did isn't like Lionel not coming out to Roseline. It isn't like Abe keeping his secret. I totally fucked Ramona over. She could have gone to Yale, but I let her tie her future to mine and then dragged her down with me. I brace myself for whatever Abe's going to say next, because whatever it is, I deserve it.

But he just puts the scissors down. He gently brushes clippings off my shoulders, and leaves his palm in the middle of my back when he says, "You're being mighty hard on yourself. Ramona lost her aunt, but you just lost your parents."

I have to laugh. "I mean, they're not dead. I've always known where they stood on this stuff, so it wasn't a big surprise or anything."

"'This stuff' meaning their child?"

"It's fine."

"It's not fine. Your parents did the cruelest thing they could ever do to you. They're the two people in this world who should love you unconditionally, but they made you feel hard to love. It makes sense you were scared to tell Ramona."

I shrug and fold into myself, but I kind of want to turn around and hit him. I've succeeded for so long in numbing myself, shoving it all down, but now rage and sadness and guilt and regret are all crashing through me in hot waves.

"They didn't even let me say goodbye to my dog," I say.

"Nugget?"

"Yeah. I'll never get to see her again."

It takes every last drop of energy to stop myself from sobbing, and I can feel Abe's hand on my arm now, trying to get me to turn toward him. But I know if he tries to comfort me, I *will* start sobbing, so I swing my leg back over the bench so I can subtly move away from him. He does the same, and when I dare to glance at him, I'm relieved to see he's looking at his watch instead of me.

"I'm so sor—" he starts, but I cut him off.

"Anway. Enough about me. What do you—"

"Wait. Can I ask one more thing about you? Or us, I guess."

Us?

"Um, sure."

"You mentioned a few times now your parents found 'trans stuff.' What's . . . what's that?"

I smirk. "Asking for a friend?"

"Um, no, for me."

"Sorry. Never mind. Trans stuff. Well, you've heard about the internet, right?" Abe nods. I explain the forums, the videos, articles. "If I'm honest, a lot of pornography. I don't know. It made me feel less ashamed, to see trans people at home in their bodies. To see queer people wanting things. Being wanted. Being loved. But I also read a lot of poetry." My eyes go to a book on his highest shelf. "Does that book work like the ones in the living room?"

When he nods, I get up, pull it down from the shelf, and flip it open. "Do you want to hear some of my favorites?"

"Please."

"Poetry might be perfect for you to practice reading. It's always been my favorite because . . . I guess I'm kind of a jock, ha. It's quick to read. It speaks to me."

The first poem that appears is Andrea Gibson's "Your Life." Because of course it is. I almost don't want to read it. It's too intimate, with Abe only inches away from me in the almost-dark, the shed's blinds pulled low. I can hear the hint of his heartbeat. Or maybe it's just my own heart doing double time. I'm grateful he looks at the floor when I start to read: "It isn't that you don't like boys. It's that you only like boys you want to be."

He doesn't flinch or recoil or laugh. He just listens. When I speak the last line of the poem, he finally looks at me, and my stomach tightens waiting for his reaction. "They put this in books you can buy?" he asks. "In 2026?"

"Yeah," I say, smiling. "This collection's from 2018, actually."

He lets out a low whistle. "Could you read me some more?"

I do. With its still-surreal Amaranth magic, all I have to do is shut the book and open it back up to find new collections by some of my other favorite trans poets: K. Iver, Ryka Aoki, KB Brookins, Jennifer Espinoza, and Kay Ulanday Barrett.

I read Cameron Awkward-Rich for what feels like an hour. Each time Abe hums in recognition, it chips away at my shame. Each time he asks me to repeat a line, it makes me feel—to use his word—unlonely. And I can't help but notice that anytime one of us shifts to get more comfortable, we inch closer to each other. Eventually we're close enough that he can put his hand on my knee, and I'm shocked by how natural it feels. I don't have time to overthink it, can't spiral and read at the same time. So I put my hand on his. I move my thumb back and forth across his knuckles.

When I finish reading "Coming Out," by Jennifer Espinoza, the light outside is fading.

"Wow," is all he says.

"Knock-your-teeth-out good, right?"

He studies my face, and we're so close I can feel his breath on my cheeks now.

"These poems," he says. "They're miracles."

"I know. I just love them."

"You'd have to be a fool," he whispers, "to not love them."

I dare to meet his eyes, and I fall right into them. He tightens his grip on my knee, and I lace my fingers into his, and my heart is up in my throat, *thumping, thumping, thumping*. He puts his other hand on my cheek, and for a surreal second, I think we're about to kiss. I hold my breath. Close my eyes. Lean in for it. Waiting.

But then he stands up quickly, ripping himself away from me.

"I'm sorry," he says. "I don't know what I was thinking."

He starts busying himself with his tools, and it's like he can't even look at me. My cheeks burn hot, but the rest of me is cold without him near me.

"Yeah, uh. Me neither." And I don't. I just broke up with Ramona. He just told me he's pregnant. What the fuck is wrong with me?

"It's not that I—"

"Let's just pretend like that never happened," I snap, because I don't want to hear him pity me. He has his back to me, palms pressed flat into the tool bench, and he nods.

"That's probably a good idea."

I scramble up and out of the door, and I don't look back to see his face flash with relief.

# *distress*

I LEAVE THE SHED, blood like lava, and jog toward the house. I plan to lock myself in the first dark room available, talk to no one for several hours, and wallow in self-loathing. Maybe I'll even confess what just happened with Abe to Ramona for some bonus emotional punishment, as a treat. But I'm stopped in my tracks when I hear the animals screaming. It's a horrible cacophony; the cows moo, the chickens shriek, the rooster howls. And the goats are bleating so loudly, and with such distress, I change course and run straight for their pen.

My blood goes cold when I see one of them tipped on her side, moaning quietly and horribly—Sylvie. I jump the fence and put my hands on her fur, petting her as gently as possible.

"Abe!" I scream at the top of my lungs, over and over again. Everything that just happened between us is so unimportant now with Sylvie seizing uncontrollably in my hands.

"*Abe!*" I'm not sure he can even hear me, but I don't want to leave her side. Thankfully, he and Dash are there almost instantly. Abe kneels down, too close to me, and presses his palms gently on Sylvie's knobby, collapsed body.

"What hurts?" he asks. "What happened, Sylvie girl?"

I stand up and drag their water trough across the dirt of the enclosure, sloshing water as I go. It makes little mud puddles in the sand, and I wonder if we could run out of water here and if I'm wasting the only thing that could keep us all alive, but I don't stop. Abe tries to help Sylvie stand, to help her drink, but she's too weak. She's resigned. He lays her back on the ground, strokes her face, and talks her through it.

"It's okay, baby," he says, "you're okay." But she's not okay, and we both know it. There's no way to get help, either. No one to call. Nowhere to go.

Within moments—so quick, so slow—Sylvie goes still. Her terrible noises stop. Nellie, Agnes, and Dorothy bleat on around us, and I swear it sounds mournful. I don't know what to say, so I sit in the dirt and touch her soft fur. Her heart isn't beating. She's not breathing.

"She's dead," he says.

"I'm so sorry," I whisper. "This is all my fault. I should go—" He grips my arm lightning quick, and glares at me.

"Don't you dare," he says. I stay.

Soon enough, all the others show up, summoned by my shouting. They stand around the pen, where we still kneel beside Sylvie. Ramona gasps, Sunny weeps, and Ambrosia and Lionel trade a meaningful look I can't decipher.

Kiyo starts, "Maybe if Cal had left—"

But Abe—always so soft-spoken—growls, "I swear to *God*,

Kiyo. Not here. Not now." Everyone is stunned into silence, even though there are so many questions that could be asked. What does this mean for poor, sweet Sylvie? For the other animals? For Ambrosia and Lionel? For the rest of us?

# *funeral*

WE COVER SYLVIE'S CORPSE in soft blankets while everyone argues about what we should do with her. Throw her over the edge of the field? Cremate her? But Abe insists on a proper burial, and everyone eventually folds.

"You two will dig the grave?" Sunny looks between us.

"Yeah, Frog and Toad," Ambrosia sniffs. "Hop to it."

"I can do it alone," Abe says.

"Nonsense," Sunny says. "I'm sure Cal would be happy to help. Wouldn't you, Cal?" I can't think of a single excuse as to why not, so I just nod.

We dig. We don't talk. I barely even look at him. And when it's done, when the night is dark, we go our separate ways.

In the morning, we all dress in black and march outside together. Abe, Kiyo, and I carry Sylvie—sweet, sweet, Sylvie—across the field, where everyone else waits for us at the empty grave.

She's heavy, and it's hard to balance her gangly limbs, still and soft. My arms get tired but it doesn't matter. I don't want to put her down. I don't want to say goodbye. I can only imagine how Abe feels.

But we do eventually reach the others, the grave. We put Sylvie gently in the earth. We take turns reaching down to touch her one last time, to grab a fistful of flower petals to sprinkle gently on her body. Abe wants to speak but finds that he can't. He plants seeds around her instead, and then Abe and I pick up the shovels and get to work again. We're careful to make the dirt fall slowly and softly, though she can't feel a thing; careful to cover every inch, every foot, so the next storm won't come to resurrect her.

"I can't believe I'm weeping over a goat," Lionel howls, and we all have to laugh. Even Abe, though he whispers, "She was more than just a goat." And we all have to laugh again when we move inside to eat the funeral lunch he's prepared, and there's a bowl of hay front and center with a sign that reads: Sylvie's Favorite.

Once everyone's seated at the kitchen table, Lionel uses a fork to *ping* his glass. "A toast. To Sylvie," he says and we all raise our blue crystal glasses.

"To Sylvie," we repeat.

We move to get food, but then Lionel *pings* his glass again. We all look to him, and he takes a deep, staggering breath. "And an announcement. Darlings. My longtime loves. I've decided."

"Decided what, Lion?" Ambrosia asks, shifting uncomfortably in her funeral dress. He looks at her, at all of us, with tears in his eyes.

"I'm leaving in the morning."

# *chaos*

AMBROSIA, FOR ONCE, IS speechless. Grief-stricken. Her hands fly to cover her mouth.

"Lionel," Kiyo whispers. "You can't mean that."

"I do, love," he says. "I'll finish my cookbook tonight, and then I've done my part. I can't take it. I'm at a funeral for a goat while all my friends die at home? What am I missing back there? *Who* am I missing? I want to live, even if I'm going to die. I want to know what happens to me in the end. I'm tired of hiding. I'm tired of feeling trapped."

"But we're going to fix forever," Sunny assures him. "We will."

"Even if we do," he says. "I've been thinking about this for a long time. I miss my sister. I miss my parents and my grandmothers. I miss my apartment and New York City and diners and night clubs. I miss the random old lady that sits outside the bodega with a cat on her head. I miss home. I want to go home."

Silence floods every inch of the room, broken only by the ticking of the grandfather clock.

"Lion, you'll die," Ambrosia speaks finally. Her voice is serious, etched with desperation. I hardly recognize her.

"Then I'll die!" Lionel yells, throwing up his hands. "But at least I'll have lived a full life. Not this half-life. Not this fucked-up, lonely, deluded illusion. This place is nothing but a pretty, sugarcoated prison."

Sunny goes pale, and even I know he's gone too far. Kiyo lunges for him, murder in her eyes, and I'm in just the right spot to intercept her. I hold her back from Lionel and she struggles to get out of my grip.

"Ungrateful!" Kiyo screams at Lionel when she can't escape me.

"I am grateful," Lionel yells back, the veins in his neck bulging. He grips the back of a chair and takes a deep breath to calm down. "Believe me, I am. I've loved being here for so long. But this isn't enough. How can it be? I need to know what else there is for me."

"But we *know* what happens back there, Lionel," Ambrosia says, standing abruptly, she and Lionel now face-to-face. "The lesions. The skeletons. The grotesque, agonizing, unbearable pain. I refuse to let you . . ." She shakes her head. "You can't do this to me. Lion, I love you."

"You have Ramona now. You don't need me anymore."

"She's not going to stay, either! And anyway, she's not you."

A tear streams down Lionel's face, but his voice is firm as he takes Ambrosia's hand. "I have to do this. I *want* to do this."

"You promised," Ambrosia hisses. "You promised you'd

never leave me behind." Ambrosia rips her hands from his and runs out of the room, Ramona right behind her.

"Some gift this is," Kiyo mutters under her breath as she finally twists out of my arms.

"It's not Cal's fault," Abe says.

"So you're on their side?"

"Yes. I mean, no. I'm not on any side. But they didn't ask for this. Stop blaming them when it was our precious Amaranth that did this."

Sunny's eyes fill with tears. They fall silently down her cheeks. But Kiyo doesn't even notice, because she's still focused on me. She lets out a dark laugh.

"Wow, Abe's pretty stuck on you. Does Ramona know you already have a boyfriend?" she asks, her voice venomous.

"He's not my boyfriend," I say, face on fire.

"Then fight your own battles," Kiyo continues, leaning toward me.

She looks like she wants to strangle me. She looks like she wants to punch my lights out. She looks exactly how I felt when I was a kid, backed into a corner, losing it all.

So I know she wants to hurt me. I know she wants me to feel just an ounce of what she's feeling right now, and I see her for what she is: terrified and lashing out, mourning and afraid and angry. I don't need to defend myself. I don't need to fight her. She's carrying enough.

"It sucks that time started," I say, working to keep my voice steady. "It really fucking sucks. And I get it: You're scared of losing Sunny and Amaranth and forever. The time you have to go back to is terrible and racist and homophobic and impossible for people like us. I wish I could change that. I wish I could be there for you if we go back. I wish we all could."

"Don't condescend to me, Cal. You've been here for what, a week? You know nothing." Kiyo's hands are balled into fists, trembling. Red creeps up her neck. "And you," she spits at Lionel. "Know *nothing* of prison." I study the emotion written all over her face, and remember what she told me that day in her studio: that the first time her world ended, she didn't even feel like she was allowed to cry. Now Kiyo should be allowed to rage.

I step toward her. "Hit me," I say.

Kiyo leans back in surprise. "What?"

"Just punch me in the face. It'll make you feel better."

"Don't even think about it," Sunny warns Kiyo, but Kiyo looks like she's considering it. Like she's building up the courage to do it.

We stare at each other, faces only inches away, and I think for a second she's going to hit me—and part of me actually wants her to. Instead, she grabs her cup, turns, and hurls it at the wall.

Sunny yelps. The glass shatters through the air, falling to the floor in little blue shards. One nicks my cheek, the pain fast and sharp, and I instinctively put my hand up to check for blood. Sunny runs out of the room, and Kiyo nearly trips over a chair trying to follow her.

"Sunny, I'm sorry!"

Lionel, Abe, and I stand there in silence, looking at one another.

"Well, that went well," Lionel says, giving us a sad smile. "Sorry for raining on your goat's funeral, Abe."

Abe nods, then says, "For what it's worth, I see it too. What you see."

Lionel blinks back more tears, and looks at the table.

"I'm not ungrateful," he says quietly. "I'm dying. And I just want to know what it's like to live. None of you know what that feels like. And I hope to God none of you ever do."

I don't know how to comfort him. Everything I almost say seems too small in the face of his fear, his grief, his longing.

"You're right," I finally settle on. "I don't know what it's like. Not even a little bit. But I do know what it's like to choose something that's right for you but hurts someone you love."

Lionel pulls me into a side hug, his arm over my shoulder and mine wrapped around his waist, both of us holding tight. "It sucks."

"It does suck. And I know I'm probably, like, the last person you want in your corner right now, given all this is my fault but—"

"It's not your fault," Abe says again.

"—how can I help?"

Lionel does want help finishing his cookbook, but first he asks me to check on Ambrosia. After he piles a tray full of the funeral food nobody touched, I search the house but find Ambrosia in the field with Ramona. Ambrosia has her head in Ramona's lap.

"Knock, knock," I say as I get closer.

"Hi, Cal," Ramona says.

Ambrosia only sniffles, sitting up as I put the food down in front of them. She sighs and takes a big bite out of a chocolate croissant. "That bastard knows I can't say no to a pastry."

"I also come bearing a message," I say, and hurry to get the words out before she can stop me. "Lionel wanted me to tell you he loves you. And that he's sorry. And that he wishes he felt differently."

"Don't make me kill the messenger," she says. But she just takes another bite, and keeps talking with her mouth full. "He was supposed to be my ride or die. He promised me, you know? He promised. He promised me he'd never leave me behind." Ambrosia's face twists, and she chucks the croissant across the field. "Why is everybody always fucking leaving me?" she whispers, putting her head on her knees, tucking herself into a ball. She looks small. She looks broken. I can hardly hear her when she says, "It makes me feel like I'm . . . nothing."

"Hey," Ramona says. She moves closer to wrap her arms around Ambrosia. "Ambrosia, you're one of my favorite people I've ever met. You're so fun and creative and full of life. You're *everything*. Lionel has to do what he has to do, but I'm here for you."

"Me too," I add.

Ambrosia pushes Ramona's arms off her and folds into herself again. "You may be here now," she says. "But you'll be gone soon enough. And then you'll forget me, just like everyone else."

"Ambrosia, it'd be impossible to forget you," I say, and I mean it.

Ambrosia looks beyond the field, through the trees holding our pasts. "You'd be surprised."

# AMBROSIA

## 1979–

Amy Smith was the fourth kid born to a family that couldn't keep food on the table. It was just Amy's mother, Angela, trying—perhaps not her best, but she was trying, or at least surviving. All four fathers were long gone. "Each one worse than the last," Amy's mother always said, and Amy never knew if she was talking about her lovers or her kids.

Angela worked two jobs with odd hours, disappearing late into long, loud, and bright New York nights. And so she was either not around or holed up in her bedroom, smoking cigarettes, messaging in AOL chatrooms. She hated men, that much was clear, but she wanted their attention. She hated her kids, too, or at least Amy. She didn't want anything from her except quiet.

Amy's siblings were only a little bit more helpful. A little bit kinder. All three of them—Ashley, Aaron, and Alexis—were at least six years older than their youngest sister. They called her things like dork and dipshit. They made her watch *The Exorcist* when she was only five, and when something was funny on *Ren and Stimpy* they refused to explain it to her. They ate McDonald's every night, bags and bags of stale items dumped out on the table thanks to Ashley's job there. She always brought home the little Happy Meal toys for Amy too—all of them, every time the theme changed. It was the best love Amy knew.

For years, she didn't have her own room; she mostly slept in her mother's cigarette-drenched bed, or cuddled up with Ashley when she didn't lock her door. Amy dreamed of having her own room—until it came true. When she was fourteen, Ashley left. Soon after, Aaron. Soon after that, Alexis. None of them ever stayed a day longer in that apartment than they had to, and Angela was glad.

But Amy was alone. She dropped out of high school after freshman year, not because she couldn't keep up, but because she couldn't see the point in any of it. She lied about her age and got a job at the bodega down the street, hoping one day she could save up enough to get out of that apartment too. But mostly, Angela took her money, and what could Amy say? They needed food. They needed to pay rent—more and more each year. They needed to survive.

Any wispy dreams Amy had of a life worth living slipped away, dollar by dollar, day by day. Her siblings never called, never visited. She was forgettable. She was invisible. Most days she thought: *I might as well not be alive.*

The only reasons she stayed alive were Skittles, Diet Coke, and MTV. If she wasn't working or sleeping, she was glued to her television. She was popping blank VHS tapes into her VCR so she'd be ready to pounce on the record button when a new favorite came on. She was bewitched by Mariah, Celine, and Whitney. She was intimidated by Madonna, Alanis, and Cher, which only made her more obsessed. These women made her heart storm. She wanted to be them—known in an instant, by just one name. Loved by millions. Sexy, strong, and angry. Absolutely unforgettable.

Amy Smith could be anyone, or more accurately, no one. She'd recently started thinking that Angela fudged her last name just so Amy could never find her father. Smith. A total throwaway. It meant nothing. She meant nothing.

But she practiced being someone. She sang in the mirror, tossing her hair like she meant business. What little money she hid from her mom she used to buy glitter makeup and curly hair products and tube tops. She changed into them in the back room of the bodega hoping . . . what? That someone would notice her? She was not worthy of her dreams. She was not eye-catching or talented or unforgettable. That was a fact.

Then a blonde girl named Melody walked into the store wearing a choker necklace, low-rise jeans, and butterfly hairclips. She bought Skittles and a Sprite.

Amy said, "Almost perfect."

Melody met her eyes then. "Aren't you, like, my age?" Melody asked, looking Amy up and down suspiciously.

"No," Amy lied, "you have to be eighteen to work here." Melody didn't seem at all convinced.

"Right. So, which part was perfect and which was almost?"

"The Skittles are perfect. The Sprite was your mistake."

"Okay, but have you ever mixed these two?" She shook the Skittles bag and popped her gum. Amy shook her head. "It's a whole new world."

"I bet."

Melody considered Amy for a minute, and Amy considered her. Melody looked like Sophie B. Hawkins. Melody looked like she might eat Amy alive. And Amy liked that.

"You seem cool," Melody said eventually.

"I am."

"What's your name?" Melody asked.

After all this time, she doesn't remember where she learned the word, or why she chose it. Later, she'd find out it meant "food of the gods." It meant immortal. But had she known that then? She could never remember. She only knew it was her first real chance at being someone besides Amy Smith.

"Ambrosia."

"Okay, fly."

Amy—no, Ambrosia felt like she'd won the lottery. She felt special and chosen when Melody invited her over to her place, when they made out in Melody's fluffy, pink twin bed, when they passed War-Heads back and forth with each kiss, laughing. Ambrosia knew long before she was asked that she'd do anything for Melody. That she'd follow her anywhere. That Melody was worth dying for, because she was the first girl who'd ever made her feel like a person to begin with.

So, yes. Ambrosia did drugs with Melody at a party without even knowing what they were. It felt gorgeous and weightless and empty. For the first time in Ambrosia's life, she felt no pain. She felt free. She felt Melody's hands wrapped up in hers. She felt dragged to a bed. Whose bed? Who cared?

"You'll never leave me, right?" Ambrosia yelled over the thumping music of the party.

"No way."

"You'll never forget me?"

"Never, ever, ever, ever, ever, ever, ever," Melody said as her eyes rolled with her voice.

Ambrosia sank right into her words and the bed and her friend. *This is happy,* she thought. *This is love.*

But weeks later, when Ambrosia had a violent sickness she couldn't shake, Melody didn't pick up her phone calls. She didn't bring soup or Gatorade or magazines. She didn't drop off Sprite or Diet Coke. She didn't check in at all. And when Ambrosia got tested—a new thing, a scary thing—she had to walk fourteen blocks to do it, shivering and sweating. She found out the news alone. She walked home clutching a brochure for a support group, sobbing, thinking, *Everyone will say I deserved it.*

Did she deserve it? She'd only wanted a friend. She'd only wanted to feel like she mattered to someone. Like she belonged.

She thought, *How could I deserve it? I'm only sixteen. I'm only sixteen and I'm going to die.*

But first she was going to kill Melody. Not literally, but at the very least she wanted to chew her out. Pull the choker off her neck. Dump a bottle of Sprite on her head. Was Melody positive too? Was that why she was hiding? Ambrosia called her and called her and called her. She showed up at her door. She was never there. She never answered. And she never came into the bodega again.

It took her a year, but eventually Ambrosia went to the support group she learned about in the brochure. Why the fuck not. She sat next to a Black boy with tall hair and a colorful sweater. He smelled like sugar, and the two of them were the youngest people there. By far.

"Lionel," he said, his hand outstretched. She went to shake it but realized too late that he was handing her a cookie, which was better, really. "Sugar cookie with a little lemon and a lot of love." It was absolutely delicious. It calmed her nerves. Better than Skittles. Better than Diet Coke. So much better than Sprite, which tasted like a headache.

"Damn that was good. Can I get another one?" she said.

Lionel handed her another. "My secret ingredient is lemon extract. And these days, tears."

Ambrosia gaped. "You made these? They're the best thing I've ever had. They make me want to live through all this," she said, sweeping her arms around the room, and Lionel excitedly jumped up and down in his seat.

"Oh, we're going to be good friends, aren't we?" he said.

Ambrosia smiled, nodded, doubted it. She was never that lucky.

Only she stayed lucky. Lionel, too. And more importantly, they stayed alive. One by one, the people in their group passed away. Month by month, Ambrosia felt luckier and luckier to have him by her side. They gripped each other's hands at every meeting, and went together to hospitals, to funerals, to protests.

"Where do your parents think you are during all this time we spend together?" Lionel asked her once. She had to laugh.

"My mom doesn't care where I am. Doesn't ask questions."

"Really? Well, I told my parents I have a girlfriend, so they think I'm out with her. With you. I hope you don't mind."

Mind? Her heart fluttered.

"Did you tell them how drop-dead gorgeous I am?"

"Of course, cupcake."

She knew it was just for pretend, but they did feel like partners, and she could admit she was at least half in love with him. But then, wasn't that always the way with friends? It's all she'd known, with her eager, impossible heart. Still, it felt like they were each other's anchor to this world as they watched their friends die—*God,* none of them deserved to die—painfully, horribly, loudly. Invisibly. They watched their fates unspool before them over and over and over again. What bond could be stronger? What love could be deeper?

She mattered to someone. She mattered to Lionel, who waited for her by the door before group every single time. Holding out a cookie, baked special just for her.

"You don't have to wait in the rain, Lion," she told him one day when he was looking particularly handsome, standing on the steps of the hospital with a pink umbrella. Why did it always feel like it was raining? He just smiled and held out a cookie, this time, double chocolate chip.

"Psh, please. Ambrosia. Angel, baby, darling, muffin, sugar. You think I'd leave you behind?"

It was New Year's Eve, and after group, a few of them decided they should go out dancing. It was still raining, harder yet, but they had so much they wanted to forget. The gaggle of them walked down the street together huddled under their three umbrellas. Ambrosia felt a hot thrill. She belonged to these people and they belonged to her. This thought kept her warm in the icy air.

"Let's just live it up!" a woman named Francesca yelled, twirling through the streets, arms out to catch the rain on her palms. "We're all going to die, anyway!" She was a grad student at NYU, studying, of all things, infectious diseases.

"Let's go to Chelsea!" someone shouted.

"Pyramid Club!"

"Sound Factory!"

"Oh, boo," Tommy, a too-handsome, recently diagnosed ballet dancer, said. "I forgot we have the kids with us." Everyone turned to Ambrosia and Lionel.

"So what? We'll sneak 'em in the back door!"

So they hopped on the subway to a neighborhood neither Ambrosia nor Lionel had ever been to. They waited behind the club for half an hour in an alley that smelled like urine and cigarettes while the freezing rain whipped around Lionel's pink umbrella. And no one ever came. So they left.

"At least we're together," Lionel said, as they walked through the city streets trying to figure out where they were. How to get home. They slipped into a random train station seeking shelter, and a group of men tumbled past them, dressed in glitter, fur coats, and little else.

One of them looked Lionel up and down. "You want to come out with us, bambino?"

Lionel blushed, and Ambrosia's heart sank. Not again. Not him. Not tonight. But instead of leaving, he grabbed her arm.

"Sorry, I'm with my Good Judy," he said, smiling at her. "And I promised her I'd never leave her behind."

Ambrosia beamed. She remembered with a quick pang that Melody had said that too. But Lionel actually meant it. Lionel had proven it, time and time again. Ambrosia had never felt so chosen. She had never felt so safe. Suddenly, the thought of going back to her sad, lifeless apartment alone was unbearable.

"Hey, I have an idea," Ambrosia said. "We're lost anyway. Let's just jump on any train and see where it takes us."

Lionel's eyes went wide. "What if we go too far? What if we end up somewhere, you know, sketchy?"

"Aw, come on. We'll be fine! We can always just come right back. It'll be an adventure."

"And if we can't get back?"

"Then what's the big deal? Who would miss us?"

"Um, my family? My parents, my sister, my grandmothers—"

"Psh, they don't even really know you, Lion," she said. "You think they'd miss you if they knew the truth?"

Lionel ducked his head, crossing his arms over his chest. Ambrosia knew what she said was fucked up, or at least unfair, but what about life was ever fair? Still, she felt bad.

"Hey," Ambrosia said, trying to get Lionel to look at her. "I'm sorry. I just meant that we only need each other."

He shook his head, but there was a train coming, howling down the tracks, fast.

"Do it for me?" she pleaded as the car doors slid open. She started backing into the car. "What did Francesca say? We're all going to die anyway! Why not make the most of the time we have left?"

Lionel sighed, and followed her through the doors, into a night where thunder rolled above them. And the storm was only building.

# *heart like a bruise*

"AMBROSIA, I . . ." *I get it.* That's what I want to say. I get what it's like to feel worthless. I get what it's like to feel hard to love—I mean, Jesus, even Abe ran away from me as fast as he could. And I get what it's like to have the one person who always promised they'd be there for you change their mind.

But that person is stroking Ambrosia's long hair right now, and I don't want to make Ramona feel bad. I don't finish my sentence.

"When we got off the train and the storm led us to Amaranth, I thought I'd finally found a place where I'd never have to say goodbye," Ambrosia says, her voice small. "But even forever can't get people to stay."

"I'm so sorry," Ramona says, Ambrosia's head in her lap once again.

Tears start to stream down Ambrosia's face, and as much as I want to help, I think the best thing I can do is leave the two of them alone.

I return to the kitchen and find Lionel working on his cookbook.

"Did it go okay?" he asks me, eyes filled with concern.

"She's hurt, of course," I say, "but she did really like the croissant." I don't tell him the croissant was thrown angrily into the amaranth. Or what she told me about their other life. "She probably just needs time."

"Don't we all."

Lionel starts swirling around the kitchen, throwing pots and pans on the counter in a manic storm that seems at once euphoric and deranged. He instructs me to start on the mashed potatoes, but after a while he's side-eying me as I try to muscle my way through.

"For someone with biceps like yours, there's very little mash happening."

"They're like rocks, I'm trying."

"Let's see." He rests his head on my shoulder, then shrieks. He puts his hands over his mouth.

"Did you even boil them, Cal?"

"What? No, I just peeled them."

He does the sign of the cross. "Jesus, Mary, and Joseph."

"Lionel!" I laugh.

"Man up! No excuses!"

"I'm learning!"

"Well, you better learn quickly," he says, and the *why* of it makes me sick to my stomach. I grab a carrot to chew nervously like a cartoon bunny.

Lionel sweats as he scribbles the recipes into his cookbook, tasting and adjusting the ingredients and quantities as we go. We make vegetarian ceviche, a chopped salad—that I totally contributed to—three different pasta dishes, chicken marsala, a seafood stew, braised and battered tofu, a chickpea curry, lemon garlic rice, paneer tikka, caprese salad, steak and mashed potatoes, and at least six desserts I want to put my whole face in.

I clean while he puts the finishing touches in the leather-bound book. Then I set the table, more of a prayer than promise that the others will join us. Lionel deserves a send-off dinner, but the mood of the house is still sour.

When only Ramona and Sunny appear in the doorway, my stomach sinks. The sunset is casting pastel shadows through the windows, and they both look like they've been crying.

"She's still that mad?" Lionel asks Ramona.

"It's not that. Ambrosia is sick," Sunny answers. "She's out in the barn. We couldn't carry her, and she doesn't have the strength to walk."

"Sick how?" Lionel whips his apron off.

"Wild fever," Sunny says. "I swear she's getting hotter."

"And there's no thermometer or medicine," Ramona says. "We looked everywhere."

"We've never needed it."

"Well, we do now."

"No. No, no, no, no," Lionel says. He starts spinning around the kitchen again, starting a new soup, throwing ice in a bowl, running a towel under hot water. "This wasn't supposed to happen now," he says. "Not her. Not here. Not like this."

Lionel whips into a panicked frenzy, and I catch him by the shoulders to try and calm him down for a moment. "What can I do to help?" I ask.

"Short of stopping time," Lionel says. "I don't know."

"It'll be all right," Sunny says. But her words do nothing to help.

"You don't understand, Sunny! You have no idea. *None*." Lionel angrily whips a towel into the sink. "It can happen so quickly. It's torture. It's hell."

"I'll remind you I lived through the Spanish flu," she says defensively. Ramona and I share a look that says, *This is not the time to mention COVID-19*.

"It's not the same," Lionel says. And again, "You have no idea. It wipes people like us off the face of the earth. Like we were never even here. Like we didn't even matter. And Ambrosia could be next."

We help him carry the ice, water, and broth out to the barn, Kiyo and Abe already there, and we all crowd around Ambrosia's makeshift bed in the middle of Kiyo's art studio.

Ambrosia looks like shit, to say the least. She's shivering violently under the covers, face flushed, hair glued to her forehead by sweat. I'm rattled, seeing her like this. I have to fold my arms to stop my hands from shaking. I want to take her to a hospital, to run for help. But there is no help. All we have is each other.

Dash lies at the base of her blankets, curled into the smallest ball he can be. Ramona and Lionel sit at her bedside, stroking her hair, feeding her ice. The rest of us hang back to give her space, and I feel the tension between me and Kiyo, me and Abe, so acutely. Kiyo is right to hate me. Abe was right to pull away. I ruined everything for everyone.

If only I'd never come here. If only I'd just signed the commitment papers and smiled and took photos on the stage with Ramona. None of this would be happening. Everyone would be okay.

"You need to leave with me," Lionel says to Ambrosia. "We need to get you help."

"I don't want to go," Ambrosia says, through chattering teeth. "I don't want to die. I want to stay here. I want to live forever."

"I don't think forever exists anymore, honey. Not for us. Not anymore."

All I can think is *my fault, my fault, my fault.*

"There's still time," Kiyo says too loudly. "And we're close, aren't we? I'll stay up all night to finish my mural."

"Yes," Sunny says. "I could finish a draft tonight, I think, if I don't edit and don't sleep and don't overthink it."

"We only have one song left to record," Ramona says.

"I finished my project just minutes ago," Abe says, and Kiyo tilts her head.

"Are you going to tell us what it is?"

He looks at the floor. "No."

"That's creepy. You know that, right?"

I want to defend Abe, even with the coldness between us. But I don't want Kiyo to accuse us of something again, or throw another glass, or actually hit me.

"At least he finished," Sunny says. "Let's be next."

Kiyo nods once, definitively. "We will be. Abe, if you're done with whatever your screwy project is, will you help me with the final coat?"

"Well, sure, but I don't want to ruin it."

"I've already outlined it all, you just have to fill it in. Even a goat could do it."

"The goats can do a lot of things I can't do."

She rolls her eyes and grabs him by his jacket sleeve. "Chop-chop. Let's keep it moving."

Lionel says he'll bring dinner around to everyone. Sunny says she just needs quiet. Ambrosia starts talking about the final song, but falls asleep mid-sentence.

Everyone files out of the barn, but Ramona stops me. "Cal, will you stay here with me? Help me keep an eye on her?"

"Of course."

I move to sit beside her, and she hugs me so hard I nearly fall over. I hug her back as tight as I can. Such a familiar thing made strange now, but still comfortable. Still welcomed. I love the silk of her hair on my chin. I love the warmth of her. I miss her, I fucking miss her, even though we've barely been apart. Even though she's right here in my arms.

"It's so scary seeing her like this," Ramona whispers when she pulls away. "She's been gripping my hand so hard I thought she was going to break it."

We both look down at Ambrosia, watch as her chest rises and falls. "She must be terrified. She's been there for others when they were suffering like this, she knows what it means. And now . . ." I let my voice trail off. Now it's come for her.

Ramona and I have heard about the HIV/AIDS crisis, obviously. How it decimated the queer community. How it devastated bodies and families. But to see it—even a hint of it—is a whole other nightmare entirely. Their reality could have been ours if we were born a few decades earlier. We just got lucky, and Lionel and Ambrosia did not, and my heart feels like a bruise when I think of how unfair that is. Of how desperately I want them both to be okay.

"Let's let her sleep through the night, if she's able," I say.

Ramona nods in agreement, not taking her eyes off Ambrosia. "Okay. We'll finish the song in the morning. But if it doesn't work, if time doesn't stop . . . Ambrosia is going to have to go with Lionel. She doesn't have a choice."

"I'm sorry. I know she's your closest friend here."

Ramona is quiet for a moment. "You probably know what I'm about to say next, right?"

I do. Because I know her. "You're leaving with them."

"I have to. We don't know if we're losing time at home now, too. I don't know if my family is missing me, or if people are looking for me . . ."

I open my mouth to protest, but she stops me and reaches for my hand. "I'm ready to go, Cal. I got what I needed here. Having this time to work on my music again has given me answers—or maybe more questions, I don't know—about what I want for my future. I realized I don't want to go to Alcott, not without you."

My stomach drops. How many times and in how many ways can I ruin Ramona's future? The chorus starts up in my head again: *my fault, my fault, my fault*. "Ramona, I'm so sorry, maybe if you contact Yale they—"

"I don't want to go to Yale either," Ramona stops me again. "I only wanted to go there because of Luíza, because I wanted to continue her legacy. She lived an amazing life, but I'm realizing that I don't have to copy it to honor her. I'm realizing that I need to stop living my life for other people, to stop tying my path to others'. Luíza would want me to be happy. And I'm happiest making music."

She smiles and squeezes my hand, and my lingering, haunting guilt melts away. Ramona and I weren't meant to be together, but we were meant to find each other. We were meant to visit this place. To meet these people. To be changed by a dream that isn't a dream. And no matter what happens between us, we'll share this for the rest of our lives.

"There's a spot for you tomorrow morning, too, just so you know," Ramona says. "If you do want to come home with me."

The thought of her leaving without me makes me panicky. I'll be left alone with Abe, who's avoiding me, Kiyo who wants to strangle me, and Sunny who will take Kiyo's side every time. Still, my answer is easy.

"I'm not ready to leave," I say. "I'm not done with Amaranth."

Ramona nods. She isn't surprised, because she knows me, too. "Okay," she says. "I understand. We'll meet on the other side."

"But what if we do stop time again and I stay here forever? Or so long that when I get back you don't recognize me? What if I change so much it's like I'm a different person?" I'm talking too quickly, holding on to her hand too tightly. "What if I get home and it feels like you don't know me?"

She puts her hands on my cheeks. "I hope that happens. I hope you get to stay here for as long as you want, and I hope you change in all the ways you want to. I hope you fall in love with yourself. But I hope you come home, too. Because I'd really like to see it."

## RAMONA SILVA

## 2008–

During the first nine years of Ramona Silva's life, the world gave her so much to love. She lived in a clean, pink house near Miami Beach with her younger brother Auggie; kind and warm parents, Sofia and Matias; and her tia Luíza, her father's sister, who followed her big brother to the United States and opened up Ramona's whole life.

See, Luíza was a lesbian who turned her homophobic, Catholic family into one of acceptance and celebration. "Love me or lose me," she'd told them. "This is who I am." And they were nothing if not loyal. Silvas stuck together. They chose each other, always. No questions asked.

So when Ramona came out as a lesbian, too, at only eight years old, her parents weren't worried. Sure, they were skeptical. How could an eight-year-old know? Wasn't it more likely she just wanted to be like her favorite person, her tia, who took her to the beach and taught her to skateboard and let her ride the Ferris wheel as many times as she wanted? Luíza had just moved from Florida to D.C., Matias reasoned. This was Ramona's response to missing her. This was Ramona's attempt to keep her close.

Maybe it was, a little. But also, Ramona just liked girls. She liked their softness. Their colorful clothes. The way they were fierce and feminine all at once. She liked how they talked, and flirted, and gossiped, pulling each other close. She had a crush on her third-grade teacher, Ms. Dalton, a cheery redhead with a strong collection of sundresses and cardigans. Ramona begged her mom to pack extra candy in her lunch box, just so she could sneak one onto Ms. Dalton's desk when she wasn't looking.

Every day without fail, Ms. Dalton would put her hands on her hips and look at the class. She'd say, "The candy fairy strikes again!" and look right at Ramona and wink. Ramona—young as she was—melted right into the floor.

And, sigh, yes. Deep down, Ramona knew she and Ms. D didn't have a future together. So thankfully, by the time middle school rolled around, she had other crushes: Nia from dance class, with her long, long legs and perfect pirouette. Carly from swim class, who had no problem changing right in the middle of the locker room. Evangelina from the neighborhood, who always slicked her hair back into a bun. Who wore soccer shorts and bikini tops. Who invited Ramona to a sleepover with a bunch of other girls from school.

Matias and Sofia went back and forth, back and forth, on whether they should let their daughter go to the party. She begged them for days, and finally they caved, on the condition she do the dishes for a week and text them every hour on the hour, letting them know she was okay.

And it was so worth it, Ramona thought, because Evangelina's house was *awesome*, and she got to see all the little intimate details of how Evangelina lived. How she neatly set her sneakers at the door, then straightened everyone else's. How she took the stairs three at a time, like some athletic goddess. How her parents let them eat pizza in her bedroom and didn't check on them every ten minutes. The girls all did each other's makeup, choreographed dances, and performed them with dramatic flair, jumping and twirling, standing on the desk like it was a stage.

Ramona got to do a duet with Evangelina. In nightgowns. Their fingers intertwined. Evangelina's hair let loose from its signature bun, her curls rolling all the way down to her waist. Ramona would do dishes for eternity if it meant this sleepover would never end.

But it didn't even last through the night. Because the next thing the girls did was throw themselves into a heap on the bed, bowls of snacks planted between them.

"Okay," someone said. "First crush and current crush."

"Obviously Harry Styles. And Aiden H. from the basketball team."

"Shawn Mendes and . . . ugh, can it be two celebrities? Tom Holland."

Ramona wasn't completely sure if she should share her crushes, since she didn't know these girls. But Evangelina said, "Tom Holland *and* Zendaya. Specifically as Bruno Mars. Tom's 'Umbrella' video changed the world."

Everyone agreed, and Ramona felt warm inside. No one laughed or made it weird. No one said anything hateful. And Evangelina was bi? This was Ramona's chance to let her know she was into girls too.

"My first crush was on my third-grade teacher," she said, and everyone nodded and whooped and giggled. "Cringe, I know. And currently? Um, probably Jenna Ortega and Hailee Steinfeld. And I mean, I love Zendaya, but then there's Hunter Schafer, and she's just everything."

The room went quiet. The playful smile on Evangelina's lips dropped completely.

"Wait you're . . . you're into girls?" she said, literally putting inches between the two of them. Ramona looked around at them, confused.

"Um, yeah? I'm a lesbian?"

"Ew," someone said. And another someone leaned over to whisper into Evangelina's ear.

"What do you mean, ew? I told you about my teacher and you were fine with it."

"You didn't say it was a girl."

"And you said Zendaya." She pointed at Evangelina. "And no one blinked!"

"I was just joking," Evangelina said. "Obviously."

"Wait, wait, wait," a spacy girl said as she stopped painting her nails. "Have you ever even had sex with a guy?"

"What? No! I'm eleven."

"Then you can't know you're a lesbian," the girl said. "You're just looking for attention."

Ramona stormed out of the room and planted herself on the front steps. Her hands shook with anger as she texted her parents to come get her, and they texted back right away. While she waited for them, she called Luíza and realized quickly she was out somewhere grown-up and fabulous. There was laughter and music clattering on in the background, but Luíza said, "Hold on, Moni," and immediately set off to find somewhere quiet.

"I'm here," she said when the noise dulled. "What happened?"

Ramona told her through tears.

"And, you know, I hear my parents talking too, when they think I can't hear them, about how they're afraid. I know they want to support me, and I know they love me, but that maybe I should stay quiet about it until I'm older. They don't want people to be mean to me. And they don't want me to scare boys off, either."

Luíza laughed out loud at this. "The patriarchy strikes again." Despite it all, this made Ramona giggle. "Listen, Moni. I have an idea. If your parents are okay with it, would you maybe want to spend this summer with me?"

Ramona doubted, very much, that her parents would allow it, given how hard she had to work to convince them to let her have a sleepover. But Matias and Sofia barely even had to consider it.

"Well, sure," Matias said. "She's family. Silvas stick together."

Luíza's apartment in D.C. had a roof deck with a firepit and her fridge was always stocked with at least three flavors of seltzer. She had a girlfriend at the time, a model named Collette who made elaborate fruit salads every morning and practiced sun salutations as the sun set. They prepared a bedroom for Ramona with soft bedding, tampons and pads (just in case!), and a caddy with organic toiletries. The walls were covered with framed photographs of women holding each other. Kissing. Protesting.

An Audre Lorde quotation hung, framed, above the queen bed: CARING FOR MYSELF IS NOT SELF-INDULGENCE. IT IS SELF-PRESERVATION, AND THAT IS AN ACT OF POLITICAL WARFARE.

"That one's a little bit ironic, isn't it?" Collette asked Ramona as she took it in for the first time.

"What do you mean?"

"I mean, your tia works herself into the ground. Sets herself on fire to make sure others feel warm."

"I heard that," Luíza said, coming through the doorframe too and playfully mussing up Collette's short hair. "Is it so wrong to want to leave this world better than I found it? For women and gay kids and immigrants? It's all for you, Moni. I work hard every day to build a better world for you. And one day you'll do the same for the next generation. *That's* self-preservation."

Sure, Luíza had to work late, late, late into the evenings—she was an established, successful, in-demand lawyer by then, and there was always more work to do. But Ramona had fun going to vegan restaurants and farmers' markets with Collette. She enjoyed reading lesbian books on the rooftop as the sun set, the city sprawled out in front of her. The city where Luíza had fought for gay marriage in the United States of America as a first-generation immigrant—and won. The city where Luíza made a home, and found love, and had a whole, vast network of queer friends.

And even though Luíza worked ungodly hours, she made sure to protect her weekends. She took her Little Moni to the D.C. Dyke March, and Pride on the Pier, and author readings at Politics and Prose. And perhaps more formatively, Sunday brunches at Luíza and Collette's various friends' homes. They were artists and activists and writers. They were business owners and actresses and academics.

Ramona watched these women prepare food for each other. Set their tables with beautiful flowers. Dance in the kitchen, and walk around braless, and cut their hair and wear men's clothes and talk about women and love women and center women and keep the toilet seat down and wash their hands with lemon-scented soap. And drink fruit-infused water. And talk too loudly about revolution. And blast Tracy Chapman and The Chicks and Tegan and Sara and Brandi Carlile and Janelle Monáe and King Princess and Hayley Kiyoko and—

And *wow*. How Ramona loved to hear all these women scream the words to songs about people like her. Songs *by* people like her. What a holy, holy thing. She dared to imagine them singing one of her songs, the ones that only existed in her journals at home. It was an impossible dream: to share her words, to hear these girls scream them. But the thought of it thrilled Ramona. It lit her all the way up. She wished she could wrap the dream around her like a blanket.

And how Ramona loved to see Luíza dancing, and okay, maybe it took her at least three mimosas to get there, but she loosened up. Her shoulders released. She grabbed Collette by the hand and spun her around, and then the two of them motioned for Ramona to join them. They held her hands, and the summer world of flowers and music and girls who loved girls streaked around her, and Ramona felt euphoric. She'd never felt this good in all her life. These were her people. This was her heaven. She wanted to stay there forever.

"You believe me, right?" she said, while she tried to get un-dizzy. "That I'm a lesbian, even if I'm just a kid?"

"Moni," Luíza said, "kids are real people with real hearts, and you know yours better than anyone. So I will always believe you when you tell me who you are. If it's about what makes you happy, it's who you are. If it's about who you love, it's who you are. And I know I moved out of Florida, but I'm only a phone call away. Sure, Silvas stick together. But guess what? Women do too. Dykes do too. So I'm here for you times three. Thrice. Triple."

Ramona thought, maybe, the mimosas were hitting her tia now, but she saw it as a window of opportunity.

"If I become a lawyer like you, could I live with you, here in D.C. when I grow up?"

Luíza kept dancing to the music. Smiling, laughing, feeling herself. Looking free in a way she never did. Ramona loved her always, but she loved her best like this.

"Of course you can, Moni," she said, her face catching the sun. "You'll be my echo. My mini. My legacy. We'll change the world together."

Ramona copied her. She looked to the sky too. She let the song and the sun and the sweet citrus scent of someone's perfume soak her all the way through. She wanted middle school to be over. She wanted to skip ahead to a future where she could feel this way every day, to when everyone would believe her about who she was and what she wanted, just like Luíza did. Where she could be surrounded and supported and celebrated by girls who were in love with each other and themselves. Who were unapologetic and unafraid. Who were singing at the top of their lungs, sun-kissed and bronze, fruit sugar lingering on their lips until a girl came along to kiss it away.

# *last note*

AMBROSIA LEANS ON ME and Ramona as we cross the field to the house, our arms wrapped around her waist, the sun rising.

"This is the bisexual dream," she jokes weakly, waggling her eyebrows at both Ramona and me.

"Glad to see you're feeling better, Ambrosia," I say dryly, but I really am beyond relieved. A full night's sleep seems to have done her some good, even if she is still too weak to walk by herself.

She stutters out a laugh. "Look, even the sky is waving my flag."

We turn our eyes upward, and she's not wrong. The dawn is a punchy swirl of pink, purple, and sky blue. Ambrosia watches it the whole way to the house.

Down in the recording studio, Lionel is waiting with, naturally, plates of food for all of us. Ambrosia motions for us to let her go but stumbles, and he catches her in his arms. She melts into him, all of yesterday's animosity forgotten.

"Hi, baby," he says. "Good morning. How are you feeling?"

Ambrosia shrugs in response, then says, "You came to listen?"

"Wouldn't miss it for the world. The others will be here soon too."

Ambrosia smiles, and it's like I can literally see her spark back to life. "Well then, let's get this show on the road."

I sneak bites of strawberries and cream while we help the girls set up, but I can't stomach much more than that. A goodbye hangs in the air like a balloon ready to pop. I can't believe—if this doesn't work, if time doesn't stop once everyone's projects are complete—that the three of them are leaving. I can't believe that I'm staying. I can't believe that I'm letting Ramona go.

But for now, they're still here, and both Ambrosia and Ramona are glowing as they bounce last-minute ideas back and forth. I soak it all in, and even when Kiyo, Abe, Dash, and Sunny enter the room, all of us are quiet. Reverent. We're here to bear witness. We're here to hope.

I dare to look at Abe, and I see he's stroking the face of his watch like a worry stone.

"Thanks for coming out this morning," Ramona says like a rock star when they're finally ready to take the stage.

"This one," Ambrosia starts, but gets choked up. She locks eyes with Ramona, who with just a glance gets Ambrosia to smile. "This one's called, 'Even in Another Time.' "

The opening notes send goose bumps up and down my skin. The song sounds much different from their other tracks. Usually all I hear is Ramona—darker acoustic pop—but this one is a ballad. This one's built for Ambrosia's hungry, wild soprano. This one could stop the world from spinning.

When the song is over, when the final notes and our applause fades to the longest silence, the album is finished.

"The mural's done too," Kiyo says eventually.

"And my cookbook," Lionel adds.

"My novel, as well," Sunny says.

"Is your watch still ticking, Abe?" Kiyo asks, nervous and hopeful.

He holds it up for all of us to see. But the second hand still jumps from line to line. Soon, the minute hand marches forward.

"That's it, then, isn't it?" Ambrosia says, and Ramona hugs her.

"That's it, then," Lionel says, and reaches out to take her hand.

# *goodbye*

UPSTAIRS, WE ALL LISTEN to the album while we pick at the leftovers from Lionel's forgotten feast, pretending to have an appetite. Ambrosia puts on her Jessica Rabbit dress for the occasion, even though she can hardly stand.

"At least I'll go out feeling drop-dead gorgeous," she says. Then she threateningly points a butter knife at each of us. "Don't you dare forget me. Any of you."

Sunny takes Ambrosia's face in her hands, then hugs her as she starts to shiver again. "Ambrosia. You are an *icon.* How could we ever?"

"You're memorialized on the wall," Kiyo says, motioning toward her portrait. "I won't move it to the barn. Promise."

"And you just sang your heart out," Abe says.

"I'll always remember that," I say. "Always."

Ambrosia smiles, her head held high, looking like she's found something close to peace.

When the record stops spinning and the sun is high and hot in the sky, we all go to the edge of Amaranth, to the clean ring of angry red flowers that mark this place and the next. Wherever that is. Whenever that is.

I hug Lionel goodbye first.

"I hope there are great things waiting for you," I say.

"You too, cookie dough." He holds me at arm's length, and looks suddenly, gravely serious. "Don't let them eat boring food again, okay? *Please,* Cal. I left you a whole cookbook. Life's too short, even here." I can't help but smile.

"All right, all right," I say. "I'll do my best to carry on your culinary legacy."

Lionel goes to hug Kiyo—who begrudgingly accepts—and I turn to Ambrosia beside him. We look at each other for a moment, and then she throws her arms around me. I unexpectedly don't want to let her go.

"Sorry I voted you out," she says.

"Sorry I started time," I say. "But you'll be okay. You have to be."

"I won't," she says, pulling away. "But at least I lived a little, right?"

"At least you were too much," I say. "Pretty much all the time."

"Speaking of too much," she says. "Will you murder me if I kiss Ramona?"

I'm stunned for a second. Her eyes are pleading, her voice sincere. I'm sad to realize there was a whole side of her I never really got to know—soft and compassionate, creative and vulnerable—but I'm so glad Ramona got to see it. I force myself to take a deep breath before responding.

"No, I won't murder you. But it's also not up to me."

Ambrosia nods, then punches me on the arm. "Come visit me in the future, okay? When I'm old and famous, no doubt."

"No doubt," I say. "I'll see you then, Ambrosia."

"I'll see you then," she says. She ruffles my hair, and walks away.

Next—last, hardest—is Ramona. My heart feels as big as my whole chest as we hug each other for as long as we can.

"I love you," she says. "You're still my person, okay? For life."

"I know," I say. "I love you too. I'll miss you like crazy."

"How could you not?"

I laugh and hold her tighter. It feels like I'm saying goodbye to more than just Ramona—it's like I'm losing half of myself. A part of who I was that I tried to hold on to for so long. But maybe that's what's right. Because with time, I'll fill that space with everything I need to be, everything I am.

I pull away and try to wipe my tears before she can see, and I notice her do the same. "I don't know how to say this, but Ambrosia just asked me if she could kiss you."

Her eyes go wide. "She *what?*"

"I told her it's up to you."

She nods, looking a little flustered. "Well, for the record, Abe's totally smitten with you."

"No, he's not," I say, heart falling, remembering him jumping away from me in the shed.

"I think I know what it looks like to be in love with Cal Quick."

I just grin and pretend, because maybe it makes her feel better to believe someone else could want me even if she couldn't.

"I'll see you on the other side, Ramona."

She kisses me on the cheek and says, "I'll see you on the other side." And then she walks away from me. Maybe forever.

Ramona meets Lionel and Ambrosia at the edge of the woods and my whole body goes numb. After a beat, Ambrosia kisses her, hard. Lionel turns around to give the rest of us the thumbs-up. Then the three of them join hands and step forward together.

Like a flicker of a firefly, they're gone.

"Poof," Kiyo says, and I realize she, Sunny, and Abe have all gathered around me.

"And then there were four," Abe says, but Dash barks in protest. "And then there were four, and a whole lot more."

# *after*

THE REST OF THE day is nothing like I expect it to be. I don't know what I thought; that the four of us remaining would trauma bond? That we'd sit by the fire together processing the loss of our friends, planning for the future, brainstorming other ways to stop time? That a group therapist would appear, set us up on chaise lounges, and help us unpack everything happening?

But the day is nothing like that. Sunny and Kiyo are nowhere to be seen. I don't know if they're together or apart, if they're mourning or creating or just trying to hold themselves together.

I go to put my boots on to help Abe in the yard, but he's already walking in through the back door. When he sees me, he freezes.

"Hey," I say.

"Hey." He inhales like he wants to say something, but stops short, running his hand through his hair.

"What's up?" I ask, unable to keep the edge out of my voice.

His words come out in a rush. "I think we need to divide the chores differently now. I'm well enough to take care of the animals on my own. It doesn't really make sense to have both of us out in the yard when someone needs to cook, and plus Ambrosia did a lot around the house, and—"

"Fine," I say, sharper than I want to. What he's saying makes sense. So why do I feel hurt? Why do I feel embarrassed, and even a little mad?

"We can take turns if you want. It's just Sunny and Kiyo won't really leave the barn, and I heard you promise Lionel—"

"It's fine, man. I've got it," I clearly lie.

Abe squints at me and once again inhales to speak but doesn't. He just shakes his head and walks out of the house, leaving me alone in the kitchen with one boot on, ready to tackle my own culinary incompetence and shame.

When I open the door to the pantry, I find heavy cream, vegetables, potatoes, flour, soy chicken, garlic, salt, and spices.

"Fuck." Why couldn't it be a microwave meal? We don't have a microwave but . . . couldn't that have been my gift, house? Honestly, Amaranth.

I open Lionel's cookbook and find his loopy handwriting in the pages. It says Recipes in script across the front. And: By Lionel Toussaint ♡ Oh, my heart. Only one entry appears to me for now: pot pie. It lists all the ingredients in the pantry, plus butter.

"Do I have to . . . ?" Goddammit. I do.

First, churn the butter by putting fresh heavy cream in a jar. Shake well for 20–30 minutes until a solid ball of butter forms. Get those biceps, handsome! Remove butter from buttermilk, rinse, and store separately. Then *leave in the fridge to chill—dance party recommended while you wait.* I smile and groan at the same time and wish desperately that Lionel was still here to teach me more. Or that Ramona was still here to help. Or that Abe would have stayed in the kitchen, would have thrown flour balls at me until he paused to wipe my cheek and—

"I'm pathetic," I say under my breath.

More pathetic, I put on Ambrosia and Ramona's album to further torture myself. And as if it's got an algorithm, the record player puts on angry '90s girl rock next. I scream along to "You Oughta Know." It's a good soundtrack for shaking the cream and getting out my aggression until I finally feel a solid mass bouncing around in the jar. I follow Lionel's instructions to rinse out the remaining buttermilk before popping my butter—MY butter! That I churned!—into the fridge to firm up.

I cut the carrots like I'm sharpening a stick. I dice all the vegetables like I'm chopping down trees. I peel the potatoes with a motherfucking vengeance and nick my knuckle on the peeler. I suck the blood off and keep going, until I have a pile of vegetables that look crooked and bruised. Good enough. I start on the crust, then assemble everything together.

The first pie is a complete mess. It comes out soggy and undercooked. I can tell even before tasting it that it's inedible. All that churning and chopping and mixing for nothing. It's depressing.

More depressing: I get the same ingredients again. Amaranth clearly isn't going to give me a break.

I make the pot pie again, and leave it in the oven way too long, and it's burnt to a near crisp. The kitchen fills with smoke, and I choke on its acid. And this shouldn't make me lose my whole shit, but I sure do. I break a plate. Not on purpose, exactly, but because I'm rushing around, frustrated and careless.

I pick up the pieces as quickly as I can, and promise myself I won't cry. I can't. I won't. I have to get food on the Goddamn table. I promised Lionel, after all. It's the least I can do. It's the most I can do.

I make the pie one more time, my eyes still watering from the lingering smoke and emotional meltdown.

"Amaranth, play 'You Oughta Know' on repeat," I say, like it's 2026. But Amaranth obliges. I hear the record start to spin. I wrestle the dough into submission, chop the vegetables with an alarming fury and this time nearly lose a thumb. But I bake it right.

I set the kitchen table, now home to just four lonely chairs, and serve four gloppy wedges on plates.

I sit there and wait. Despite myself, I really hope they like it, and I hope, somewhere, Lionel is proud of me. The crust is cooked through at least, and only a little blackened on the edges. I try a bite and find the gravy is pretty damn good, actually, and the vegetables are . . . chopped. It's edible. It's a start. And I can be proud of myself for that.

# *dinner*

THEY COME HOME TO eat eventually. All three of them. I'm not exactly happy to see them, but I am relieved. And oddly excited for them to try my D+ dinner, even though it ruined my life at least three times.

"Is something on fire?" Sunny asks as she opens all the windows.

"Uh, yeah, sorry. I burned the second attempt."

"Thank you for cooking," Kiyo says awkwardly. She hands me something wrapped in watercolor paper, and then she does the best and worst thing she could do. She throws her arms around me. I'm so stunned it takes me at least five seconds to react, and I awkwardly hug her back.

"I've been crummy to you," she says as she pulls away.

"It's okay," I say. "I get it."

"It's not okay. And you haven't deserved it. Losing the others made me realize how much we need each other. So, I really am so sorry, and this is my apology." She motions for me to open the gift.

I unwrap it to find a royal blue glass veined with chalky, rainbow colors. It's jagged and reminds me of the stained glass of the grandfather clock. It's not nearly as tidy as her kintsugi. I like it so much better.

"Is this the cup you shattered?"

"Yep," she says. "It might fall apart eventually, if I'm honest, but I tried something new—or maybe something old—instead of the gold foil. I copied Lionel's gingerbread house recipe and melted sugar, then mixed it with crushed wildflowers. Because they're growing outside now. And because, well, who has gold just lying around?"

"It's perfect," I say, cradling it in my hands, remembering the corsage I made for Ramona. "Even if it falls apart eventually."

She nods. "I know I said you're broken, but I think I'm still broken, too. I'm working on it, though. Trying to put all the pieces back together. Et cetera."

"Thank you, Kiyo," I say. "Me too. If it makes you feel better, I just shattered a plate because I was emo about pie."

"You want me to show you how to mend it later? Not with gold. Just with . . . ugh, don't make me say it."

"Just love?" I say with a wink, and though she pretends to gag, she smiles, too, and punches me on the shoulder.

We sit at the table, where Sunny beams at Kiyo—probably proud of her out-of-character apology—and Abe refuses to meet my eyes.

"The vegetables are kind of hard, the crust is kinda fucked up, and honestly, Kiyo, you could probably use the gravy as glue, but—"

"It's delicious," Sunny says, rubbing my shoulder. "Much better than anything we had before Lionel, right?" Kiyo nods quickly, and Abe mumbles something, and my chest tightens.

We eat in silence for a while, the only sound forks scraping on plates, until finally the question bubbles out of me. "So . . . now what?"

They all consider this for a moment.

"Time may still stop yet," Sunny says, ever the optimist. "Perhaps we'll figure it out, or perhaps it will just happen. Could be tomorrow, could be twenty years from now. Maybe another houseguest will come, and that will be their gift."

"And if it doesn't stop?" Abe asks, eyes trained on his plate as he pokes at his food.

"Well. I know it's morbid, but in that case, I'll be here until I die," Sunny says. "I'd rather live out my days at Amaranth. Even if it's changing, it's still paradise to me."

"Me too," Kiyo says. "The other world isn't built for us."

"You can bury us in the flowers," Sunny says, holding Kiyo's hand, a whole future in her eyes.

"We're all pretty much the same age, though," I say. "Who's to say you'll go first?"

"Fair point," Sunny says.

"And that's assuming you two hang around that long. What do you think, Cal?" Kiyo asks. "Will you stay?"

Kiyo's question catches me off guard for some reason. *Do I want to live my whole life here?* I know I'm meant to be at Amaranth now—feel it deep in my bones—but I don't feel any more prepared to decide on my future than I did when I got here.

"For now, yes," I say. And I leave it at that.

"What about you, buddy?" Kiyo says, turning to Abe. "Will you stick around?"

He stops eating. Holds his fork midair. Looks at his plate. "I can't."

"Well, sure you can," Sunny says. "This is as much your home as it is ours."

"I wish I could, but I can't," he says.

"But why?" Kiyo asks, her usual edge returning to her voice. "What aren't you telling us?"

Abe doesn't respond. I keep my eyes trained on my plate, too, not wanting to give anything away, but I can feel Kiyo's eyes volleying between us.

"Cal knows why. I can tell," Kiyo says, her voice unexpectedly gentle.

I almost protest, almost lie. For Abe. But he says, "Please don't ask them."

"All right," Sunny says, exchanging a look with Kiyo. "But, Abe, I hope you know you can trust us."

"After all," Kiyo says. "We're all we have now."

# *inevitable*

EVERYONE HELPS ME CLEAN up after dinner. Then Sunny and Kiyo leave for the barn again, and I expect Abe to head to his shed with Dash. But he stops in the doorway and turns to me.

"Cal, do you want to . . . would you mind . . . would you want to build a fire tonight? Look at the stars? With me?"

"Oh. Okay," is all I say. I try to keep my face stony. I try to keep my voice neutral. Because this doesn't mean anything. Maybe Kiyo's words just got to him—we're all each other has now, and we need to make nice. I can't believe it's more than that. It would hurt too much to believe it's more than that. But still, I follow him outside.

We build the fire in silence. Once it's raging, we wrap ourselves in blankets to hide from the cutting wind whipping around us, sending the flames dancing in every direction. There are only four chairs now, and it makes me desperately sad. Abe must feel the same, because he stares at them for a minute before sitting on the grass instead. I join him, but make sure there's plenty of space between us. Dash plops himself smack-dab in the middle.

"Windy," I say.

"Mmm," he murmurs.

"Do you think that means a storm's coming?"

"Not sure." He pulls the blanket tighter around himself, and I half wonder if I imagined his invitation because Abe will barely look at me. I almost want to scream or shake him but I don't.

A cricket choir creaks and fireflies flicker at the edge of the trees. The bugs are new. Part of my gift too, I guess.

"Listen," I say finally. "I know you've been avoiding me because we had that moment where I almost kissed you and . . . I'm sorry. I don't know what happened, but it won't happen again. We can still be friends. We should be friends. There's only the four of us now."

"I haven't been avoiding you," he says, shaking his head. "Or maybe I have. I just—" He takes a deep breath, and finally looks at me. "I feel . . . so . . . *good* when I'm around you. I'm scared to get close to you, because it'll make me want to stay. And I shouldn't. I can't. I feel so guilty, being here. Putting myself first. Trying to stall their life. Messing with it. Risking it." He's talking about the baby, though he can't say it. And while I want to comfort him, to tell him he's being ridiculous, I can't. Because he's not wrong.

"I don't think you should feel guilty, Abe. You're doing the best you can with the information you have. And, I mean, what kid wouldn't love it here?" I say, gesturing to the sky and the land around us.

"This is no place for a child. It's beautiful, but it's . . . what did Lionel say? A prison." Abe stares at the edge of the amaranth field with a focused intensity.

“Are you thinking of leaving . . . soon?” I ask, scared of his answer.

“Yes. No. If I stay here, I’m ruining someone else’s life. But if I go back as Abe, as me, I think I’ll be killed. There was a boy just like me a few towns away and . . .” he trails off. Doesn’t want to say it. Doesn’t need to. “But if I don’t get to live this way, if I have to go back to pretending, I couldn’t take it. I think I’ll die, one way or another.”

I want to tell him it doesn’t have to be like that. I want to tell him it’s not true, that he’ll make it, that he has to. But the truth is, I’m terrified for him. If it’s this hard for me, I can only imagine the impossibilities of the 1950s.

“So you can’t stay. And you can’t go.”

“I know, it doesn’t make sense.”

“No,” I say. “I get it. It’s an impossible choice. I know it’s different, but I felt that way too when I had to choose between losing Ramona or losing myself.”

Abe turns to me. “What was it in the end? That made you choose yourself?”

I’m about to say that I didn’t have a choice. That when my parents found what they did on my iPad, the choice was made for me. That I would have kept hiding if I could have, because it would have made everything so much easier. That I could have had everything I ever wanted.

But that’s not true, is it? Because in the end, it *wasn’t* what I wanted. Maybe I was powerless in what happened with my parents, but I chose to come out to Ramona in that men’s bathroom. I chose to tell everyone to call me Cal here, to use they/them pronouns. I chose to walk away from Alcott. And I was brave enough—even though it broke my heart—to admit Ramona and

I can love each other better as friends. Maybe I wanted to feel like I didn't have a choice because, if I didn't, then I wouldn't have to take any responsibility for blowing up my whole life.

"I think there were a lot of small things that eventually added up," I tell Abe. "But honestly? It was the tux." I laugh, because it sounds absurd. "I hated myself so much for so long, and then I saw a glimpse of who I could be and it just made me so *happy.* I found other things that made me feel like myself, and when everything came together, it all just seemed so . . . inevitable. So right."

"Like the poems. And the button." He winks. I pull it out of my pocket to show him I still have it, and he smiles.

"Exactly. And once you feel that way, after you've waited for so long, it's hard to imagine giving it up, no matter the cost." The next part comes out quiet. "What you said about dying either way? I understand what you mean. There were moments where I thought if I had to keep living that way, I'd rather just not live at all."

His smile drops. "I've been feeling so terrible about feeling that way, thinking those thoughts, especially these past few days. Ambrosia and Lionel want to live so badly and I . . . I was starting to think the devil lives in me."

"Abe," I say, and move close enough to put my hand on his shoulder. "No. It's hard living in the world. It's natural to dream of escaping—why do you think I stayed today? But you can talk to me about it. It's not something you should carry alone."

"So you're not scared of me? You don't think I'm a bad person?" he asks, voice tight.

I shake my head, but he seems unconvinced. So I tell him something I've never told anyone before, not even Ramona.

Something I've tried hard to forget, because I guess I feel ashamed of it too.

Turning away from him, I say, "You know, I almost did it once, for real, when I was in middle school. I came really close."

"Really?"

"Really."

"I'm glad you didn't," Abe says quietly. "Do you wanna talk about it?"

And I find that I do.

## CAL QUICK

## 2008–

Calla ran away from her mother and that car, from that afternoon in the hallway and the principal's office and the counselor's office. She ran away from Jackson and the boys in her class who tormented her, the girls in her class who said nothing, and the teachers who did nothing except make *her* apologize. Snow was falling fast and wet, and she'd left her jacket in her mom's car, so she got onto an IndyGo bus and begged the driver to let her on for free.

"Sorry, baby girl," the driver said, "rules are rules. Do you know how many people ask me for a free ride? You don't even have a mask." Calla touched her face, realizing. She'd left that in the car too. She covered her mouth with her cotton shirt, and dug around in her jean pockets.

"Do you want my earrings? They're . . . what is it? Karat gold."

The driver considered but shook her head.

"This bus has places to be," she said. "Go on."

Calla turned to leave, dread ripping through her, but an old man with a cane slowly made his way up the aisle. He reached into his pocket, pulled out an extra mask, and tapped his bus pass on the reader. Then he walked back to his own seat and sat down.

Calla mumbled a thank-you, put the mask on, and found her own seat. She pulled her knees up to her chest and wept as the bus went round and round the city.

She tried to think of ways to die, and came up with three.

She tried to think of ways to live, too, and, well. She couldn't.

*The rest of my life is on this bus*, she thought. *When I get off, it's over. I'll find a way for it to be over.* She couldn't go home. She couldn't go back to school. Not ever. She dreamed of escape and planned what it would look like. But she wasn't quite ready to get off and go through with it—and she so regretted not saying goodbye to Nugget—so she rode the whole route, multiple times, for hours, until that driver's shift ended and another one's began. Until she fell asleep and woke to darkness, to find the bus idling in front of a diner. And to find a jacket folded next to her on the seat.

It was the old man's, she realized. He was still on the bus, holding a newspaper, sleeves rolled up to his elbows. She liked his glasses. They made him look smart. She liked the way he poked at the paper with a pen. A crossword puzzle, if she had to guess. With his skin exposed, she could see one of his arms was covered in red, feathery scars that reminded her of fern leaves. She wanted to ask him what happened, but she knew better.

He noticed her staring and looked up from his puzzle.

"Thank you for the jacket, sir," she said quickly, and looked down. Not that she'd need it where she was going, but it was the polite thing to say.

"You know," the old man said, "this bus is almost done for the night, and this diner has marvelous hot chocolate. What do you say

I buy you a cup, and then we'll call someone you trust to take you home?"

"I can't go home," she said, voice breaking, her tears spilling. She hated herself for it. She had promised herself to never feel anything ever again. "Not anymore."

"Or maybe you just can't go home *yet*," he said. "Why don't you tell me about it in there where it's warm?"

# *heartbeat*

"IN RETROSPECT, IT WAS probably not very smart of me to say yes, but I mean, what was the worst that could happen? I'd die? That's what I wanted anyway. But I'd never had an adult listen to me like that before. It made me feel like I mattered. I told him I was thinking of killing myself, and he didn't freak out or call the cops or my parents. He just made me promise that I'd make it to my high school graduation. Just put my head down and do whatever I needed to do to survive until then. And only then, if I still wanted to die, I could make that choice. I still have his jacket—he wouldn't let me give it back. My friends make fun of me for how much I wear it, but sometimes . . . sometimes having that reminder was the only thing that kept me going."

"And now you're almost at graduation," Abe says. "Maybe that's why you finally decided. To pick your head up again. To do more than just survive. To be yourself. You made it."

I hadn't thought of it like that, but he's right. The thought takes my breath away. I'm finally fighting for that little kid on the bus. Letting them live. Letting them be free. Things aren't perfect by any means, and I'm still figuring things out, but I made it out alive. I made it here, to this impossible place, fire-warmed and starlit, my hand on Abe's shoulder.

"You're really smart, you know that?" I say, but Abe shakes his head. "No, you are. You'd be such a great parent, Abe."

He shakes his head again. "Who would want me as a mother? I'm a freak."

"You're not a freak," I say. "In my time, all sorts of people get pregnant. Men too. Fathers too."

"Well, I'm not from your time, Cal. In my time, I'm a freak."

"You're not a freak," I shout again, then remember myself and lower my voice. "You're nurturing and kind. You're helpful and open-minded, and you're really fun to be around when you're not icing me out." He narrows his eyes like he wants to fight me but I keep going. "In our short time together, you've made me feel like I can be myself. And I know I fucked it all up, trying to kiss you but—"

"You didn't," he says. "I just got scared. I've only ever been with my husband and . . ." And that was violent. That was traumatic. That was assault.

"God, Abe, I'm sorry. I didn't even think—" He waves me off.

"I'm broken, I reckon. But I'm grateful still, that you tried. I never thought someone would want me, especially knowing . . ." He shakes his head. "Anyway. I'm the one who messed it all up. You made me feel like someone could love me—uh, I mean, not *love* me, but want me one day. So, thank you for that."

I stare at him, so close to me. His handsome face. His freckles. The blanket slipping off his shoulders. His corduroy jacket and his canvas shirt and his blue jeans. His nervous hands, plucking grass from the ground, tying the blades into little knots. My heart beats louder and louder, and I feel the walls between us falling, falling. Breaking.

"It's easy to want you, Abe," I whisper. "It's easy to love you. You'd have to be a fool not to."

We stare at each other for so long, but I don't dare move a muscle. Then he puts his hand out, and when I take it, he pulls me to him. He hugs me so hard that there's no way he doesn't feel my heartbeat on his chest. Or is it his I'm feeling? We're pressed up together so tightly, I worry I might be hurting him. But he only hugs me harder, like it can anchor us here forever. Like we might fall into each other and never have to leave.

"Can we try again?" he whispers into my hair.

I sit back and take his face in my hands. Rub my thumbs across his freckles.

He presses his forehead to mine, and I can feel his breath on my skin. But I don't make the same mistake. I give him space. I give him time. I wait for him to choose it. And soon, he does.

He kisses me, and I kiss him back, and I feel hungry and breathless. And yes, of course I miss Ramona, and I feel a pang of longing when I think of her, but it's fleeting. This feels different, so different—me as Cal, wanting. Wanted.

When I pull away to check on him, he grabs me by the front of my shirt and kisses me again, this time harder. This time longer. It feels like time stops to hold us right here, just like this, safe from all the world.

When we settle into each other, his head on my chest, I even grab his wrist to check his watch, just in case. The hands are still moving, and it's a damn shame, because I could spend forever running my fingers through his hair. Dash licks my face, then puts his head on my shoulder and licks Abe's cheek too, and we can't stop laughing.

"I guess he approves," he says.

"Thank God," I say.

"God approves too. I asked him."

"Oh yeah? I must admit, I've never been religious."

"Is it okay if I'm keen on a heathen?" he shouts at the sky as he sits up. He smirks, gray eyes sparkling down at me. "Good news. He said yes."

"Lucky us," I say, laughing.

"Lucky us," Abe echoes and puts his palm on my sternum, the only part of my chest that feels like me, and I feel seen all over again.

"I've been praying for a miracle," Abe whispers.

"To stop time again?"

He nods, sadly, and lowers himself down to kiss me again. "Because if we leave here . . . when we leave here . . . I'm going to lose you. And it already breaks my heart."

# *passing the time*

DESPITE THE DREAD OF time marching on, Sunny, Kiyo, and Abe are delighted to have seasons. And I am too, because summer at Amaranth is a dream. It's heat and crickets and crushed strawberries frozen into popsicles. It's fireflies and grilled peaches and water balloon fights. Wildflowers burst across the field, dueling with the amaranth, but they can't be tamed no matter how many bouquets we gather for the kitchen vase. Kiyo couldn't be happier about it.

Summer days are lazy. We use blankets to make hammocks. Sunny sacrifices some of her books to make us fans, and we sit around picnic baskets fanning ourselves and each other dramatically. We use posh accents to match, pretend to be socialites on a holiday.

"Would you pass the berries, Sunshine?"

"It would be my pleasure, Abraham."

"Callan, you look so handsome today with your ascot."

"Thank you, Sunshine, Kiyoko picked it out for me. It makes me look quite distinguished, doesn't it?"

"We never used to spend this much time together," Sunny muses, as she drinks her lemonade pinkie up. "Before we had time, I mean."

"It was different, wasn't it?" Kiyo says, breaking character. "Things feel more precious, now."

Which is, I guess, why we orbit each other more tightly. We eat every meal together. We tell each other stories of our other lives. We play cards and let Sunny style us in all kinds of outfits and have baking competitions that I usually win (if only Lionel could see me now). We make sailboats out of art supplies, man them with Abe's whittled animals, and make them race (at a snail's pace) across the pond. We make wishes on pebbles and toss them in the murky water, and I know for sure we all have the very same wish.

Summer days are easy and childish and joyful. And the nights are . . . wow. Abe and I try to map the sky, though it's now an impossible, Sisyphean task. And in the dark of the shed, we map each other's bodies too. We strip them of the words they were given; all the wrong words. We tell new stories all over our skin. We relearn what we like, what we want. *Touch me here, like this. Not there, not that.* Until it's only nights of *Yes. Yes. Yes.* Until we are lit up like constellations.

Until we guide each other home.

But still, time passes, and we all grow restless in the heat.

"I'm not meant to melt like this," Sunny says, draping herself dramatically over the green velvet couch. "I can hardly focus on anything at all."

"What if we each teach a class, like it's summer camp?" I

suggest. "Run a workshop of some kind? Maybe it'll help distract us from the heat." And, I don't say, distract Abe from his persistent fatigue, nausea, and the growing stomach he's still taking great lengths to hide.

"You first," Abe says.

"Are you sure you're up for—"

"Bring it on, Quick," he says in his deepest voice. "I'll see you on the field. Pitch? Court?"

"Oh, it's on, Turner."

I teach them how to play field hockey, and they take to it right away. Especially Sunny, who turns her jersey into a belly shirt and picks the shortest skirt she can find.

"Gee, you're good, Cal," Kiyo says, at the end of a scrimmage. "I understand now. How you got a dish like Ramona to go steady with you."

I bark out a laugh. "Mystery solved!" And I smile, mostly to myself, because it doesn't hurt to hear Ramona's name. It doesn't hurt to remember. I just miss her. I just wish she were here.

Abe has us all build a miniature Amaranth together using wood scraps. Kiyo tries to teach us how to paint landscapes. And while I'm slopping paint on a canvas in a way that is truly aesthetically displeasing, she taps me on the shoulder.

"I've got a surprise for you, Cal," she says.

When I turn around, she's holding my portrait. My new one—my real one. It's me in the navy tux, on the night of the welcome party. And now I understand what was wrong with her first attempt. It looked like me, but it wasn't me. This, though . . . this captures me perfectly, in a way I never could have imagined. All I can do is stare at it, stunned.

"Sorry it took me so long. I wanted to get it just right," Kiyo says. "I wanted it to feel like it was really you."

"How did you—?"

"I did it from memory," Kiyo answers. "For as long as I live, I'll never forget your expression coming down those stairs. It was you and only you in that moment, Cal."

It's enough to make me tear up. "Kiyo, I can't thank you enough. I wish I had something for you, too," I say.

"Please, I'm begging you. No more gifts from you!" She puts her hands up, grinning. "Now let's go hang this up."

# *echoes*

FOR SUNNY'S LESSON, SHE suggests we teach Abe to read, which makes him groan, but he shows up in the living room in the morning as requested.

"I don't want to read picture books," he says, grabbing one of the letter-shaped sugar cookies I've laid out and sprinkled within an inch of their life.

"Oh, but there are some gorgeous ones," Sunny says, clutching a leather book to her chest.

"I'm sure there are," he says, "but I'm already embarrassed enough."

"Well, you shouldn't be," Sunny says. "We all started somewhere. It took me longer than all my brothers to learn, but I was determined to read because my mother couldn't. And now I'm a writer myself!"

"I bet your mom is so proud of you," I say. "Wherever she is."

Sunny gives me a small smile and runs her fingers along her

pearls. "It's pretty to think so," she says, eyes straying to look out the window where the first signs of fall are visible on the tips of the leaves. "This was always her favorite time of year. She loved when summer hadn't quite left and autumn hadn't quite arrived. I think that's why she and I had such a special connection. She knew how to love the in-between, whether it was seasons or people."

Sunny's gaze stays glued on the trees outside, and I'm about to ask more about her mother when Kiyo says to Abe, "So, what *do* you want to read, cowboy? The dictionary? A phone book? The *Farmer's Almanac*?"

"The what?" Abe says, and I can tell by his voice and the pink of his cheeks that he's getting flustered. Dash must notice too, because he starts awkwardly licking Abe's legs. I stand up from the couch to drape my arms over his shoulders, and he relaxes at my touch.

"What about your novel, Sunny?" I suggest, snapping her out of her trance. "It's finished now, after all."

"No," she says sharply. "I'm . . . It's not ready to be shared." She turns away from us toward the bookshelf, and jams the leather book back into the shelf like she's trying to murder it. Both Abe and I jump in surprise. I look at Kiyo to search her face for clues, but she just stares at the floor.

"Hey, that's okay," I say calmly. "How about I read my favorite poem instead?"

Sunny nods quickly, and sits in a chair without looking at me or anyone. I grab a book and pull Abe onto the couch with me, open the pages and watch it appear. I read Andrea Gibson's "Your Life," again, and Abe puts his hand on my knee, and this time I know he won't let go. I move my finger under each word as I read it so he can follow along, and he squeezes my knee when I hit his favorite lines.

When I finish the poem and look up, I hope to see that Sunny and Kiyo loved it as much as Abe and I do. But Sunny is silently crying, and Kiyo is stroking her hair from where she's perched on the side of the chair.

"Sunny?" I say. A pang of guilt flashes through me, and I look back at the pages to see what might have hurt or offended her.

"I'm sorry, Cal," Sunny says, wiping her tears. "The poem was beautiful. Perfect, in fact." She stands up and smooths her skirt before pulling a book from the bookshelf. "You can't read my novel because I didn't write one. I wrote a memoir. About my hard, sweet, beautiful life."

Her words echo the last lines of the poem, and suddenly I understand. "That must have been so hard. I know how difficult thinking of your old lives can be," I say, even though it doesn't feel like enough.

Sunny runs her thumb over the leather book cover. "I had rushed to finish it when I thought we might stop time, but I've been going through it more thoughtfully now. Revising. Revisiting. It brings back so many memories . . ."

"I told her not to," Kiyo says, folding her arms across her chest. "What good does dredging up the past do?"

"I think it does some good, actually," Sunny says, looking at me. Her eyes fall to the book in her hand. "Perhaps it would do more good to share what I've written."

"I'd love to hear it," I say encouragingly. "And you might feel lighter if you have us to help carry the weight of it all."

Sunny takes a seat and looks to Kiyo, communicating in their silent shared language. Sunny opens the book.

"I'm sure you know it by heart now, Abe, the story of how I came to Amaranth. You've heard it a dozen times."

"Sure," Abe says. "Your brother found you wearing women's clothes, and you ran toward Harlem. You got caught in a storm and dreamed of Amaranth until it wasn't a dream."

"That's right," she says, "but that's only half of the story." She finds the page she wants. She takes one more deep breath. And she begins.

## SUNSHINE (SUNNY) RUFFIN

1911–

Sunny left her family house in Philadelphia with only the clothes on her back—most notably, her mother's treasured wedding pearls—a handful of coins she grabbed from the kitchen money jar, and her precious doll, who she'd named Ruthie. She felt ashamed and ridiculous, holding the toy, walking through the streets of the city in a silk dress, full makeup, and the hand-me-down men's shoes she hastily threw on as she scrambled out the door.

*Who will take me in?* she thought. She couldn't think of a soul who wouldn't take one look at her and throw her right back out again. *Where can I go?*

Her next thought was, of course, Harlem. A place for fairies and sinners. *A place for people like me*. She would have to find Florence, somehow. How big could Harlem be? She would have to tell her everything that happened. Maybe she would let Sunny stay for a bit, just until she could save enough money for her own place. She'd help around the house. She'd cook and clean and run errands. She'd earn her keep.

And she'd dress like a man, out in the world, and find a job. She hated the thought of it, but she'd been doing it for so long anyway, and what choice did she have? She repeated the word in her mind like a prayer: *Harlem, Harlem, Harlem,* as she wandered in the direction of Broad Street Station.

Women hurried their children past her as she walked. One man spat at her feet, and another hit her on the behind and called her a word that cut her into pieces. She hugged Ruthie tighter, put her head down, and walked faster, and only when she reached the station did she finally exhale. A huge clock tower loomed above her, big as the sun. Everything about the building, actually, was enormous, with its stone face and its high-vaulted ceilings. The intricate iron work and big glass windows. She caught her reflection in the glass of the doors, and couldn't help but think how haggard she felt. Her heels were chapped. Her mascara dripped down her cheeks. Had she been crying? Or just sweating? She didn't have the wherewithal to say.

She approached the ticket counter with the coins clinking in her shaking hands. The white attendants looked at her with contempt and the man in the booth leaned over to whisper something to his colleague.

"One ticket," she said as boldly as she could muster, in the highest voice she could manage, "from here to New York City."

"Twenty dollars," the man said. "Actually, for you? Let's make it thirty. And you ride in the Jim Crow car."

"Thirty dollars," she whispered with despair. She didn't know how much she had, but she knew it wouldn't even come close. "Gosh. I . . . I don't have that."

"You could trade your pearls," the man said, reaching out to touch them. "My wife would love 'em." She wanted to slap his hand away, but she knew better.

"Oh, anything but those. They were my mother's. You can have my shoes, here, see? They're real leather. I have this doll, too, it's vintage. Or . . . you can put me to work. Surely someone needs help around here?"

"I can think of one way she can earn her way," the colleague snickered (and of course did not say *she*) and fear rippled down Sunny's body. But the attendant in front of her just punched his friend in the arm and glared at her again.

"The pearls or you don't ride," he said.

She ran her fingers along each bead, considering. They were worth more than thirty dollars, that was certain. And again, they were her mother's. How she missed her—there were not words for how much. The pearls and the doll were all she had left.

But, again, what choice did she have? She unclasped the necklace. She slid it, as slowly as she could, across the counter. The man grabbed for it with his dirty fingernails, and Sunny felt it leave her hand, and goodness, the pain of it. It was like she had given away her heart.

But she got a ticket in return. She boarded her car, and took a seat far from the other passengers. The bench was wooden and uncomfortable, with almost no leg room at all. People looked at her as they passed her, muttered things to one another, until finally she covered her face with her hands and prayed they'd just leave her alone. Let her be.

When the train pulled out of the station, butterflies fluttered in her chest. She was really going to Harlem. She was really headed toward somewhere better, somewhere safer. She let herself dream of what it could look like: an apartment full of inverts. All of them masquerading through their days, coming home to themselves and each other at night. She pictured the dresses she would make. The hairstyles she would try. She thought about jazz salons and poetry readings, restaurants and speakeasies where she could dance the night away, her skirt twirling out, her hands in someone else's.

Because maybe—she barely let herself think it—someone would love her there.

Her dreams were cut short when, three stops later, two white men in uniforms boarded the car. Sunny's blood turned to ice. They headed straight for her, pushing a woman out of the way just to get to her. One man grabbed Sunny by the arm, pulled her to her feet with a grip so hard she knew it would leave bruises. She clung to Ruthie as they dragged her out of the train, onto a platform in a town she'd never heard of, and cuffed her.

Sunny wanted to fight. To scream. But she stayed silent. Her parents had taught her to never say anything to men like these, because they wouldn't hear her anyway.

"We had some complaints," one man said as he smirked, "about someone impersonating a female. Have you heard of the three article rule?"

Sunny nodded. She had, from Florence. It meant she was supposed to be wearing three items of men's clothing. Could her shoes count as two?

"Then you know we have to charge you for being a public nuisance."

"Now, we could just fine you," one of them whispered, "if you could pay up, right here right now." Sunny couldn't reach her coins, but it didn't matter. If it wasn't enough for a train ticket, it wouldn't be nearly enough to buy them off.

They threw her in the back of their car. They took her to a men's prison. They stole everything she owned, made her wash her face with brown water, and forced her to dress in a black-and-white striped jumpsuit. They booked her, pushed her into a crowded cell, and blew her a kiss before leaving her behind. They didn't tell her how long she'd have to be there, but she imagined the worst.

She didn't want to die there, in these ugly clothes, in this cage where the stench of neglect could knock you over. Every surface was cold to the touch, and the floor was crawling with rats. The men around her sobbed, yelled, and fought over bug-riddled food and dirty water and inches of space. Over everything and nothing at all. She tried to stay out of the way.

Sunny tucked herself in a corner and made herself as small as she could. She stayed there until her body ached, until she didn't know how long she'd been in there, only that she'd lost all sense of time. Was it night or day? Would she be in here forever? It was so unjust, inhumane, unfair—there really wasn't even a word for it. She was so close to freedom, and now . . .

"I don't want to die here," she whispered. When she closed her eyes, she saw her mother's face, more clearly than she had in years. She heard her voice say: *Don't let anyone take your light, Sunshine.*

This world was cruel. This place was hell. She was determined to survive it.

So she started to dream of escape. *An apartment in the city. No, a house. It would be a house somewhere beautiful. Maybe in a field with a glittering pond and a willow tree and evergreens as far as the eye can see. Stars at night. Bright, bright, bright.*

A crack of thunder ripped Sunny from her imaginings. It was so close it shook the concrete building, and within minutes, rain poured through the leaky ceiling in multiple places, splashing against the floor and soaking the inmates' clothes. The rats squealed as they scattered, and the men started shouting louder and louder as the water poured and pooled until they were standing in two inches of water.

*On the porch, there would be a friendly dog, tail wagging. Behind the dog, there would be a fire to warm her. And, oh, a closet the size of a bedroom, filled with clothes soft as butter. And pearls! She would have as many pearls as she could handle.*

Only inches away from her, a man stumbled by her, blood dripping down the side of his head. In seconds, it was everywhere, all over his shirt. He fell, and used her shoulder to catch himself, and soon, his blood was all over her too. All Sunny could see was red, red, red.

She shut her eyes as tightly as she could as the water filled her slippers. She dreamed of flowers. Red, red, red flowers. And when she opened her eyes . . .

# *storm*

"AMARANTH," SUNNY SAYS, PUTTING her book down. She pushes the sleeve of her gown up, and shows us her arm. "After all these years, the bruises they left are healing. Time. What a gift."

I turn to Abe, who looks as stricken as I feel.

I think about Lionel calling Amaranth a prison. Sunny's face falling. Kiyo, lunging for Lionel, ready to rip his throat out. At the time, I thought her fury had stemmed from her own hurt, her memories of imprisonment in the internment camp, but it was more than that. It was so much more than that.

I cross the room and almost bend down to hug Sunny, but she stands up to meet me. She takes me into her arms, and cries into my shirt, and Kiyo and Abe pile onto us, and I feel Dash's paws on my back.

"I'm so sorry," Abe says. "I never knew . . ."

Sunny pulls away from me to pat him on the head. "We're all entitled to our secrets, aren't we?"

He blushes, and opens his mouth like he's about to share his in return, but a loud boom sounds above us. The floor beneath us literally drops an inch, and we fall to the ground. The rush of rain crashes outside the window.

"What's happening?" I shout, as we all scramble to sit up, to reach for each other.

"A storm," Kiyo says. "New guests."

My stomach flips and ping-pongs around, bouncing from emotion to emotion. Fear and longing and jealousy and shock and hope. Could they stop time? Is this what we've been waiting for? The house shakes with another deafening boom.

"Are the storms always this violent?" I shout.

"Well, not *quite* this—" Sunny's drowned out by another crashing roar. The steady booming outside makes everything inside shiver even harder. It sounds and feels like every tree around the property is crashing to the ground, and when I rush to the window and throw the blinds open, I can see that I'm not that far off.

"Oh, but someone new!" Sunny says as she places her hands on my shoulders, hoping the same hope. But it's hard to feel optimistic when outside, the chickens are jumping around screaming bloody murder. The rooster is practically yodeling, and the goats are bleating along. Beside us, Dash is howling, and it sounds like the choir from hell. Uncertainty rises in me like a tide.

But . . . new guests. I'm weak with anticipation. Are they from 2026 too, only a few months later? Or has time warped further, sending us someone from decades down the line? I try to prep my questions for them: The classic, what year is it? And, is the United States still a country? And, what's going on with gender, anyway? And, have you ever heard of someone named Ramona Silva?

"We have to get ready!" Sunny claps.

We hang the welcome streamers and balloons—the same from my and Ramona's arrival. I can't help but remember how young I was then—though it wasn't really so long ago. I was so unsure, so confused. So terrified to say who I am, to lose Ramona. I've been here for what feels like so long. I've been Cal for what feels like so long. It's thrilling to think these guests will never know me as anyone else.

As the storm rages on, we bake a lopsided, melty pink sprinkle cake.

"Somewhere," I say, "Lionel is weeping."

We wait in what feels like an endless night, the storm lashing down around us, the temperature dropping. We huddle around the fireplace and Sunny reads us more of her memoir. This time she reads pages from the happier moments. Helping her mother pick out her Sunday church clothes. Philadelphia festivals. Her brothers pulling her in a wagon to buy candy at the nickel-and-dime store.

"Oh, and this was the first time I put on a dress. And I knew, I just *knew* I looked—"

Outside, there's a hiss, crack, and crash, as loud as an explosion. We all jump up, and turn to look out the window. A lightning-struck tree has crashed into the barn and set a corner of its roof on fire. Within seconds, the whole second level is engulfed in flames, and though I can *feel* all of us scream out in horror, the world goes quiet, muddled, drowned.

# *inferno*

I'M FROZEN TO THE couch, watching the barn burn. All sound comes rushing back at once, and I spin around to find Abe running out the door, Dash hot and hobbling on his heels. Kiyo's scrambling to find boots.

"The cows," Sunny says, and her hands cover her mouth.

"My art!" Kiyo's given up and is pulling on my boots, which I can only imagine are at least three sizes too big.

My brain is saying, *Cal, DO something,* but I can't move. Finally, Sunny drags me by the hand up to the closet so we can find shoes, too. And then we're back down the stairs, out the door, and the rain pummels me back into my body.

Yards ahead of us, Bert and Ernie run through the big barn door, and I stumble forward, weak with relief. But Kiyo and Abe keep running in and out of the barn, as the flames spread wider and higher. *Leave the art,* I want to scream. *Leave the portraits.* I'm fast across the field, but by the time I get to the fire, Kiyo and

Abe are nowhere to be found. Thick, black smoke puffs out of every window, every opening, and heat pulses around me.

"They've been in there too long," Sunny says, and I can't tell if it's rain or more tears streaming down her face.

"Abe!" I call out. "Kiyo!" When they don't answer, I take a deep breath, put my arm up to shield my nose and mouth, and I go in.

I fight my way across hay bales, an inferno screaming and raging in the rafters above me. I can barely see, but I make out the shape of the two of them and head toward them, the heat beginning to make my skin sting. When I'm close enough, I see why they're still here. A large panel of wood has fallen, trapping Dash in a corner of the barn.

He's too big to go under it, though he's spinning in circles, whining, trying. It's impossible for any of us to go over it because it's far too tall. I grab Abe by the back of his jacket and yank him away from the wall.

"Get out of here!" I yell. "I'll get him out! I promise!" I have no idea how, but I'll do it or die trying. I can see Abe start to protest, but he puts his hand on his stomach and nods. He presses his sweaty forehead quickly to mine, and yells, "I love you." I try to say it too but start coughing, and he's gone before I catch my breath.

Kiyo and I try to muscle the wood apart, but it doesn't budge at all. We try to kick it, and that doesn't help either.

"I have an idea," I call. "It's risky."

"Tell me."

"We set it on fire."

"We *what?*"

"It'll compromise the wood. It'll weaken it. But then we'll

have to move quickly. We'll only have a few seconds to try to break it down."

"Well, I don't have any other ideas," Kiyo says, already moving. She grabs a fallen beam glowing with embers. She runs back to me, and the two of us hold it against the panel until it catches, until it sparks. Flames shoot upward and sideways, a beautiful, horrible map of fiery rivulets. The wood starts to char and splinter.

"Stand back, Dash!" I call, as if he knows what that means. "On the count of three," I yell to Kiyo, and she nods once. We kick at the panel, and it budges. Only an inch but it's something. "Again!" We kick it harder, and it angles. And Dash has enough room to crawl under, and the three of us are out, running through smoke with our eyes closed as wood falls around us.

Outside, we gasp for breath and Kiyo and I throw ourselves onto the grass. Sunny is screaming for us, running to us, grabbing us both by the back of our shirts and pulling us farther away from the flames and smoke. Rain drenches us, cools us, cleans us. It does not put out the blaze.

I wipe at my eyes, and through the hot, acid tears that cloud them, I see Abe running from his shed to the barn, an axe in his hand. He slows when he sees us, folds into himself with relief, and starts to lower the axe to his side.

Then a hot, blue streak of light bursts above him. Lightning connects with the metal of the axe and Abe falls forward, crumpling into a ball on the ground. And for an instant the whole world falls away.

# *lightning strike*

FOR ONCE, I DON'T freeze. For once, I leap to action. I run to him and open his body so he's lying on his back. He's not breathing, and my heart is beating too hard to tell if his is beating at all. I do CPR—God bless Miss Stone's curriculum—as rain washes down my face and onto him.

I press his chest thirty times. And I breathe into him, two breaths, each a second long. Thirty compressions. Two breaths. Thirty. Two. Thirty. One—

Abe coughs, and starts to breathe, and I press my cheek to his chest just to hear his heart.

"Let's get him out of the storm," Sunny yells.

"Or should we throw him over the edge of the flowers?" Kiyo calls.

"He wouldn't want that," I say, and I'm confident it's true. Together, we all lift him up, carry him back to the house. He's only half conscious when we get him to the bedroom and help him sit up. I hold him against me, and stroke his hair, and say what I didn't get to say in the barn, as many times as I can: "I love you, Abe. I love you. I love you—"

I don't know if he can hear me, but I need him to know it. I never want him to forget it.

"Let's get him into dry clothes," Sunny says, entering the room with towels and more blankets and flannel. "He's shivering." I'm holding him so tightly I barely noticed, but she's right.

I try to change him alone, Sunny and Kiyo turned away to give Abe some privacy, but he can't sit up on his own, and I'm unable to wrestle his shirt off.

"I'm sorry," I say to him. Then to the others, "I need help, please."

"Abe, forgive us," Sunny says as she sits next to him on the bed, and Kiyo stands in front of him.

When his shirt comes off, we all gasp. I don't mean to, but I do.

"He's pregnant," Kiyo whispers.

"*Oh*," Sunny says.

Because, yes, it's visible now, but I've known that for some time. I gasped because on his right arm, where the lightning struck, there are bright scars. They're a hot red, fresh, and horrible. But they're beautiful, too. They look like feathers. They look like fern leaves.

And I know, without a shadow of a doubt, that I've seen them before.

# *thank god*

ONCE ABE IS STABLE, dressed, and propped up against me in the bed, he falls asleep. Dash is, too, at our feet. I don't sleep, of course. I just make sure Abe's still breathing. That his heart is still beating. I place my hand on his stomach and wait for a kick or movement or anything at all, and only when I feel the baby kick not once, but twice, do I dare to relax even a little.

We stay there like that for the rest of the night, until the storm finally quiets. Until Abe wakes, fully this time, and sits up on his own.

"Dash," he says frantically, but calms when he sees him. "Cal. What happened?"

"It's okay, you're okay. Lightning hit your axe."

"My God." His hands fly to his stomach too. "Oh, God. Are they . . . ?"

"Yes," I say quickly. "They've been moving. I keep checking."

"Okay. Okay, good."

My gaze shifts down, unable to meet his eyes. "Sunny and Kiyo know. They had to help me get you into dry clothes."

He exhales. "I see." He's quiet for a second. "It was probably time I told them anyway." He shifts and immediately winces. "Ow. *Ow.*"

"Abe," I say. "There's something else." I help him pull up his right sleeve, and peel back the bandage I'd wrapped carefully around his skin. His mouth gapes as his other hand traces the blistering skin.

"The man you met on the bus," he says eventually. "The one who saved your life."

I nod. "It's you. Or it will be."

I don't know how I expect him to react. To learn that we've met before; that we'll meet again. Another impossible thing. But I'm still surprised when Abe says, "I get old?" Then louder, "I get old!"

I can't help but laugh. "*Really* old."

There's tears in his eyes—happy ones—when he says, "I make it, Cal. I live. I fucking survive."

I put a hand to my chest in mock outrage, even as tears flood my vision too. "Did you just swear, Abe Turner? What does God think?"

He shrugs, then hugs me close, fresh wounds and all. "He thinks I needed a sign I'd be okay." He pulls back and takes my face in his hands. "And this is it."

# *the lavender room*

"IS THE PATIENT ACCEPTING visitors?"

Abe and I turn to see Sunny and Kiyo standing in the doorway. Abe throws open his arms and they both run to us, piling onto the bed in one big group hug.

As we hold each other, I'm crushed by memories of the night before. The barn is gone. Abe is hurt. Even Dash has a small patch of fur that's been singed to black. But everyone survived, and the storm is over.

"Have you met the new guests?" Abe asks as we all disentangle ourselves.

I whip around to face Sunny and Kiyo. I'd been so worried about Abe, I hadn't even thought to ask if anyone had finally shown up last night.

But Sunny and Kiyo just exchange a look.

"No one ever came," Kiyo says.

"But the storm . . ." I say.

"Odd, isn't it?" Sunny hugs a pillow to her chest.

We were hoping for a savior. We've been wishing. Asking. Praying. And nothing. The letdown is palpable, so I stand up and stretch.

"All right, well, more breakfast for us, then," I say, trying to lighten the mood. "Taking requests."

"Chocolate chip pancakes," Sunny says.

"What's that thing Ambrosia used to love?" Kiyo asks. "And Lionel used to hate?"

"Ah yes," Sunny says. "I'm forgetting the name, but it was a 1990s delicacy."

"Puppy . . ." Abe offers, and Kiyo shakes her head.

"Pop Tarts?" I smirk.

"Yes!" Kiyo shouts. "They're swell."

"I'll just have oatmeal," Abe says, and the girls look offended.

"Abraham," Sunny puts on her accent. "You're eating for two!"

"Okay, fine. Oatmeal and eggs."

"On it," I say, and head into the hallway.

But I don't even get to the stairs before I'm stopped in my tracks. Because there's a new door. To a new room. I stand there for a few beats just staring, scared, like something is going to burst out of it.

Finally, I find my voice. "Friends? There's something you need to see," I yell, and within seconds, all three of them crowd behind me.

"A new room?" Abe questions.

"There's never been anything new without *someone* new," Sunny says, awed but still keeping her distance.

"Go on, Cal," Kiyo says. "Open it."

"Me?! Why do I have to do it?" I ask.

"You found it," Kiyo says simply, and gives me a light shove forward.

I stumble but catch myself. Apprehensively, I reach for the knob. I pull it slowly, then quickly, and all I see is—

"*Purple*," Sunny gasps.

I step in, everyone right at my heels, and find it's almost more of a corridor than a room. It seems to go on and on and on. The walls, ceiling, floor, and furniture are all lavender, violet, orchid, and indigo.

"My favorite color," Sunny says, as she steps toward the dozens and dozens of desks that line the walls. Books are spread across them, and above each one, a portrait.

I read the inscription on the first one out loud. "Chaska, 1642–1650." On the desk, there are piles and piles of pages with loopy handwriting.

"Ernest Montague, 1888–1909," Abe says from where he's standing.

"Margaret Donahue, 1920–1929," I say, moving down the line. I pick up a piece of paper from the pile below Margaret's portrait. *Margaret Donahue proudly described herself as a suffragette, though her father often begged her not to get wrapped up in such frivolities. If only he knew, for Margaret, the real appeal of the meetings in Worcester, was the outspoken, fire-hearted, beautiful Elizabeth Shore.*

"Wait. Are these—?"

We all realize it at once. "—other houseguests?"

"No," Sunny whispers. She runs her fingers along a golden portrait frame. "No, no, no. This can't be. I was the first. I dreamed this into being, all this. I took something terrible and made something beautiful. I thought—" Sunny's voice cracks. "I'm such a fool."

"You're not a fool," Kiyo says, putting her arm around her. "You're the one who made this a home. For all of us. You *did* make something beautiful."

"Amaranth appeared to you when you needed it the most," I say to Sunny, echoing what she told me on my first day. "It brought you here for a reason. It called you home."

Sunny's eyes shine with tears. "It's just . . . no one else was here when I got here. No one else was here except—"

"Dash," Abe says, walking all the way down the hall to not just one, but dozens of portraits of Dash. "It says, Dash, and then there's just a, well, a dash." He laughs. "He's been here forever. Wait—come look."

Sunny loops her arms through mine and Kiyo's and we go together. All of Kiyo's portraits hang, framed, over the desks where Abe is standing.

"I thought these were lost in the fire," Kiyo says. "But they're here. Restored like magic."

There are people I never met, but then there are those I have: Ramona Silva, 2026–2026. Lionel Toussaint, 1998–2026. Ambrosia, 1998–2026. And on the looseleaf pages, their stories. In penmanship that could belong to a toddler. Handwriting that left teachers frustrated my whole life.

"Why is this in my handwriting?" I ask.

"Great question," Kiyo says. "It's really not good."

Sunny skims the pages with a hand on her heart. Then she looks up and smiles at me. "Because you're a keeper."

"Like . . . in field hockey?"

"Well, yes," she says, and laughs. "But you've been keeping

our stories too. You encouraged us to remember, to talk about our lives. I suppose this is Amaranth's way of giving you credit, because you deserve it."

"It's that face of yours," Kiyo adds. "Those big buck eyes."

"Do bucks even have big eyes?" I say.

She throws her hands up in the air. "Just trying not to doe you. But you are a good listener. You make people feel safe."

"Amaranth is what makes us feel safe, I mean—"

"You do too, Cal," Abe cuts in. "I kept my secret for decades. But when you showed up, I knew I could trust you with it."

"And you think I tell everyone my storied past on day one? Hell no," Kiyo says.

"You have a gift," Sunny says, squeezing my arm.

I shake my head. "I really didn't do anything special."

"*This*"—Sunny picks up the pile of looseleaf pages from Ramona's desk—"is special. If we ever leave here, our stories—our lives—will be preserved forever. Amaranth gave you time, but you made us timeless."

Tears well in my eyes. "If that's true," I say, "it's only because you made me feel like I'm home for the first time in my whole life. At Amaranth, obviously, but in myself too. You all opened doors inside me I didn't even know existed."

"Kinda like this room," Kiyo says, running her hand gently over one of the portraits. "But why now? Why did Amaranth open this door now?"

As if in response, Dash barks from the back of the room.

Along the wall are four empty desks. There are no portraits hanging above them yet, but there are nails and gold brackets where they'll go someday. And there, etched on golden plaques, are our names and the year we entered followed by a dash and then—nothing. Nothing yet. There are no thick piles of paper on our desks like there are on the others. There is only a card on each table, our names printed on top.

Sunny reaches for hers. "What do you think these are?"

She opens it, and her expression shifts to confusion. Abe, Kiyo, and I reach for ours, too. Inside, I find two words in handwriting I don't recognize. There are only two words: *It's time.*

Abe tilts his letter to show me. "Even I can read this." Kiyo and Sunny hold theirs up too. They all say the same thing.

"This isn't Cal's handwriting, that's for sure," Kiyo says. "Is it a message from . . . Amaranth?"

"It's not just a message," Sunny says. "It's an eviction notice."

We're stunned into silence for a moment as we read the two words over and over again.

"It's time," Abe says, breaking the silence. "For me, at least. The baby's alive, but what if they're hurt? I need a doctor." He looks to me, eyes shimmering. "I don't want to leave you. I don't want to leave any of you. But . . ."

"It's time," I echo. But all I can think is: *It wasn't enough time,* and, *Amaranth was supposed to be forever*, and, *How can I leave now? How can I leave ever?* and *How can I go back to my old life? The old me in a dress, at prom, at Miss Stone's?*

I walk toward the portrait of Ramona, and in the instant before I reach her, I catch my reflection in the glass of the frame. And I feel it all over again—the thrill of self-recognition. Of looking in the mirror and not wanting to disappear. I run my hands through my hair, then put one palm on my sternum. I feel the beat of my heart, and it's the same heart, but I am a new person. Things grow here, now. I roll my wrist. Things heal.

When I came to Amaranth, all I wanted was more time to

figure out my future. To figure out myself. But maybe it wasn't more time that I needed. It was more confidence, trust, and questioning. It was more mistakes, and risks, and mourning, because in one sense, I lost everything. But I gained clarity, too, even if my answers are mostly questions. I built an honest friendship with Ramona where we can both be our full selves. I found new love with Abe. I gained support and acceptance and perspective.

And hell, I even learned to cook. Sort of.

"Cal? What are you thinking?" Abe asks.

I turn to him. Step to him. Take in his handsome face, his freckles, his soft smile.

"I'm thinking," I say slowly, "that Amaranth has been paradise. That you have all changed me completely. But it's time for me, too."

Abe nods, and takes a deep, shuddering breath. "I wish we could have had forever," he whispers.

"Me too," I say, "but it's because of you that I got more time at all."

There's no world where we will be together again, but because of Abe, I made it this far. And I think I have what I need now to make it on my own.

"It's strange," Sunny says, walking back and forth around the corridor. "If you'd asked me just this morning if I would ever leave, could ever leave, I'd have said no. How could I? I'd rather die here than go back to that prison, to that moment."

"Sunny—" Kiyo begins, eyes panicked.

"But," Sunny continues. "I've always trusted Amaranth has the best intentions for us. I've always believed it wants to keep us safe. To give us just what we need the most, when we need it most. I must say, I trust it still. I believe it still."

"So what are you saying?" Kiyo asks, voice already cracking.

Sunny sighs. "I'm saying I don't think that was a welcome storm at all. I think Amaranth meant it as a goodbye, and what if that means it's for the best? For all of us?" Kiyo and Abe are quiet, so Sunny turns to me. "Cal? What do you think? Time was your gift, after all."

What a question. Because the truth is, even if we were from the same time, Sunny will face things I'll never have to. I could ruin her life with my answer. But I know by now the best thing to do is to tell the truth, even if it's hard.

"I would never tell you to go back," I say. "I can't imagine the suffering, and I'm so sorry you've had to endure it. But for what it's worth, I do think the world outside here desperately needs people like you in it."

"People like us," she says. For a few minutes, she's quiet. Solemn. Considering. Then she breaks into a bittersweet smile, her eyes glittering with tears as she takes Kiyo's hands in hers. "It's time for other writers. Other artists. Other houseguests. It's time for other kids who need it more. Oh, darling? What do you think?"

I expect Kiyo to protest, but instead she pulls Sunny in for a kiss. Then with only love she says, "You trust Amaranth, Sunny. And I trust you."

Sunny puts her hand on Kiyo's cheek. "We'll find each other in another time, my love."

"I know we will," she says. "And before that, I'll go back to California. I never did say goodbye to my parents. I never actually wanted to."

"You should probably check on Marion too," Sunny says.

Kiyo opens her mouth to protest, but Sunny cuts her off. "Don't fret. I'm not the jealous type."

Kiyo looks at the floor but nods.

After a moment of silence, Abe asks, "Do you think there are other Amaranths?"

"There must be," Sunny says, "because, well, we're everywhere. Every time, every place. I'd bet there are magical havens hidden all over the world."

"But none quite like this," Kiyo says, kneeling down to pet Dash.

"No, we were a once-in-many-lifetimes thing," Sunny says as she joins her.

"A once-in-forever thing," I say, and lock eyes with Abe. "A should-be-impossible thing." He gives me a small smile as I close the space between us and slip my arm around his shoulders. He leans into me, hand on my back, head near my heart.

"You know," he says, "where I come from, they call that a miracle."

Sunny looks up and past us, through the still-open door that leads to the hallway, to the house she dreamed of, to the worlds that wait beyond it. "And I'll call us that too," she says, voice steady, eyes bright with wonder, "wherever I'm going next."

# *leaving*

WE THROW ONE MORE party. We dress in the best clothes the house has to offer. Sunny tailors our suits to perfection, and drapes herself in pearls.

"Now that is one attractive man," Sunny says, as she helps Abe pull his coat on.

"And one good-looking family," Kiyo says, as we all pose in the mirror together.

"Family?" I tease. She ruffles my hair. To my shock, she kisses my cheek.

Sunny drapes her arms around us. "What is family if not the people who help you survive the world, love yourself, and when it's time . . . let go?"

I straighten my tie in the mirror and take myself in. I'm handsome and sturdy. I'm masculine and strong. I'm soft, and girlish, and maybe I'm not how I dreamed still, but I'm close. And what's more: I'm home. This body I've hated so much and for so long brought me here. I know now it'll bring me anywhere.

We set up a picnic at the edge of the amaranth field and eat the cake we made for the guests who never came. We sit on the edge of this world and take it all in like astronauts looking homeward. The soft autumn sun lights the field of feathery, bloodred flowers, the weatherworn house with a door that same bright, unforgettable color. Every window dark now. The pond, the weeping willow tree, the charred and ruined barn, with all its buried treasure.

Our cake eaten, we say our goodbyes to the cows, chickens, and goats, but when we open their gates, they wander to the edge with us. They want to follow us home.

All except Dash, who lingers closer to the house. Who seems to understand. Who has done this again and again, and will be waiting for the next guests who need him, in his timeless, forever home. He licks my face when I bend down to scratch his ears.

"Thanks for being the best boy," I whisper to him.

Then I say goodbye to Kiyo. "I'll see you soon," I say.

"You seem pretty confident I'll still be alive in 2026."

"You will be. You're going to live forever purely out of spite."

She puts her hand on her chest. "You know me so well."

"I know. So, I'll see you soon."

"I'll be a geezer," she says, "and you'll be a fetus. But yes, Cal. I'll see you soon."

Next, I hold Sunny long and hard. I say, "Thank you, thank you, thank you," until she yells, "Stop, stop, stop, stop, stop."

"Thank you for your gift," she says, holding my hands in hers. "I thought it was a mistake at first, of course. I thought it was terrible but . . . oh. Now I wonder. What will the rest of my days bring?"

Finally, Abe and I stand face-to-face. It's the hardest thing, and the best.

"I love you," I tell him one more time.

"I'll see you again," he says, "when I'm old and gray."

"And really good at crossword puzzles."

"You know," he says, blushing. "I used to wonder, when I just had a silly little crush, what could Cal and I be together? If you weren't with Ramona. If you stayed. If only we had time. If only . . ."

"Now you know," I say, brushing the hair out of his eyes. "You'll save my life."

"And you've saved mine," he says. He breaks out into a teary smile. "We fucking make it, Cal."

"We fucking make it, Abe."

He hugs me and I don't want to let go. But I do. I kiss Abe one more time. I hold his hand and give it an extra squeeze when he takes one last look at Dash and turns back with tears running down his face. We stand beside Kiyo and Sunny, who takes my free hand in hers, and the four of us line up at the edge.

"Together?" Sunny asks.

My heart thrums in my chest. I hold my breath. I look back one more time.

And we step forward.

# 2026

AND JUST LIKE THAT, I'm back in the woods, barefoot, long haired, in my borrowed, tattered prom dress. The rain has stopped, and Ramona is in front of me soaked to the bone, and it's like we never left at all. A total reset. Except my wrist doesn't hurt anymore. Except I still have the white line on my thumb where I nicked it with a kitchen knife, and the divot in my cheek from the shard of Kiyo's broken glass. The healing stuck. But so did the scars.

"Did we—?" I start.

"How long were you—?" she gasps.

I was gone for an instant and for so long. And it's like it doesn't matter. We hug each other and don't let go. We hold on for dear life.

"We're not old!" I laugh.

"We're not dead!" she cries.

"And we didn't lose time. At least I don't think so?"

Ramona pulls away and looks me up and down. "Oh, Cal. You look so weird in that dress."

We burst out laughing. When our giggles die off, I turn to look down the path, past the flowers, to the bend where Amaranth sat. But there is no more path, no more flowers, no more house. There is only a wall of trees. And my relief at being back with Ramona unchanged, unscathed, is washed away by a horrible, gaping sadness.

"It's gone," I say. "They're gone."

She clutches my arm, and I put my hand on hers. With my other, I go to reach for my phone. I want to know that they all made it, I want to google our friends, our family. Abe. But I remember it's in Ramona's purse back at the country club. At prom. Prom. Wow. Damn. A million years ago. In another life. This life.

Maybe it's for the best that we have to limp back together, quietly grateful for each other and what we went through, still reeling and unmoored. We have time to remember. It was real, it was real, it was real.

"Remember the time Lionel made the pineapple upside-down cake upside down?"

"And oh my God, how are we going to go through life without Sunny's smile?"

Sunny, who is almost definitely dead, here, now. Unless she's 115 years old, which seems unlikely, but more impossible things have happened. We're proof of that.

When the lamplights of the country club appear on the horizon, like lightning bugs and nothing like them at all, we stop in the middle of the woods.

"You ready?" I ask.

"No," Ramona says. "I think this will be hard—I *know* it will be hard." She takes my hand then. "But just know, whoever you are, I love you. You're my best friend. And that will never change."

"You're mine too," I say.

"No one is going to believe us," she says, and laughs hysterically at the new night sky.

"But we know," I say. Thank God we both know.

Perhaps we've lost all sense of Miss Stone's decorum, because when we make our way back, hand in hand, we walk right in with our shoes off.

"Ew, why are you all wet?" a random girl asks us.

Ramona yells, "Mind your own business, princess."

We burst into the ballroom where people are dancing, and beeline to our table where our friends are sitting.

"Calla, you okay?" MK asks. "Did you . . . was it raining?"

"You were gone for, like, half an hour," Minali says.

Ramona and I look at each other and start laughing hysterically again. We laugh so hard my stomach hurts, and all the girls stare at us with twisted expressions.

"What the fuck is going on?" Lyndsey asks, half a cupcake still in her mouth.

"A few things," Ramona says, and collects herself. Leans on the chair to breathe. "For starters, we broke up."

"Oh my God, what?" Minali cries, and grabs on to Lyndsey's shoulders.

"Shit, I'm sorry," Cho-Hee groans.

"It's okay," Ramona says, shooting me a smile. "It's great, even."

"Also, I'm not going to Alcott next year," I say.

“Me neither!” Ramona says, and throws imaginary flowers in the air.

“Also . . .” I take a deep breath. It’s scary, doing this in the real world, but I don’t actually feel all that scared. I feel ready. “My name is Cal. And I use they/them pronouns. And I’m trans, and I don’t really know what that means yet but I’m just, like, excited about it.”

“Bro, what?” Lyndsey says, practically knocking her chair over to stand up, circle the table, and slap me on the back. “Yes! I’m so happy for you, dude.”

“I’m . . . so confused,” MK says. “You were only gone for thirty minutes. And you broke up, came out, made up, and changed your whole plans for the future?”

“Pretty much, yeah,” Ramona says. She reaches for her purse draped on the back of her chair. “And now if you’ll excuse us, we need a few minutes alone.”

# *in memory of*

WE SIT ON THE floor of an empty conference room and lean into each other. We both take our phones out, but my hand shakes too hard to open my lock screen.

"Let's read everything together, okay?" Ramona says.

"Yeah," I say. My voice comes out small. I don't want to know, but I do. I have to. We should learn what happened together.

We look up Sunny first, and find her obituary in the *BLACKlines* digital archive.

SUNSHINE "SUNNY" RUFFIN (1911–2003)

Sunshine "Sunny" Ruffin, beloved educator, writer, and lifelong advocate for LGBTQ+ youth, passed peacefully in Chicago, surrounded by people who loved her. She was 92.

Born to George and Ruth Ruffin in Philadelphia, Sunny was bubbly and bright from the very beginning. In a cruel act of injustice, Sunny was imprisoned for two weeks in 1929. But as always, she turned something terrible into something beautiful. During that time, she took it upon herself to teach other inmates to read. As fate would have it, one of them sang her praises to a friend, a very wealthy man in Chicago. He employed Sunny as a tutor for his twelve children all through the Great Depression, and she continued her career as a teacher for 35 years before founding Sunny's Place for homeless and at-risk LGBTQ+ youth.

She loved fashion, fearless dreams, and family. She wrote three novels and an autobiography, which were never published but well read and well loved by her partner, Kiyo Tamura. She's survived by Tamura; her dearest chosen ones, Abe Turner, Lionel Toussaint, Ambrosia; and the many, many others who loved her. Whose lives were changed by her. And, somewhere, a dog named Dash.

Even though I expected it, I'm still leveled by sadness. She was just there, right next to me. She was just hugging me goodbye, and holding my hand, and telling me everything would be okay. Now she's gone. I can't call her. I will never talk to her again. It feels . . . impossible. And yet. Everything about Sunny Ruffin has always been impossible. That was always the magic of her.

"I can't find an obituary for Kiyo," Ramona says with a sniff, "though there's a ton of stuff about her art, landscapes and portraits and mosaics all made from upcycled, repurposed materials. Wow. She's huge in Japan, and in California, but she had a gallery in Chicago for many years, too." Hope pops in my chest. Could she still be alive? Could the rest of them? But she gasps, and puts her hand on her cheek, voice breaking. "Oh, Ambrosia."

> AMBROSIA (1979–2020)
>
> This perfect, angelic, starling diva lived a life I will never forget.

"All right, well, I think we know who wrote her obituary." Ramona laughs through her tears, and I rest my head on hers.

> If you think she needed a last name, then you are foolishly, desperately mistaken. She had the voice of an angel, and though she struggled through the first chapters of her life, she found herself when she found her name—Ambrosia. Girl of the Gods. Girl of forever. She found herself when she found her voice, and made music none of you even deserve to hear.
>
> She will be remembered as a fierce friend, dedicated AIDS activist, and leader in both ACT UP and the Lesbian Avengers (though even from the grave, she'd like to remind you she's bi, okay, don't you get it twisted). She was fashionable and gorgeous and raw.
>
> She changed the lives of the many she cared for, the many who loved her, and the people who will

never forget her. Not ever. And yes, for anyone in the future asking, she went to Lilith Fair. Thrice.

Ambrosia succumbed to complications from AIDS and COVID-19 at the age of 41 in Chicago, Illinois. In a final letter, she wrote, "It took me a long time to learn to love this world. But I did. How grateful I am to be so sad to leave it." She is survived by her partner, June Michaelson, the Toussaint twins, the Turners, and Kiyo Tamura. And, somewhere, a dog named Dash."

We cry harder.

"Kiyo!" I say, hoping again. "And the Turners . . ."

I type in Abe's name, hold my breath. But I find it there. In the *IndyStar*.

ABE TURNER (1941–2021)

It's a punch to the gut, making me double over and lose my breath completely. Ramona rubs my shoulders as she reads silently.

2021. He's been gone for five years. It's so final. It feels so wrong. "I can't read it," I whisper. "I can't." Ramona reaches over to hold my hand.

"I know you don't want to, Cal," she says, "but I really think you should hear this. It's short."

"Just tell me this. Was he happy? Was he loved?" Please, please, please, I pray to anyone.

Ramona reads out loud.

Abe Turner worked in animal medicine across Illinois and, in his final years, Indiana. He is survived by his wife of fifty-five years, Lillian Turner, as well as their two children, two sons-in-law, three grandchildren, and beloved friends.

Ramona and I say the last line out loud together. "And, somewhere, a dog named Dash."

"But Indiana?" she says, turning to me. "Maybe you ran into him and didn't even know it."

I realize I haven't told her. Not about the man and the bus. Not about Abe and the lightning. I'm about to, but a voice from the edge of the room interrupts us.

"Calla? Ramona? Are you all right?" Ms. Sinclair, our head of school, stands in the doorway, a stranger in a suit beside her.

"Yes," I say, though she still looks alarmed by our appearance.

"This is the manager of the club. There's a phone call for . . . both of you?"

He holds up their wireless landline phone. "Someone named Lionel Toussaint?"

We look at each other in disbelief.

"Yes," Ramona says, and we scramble up and to the phone. Ramona takes it, puts it on speakerphone, and holds it up between us as Ms. Sinclair and the country club worker politely fade away.

"Lionel!" we say at the same.

"Hello, cupcakes." His voice is deeper, older, but still warm. Still bright. "I've been waiting for this night for so long."

# *family*

LIONEL COMES INTO TOWN to visit us. Ramona and I sign ourselves out of our dorms and wait nervously at the edge of campus, holding hands. Right on time, a red car pulls up to us and the person inside rolls the window down.

"Don't tell me you lovers are back together." Lionel's older. His hair is salt-and-pepper handsome, and he's wearing very hip glasses. His face looks sun-kissed and his eyes sparkle. He puts the car in park, gets out in the middle of the road, and runs up to pull Ramona into a hug.

"Not back together," Ramona says into his chest. "Just nervous."

"Sharp jacket," Lionel says before crushing me to him next. He smells amazing. "A family heirloom, right?"

I smile so big my cheeks hurt. I show off the jacket Abe lent me on the bus all those years ago, the one he wouldn't let me give back. Navy with black details, just like my Amaranth tux. And a detail I never noticed before Amaranth but is now my favorite part: one black pearly button sewed onto the sleeve.

"I had to tell them it was a little weird to sleep in it in the middle of June," Ramona teases.

"Anyway," I say loudly. "Forty-seven looks good on you, Lionel. What are we doing for your fiftieth?"

"Don't remind me," he says, and locks eyes with me. "I'm kidding. Every year, all this time. What a gift."

Lionel takes us out to the fanciest restaurant in town, Oak & Orchid, a place we've only been with our parents or other people's parents.

"My partner's joining us," he says, "but something tells me you won't mind."

"Of course we don't," Ramona says.

"Yeah, we can't wait to meet him."

We order a bunch of appetizers to share—luxury of luxuries—and Lionel side-eyes the Mexican-Thai fusion spring rolls.

"I could do this better," he whispers, and winks at us, and even though they're kinda delicious, after a few bites I have to agree. As we eat, he gets us caught up on everything.

"When Ambrosia and I got back to 1998, Kiyo, Sunny, and the Turners tried to get us into a HAART program right away. It took us a while, though, and Ambrosia really struggled. It wasn't like it was at Amaranth. She was angry with me for a long time about how everything went down at Amaranth." He says he stayed in New York while she followed the others to Illinois.

"We spent twelve whole years apart, but then she met her partner, June, and that woman made our Ambrosia as soft as an angel food cake, and we made up. And thank God, because in the end . . . well. In the end she was the one who did the leaving."

Ramona gets up to hug him for a good few minutes, until the server comes to take our order.

"Anyway," he says, dabbing at his eyes. "I eventually moved to Chicago too, to help with Sunny's Place, which I now run with Roseline. Let me tell you, those kids eat *good*."

"Roseline!" I say. "How did it go when you told her everything?"

He grins and leans forward. "I said, Rosie, I'm gay. And I got scared for a minute because she just froze. Then she said, 'You can't be gay. *I'm* gay!' "

"No way!"

"Hand to God. My HIV status was a tougher conversation, but she really stepped up for me. My whole family did. My mom is a nurse, as you know, so she helped us get in touch with all the right people."

"And you're in Chicago now?"

"Yep. I live in Andersonville, only a few blocks away from Kiyo's assisted care home. She's ninety-six! Can you believe it? She has dementia—started as soon as Sunny passed, almost like she couldn't bear to remember she was gone—but she still paints. And she's so damn *friendly* now. She has so many friends in that home, you wouldn't believe it. Ambrosia spent the last year of her life there, too."

"And what about this partner of yours?" Ramona asks, raising her eyebrows. Lionel's face breaks out into a huge smile as he looks beyond us and stands up to pull the fourth chair out.

"Speak of the devil," he says, and we turn to see a man with sandy brown hair, deep smile lines, and freckles all across his round cheeks. He looks a few years older than Lionel. He's handsome, dressed in a sharp-looking coat, cool glasses. He looks like—

But it couldn't be—

"Dashiell," he says, extending his hand for me to shake it.

"You . . . you're . . . are you—?" I stammer.

"Named after a dog?" He winks. "Absolutely."

"Could be worse," Lionel says. "His older sister's named after a goat."

# *memory*

IT FEELS SURREAL, SO surreal, to sit across the table from Abe's son, only weeks after I kissed Abe goodbye. I can still feel his skin on my skin. I still catch the scent of him sometimes and turn around, expecting to see him. But he's never there. He never will be. It wrecks me every time.

Dashiell tells me about Abe's life—how he gave birth to Sylvia in 1960. How he became a single parent and concocted a story about the child's mother dying during childbirth.

"The hospital stay was a bit awkward, but after that, people didn't really question it," he says. "I once asked him if he worried about the karma of telling such a story, and he said, 'I've already been struck by lightning. What else they got?' "

"Of course, Sunny and Kiyo helped, along with the rest of the family they'd built by then," Lionel says.

"And when my sister was older, he went back to school. I'm talking, like, elementary school for adults. But he worked his way through it all. He became a large animal vet and moved to a more rural part of Illinois."

"Because he liked his space and quiet," I say.

"Exactly. He met my mother, Lillian, on one of the farms, and then they had me."

"And she loved him? And he was happy?" I ask, my mouth dry.

"So much. They were the happiest. Really puts us to shame, huh, Lionel?" Lionel hits him with a napkin, but nods.

"Good," I say. "Good." But it makes me miss him so intensely. I don't even try to fight the tears of it; I just let them fall while he tells me more, and Ramona holds my hand under the table.

"I wish he were still here," I say. I feel it in every cell of my body. He'll never get to see my life, my future, or who I become. When we were together, I was only potential and ideas and wishes. And Abe Turner loved me anyway.

"Me too. He was the best dad. The best man," Dashiell says, choking up. "God, is someone cutting onions in here?"

"Hopefully not Cal," Lionel says, tossing a truffle fry at me.

"Hey!" I protest, snatching the fry out of the air and taking a bite. "I've come a long way, thanks to you."

"I'm sure you have, sugar," Lionel says with a smile. "So, what's next for you? You're still so young, you two! You still have so much time."

"I deferred Alcott for a year," Ramona says. "Just to keep it as an option. But I want to spend more time on my music and consider other colleges."

"We contacted all the people who donated to my college fund," I say. "We told them I'd had a change of heart. I said I'm trans, and no longer want to play field hockey at an all-women's school, and said if they wanted to take their money back, I understood. But if they didn't, I'd use it for housing while I figure everything out, and, um, maybe top surgery? I made an appointment for a consultation."

"Top surgery!" Lionel raises his water glass to cheers, and Dashiell and Ramona join him. I clink my glass against theirs, and I must be blushing, because Lionel ruffles my hair.

"Anyway," Ramona says, "guess how many people pulled their money?"

"I'm scared to ask," Lionel says.

"ZERO! Absolutely no one. Isn't that incredible?"

"Damn straight. It's what you deserve, muffin."

"And what's more," I said, blushing again, "once word got out, I started getting emails from alumni who had come out as trans later in life. And from current students who were questioning, and too scared to tell anyone. It's been nice to hear other people's stories."

"That's my Cal," Lionel says, beaming. "Sunny would be so proud."

"Dad would be too," Dashiell says.

"Thank you," I say, my voice barely steady.

"Lord," Lionel says, wiping at his face again.

"So where will you two live during your gap year?" Dashiell asks. "What will you do?"

"I'm going to live with my parents in Miami while I intern with Equality Florida. Actually, I'm going to work on their HIV advocacy project," Ramona says.

"Right on," Lionel says, through a full sob, but he's smiling too. Dashiell gives him his napkin.

"And I'm going to record our album again," Ramona adds. "Don't worry, Ambrosia will have full writing credit. I'm going to make her famous if it's the last thing I do. And then next year I'll reapply to the schools I actually want to go to."

Lionel gestures at me, but can't even speak now, so Dashiell speaks for him. "And you, Cal?"

"I'm going to live with the Silvas until I find a job and my own place. I'm not sure what I'll do next, but I'm grateful to have a minute to figure that out."

"Well, no pressure," Lionel says, having collected himself. "I know we're still sort of strangers, weirdly, but Dashiell and I have an extra room at our place and we'd love to have you."

Dashiell nods so sincerely. "We would," he says. "Absolutely. If it sweetens the deal, our condo is basically a Kiyo Tamura museum."

"Chicago," I say, reeling. A place I've never been. A place where no one knows me. A place I could become someone new. All over again.

"And it pays modestly, but we could use some help at Sunny's Place," Lionel says.

Ramona and I look at each other. "You should go, Cal," she says, bumping my knee with hers under the table.

"Soooo what do you think?" Lionel asks expectantly.

I think it's hard not to feel like a burden. I think it's hard to feel like they actually want me there. But I know by now that I'm worthy of kindness. Good things. Love.

"Okay," I say, smiling. "Okay. Count me in."

# *lake michigan, two months later*

SUMMER IN CHICAGO IS hot and busy and sparkling, and I feel bigger than I could have ever imagined. Ramona's coming to visit soon, and I can't wait to show her my room at Lionel and Dashiell's. It's small, but filled with books and pillows and pictures of people I love. And someone I love, too.

I built a little flight of stairs so Nugget can climb up on my bed—because, yes, I drove to Bakersville and took her when my parents were out. They'd changed the locks, but just as I'd hoped, they left the garage code the same (Nugget's birthday. Honestly.). She fits in perfectly, sprawled out on my bed, her little chest rising and falling peacefully in pools of morning light.

All around us, the walls are decorated with Kiyo's original art, and I framed the letters Lionel left on my bed my first morning. Ambrosia's says, *Thanks for letting me steal your girl, xoxo.* Sunny's is signed, *You were the gift, love.*

And in Abe's letter, in confident, blocky handwriting, he

wrote (among so many other things): *Even when I'm gone, I know you'll find me.*

And I do find him everywhere. I find him in my work at Sunny's Place, where I help Lionel coordinate treatment for kids, run community programming, and interview elders for our queer history archive. I think of him when I dream of expanding it someday, to Indiana, where kids like me could use a place to call home. I think of him when I write they/he on my nametag at the trans support group I go to twice a month at The Center on Halsted. I think of him when I ask a girl from the group out on a date and she says yes. And most of all, I find him in every animal I see, and when I stop to pet them, I feel his gentle hand in mine. Abe Turner. One of my greatest loves. I will always, always miss him.

Most mornings, I cook breakfast with Lionel, and then we go with Dashiell to visit Kiyo. We pick up small canvas-wrapped bouquets of wildflowers from a shop along the way. I touch my fingers to the framed photo of her and Ambrosia in the home, both using wheelchairs, holding hands. Both smiling. The nurses sometimes catch me staring.

"They were an odd pair," one says, "but thick as thieves."

There are photos, too, of Marion, who became a lifelong friend. Of Sunny, Abe, Lionel, and so many other people whose stories I will never know. Kiyo was so loved for so long, and still is. We check her out of her home and I push her wheelchair down the sidewalks, past tall, blue-glass buildings that are becoming more and more familiar. Most days Kiyo doesn't remember who we are, but she lights up and claps along when I play her Ramona and Ambrosia's music, and she's always happy to come with us. She always turns her face up to the sun.

"Are we going to the lake? Oh, my, yes," she says every day like it's the first time, and when we get there, we all take our shoes and socks off and help her wade into the sky-blue water. The sun puts on a spectacular show and I think: All this is impossible. All this is strange and precious and impossible. I disappeared. I started over. And I found myself, and I'll keep finding myself, in all this perpetual searching.

And so, one morning when Kiyo tugs on my arm, her eyes clear with recognition, and says, "Cal Quick, after all this time, there you are," I smile and kiss her cheek. I catch my reflection rippling and breaking in the soft waves. And I believe her.

# *in another time*

## ABE TURNER

1941–2021

Abe got his cancer diagnosis in 2018. "It's terminal," his doctor said. "I give you weeks to months."

"Okay," Abe chuckled. "Well. We'll see." Because although he knew he wouldn't live forever, he knew he'd live to at least 2020, because he had a bus to catch in Indianapolis. He knew the route, at least, because he knew it ended at The Porchlight Diner. But he didn't know the day or time. So, every morning, even during the pandemic, he brought his tea in a thermos, his newspaper crossword puzzle and a pen, his cane, and extra masks. He loaded up his bus pass. And he climbed aboard the IndyGo bus #349.

Most days were the same, until the day that wasn't. He heard Cal before he saw them, and when he looked up, he was certain. Their young face, wet with tears. Their voice, shivering, and full of desperation. *Cal.* His Cal. Only not at all. Not yet.

He wordlessly walked up the aisle and tapped his card for the child, offered them a mask. He heard their small thank-you before they put it on, found a seat, curled up and wept. The bus went round and round the city for hours, and Abe put his head down and kept it together. Because he wanted to hold them, that sweet, scared kid who had never been loved in their whole life. He wanted to wipe their tears away like he did with his own children, who were grown now. Who still called him every morning, every night.

But he knew how this day went. He waited until they were asleep, then he folded his coat and placed it on the seat beside them. He waited until they were in front of the diner. Until he heard young Cal say, "Thank you for the jacket, sir." Abe looked up from his puzzle.

"You know," he said, "this bus is almost done for the night, and I've been told this diner has marvelous hot chocolate. What do you say I buy you a cup, and then we'll call someone you trust to take you home?"

"I can't go home," Cal said, voice small and high, tears spilling down their cheeks, soaking their mask. "Not anymore." They shoved their fists into their eyes to try to stop sobbing, but it didn't work.

"Or maybe you just can't go home *yet*," Abe said, as gently as he could, and it took everything in him not to cry too. "Listen, kiddo. Why don't you tell me about it in there where it's warm?"

Cal dropped their hands and looked at Abe wide-eyed. They nodded quickly and caught their breath. They followed him off the bus, still hugging the too-big jacket against their chest, and the two of them slid into a red plastic booth. Cal started nervously scribbling on a children's menu, and Abe could feel every single beat of his own heart.

The server brought them two hot chocolates, extra whipped cream, extra sprinkles.

"Can I take my mask off while I drink this?" Cal asked.

"Of course. Cheers. My name's Abe, by the way." He knew Cal wouldn't remember it, but he wanted them to feel comfortable. And they did. They told him everything, about the earrings and the boys, the cartoons and the punch. About the principal's office and the counselor and their mother.

"He told them I said I was a boy," they whimpered, their bottom lip trembling. "And. I mean. I did."

"You know," Abe said. "When I was born, they thought I was a girl too."

Cal studied him, and then looked down at their hands, clearly scared of giving away too much. But their voice was desperate and earnest when they looked back up and said, "Really?"

"Yes. And it was hard for such a long time. Really hard. But now I'm happy. Now I'm okay."

"You promise?"

"I do. Will you promise me something too?"

Cal had whipped cream on the tip of their nose when they nodded, but Abe didn't laugh.

"Promise me you'll do what you can to survive. Promise me you'll choose to live, at least until you graduate high school." Cal stared at him, wide-eyed again. They sipped the last of their hot chocolate. They didn't respond. At least not out loud.

Instead, Cal flipped their menu over and scribbled. They slid the paper across the table, and Abe held it up between them. He had to smile because the handwriting was worse than ever, but he could read it easily.

"I promise," he read out loud, and looked up at the kid, who was smiling too. "You promise." Abe said it like it wasn't a question, like he trusted them, and Cal nodded. "Is it okay if I keep this?" Abe asked as he folded the paper carefully. "Your promise means a lot to me."

"Sure," Cal said, blushing, and so Abe tucked it into the front pocket of his shirt. He patted it, right over his heart. This final, perfect gift.

But Cal's face fell as they glanced at the clock ticking above the diner door. They said, "Shoot. It's getting late, and I'm probably already in big trouble. But thank you, sir, for everything." Abe looked out the window to see the streetlights were still out, but the stars had already risen. Even in the city, they were bright. So bright. Too bright. Impossibly bright. It took Abe's breath away. It reminded him of somewhere from long ago.

It reminded him of someone here, now, across from him in the booth, young and scared and at the beginning of it all, although they didn't know it.

"You're right, Cal," Abe said, as the kid pulled the old man's coat around their shoulders to protect them from the still-falling snow. "Let's get you home."

# *acknowledgments*

Thank you to:

Our queer ancestors and elders. For being who you were, who you are, even when you couldn't say it out loud. For carving out spaces in the world with your art, words, anger, defiance, and hard-won joy. For pressing the petals of yourselves in the pages of history. Thank you for guiding me home.

Alex Borbolla, for jumping into this story with enthusiasm, thoughtfulness, and a clear vision for how to make it the strongest version it could be. I'm blown away by your editorial insight and efficiency. You're brilliant. I will always be grateful for the ways you transformed this story so completely and so quickly. And Cal will always be grateful for the baking tips; they would have been completely lost and butterless without you.

Cameron Kellogg, who is so deeply good. Publishing a novel was my wildest dream, and you opened the doors for my stories. You made me feel safe to write things I was terrified to write. You helped me dream up impossible worlds and impossible lives. It's been wonderful to know you first as my incredibly talented editor, and now as my [officially official] friend. I hope we really do share stories forever or, at the very least, until we are extremely old and inevitably gayer.

My team at Bloomsbury, for publishing and supporting my queer and trans stories in a time when it's risky to do so. My books have been in such good hands, and I have been too. Special thanks to Faye Bi, Erica Barmash, Jennifer Choi, Beth Eller, Phoebe Dyer, Lily Yengle, Tiffany Coelho, Diane Aronson, and John Candell—it has been a total dream to work with such wonderful people.

My team at Penguin UK, especially Anthea Townsend, Michael Bedo, Amy Wilkerson, Natalie Doherty, Carmen McCullough, and India Chambers. Thank you for all your beautiful work, and for sharing my books with the world.

Erin Harris, for giving me the courage to start over when I realized I was writing the wrong story, and for always being in my corner.

Mary Metzger for this breathtaking cover. You are magic.

Hugh Ryan, for your remarkable contributions to queer historical scholarship, and for your piece, "Who's Afraid of Social Contagion?," in *Boston Review* that shaped my understanding of identity. And most of all, thank you for jumping on a call with me two years ago to talk through my characters. I could not have written this book without your abundance of knowledge and generosity. I owe you, like, ten dinners. And so much more.

Hannah (@soupgirlreads) and my other authenticity readers for your smart, thoughtful notes and professionalism (and on such a quick timeline!). You added so much to these characters and their histories, and I will never forget the ways you shaped this world.

Jas Hammonds, L.T. Thompson, Abdi Nazemian, Kelly Quindlen, Tucker Shaw, Aiden Thomas, Adrienne Tooley, Trang Thanh Tran, and Justine Pucella Winans for taking the time to read and blurb (I wish there was a word for this that felt less goofy, because it is such a generous and kind act). I have been inspired by each and every one of you, and admire you all in so many ways.

The group of MVP readers (/friends) who gave me feedback when I needed it most: Artemis Crystal, Gabbie Kay, Jessica Kent, Heather Lo, Chloe Maron, Bri Miano, Diana Perry, August Ryan, and Jessica Valeske.

The friends who helped me with brainstorming, body doubling, and emotional support: Lara Ameen, Kay Ulanday Barrett, Terri Bello, Aislinn Brophy, Kate Cochrane, Kirt Ethridge, Jordan Francoeur, Kate Fussner, Lakshya, Jas Hammonds, Jessie Hansen, Caroline Huntoon, Briana Johnson, Sacha Lamb (thank you for naming Amaranth!), Aleycha Landrau, Isla Lassiter, Nicole Lovell, Tess Malone, Amanda Maynard, Avery Mead, Jenna Miller, Christen Randall, Ronnie Riley, Octavia Saenz, Izzy Sanders, Birdie Schae, JD Scott, Steph Scott, Neha Shah, Jordan Silversmith, Brett Solimine, Anna Sortino, Leah Stecher, Lin Thompson, Chaloe Tyler, and Ann Zhao.

My family—Andrew, Tony, Dad, Mom, The Shahs, The Clements, The Rusczcaks, and so many others—for years of care and support.

Juni, for being the curmudgeonly dog to welcome me home.

Krupa Shah, for the endless gifts of our shared life and precious family. For supporting me through tight deadlines and sleepless nights. And most of all for loving every version of us in every season. We still are, and always will be.

Z, for everything, everything, everything. It is the honor of my life to witness yours, and to love you, with all your energy, curiosity, humor, and kindness. I am so proud to be your parent. I adore every single thing about you. I treasure every second with you. If I could live forever, it would only be to know you more and more and more. I'll meet you in the ocean and the igloo and maybe on some impossible day, at our own kind of Amaranth. You are a miracle, a dream, and the brightest, most beautiful star.

And, finally, thank you to you, reader. Especially if you're young, especially if you're trans. Especially if you feel broken and hopeless. Especially if you're searching for a place to call home. I hope you find it, but until then, please stay, if you can. I think we fucking make it, or at least I hope so, because I need you—we all do—wherever we're going next.

# RESOURCES

If you have been affected by issues raised in this book, these organizations can provide information and support.

## UK

### TRANS ACTUAL

TransActual are a UK based, trans-led and run organization. They are a national advocacy and education organization focused specifically on working for trans adults in the UK, with a particular focus on healthcare and trans people's legal protections.

### MERMAIDS

Mermaids supports transgender, non-binary and gender-diverse children and young people, as well as their families and professionals involved in their care. They provide services directly to trans children and young people, and work to educate and inform professionals and organizations who want to be part of a society where trans children and young people are safe, included and empowered to be their best selves.

### STONEWALL

Stonewall provides support and advice to people in the LGBTQ+ community. It also supports individuals and organizations to work out how they can make a difference for LGBTQ+ people at work, at home and in their communities and campaigns for LGBTQ+ equality.

### THE PROUD TRUST

The Proud Trust is an organization that helps LGBTQ+ young people empower themselves through youth groups, national and regional LGBTQ+ youth networks, managing the LGBTQ+ centre for Manchester, delivering training, running events and campaigns, undertaking research and creating resources.

### SWITCHBOARD

A helpline for anyone to discuss anything, including sexuality, gender identity, sexual health and emotional wellbeing.

### MIND

Mind provides advice and support, to make sure no one has to face a mental health problem alone.

### SAMARITANS

Samaritans is a unique charity dedicated to reducing feelings of isolation and disconnection that can lead to suicide. They provide support to anyone in emotional distress, struggling to cope or at risk of suicide.

## AUSTRALIA

### MINUS18

Minus18 are champions for LGBTQIA+ youth in Australia. Through awareness and visibility, LGBTQIA+ education, and life-affirming programs, they are creating an Australia where all young people are safe, empowered, and surrounded by people that support them.

## TRANSCEND AUSTRALIA

Transcend Australia support Australian families and their trans, gender-diverse and non-binary children and young people.

## TRANSHUB

TransHub is a ground-breaking digital platform for trans and gender-diverse people, their loved ones and health providers.

## CHARLEE

Charlee is a suicide prevention hub made by LGBTIQA+ people who have thought about suicide, lived through suicide attempts, supported others in distress and live with the pain of loss through suicide.

## QLIFE

QLife provides Australia-wide anonymous, LGBTI peer support and referral for people wanting to talk about a range of issues including sexuality, identity, gender, bodies, feelings or relationships.

## LIFELINE

A national charity providing all Australians experiencing emotional distress with access to 24-hour crisis support and suicide prevention services.

## KIDS HELPLINE

A free, confidential 24/7 online and phone counselling service for young people aged five to twenty-five.

### THE SUICIDE CALL BACK SERVICE

A free nationwide service providing 24/7 phone and online counselling to people affected by suicide.

### BEYOND BLUE

A mental health organization, focused on supporting people affected by anxiety, depression and suicide.

## NEW ZEALAND

### AVIVA

A charity that strives to create safe homes for all individuals.

### INSIDEOUT

A national organization that works with youth, whanau, schools and communities to make Aotearoa a safer place for all rainbow young people to live and be in.

### LIFELINE

Lifeline Aotearoa has been helping New Zealanders in distress and crisis for over fifty years, supporting those with issues ranging from anxiety and depression, and aiding victims of domestic violence and abuse.

### TAUTOKO SUICIDE CRISIS HELPLINE

TAUTOKO is operated by trained and experienced social service practitioners who have undergone suicide prevention training. It is a free nationwide service available 24/7.

### OUTLINE

OutLine is an all-ages rainbow mental health organization providing support to the rainbow community, their friends, whānau and those questioning.

## SOUTH AFRICA

### LIFELINE SOUTH AFRICA

LifeLine offers mental and emotional health human rights services, through programmes that are preventative and responsive.

### SADAG

South Africa's premier Mental Health non-governmental organization, dedicated to providing free and accessible support resources and education to individuals and communities nationwide.

### OUT

Provides stigma-free services to gay, bisexual and MSN communities. They also work to eradicate LGBT+ hate crimes and discrimination while assisting and supporting victims.

### SOUTH AFRICAN FEDERATION FOR MENTAL HEALTH

The largest national mental health federation in South Africa, promoting community mental health care.